Praise for *Capital Crimes*

"Sanders' plot is fast forward . . . A cautionary tale."
—*New York Daily News*

"A fascinating central figure . . . A suspenseful story that doubles as an essay on the corruptions of power."
—*Los Angeles Times*

"The sordid background is believable."   —*Newsday*

"Sanders is always good . . . "   —*Chicago Tribune*

LAWRENCE SANDERS

"A master storyteller."   —*King Features*

"A writer who has matured into one of our great ones."
—*Pittsburgh Press*

"One of the most consistently satisfying 'entertainment' novelists in America today."   —*Washington Post*

"The amazing thing about Sanders is that he never disappoints his reader."   —*USA Today*

"It's a sin not to enjoy Sanders!"

—*Columbia State* (S.C.)

Berkley Books by Lawrence Sanders

THE ANDERSON TAPES
CAPER
CAPITAL CRIMES
THE CASE OF LUCY BENDING
THE DREAM LOVER
THE EIGHTH COMMANDMENT
THE FIRST DEADLY SIN
THE FOURTH DEADLY SIN
THE LOVES OF HARRY DANCER
LOVE SONGS
THE MARLOW CHRONICLES
THE PASSION OF MOLLY T.
THE PLEASURES OF HELEN
THE SECOND DEADLY SIN
THE SEDUCTION OF PETER S.
THE SIXTH COMMANDMENT
STOLEN BLESSINGS
THE TANGENT FACTOR
THE TANGENT OBJECTIVE
THE TENTH COMMANDMENT
THE THIRD DEADLY SIN
THE TIMOTHY FILES
TIMOTHY'S GAME
THE TOMORROW FILE

CAPITAL CRIMES

Lawrence SANDERS

BERKLEY BOOKS, NEW YORK

CAPITAL CRIMES

A Berkley Book / published by arrangement with
the author

PRINTING HISTORY
G. P. Putnam's Sons edition / May 1989
Published simultaneously in Canada
Berkley edition / July 1990

ISBN: 0-425-12164-X

A BERKLEY BOOK ® TM 757,375
Berkley Books are published by The Berkley Publishing Group,
200 Madison Avenue, New York, New York 10016.
The name "BERKLEY" and the "B" logo
are trademarks belonging to Berkley Publishing Corporation.

PRINTED IN THE UNITED STATES OF AMERICA

10 9 8 7 6 5 4 3 2 1

CAPITAL CRIMES

ONE

=1=

The roads dwindle down: Washington through Manassas
to Culpeper. Then south to Goochland, and from there
a straight and narrow trail rutting through scrabbly fields
glinting with hoarfrost. A glaucous moon floating, hard
stars, and a wind with teeth.

In unremembered days it was a tobacco barn; the tang
still lingers. Splintered drying racks sag; winter seeps in
through weathered clapboard. Parked around are a dozen
cars, a pickup truck, two motorcycles. Within the barn,
pilgrims huddle on rude benches in overcoats, parkas,
furs.

There is a makeshift stage: sides of a large packing crate
laid flat and supported on bricks. A smaller wooden box,
covered with a scrap of worn velvet, serves as pulpit. Kerosene lanterns illuminate with a flickering glare, wicks
smoking, shadows dancing. A bleached hound, shivering,
huddles close to the man on the stage.

Brother Kristos speaks:

"We are all created in God's image. It is written. And
since God is without sin, so are we. Men and women are
divine. The only hell is to resist your will."

He stands planted, a blocky man in a rough robe of burlap belted with a rope. A scraggly beard hides cheeks and
throat. Greasy hair, parted in the middle, falls to his
shoulders in crusty wings. Fingernails are grimed, bare
feet soiled with punk.

"If you cannot accept the pain of your existence," he

says, "believe in me, for I shall bring you grace and purification. I take unto me your crimes and vices, your sins and secret lusts. I am one with God. Believe in me, and I shall wash your soul of guilt."

The voice is flat, without timbre; it is the eyes that stun. As he speaks he turns his head slowly to stare at each member of his congregation. Fierier than the lanterns those eyes, with a scorching intensity that melts and welds.

"May you be healed and made whole," Brother Kristos says. "Go with joy, guiltless, sinless, and free. Give to me your sadness and rejoice. For I am one with God, and through me you shall enter the Kingdom of Heaven."

He makes a swift sign of the cross as blessing, then steps down from the stage. The pale hound slinks along at his heels to a doorway curtained with a length of greige. Man and dog disappear.

Two young women clad in robes of stitched white sheets pass among the congregants with lidless cigar boxes. Contributions are made in coins and bills. Worshipers leave slowly, turning up collars, pulling on gloves.

A middle-aged woman bundled in a long mink coat remains. She speaks briefly to one of the acolytes. The young woman nods, goes to the curtained doorway at the rear of the barn. She steps into a mean, cluttered chamber, formerly a wagon stall. A potbellied stove glows a cherry red. The air is fumy.

"A woman wants to talk to you," the assistant reports. "Fifty-five to sixty. Mink coat. Alligator handbag. I've never seen her before."

Brother Kristos rises from the rumpled cot and stands beside a kitchen table covered with peeling oilcloth. The doorway curtain is held aside. The woman enters haltingly, trying to smile.

"Brother Kristos," she says, voice trembly, "thank you for seeing me. I hope you will be able to help."

Her eyes are locked by his fervid stare; she cannot look away.

"Mrs. Lenore Mattingly suggested I come to you," the woman goes on. "You cured her migraine headaches. She swears by you."

"Yes?" he says in that dull voice. "Then she had faith. I cannot help those who do not believe. Do you have faith?"

"Oh I do, I really do, Brother Kristos. Your sermon tonight was the most inspiring thing I've ever heard. I'm going to come back again and again."

She is a heavy, florid woman with a raddled complexion. Rings on three fingers: chunky diamonds.

"It's so hot in here," she says, the small laugh nervous. "May I take off my coat?"

He says nothing, not helping her as she shrugs out of the mink and holds it folded over one arm. She is wearing a dress of black silk crepe. A necklace of pearls dangles between pillowy breasts. She sways on high-heeled pumps of patent leather.

"What is your name?" he asks.

"Kate Downley. Mrs. Katherine Downley. I live in D.C. My husband is an attorney with the government."

"And you came to see me because you are in pain. Physical pain."

"Yes. Sometimes it gets so bad I can't—"

"In your knees," Brother Kristos says. "The pain is in your knees. Doctors cannot help. They tell you it is arthritis, and they prescribe medication. But the drugs wear off, and the pain returns."

She is astounded. "How did you know?"

He shakes his head. "I cannot explain it."

He takes the mink coat and alligator handbag from her, drops them onto the table. He pulls up two wooden chairs, facing each other. They sit so close their knees are almost touching. His burlap robe falls open. She sees bare legs, corded and scarred, heavily haired. She is conscious of his odor.

He leans forward, takes her two hands in his.

"Look into my eyes," he commands.

She obeys, blinking at the blaze.

"Do you have faith in me?"

She nods.

"Say it," he orders. "Say, 'I believe in you, Brother Kristos.' "

"I believe in you, Brother Kristos," she repeats, her face twisted.

He releases her hands. He pushes up the hem of her dress. Her hosiery is black, almost opaque.

"Pull down your stockings."

"They're—uh, not stockings. Pantyhose."

"Pull them down."

She stands, reaches under her skirt, peels the pantyhose down until they are bunched about her ankles. She sits down again, and again he hikes up her skirt. Her bare knees are swollen.

He raises his head and recaptures her eyes with his burning stare. He clasps her fleshy knees. His hands are strong, skin rough. Wiry hair springs from the back of hands and fingers.

"Have faith," he tells her. "Let your belief in me grow. I shall take your pain unto myself. Your suffering will flow to me from you. As your faith grows, so shall your punishment become less. Believe that. Believe in me."

As he speaks, his eyes widen until she feels that piercing stare as hot and red as the stove . . . scorching.

He pulps the flesh of her knees. His hard gritty fingers move upward to the softness of her inner thighs.

"There is no sin, no guilt," he intones. "You are created in a divine image and cannot err. You may do all that you wish without fear. Your pain will not cease at once, but as your faith increases, the despair of your body will diminish. Give yourself to me, body and soul, and your suffering will wither away."

Her eyes flutter and close. His voice drones on. She hears it from a distance, faint. Feels ghost fingers stroking, then slowly, lovingly withdrawn. Her thighs are circled, clasped, caressed. Then the disembodied hands are gone.

She opens her eyes to face that fixed stare again.

"I am the Light," he tells her. "Brought on earth to show the One Way. Do you believe in me?"

She nods.

"Say it."

"I believe in you, Brother Kristos."

He rises, moves away from her. She stands shakily, tugs up her pantyhose. She puts on her fur. She fishes in her handbag, counts out a hundred dollars in small bills onto the oilcloth.

"Will that be all right?" she asks anxiously.

"It is not important," he says. "The important thing is to believe."

"May I come back again, Brother Kristos?"

He shrugs. "If you wish."

When she is gone, the curtain closed, he goes to a broken cabinet fixed to the interior barn wall and takes down a jug of vodka. He puts it to his mouth, takes two gulps. Then he pours a little into a tin dish on the floor, and the old hound rouses, pads over and laps greedily.

His assistants come into the room carrying their collection boxes.

"Almost forty-six," one of them reports, showing Brother Kristos a wad of bills, a handful of change. "How did you make out?"

He gestures toward the money on the table. "A hundred. Pearl, take the truck into town tomorrow morning. Have it gassed. And we need vodka."

"And food," Agnes Brittlewaite says.

"And more coal for the stove," Pearl Gibbs says. "And kerosene for the lanterns. We need everything."

"The Lord will provide," Brother Kristos says.

Pounds of barbecued ribs are heated in a tin platter atop the stove, along with small, spotted potatoes already boiled and peeled. There is a stale loaf of rye bread, unsliced.

They take off their robes. Brother Kristos is wearing grayish underdrawers, wrinkled and stained. The women wear cotton panties. Their breasts are bare.

They tear at the rib bones ravenously. They stuff whole potatoes in their mouths, rip off chunks of rye to wipe their lips before swallowing the bread or tossing it to the waiting hound.

All three drink vodka, passing the jug around. Only the women talk as they eat and drink. Kristos hunches over his food, head lowered, spitting pieces of gristle onto the floor. He gorges frantically, scraping greasy pork from the bones with strong, yellowed teeth.

The women attack their food just as greedily, but they pause occasionally to exchange reactions to individuals at the evening's service. All wash down their meal with swallows from the vodka jug. The potatoes are finished, the barbecued ribs reduced to a stack of glistening bones tossed onto the floor for the hound to gnaw.

Brother Kristos sits back and beckons to Pearl. She swings from her chair to sit on his lap. Kristos fondles her breast, summoning the other woman with his free hand. She comes around the table to stand alongside his chair.

Agnes is a heavy woman with pendulous breasts, no waist, spongy thighs. She presses close as Kristos thrusts his hand in her panties. She stands with legs apart, caressing his hair.

He pushes her away and stands, dumping Pearl off his lap. He puts the vodka jug to his mouth and takes a deep swallow. He rolls naked onto the cot, exhibiting himself to the laughing women.

Pearl joins him on the cot. Agnes pauses to add a small

shovelful of coal to the stove from a scuttle alongside. Then she takes off her panties and kneels close to the cot.

The air is gummy with heat, fumes of burning coal, food, vodka, sweat, the musk of the pit. The kerosene lanterns smoke and flicker; shadows loom and fade on the walls of the cave.

Kristos snarls like a cornered beast, lurching about and clawing. He uses his hard strength like a bludgeon. He savages them. He pierces, rends, splits and tears, full lips drawn back from animal teeth, claws unsheathed.

It goes on until midnight, until the liquor is gone, passion drained. Their viscid flesh cannot cool in that vaporous hell. He kicks the women aside, stands swaying. Then, still naked, he leaves by the back door, going outside.

The two women rise unsteadily, pull on their white robes.

Pearl: "Where is he?"

Agnes: "Outside."

Pearl: "In the privy?"

Agnes: "I don't know."

Pearl: "Maybe he passed out."

Agnes: "Never."

Pearl: "Maybe we should go see."

They step outside. Cold strikes like a blow. A frosted moon still makes milk glass of the sky. Stars turn and wind bites.

"There he is," Agnes says. "Up the slope."

They see him naked on his knees, head bowed, close to an ancient oak, now barren and black. The arms of Brother Kristos are clasped around the rough wood. He looks small, defenseless, his body whitish in the moon glare.

"What is he doing?" Pearl asks.

"Praying," Agnes says.

Pearl laughs. "He's crazy," she says.

Agnes whirls on her. "Don't you ever say that, you stupid cunt!" Then, voice softening, "But we did have fun, didn't we?"

=2=

They're inside, comfortably warm, but the Chief of Staff stands hunched, hands thrust into his pockets as if he's standing on the portico. The Marine guard out there is wearing overcoat and gloves.

"The son of a bitch," Henry Aaron Folsom says bitterly. "He shows up every three months, right on schedule. You know why? So he can have his picture taken with the Boss. He sends the photograph to his piss-ass country, and it's printed in their newspapers—all two of them. That's supposed to show how buddy-buddy he is with the President of the U.S. of A. You've alerted a photographer?"

"Standing by," John Tollinger says.

"Good. We'll whisk that miniature shithead in and whisk him out. Heavy schedule today. The counsel from State is due in ten minutes."

"Yes, sir," his executive assistant says. "The briefing on the legal situation in the Marianas."

"I wish I could remember things the way you do."

"I take memory pills," Tollinger says.

"No kidding? What are they?"

"I can't recall the name," the EA says solemnly, and Folsom snorts a laugh.

A black stretch limousine pulls up outside.

"Here's the little pipsqueak now," the Chief of Staff

says. "That car of his could feed half of his country for a week."

The two men go outside. The chauffeur hustles to open the back door of the limo. A small lemony man comes hurtling out and bounds up the steps.

"Mr. Ambassador!" Folsom says, extending his hand. "How nice to see you again!"

The ambassador giggles. "All is well with you and Mr. President, I trust?"

"Couldn't be better," the Chief says heartily. "I know how much he's looking forward to your visit. This way, sir."

They conduct him down the corridors to the Oval Office. President Abner Randolph Hawkins rises when they enter. He shakes the little paw offered by the ambassador. The two men stand close a moment, exchanging small talk on the horrendous winter weather and the dreadful state of the economy in the ambassador's country.

"People are starving," the diplomat says sadly.

Because, the President would like to say, our aid is being siphoned off by that gang of crooks you work for. But he only shakes his head sympathetically and promises to have the matter investigated.

The photographer is summoned; the requisite picture is taken. A dozen eight-by-tens will be sent to the ambassador's official residence: a lavish suite in the Washington Plaza Hotel. The Chief of Staff remains in the Oval Office. John Tollinger escorts the envoy back to his limousine.

Just before they step outside, the ambassador looks about cautiously, then comes close, putting papery fingers lightly on Tollinger's arm.

"Mr. President is well?" he asks in a low voice.

"The President is in excellent health," the EA says coldly.

"But he looks so worn," the ambassador persists. "So tired and perhaps worried. And he seemed distant. He did not smile or laugh. Not once."

"He has been working very hard," Tollinger says stiffly. "That business in Peru . . ."

"Ah yes," the diplomat says, having only a vague notion of where Peru is located and no notion at all of what the "business" might be. "And his son—what is his condition?"

"Responding to treatment," Tollinger answers, giving the standard, approved response to such questions.

Later that afternoon, the executive assistant enters the Chief of Staff's private office and reports his conversation with the ambassador.

"So he noticed, did he?" Folsom says. "That midget asshole! Well, it's the truth: the Boss looks like the wrath of God. John, let's cut out the photo opportunities for a while. We can't have the *Times* printing pictures of him looking like death warmed over. And we'll hold off on press conferences and put out the word that he's too busy with that flap in Peru."

"It won't fly," Tollinger says.

"In the long run," the COS agrees. "But it's temporary damage control. I'm already beginning to get questions up on the Hill. I have bad vibes about all this. The Man was moving like a zombie today. He wasn't *listening*. There are a dozen things, important things, waiting for his decision. Just a Yes or No will do, but suddenly he can't make up his mind. It's not like him."

"His son?"

"Yeah," the Chief says somberly, "and his wife. She's not helping. You mind working late tonight?"

"Of course not."

"No plans? No heavy date?"

"I think my dating days are over."

"Nah," Folsom says, "you're just going through the PDB. You know what that means?"

"Post-divorce blues?"

"You got it. But when you're thrown by a horse, you've got to get up and ride again—the sooner the better. Ask me; I know. Been through it twice. Okay, end of sermon. Why I asked if you'd work late is this: Doc Stemple is coming by at seven. At first I thought I'd have a one-on-one with him. But I've been thinking about it, and I've decided it would be smarter to have a witness. You willing?"

"What's it about—the Boss?"

"Yeah," the Chief says. "I want the doc's top-of-the-head opinion. We may have a serious problem here, John."

"I know."

"So you'll sit in? Just to listen."

"I'll be here. You want me to take notes?"

"Jesus, no!" the COS says. "No notes, no tapes. It'll be strictly under the sheets. So we can deny, deny, deny—right?"

"I understand," John Tollinger says.

It wouldn't do a bit of good if the media learned the administration employed a house shrink, so Dr. R. Judd Stemple is officially assigned to the National Security Council. Ostensibly, his job is to honcho a staff of five that prepares psychobiographies of foreign leaders, diplomats, terrorists, domestic revolutionaries and, occasionally, members of Congress.

Actually, Stemple serves mainly as consulting psychologist to the White House staff. He's available when pressures outweigh the perks, when alcohol and/or drugs become too important, or when some of those brainy people start brooding about the decompression that must inevitably ensue when they are cut loose from the cachet of a White House pass and telephone number.

Stemple is a breezy, baldish man, reputed to be the best three-cushion billiards player in the capital. It is said he practices every night—which may be the reason he wastes no time in small talk.

"Look," he says to Folsom and Tollinger, "you've got a guy suddenly dumped in a high-pressure cooker. Maybe the toughest job in the world. Sure, he came up through the ranks. Served in his state legislature and was governor for two terms. So what? There's no training that can prepare you for the moment when you sit your ass behind that big desk in the Oval Office."

"He's been doing okay," the Chief of Staff says. "For a year now."

"Has he?" the doctor says. "Sure, he's been functioning, and functioning well. But he's been pushing his personal problems aside. Not aside maybe, but pushing them down deep."

"He figures the country comes first," Folsom says defensively. "Listen, the Boss is a patriot. Cheap word these days, but that's what he is—a patriot."

"I'll give you that," Stemple says. "But the psychic cost has been enormous, and it's catching up with him. How old was he when his son was born?"

The Chief of Staff looks at his executive assistant. "John?"

"Forty-two," Tollinger says. "And his wife was thirty-six."

"Old for a first child," the doctor says. "You can imagine how happy they were, after all their years of trying. Then the kid turns out to be a hemophiliac. That's a crusher, but they try to cope, try to live a normal life—which is hard to do when you've got a handsome young son who might bleed to death if he tumbles off his bike. Anyway, Abner Randolph Hawkins makes it to the White House. Now he's got a million heavy problems, but none as big as his one and only son, George Powell Hawkins, whose life is constantly at risk."

"Come on," Folsom says, "it's not that bad. The kid is sick, admittedly, but he gets special treatment—you know that. There's always someone looking after him. He's never too far from a transfusion if he needs it. And now they're trying a new clotting substance."

"Is it succeeding?" Stemple asks.

"He's responding to treatment," the Chief says.

"Don't give me that garbage," the doctor says. "That's as bad as 'The operation was a success, but the patient died.' The boy is still sick, and you know it. And you're asking me why his father is showing signs of stress? Because he loves his son. Can't stop worrying about the kid's condition. It's a wonder he can function at all. I don't happen to agree with his political philosophy, but he is a mensch and loves his son deeply."

"What about the wife?" Folsom asks.

"She feels everything her husband feels—in spades! Because she thinks she's the cause of the child's illness— which, in a way, she is. Hemophilia is a hereditary blood defect that affects only males but is transmitted through their mothers. Can you imagine the guilt? Helen feels *she* is the reason for her child's misfortune. I've read that she had no idea that she was carrying a sex-linked recessive trait in her genes. Her mother had two girls. Her grandmother had three girls. Only when they went back to her great-grandmother did they find a boy. He was a hemophiliac and died at the age of four. So you know how she must be torturing herself."

"All right," the Chief says. "Thanks for the medical diagnosis. Now give it to us straight, what's the worst-case scenario? That the kid will die?"

Dr. Stemple sits back, rubs a palm over his bald head. "I wish to hell you'd relax the No Smoking regulation around here," he says fretfully. "I'd love a cigar right now. No, I don't think the boy's death would be the worst case. Other Presidents have lost children while they were in the White House and survived. There's a terrible period of grief, of course, but mourning can be therapeutic."

"Therapeutic?" Folsom says.

"Sure. It's like taking an emetic. The child's death would be shattering, but it would also free the President from his constant anxieties."

"Then what *is* the worst case?" Folsom demands.

The doctor stares at him. "He cracks up."

"Oh Jesus, don't tell me that."

"I *am* telling you that. A complete nervous breakdown is a very real possibility."

"I don't believe it," Folsom says wrathfully. "I served with the Boss in the Marines. He went through hell and never wavered. He's not going to crack."

"Chief," Stemple says gently, "in combat the enemy is trying to kill you, and you're trying to kill him. It's *action*. You fight back. But how do you fire a rifle at fate? Don't you understand? Part of the Man's problem is that he can't *act;* he can only suffer."

The Chief of Staff shakes his head. "Crack-up?" he says. "Oh God, how can we prepare for that?"

They sit in silence, hearing the late evening sounds of the White House still at work: couriers scurrying down corridors, a sudden burst of laughter, a door slamming. Upstairs, they know, the President and his wife, together for the first time that day, sitting close, holding hands, perhaps weeping.

"John," the COS says wearily, "do you have any questions?"

Tollinger turns to the psychologist. "Dr. Stemple, there's a factor you haven't mentioned: their religiousness. As I'm sure you're aware, both the President and First Lady are very devout. Won't that help them get through this?"

"I haven't spoken to either," Stemple says, "so I can only guess, but they might feel they must have sinned for God to be punishing them, and that increases their guilt. I can't give you a more definite opinion than that. I don't think anyone can—including Helen and Abner Hawkins."

"They go to church every Sunday," Tollinger persists. "They contribute heavily. Sometimes they have prayer breakfasts here in the White House. Their pastor is the Reverend Jonathan Smiley. You know him?"

"I've met him. Sanctimonious bastard."

"Regardless, if they believe in him, wouldn't it do some good to recruit him? Maybe he could convince them that their feelings of guilt are so much nonsense."

"It might do some good—but I doubt it. Have you ever heard Smiley preach? He's strictly a 'God's will be done' guy. No explanation of why the innocent starve, babies are born with AIDS, and people are gunned down on the streets by strangers. It's just God's will. You think the President and First Lady are going to buy that? I don't think so. They may not be the smartest couple in the land, but they are real practical midwesterners. They believe when you have a problem, you try to solve it, no matter what it takes. You don't just shrug and say, 'God's will be done.' No, I don't think the Reverend Smiley is the answer."

"Then what the hell is?" Folsom says angrily.

The doctor looks at him benignly. "What makes you think all problems have solutions?" he says. "They don't. But sometimes, if you wait long enough, they just go away."

"Bullshit!" the Chief of Staff says.

=3=

Many think John Tollinger a mirthless man. Actually, he possesses a fine wit, but so desiccated that only he sees the humor. On the drive home from the White House to Spring Valley, he reflects on the conference with the Chief and Doc Stemple. He is amused, but he does not laugh aloud or even smile at the image of three flunkies assessing the mental health of the President of the United States.

Before she became his ex, Jennifer said to him, "There are supposed to be two kinds of people in the world: those who see life as a tragedy and those who see it as a comedy. But not you. You see life as a disaster."

"That's unfair," he said. "And not true. I just have a very keen appreciation of the absurdity of existence."

"And you use too many long words," she added.

Recalling that conversation, he ponders once again the reason for their divorce. Not money, not sex (which both agreed was super), and not infidelity; they were determinedly faithful during their three years together.

It was, he reasons, emotional incompatibility that did them in. They should have known. But during their courtship they concurred that "opposites attract" and hoped their marriage might last forever. It didn't.

"You are a cold man," she finally accused. "You have ice water in your veins. If your pants were on fire, you might say, 'Drat.' There's no warmth to you. You go through life like Puck, thinking, 'Lord, what fools these mortals be.'"

"Seneca said it first," he observed calmly. "And you are so moody that you barely escape being manic-depressive. I've seen you weep because you've misplaced your car keys. You're so emotionally volatile that I really think you seek out crises, and when none are available, you manufacture them."

"Still," she said, "you mix one hell of a dry martini."

"And I love your pesto," he said.

So they were divorced, remaining cautious friends and meeting occasionally to enjoy martinis and pesto together. Besides, Jennifer—reclaiming her maiden name, Jennifer Raye—is deputy press secretary to the First Lady, and she and John Tollinger see each other frequently at White House functions. No awkwardness at all.

She was, he admits, reasonably generous in the divorce

settlement. He retained the house in Spring Valley, and she took most of the furniture—enough to fill a duplex in Georgetown she began sharing with a formidable woman who did something with statistics for the Department of Labor.

But their affable agreement left him, almost literally, with an empty home. One bed, one chest of drawers in the master bedroom. Nothing in the guest bedroom. The living room still boasts two upholstered armchairs and a cocktail table. The dining room: empty. But there is a wide counter in the kitchen with a high stool.

The one chamber Jennifer didn't pillage—because she knew how much it meant to him—is the den. It looks like a reading room in a stodgy men's club: leather couch and wing chairs, built-in bookcases, a working fireplace, an antique globe, a marble-topped sideboard.

"All you need in that room," Jennifer once said, "is a Victorian stereoscope with pictures of naked fat ladies wearing black stockings."

It *is* his favorite room, no doubt about it. And not only because it holds his liquor, books, and collection of James Upshall pipes. But because it's a sanctuary where he can be at peace with the world and, occasionally, himself.

He supposes he should never have married. Should have seen that he was born to be a bachelor, a man with a taste for solitude, a loner who has to make a conscious effort to entertain and be entertained. He blames his parents for that; their rancorous relationship taught him to appreciate the quiet satisfactions of singleness.

So there he is, comfortably ensconced in a leather club chair, a noggin of Glenfiddich in his fist. He is reflecting again on that meeting with Folsom and Stemple, trying to reckon where his loyalties lie. Primarily with the Chief of Staff, of course, because that coarse, profane man has been his mentor. The COS has gone to bat for him on more than one occasion, has pushed salary raises and more prestigious job titles. Tollinger owes him.

But what about the President? What does John owe him? Like Doc Stemple, he does not wholly agree with the Boss's political philosophy, but there is no denying that Abner Hawkins is essentially an honest man with all the Boy Scout virtues. But simple. Not much subtlety to him. No intellectual depth. Which are not necessarily bad characteristics for the Chief Executive. Tollinger believes most Americans instinctively mistrust intellectuals—and could quite possibly be right. And what, John wonders, is his loyalty to that huge, amorphous entity called country? Is it to that frequently mistaken and frequently violent family that John Tollinger's final allegiance belongs? He once believed so. But after a decade in the hurly-burly of politics, his faith in the nobility of public service has become a bit frazzled.

The phone rings on the drum table alongside his armchair. He's tempted not to answer, but he *is* taking the king's shilling. He picks up.

"John Tollinger," he says.

"Hello, John Tollinger," Jennifer says briskly. "How about buying a thirsty guy a drink?"

"Sure," he says gamely. "Where and when?"

"Right where you're sitting. In about an hour?"

"Sounds good," he says.

He stirs up a pitcher of dry martinis, fishes out the ice cubes, and puts the pitcher into the freezer section of the refrigerator. Martinis prepared beforehand, even two or three days, will meld and develop a velvety texture. It is one of his more profound beliefs.

Jennifer is late, as usual. But he's used to that; it no longer annoys him. When she finally arrives and he opens the door for her, she comes bouncing in wearing her beloved 1920's raccoon coat (purchased at a thrift shop) over a slinky jumpsuit of black velvet.

"You made martinis?" she demands. "Gimme gimme gimme!" Then she knocks him a quick kiss: a peck on the chin.

He gets her settled in a den armchair and pours her drink, no olive, no onion, no lemon twist. She sips and closes her eyes with pleasure. "Plasma," she says. "You haven't lost your touch." Then she takes two deep gulps.

"My God," he says, "take it easy. You know what that stuff does to you."

"No," she challenges, "what does it do to me?"

He throws up his hands. "Hey," he says, "calm down. You didn't drive all this way to pick a fight, did you?"

"Just don't lean on me," she says angrily. "I'm in no mood."

"I can see that. Tough day?"

"They're all tough. Can I stay the night?"

He takes a bite of his Scotch before he answers. "Do you think that's wise?"

"Jesus," she says, "does every decision have to be wise? Don't you ever do anything on impulse?"

"Occasionally," he says. "And always regret it later. Come on, Jen, what's the problem now? Something I did or didn't do?"

"Nah," she says, draining her glass. "It's not your fault. Sorry I hollered on you. But it's been such a lousy day. Buy me another, will you, hon, and leave the pitcher in here. I think I'm going to need it."

"Oh boy," he says. "Batten down the hatches."

She's well into her second drink before she stops fidgeting and sits quietly.

"Did you have anything to eat tonight?" he asks her.

"A tunafish sandwich. That's all I wanted."

"I can scramble up some eggs if you're hungry."

"I'm not hungry, thanks. What's happening in Peru?"

"Nothing, I hope. The feeling now is that they'll release the hostages. They got the headlines and TV exposure they wanted. Anyway, State is working on it; it's their crisis. What's yours?"

"You're not going to believe it," she says. "Maude is up in New York, talking with the Hemophilia Foundation. The idea is a good one, I think—and not only because it's my brainchild. The First Lady will become the main spokesperson for raising money for hemophilia research and treatment. It's a natural. Everyone knows her kid's got it. She gets hundreds of letters every week. We pray for you and your boy—stuff like that. Anyway, that's why Maude is in New York—to organize the operation. Personal appearances, TV interviews, cassettes, buttons, bumper stickers—the whole schmear. It will be her personal crusade, like Nancy Reagan's antidrug campaign."

"Makes sense to me," Tollinger says. "A lot of media exposure there. Good political fallout."

"Sure," Jennifer agrees. "That's the point. But while Maude is in New York, I'm holding Helen Hawkins' hand. John, it's a shattering experience. The poor woman is right on the edge. She sits at Walter Reed for hours and hours. She hardly eats a thing. She's lost weight, she can't sleep, she cries for hours."

"Not good," he says.

"That's not the worst," Jennifer says. "Yesterday I'm sitting with her at the hospital. The boy hasn't shown any improvement with that new stuff they're pumping into him, so they're adjusting the dosage. Anyway, about three in the afternoon Audrey Robertson shows up. She's the Social Secretary."

"I know."

"She's come to remind Helen that she's got an appointment at four o'clock. It's a charity tea at the Four Seasons Hotel. Well, Helen doesn't want to go, but Audrey and I finally persuade her to at least make an appearance. You getting bored?"

"Nope. I'm all ears."

"Well, the tea goes okay, with Audrey and me sticking close in case Helen goes into one of her weeping fits. But she's doing fine until the party starts breaking up. Then she gets cornered by a couple of old battleaxes: Mrs. Katherine Downley and Mrs. Lenore Mattingly. You know them?"

"No."

"You're lucky. Oodles of money and no brains at all. Naturally they ask Helen how George is feeling, and she says there's no improvement. Then they start telling her about this wonderful man down in Virginia. Apparently he's some kind of a preacher who works out of an old tobacco barn. They claim he's a clairvoyant and faith healer. He supposedly cured Mattingly's migraine headaches and Downley's arthritis."

"Oh God," Tollinger says, pouring himself more Glenfiddich. "I know what's coming."

"You better believe it. Audrey and I tried to tug Helen away from the two biddies, but no luck, she had to hear everything: exactly where this quack lived, how old he was, how many people were in his congregation, and did they think he could help George. To make a long story short—if it's not too late—the First Lady of the United States of America decided she has to consult this faker. Audrey and I tried to talk her out of it, but no soap. She insisted. She said she'd never forgive herself for not going even if there was one chance in a million that he could cure her son."

Tollinger takes a deep breath. "This time you're right, Jen," he says. "You've got a crisis. When is she going to visit this fraud?"

"Let me finish my story. The tea party was yesterday. I finally convinced Helen that before she consulted this nut, it would be smart to let me go first with a Secret Service man. We could take a look at this so-called church, see what security precautions would have to be taken, and just generally check the guy out."

"Good thinking."

"So the Secret Service agent and I drove down there this morning. It took almost four hours. I thought we'd have trouble finding the place, but all the locals knew about it. Surprisingly, the farmers we talked to swear by this weirdo. They claim he's the best man with animals they've ever met, can cure anything from a sick chicken to an ox."

"Jennifer, what *is* the guy? A fundamentalist? An evangelist? I mean, what's his religion?"

"Who the hell knows? I've never heard him preach, and those two fine, upstanding matrons, Downley and Mattingly, said he has a unique faith, all his own, very inspiring. I'm quoting their exact words. Anyway, we found the barn. It looks like a stiff breeze would blow it away. No signs, no decorations."

"A cross?"

"I didn't see one. Inside are rough benches, a kind of homemade stage, and a sad little pulpit. There's a back room where the preacher lives—with a couple of women."

"Oh-ho. Young women?"

"Not teenagers. But real bimbos. One is maybe late twenties, the other middle thirties. They both wear robes made of dirty sheets. They look like Ku Kluxers without the hoods."

"You met the preacher himself?"

"Oh yeah. A scruffy beast. John, he's not as tall as you but looks bigger. Heavy through the chest and shoulders. Greasy mustache and long beard. Huge hands and feet. Not a bad-looking guy, but it's his eyes that get you. I swear they're phosphorescent. He stared at me, and I was hooked. I just couldn't look away. You know what the first thing he said to me was?"

"What?"

"Why did you leave your husband?"

"You're kidding."

"God's truth; that's what he said. Now how did he know that?"

"Well," John Tollinger says calmly, "maybe he noted that slightly paler ring around your finger where you once wore a wedding band. Or perhaps he just made a lucky guess. In any event, he was wrong. You didn't leave me; we parted by mutual consent."

"Cut the crap," she says sharply, then takes a swallow of her drink. "I was a stranger; he had never seen me before. But he knew I had just left my husband. It shook me; I admit it. But finally I told him a well-known lady wanted to consult him in private, and because he would probably recognize her, could I depend on his discretion?"

"And what did he say to that?"

"He didn't answer. Just kept staring at me. He was coming on to me, and I didn't just imagine it. Then I asked him what he charged for a consultation. And he said, 'Nothing or everything.' Now how do you interpret that?"

"I don't."

"Well, then I got out of there. That stare of his was making me sweat. Helen has a full schedule. There's a state dinner on Friday night, and she and the President are going out to Camp David for the weekend. If the doctors okay it, they'll bring George out there in an ambulance, just to give the kid a change from the hospital. That little guy is so brave, John—I can't tell you. Every time I think of him I want to cry. Anyway, Helen is insisting on seeing this faith healer Monday. The Secret Service said they could provide security. They'll search the barn thoroughly before the First Lady goes in. Oh yes, one thing I forgot to mention—the preacher smells."

"He smells? Of what?"

"Of him. He wears a scuzzy burlap robe, and his bare feet aren't too clean. And it looks to me like he uses his beard as a napkin. So on the way out, I slipped those two tootsies a hundred bucks and asked them to try to get their boss cleaned up a little by Monday. Like sandpapering the crud off him, hosing him down, trimming that wild beard, and maybe dousing him with roach spray."

Tollinger pours what's left in the martini pitcher into her glass and adds a little malt to his.

"Now I can understand why you're so upset," he says. "You know what the big problem is, don't you?"

"God damn it!" she shouts wrathfully. "Give me credit for a little brains, will you? Of course I know. That the media will get hold of this, and the next thing you know, the Washington *Post* will be headlining 'First Lady Consults Faith Healer.' Look what Nancy's astrologer did to the Reagans."

"You've got it," he says. "You better start planning how you can put a positive spin on that to make her look good. If the Hemophilia Foundation learns of it, there goes your public-service campaign. Think about it."

"I can't think about anything," Jennifer Raye says. "I just feel wired. The way that guy looked at me!"

"You never did tell me his name."

"He calls himself Brother Kristos. Can we go to bed now?"

"Sure," John Tollinger says.

It's an austere January day, the sun out but the land still frozen. The caravan starts out from the White House at nine A.M. The First Lady's schedule, given to the press corps, notes that she intends to spend the day with her son at Walter Reed Hospital. It's of such little interest, having neither novelty nor photo opportunities, that no reporters follow the three cars.

A black van leads the way: four armed Secret Service agents with electronic equipment and a German shepherd trained to sniff out explosives. Then the chauffeured black limousine with armored side panels and bullet-proof glass. The First Lady curls up in the backseat, alongside Jennifer Raye, and seems to nap. Bringing up the rear is a black coupé with another Secret Service man and Helen Hawkins' personal physician.

The vehicles move steadily southward through the bleak Virginia countryside, close enough to each other so that no strange car can break into the line. Through Manassas, through Culpeper, and then down to Goochland.

The Secret Service agents go into the barn first, the German shepherd pulling ahead on a leash. They are inside for almost a half-hour, then the chief exits and comes over to the limousine. He opens the back door.

"All clear," he reports to the First Lady, "but it's not the cleanest place in the world. You sure you want to go in there, ma'am?"

"I'm sure," she says.

She climbs out, followed by Jennifer Raye. Three guards are posted around the barn, the others inside. Helen Hawkins marches steadily through the front entrance. She is wearing a coat of black Persian lamb in an old-fashioned cut.

Agnes, swathed in a clean white robe, comes forward. "Brother Kristos will see you now," she announces like a doctor's nurse.

"May I go in with you?" Jennifer asks.

"No," Helen says. "I want to talk to him alone."

"I wouldn't advise that, ma'am," the Secret Service chief says.

She glares at him. "I can take care of myself," she says sharply. "If I need help, I'll scream. I know how to scream."

She goes into the back room. The chief glances at Jennifer Raye and shrugs.

Brother Kristos sees a spare, determined woman, face pinched with sorrow. She sees nothing but the flame of his eyes.

"Do you know who I am?" she demands.

"Yes, mother," he says in his flat voice. "Your child is ill. A sickness of the blood."

"Can you help him?"

He doesn't answer, but pulls out a chair and motions. She opens her coat and sits down. The fire in the potbellied stove is banked; the room is cool. He stands before her, staring down.

He wears a new blue denim work shirt, still creased from the wrapper. Khaki jeans, beltless, cuffs tucked into motorcycle boots of black leather. His hair and beard are freshly washed but not trimmed. Primal eyes blaze out from a jungle. He sits down facing her, takes her chilled hands in his.

"What do you want?" he asks her.

"The health of my boy."

"Do you believe in God?"

"Yes. Oh yes."

"Why did God let this happen to you?"

"Because I have sinned?" she asks tentatively.

"You are created in God's image. Since God is without sin, so must you be. Do you believe in redemption?"

"Of course."

"But how can you be redeemed if you have not sinned?"

She is a devout woman with a taste for the mystical, but his words bewilder her. "I don't understand," she falters.

He presses her hands. "I speak for God," he says. "I am the brother of Christ, brought to earth to teach His will. Now you are confused. You live a pure life, yet this pain has been inflicted upon you. Has God forsaken you? you ask."

"Yes," she breathes, "oh yes. That is how I feel. What have I done to deserve this?"

"God tests our faith—every day, in a hundred ways. God is trying you. You say you believe, but do you truly believe?"

"I do," she says fiercely, "I really do."

"Then you must prove your faith if this grief is to be taken from you. Do you believe in me?"

She doesn't answer.

"I am God's apostle on earth. If you doubt me, then you doubt Him."

"I believe," she says faintly.

"In God?"

"Yes."

"In me?"

Her "Yes" is fainter still.

"Mother, say to me, 'I believe in you, Brother Kristos.'"

"I believe in you, Brother Kristos," she repeats in a small voice.

"If that belief is not strong and true, then I can do nothing for your son. The stronger your faith, the stronger God's powers become. You understand that?"

She nods slowly. Not once has she been able to move her eyes away from his burning stare.

"Give me a sign," she pleads. "Any sign that you are who you claim to be."

"You tried to kill yourself," he tells her. "Several years ago. Your husband found you in time."

She begins weeping quietly. "How did you know?" she asks. "It was never printed. How did you know?"

"Is anything hidden from God?"

They sit in silence then. Suddenly: "Mrs. Hawkins!" Jennifer Raye calls. "Are you all right?"

"Yes, yes!" she shouts. "Go away, go away!"

Brother Kristos stands, moves behind her. He pulls her fur coat down. He places his big hands on her shoulders.

He begins to knead her flesh, strong fingers reaching up to the back of her neck. Her head lolls forward, bobbing bonelessly.

"Will you help my child?" she asks.

"I must see him. Talk to him. Touch him as I am touching you."

"It can be arranged," she says breathlessly.

"If you wish. But nothing will happen if you do not believe in me."

"I do believe. I *do!*"

"And your husband?"

"I'll explain it to him. If there is a chance, any chance, he will agree; I know he will."

"He has many responsibilities, many duties. But does he have time for faith?"

"Oh yes. We pray together. Every night."

"Some prayers go unanswered. But that is God's answer: No."

His fingers stroke her neck, behind her ears, the sharp line of her jaw. He feels the flesh of her shoulders and upper arms.

"Believe in me," he intones, "and I will take your son's suffering unto myself, and he shall be born again."

"I'll find a way," she vows. "Somehow. I want you to see my child, lay your hands on him."

"If you wish," Brother Kristos says, and moves away.

She stands shakily, rebuttons her coat. "I have brought a contribution," she says. "For your church," she adds hastily. "For your good work."

He inclines his head gravely, and she leaves a wad of crumpled bills on the oilclothed table.

"Thank you, Brother Kristos," she says fervently. "Thank you for everything. You've given me new hope."

He remains standing when she departs. He hears voices in the barn. Then, a few moments later, the sounds of engines starting up. He opens the back door. The pale hound comes slinking in, shivering.

Kristos takes a jug of vodka from the cupboard, pours a little into the dog's dish. The animal laps slowly. His master swallows from the bottle, then goes back to the cupboard for a tin plate of peeled cucumbers. He sits at the table, gulping vodka and crunching bites from the raw cukes.

Agnes comes through the curtained doorway.

"They're gone," she says. "How did you make out?"

He gestures toward the money on the table. She grabs it up, counts it swiftly.

"Two hundred," she reports. "Not bad. What kind of a woman is she?"

"Bony. But there is a fever to her skin."

"Pearl should be back soon. She's bringing groceries. We'll have fish stew tonight. With a lot of pepper. Your favorite."

"Good," he says, and starts on another cucumber.

"Ernie McAllister stopped by," she tells him. "He's got a sick heifer. He wants you to come as soon as you can."

Brother Kristos looks up at her. Something changes in his stare; the focus flattens. "Too late," he says. "The animal is dead."

She has learned not to question his pronouncements. She moves to his side, presses her soft belly against his shoulder.

"You look so handsome in your new clothes," she says. "I wish you had let us trim your hair and beard."

He smiles cynically. "And disappoint the fancy ladies? They are excited by a savage. A shaved, civilized preacher man would make them think they weren't getting their money's worth."

Agnes strokes his hair, combing it with her fingers. "Was she really bony?"

His hand falls to her leg. He begins caressing the calf, reaching up to her fleshy thigh. She shivers with delight and parts her legs.

She is naked beneath her robe of sheets. His forefinger

rubs the furred vulva until it is moist. Then the stiff finger
penetrates.

"Deeper," she says, gasping.

But he withdraws his hand and, with a lupine grin,
stands and unbuttons his new shirt. Agnes lifts the robe
off over her head.

"You never get enough, do you?" she says.

"No," Brother Kristos says. "Never."

"He is such a devout man," the First Lady says on the
drive back to the White House. "I can't tell you how impressed I was."

"Mrs. Hawkins," Jennifer says, trying to keep her voice
calm, reasonable, "are you certain you want to go on with
this?"

"Oh yes, I'm certain. And I know that when I tell Ab
about it, he'll be willing. Jen, I realize it's only a chance,
but it *is* a chance, and we must try everything, mustn't
we?"

"Oh sure," Jennifer says. "I can understand that. All
I'm thinking of are the complications. You know: bad
publicity, political fallout."

"I appreciate your concern, dear," Mrs. Hawkins says,
putting a hand lightly on the other woman's arm. "But
we can't let things like that influence us, can we? The important thing—the *only* thing—is my son's health. And
I'm not letting anything stand in the way of trying to do
something about *that.*"

"How do you plan to handle it?" Jennifer asks, wishing
she had a thermos of John Tollinger's dry martinis.

"Oh goodness, I'm sure I'll be able to figure some way
of bringing Brother Kristos and George together. I don't
suppose it would be wise to ask the preacher to come to
the hospital."

"No," Jennifer says hastily, "that wouldn't be wise. The
doctors would resent your bringing in an outside consult-
ant—if you can call him that—and nurses and orderlies

are sure to leak the visit to the media. After all, Brother Kristos doesn't exactly look like a close friend of the First Family."

"Or," Helen Hawkins says, not listening, "perhaps we could take George down to Brother Kristos' church. The outing would do the boy good."

"I don't think that would work," Jennifer says desperately. "The press is sure to follow the ambulance to see where you're taking him. Ma'am, if this is done at all, it's got to be done very discreetly, with the risk of a leak kept to an absolute minimum."

"I've got it!" the First Lady says brightly. "We'll invite Brother Kristos to Camp David for a weekend. He can stay in one of the guest cabins. We'll have other people at the same time—for a cover, you know. And of course we'll bring George out, so the two of them can spend some time together. How does that sound?"

"Wonderful," Jennifer says miserably. The moment she's back in her office, she phones John Tollinger.

=5=

"Chief," Tollinger says the next morning, "you've got to give me some time. An hour at least."

Henry Folsom looks up from his desk. "An hour? Jesus, I don't have five minutes today. What's it about?"

"The Boss."

"What we discussed with Doc Stemple?"

Tollinger nods.

"And it's important?"

"Disaster time."

The Chief of Staff sighs, begins going over his schedule. "Cabinet meeting this morning. This afternoon I'm due on the Hill for a go-around with those hardnoses on the Senate Budget Committee. And in between, I'm supposed to have my weekly lunch with the Vice President—that whiny bastard! I'll have to listen to his complaints and tell him again that we have every intention of keeping him in the Big Picture—whatever the hell that is. And you want me to give you an hour?"

"I think you better," his executive assistant persists.

"If you say so. But if you're pissing in the wind, I'll have your cojones. All right, I'll cancel the lunch with the VP. He'll scream like a stuck pig, but screw him. Want to meet in here?"

"No," Tollinger says, "not here. Too many interruptions, too many ears. Could we use the Situation Room?"

Folsom stares at him. "That bad, is it?"

"Bad enough. I'll order us up some lunch. The usual hot pastrami on rye for you?"

"Yeah, that'll do fine. With a side order of slaw. And a dill pickle. How I'd love a beer with that. I wish to hell the Boss hadn't teetotaled this joint. Can you imagine serving club soda at state dinners? What are we—a bunch of Moslems?"

"I smuggled in a six-pack this morning," Tollinger tells him. "Carlos is keeping it cold in the kitchen. I only had to bribe him one can. But I knew you'd want a brew with your pastrami."

The Chief of Staff grins at him. "Pretty sure of yourself, weren't you?"

By one P.M. they're sitting at one end of a long conference table in the basement Situation Room. It's probably the most secure chamber in the White House, electronically guarded, swept daily to make certain it's free of listening devices. It's a neuter room, decorated in what Folsom calls "vomit beige."

The Chief is seated before two hot pastrami sandwiches on Jewish rye (with seeds), a bowl of coleslaw, another of sliced dill pickles. The cans of beer are placed on the floor, out of sight.

"No lunch for you?" he asks.

"I'll skip," Tollinger says. "I can't eat and talk at the same time."

"It never bothered me," the COS says. "Okay, start talking."

The executive assistant is good at briefings; he's done enough of them. He speaks fluently in short, complete, declarative sentences, with no uhs or ahs. His narrative is organized, with no personal opinions intruding.

He tells the Chief of Staff everything he has heard from Jennifer Raye: how the First Lady learned of Brother Kristos, her resolve to visit the reported faith healer, Raye's preliminary trip with the Secret Service agent to check out security, and then Mrs. Hawkins' personal interview with the pastor.

Whenever possible, Tollinger uses Jennifer's words to describe Kristos and the dilapidated barn in which he preaches. He concludes by telling Folsom of the First Lady's plan to invite the man to Camp David so he may meet her afflicted son and perhaps perform one of his "miracle cures."

The Chief of Staff listens to all this without interrupting. He steadily demolishes his lunch. When Tollinger has finished, Folsom pushes back from the table. He pops two beers and slides one across to his executive assistant.

"Sometimes," he says, "I wish I was back in Wichita Falls. This is one of those times."

"You had to know," Tollinger says stolidly.

The COS nods. "Sure. Thanks for telling me. You got all this from Jennifer?"

"That's correct."

"Who else knows?"

"You, me, Jennifer, the First Lady. The Secret Service

men and her doctor went along on the trip to the barn, but I doubt if they know the purpose of her visit."

"Someone else knows—Brother Kristos. And probably his tootsies. Does Jennifer know you're telling me all this?"

"No."

"How do you think she'll react if she finds out?"

Tollinger takes a sip of beer before he replies. "Infuriated, probably. She considers herself a strong woman capable of solving her own problems."

"But you don't think so?"

The executive assistant stirs uncomfortably. "She's very emotional. But the fact that she told me about the First Lady and Brother Kristos seems to me a plea for help. She knows what the consequences might be."

"Yeah," Folsom says, "like the media learning that the First Lady is hobnobbing with some schmuck in a turban who reads tea leaves."

"I don't think he's that bad," Tollinger says, "but bad enough. Chief, our first consideration can't be Mrs. Hawkins' public image. We've got to protect the Boss. If she insists on Kristos visiting Camp David, do you think the President will agree?"

"Hell yes. When it comes to shit like this—the power of God to work miracles—he's as gullible as she is. Yeah, he'll go along with her. And the press will get hold of it— you can't keep something like that covered up forever— and then we'll have some first-term congressman making snotty remarks about the Boss's mental competence. John, I can't believe you told me all this without figuring out some way to limit the damage."

"I was up most of the night," Tollinger acknowledges. "Smoked too many pipes and drank too much single malt. This is what I suggest:

"So far all we've got is Jennifer's version of what's going on. I think our first objective should be to get an X ray on this Brother Kristos. Who is he? What's his background? Where did he come from? Does he have a criminal record? If he turns out to be a complete fraud with a police rap sheet, we can take the evidence to the Boss and prove the man should be dumped."

"Yeah," Folsom says slowly, "that's a possibility."

"As I see it," Tollinger goes on, "we better keep this under wraps. Ordinarily we'd ask for an FBI check. But the fewer people who hear about it, the better."

"I'll buy that," the Chief of Staff says. "But who's going to get the skinny on this guy if we don't use the spooks?"

"You trust me?" John asks.

"Stupid question," the Chief says. "If I didn't, would you be sitting here?"

"Then let me handle it. I'll be your cut-out. All you'll have to do is sign some petty-cash vouchers, marked for research. Then if the roof falls in, you'll be clean."

Folsom gives him a wry grin. "Thanks, John, but no, thanks. I'm not going to leave you twisting in the wind. If you're in, I'm in. Handle it yourself, but keep me up to speed. Oral reports only. No tapes, nothing on paper."

"Will do," Tollinger says.

He goes back to his office, spins his Rolodex, comes up with the phone number of his contact at the Federal Bureau of Investigation: Fred C. Hechett, an assistant deputy director. He calls, and they exchange pleasantries.

"Listen, Fred," Tollinger says, "this isn't an official call—just a personal thing I hope you'll be able to help me with. You remember an agent named Marvin Lindberg? You guys bounced him about six months ago."

"Of course I remember him," Hechett says, "and we didn't bounce him; he was allowed to resign."

"He was on the sauce—right?"

"Hey, come on," the FBI man says. "You don't expect me to answer that, do you?"

"I heard that he's opened a private-investigation agency," Tollinger says. "No divorces, but credit checks and things like that. He helped us out once, and I remember him as a very savvy guy."

"The best. We were sorry to lose him."

"Well, here's my problem: I've got a friend who wants to invest in a new bank being organized in Silver Spring. But before he does, he'd like to know a little more about the guys who are pushing the deal. So he asked me for help. I can't do anything officially, but I remembered Marvin and I'd like to throw some business his way. You don't happen to know the name of his outfit, do you?"

"Sure," Hechett says. "He's working out of Alexandria under his own name. I don't have his number, but he's probably in the book."

"Thanks, Fred. I owe you one."

Hechett hangs up, stares at the phone thoughtfully. Then he picks it up again and asks his secretary to put him through to the Executive Office Building.

At four that afternoon, Tollinger is seated on a wooden bench in the Enid A. Haupt Garden at the Smithsonian Institution. He's wearing a double-breasted chesterfield, black homburg, white silk scarf, deerskin gloves.

A few minutes after four, Marvin Lindberg comes lumbering up, and Tollinger rises to greet him. The two men shake hands, then sit close together on the slatted bench.

"Great spot to meet," Lindberg says, looking around the deserted garden. "Couldn't you have picked a place with steam heat?"

"I guess I'm getting paranoid," the executive assistant says.

"Anyone in this town who isn't paranoid is nuts. What's on your mind?"

"I've got a job for you. But before I get into that, I've got to know something."

Lindberg looks at him with a twisted smile. "You mean am I still on the booze? No, but I'm an alkie and will be till the day I die. I've joined AA, and I'm taking it a day at a time. So far, so good."

He was once a beefy man with heavy shoulders and a gut. He's shrunken now, his neck too thin for his collar, spindly wrists lost in the cuffs of his shirt. He still has a boozer's nose and his voice is a whiskey tenor.

Tollinger decides to bet on this wreck.

"This is a personal job," he tells the ex-FBI man. "It's got nothing to do with the administration."

"Uh-huh. If you say so."

"I want a profile on a man. Full name, date and place of birth, education, job history, marital status, possible criminal record—everything. In other words, a complete dossier. I'm sure you know what I need."

"I know," Lindberg says, and gives him that crooked smile again. "A thousand a week plus expenses."

"That's a little stiff, isn't it?"

"Sure it is," the investigator agrees. "You can hire other eyes for a lot less."

"How long do you think it'll take?"

"I know the ropes; it shouldn't take more than a month. That includes travel if it's necessary."

"It probably will be," Tollinger says. "Can you submit daily reports?"

"Waste of time. Maybe nothing will turn up every day. How about weekly? More often if something hot breaks."

"All right. I want the reports mailed to my home."

"If you're really paranoid," Lindberg says, "you could rent a PO box under a phony name."

"No," Tollinger says. "Mail the reports to me directly. How do I get the cash to you?"

"Can you give me an advance?"

"I have a thousand with me."

"That'll do. When I need more, I'll give you a call."

"At my home," Tollinger says hastily. "Not at the Casa Blanca."

Lindberg sighs. "Give me credit for a little sense, will you? All right, we've got the sordid money matters settled. Now, who is this guy?"

"I don't know his full name. He calls himself Brother Kristos. He claims to be a preacher, a faith healer, and a seer."

"Beautiful. And where does this fruitcake hang out?"

"Down in Virginia. Listen, I've written it all out for you. Everything I know about him. His church is an old tobacco barn. Apparently he's living with two young women. Try to find out their names, will you, and what their relationship is to Brother Kristos."

"I know what their relationship is," Lindberg says. "Sexual. Okay, give me your info and the retainer, and I'll get to work."

Tollinger reaches into his inside jacket pocket, hauls out a Mark Cross pigskin wallet with gold corners. He extracts a single sheet of folded foolscap. He hands that to Lindberg. Then, from another compartment, he takes a thin sheaf of hundred-dollar bills. They're brand-new, and he has to lick thumb and forefinger to separate them.

"Did the Treasury Department send these over an hour ago?" the investigator asks.

"Something like that," Tollinger says with a thin smile. "Look, I'm not going to swear you to secrecy or anything like that. I've hired you because I trust you."

"I don't blab," Marvin Lindberg says.

=6=

Michael Oberfest, personal aide to Vice President Samuel Landon Trent, believes strongly in the conspiratorial theory of history. He is convinced that Lyndon Johnson engineered the assassination of President John Kennedy; that Gerald Ford was elevated to the vice presidency in return for a pledge to pardon President Richard Nixon; that President Ronald Reagan promised a cabal of ultraconservative Californians to balloon the national debt to the point where no President, for decades to come, would be able to initiate new social programs.

What fun is history without juicy plots?

Oberfest doesn't object to conspiracies, he just wants to get in on them and profit thereby. But in his six years on the staff of Samuel Trent, no opportunities for sharing in a major conspiracy have been offered. The VP is an obstinate, dour man who, one political pundit wrote, "seems to have had a charisma transplant from Andrei Gromyko."

Michael served Trent faithfully while he was governor of Massachusetts. Then his boss was tapped as vice-presidential candidate to balance the ticket with midwesterner Abner Hawkins. The party eked out a small victory, all the sweeter for being close, and Michael Oberfest now works in the Executive Office Building, attends diplomatic receptions, has a White House pass, and is courted by lobbyists and petitioners. Power, he has discovered, tastes of honey.

The call from Hechett at the FBI is a puzzler. Fred and Michael are casual friends; both belong to an informal group of government employees that meets occasionally to trade X-rated videocassettes. Hechett phoned to report the call he received from Tollinger.

"He wants to get hold of Marvin Lindberg because he says a friend of his is interested in putting money in a new bank being organized in Silver Spring. I know what a wheeler-dealer you are in investments, so I figured I'd let you know in case you want to get in on it. And maybe score some brownie points for myself."

"Sure thing, Fred," Michael says. "Thanks for the tip. I'll look into it."

So Oberfest, a greedy man, does look into it. He calls his stockbroker, his banker, and a contact at the Federal Reserve. They all promise to check it out and get back to him as soon as possible. And they all do, because he is the top personal aide to the Vice President of the United States of America, and not a man to be given a fast shuffle.

By four o'clock that afternoon, after listening to his informants' reports, Oberfest is convinced there is no new bank being organized in Silver Spring. That means Tollinger's call to Hechett was a cover for something else. Either Tollinger personally or the White House had need of a private investigator, someone outside official channels. And they sought out an ex-FBI man cashiered for drunkenness.

The Vice President is in his office being interviewed by a young, inexperienced reporter from Missoula, Montana.

"Sir," the lad says earnestly, "do you ever disagree with the policies of President Hawkins?"

"Of course there will be minor disagreement from time to time," Trent replies with his glacial smile. "But always over matters of tactics, never of strategy. That is to say, policy conflicts are extremely rare if not nonexistent. When there is debate over implementation of policy, a frank discussion is held—a give-and-take, you might say—and inevitably a consensus is arrived at. I am a team player, an active participant at meetings of the Cabinet and National Security Council, and I assure you my primary objective is the furtherance of this administration's plans for a stronger, happier, and more equitable nation."

"Thank you, sir," the reporter says faintly, closing his notebook.

When he exits from the Vice President's private office, Oberfest is there to usher him out into the corridor. The aide glances sympathetically at the journalist. He recognizes the symptoms of someone who has been exposed to the numbing effects of Trent's rhetoric for the first time: eyeballs glazed over, slack jaw, a slight tremor of the hands.

Then Oberfest returns to the VP's office, knocks once and enters. "Sir," he says, "a few minutes of your time?"

"Art is long, and Time is fleeting," Trent says. "What is it?"

The aide tells him of the curious phone call from Fred Hechett, and his subsequent investigation. When he finishes, he remains stationed in front of Trent's desk. The Vice President prefers to keep his underlings standing, like errant schoolboys summoned to the principal's office.

It is true that Samuel Landon Trent is more highly educated than most of the men and women running the U.S. government—and he is acutely aware of it. He is a ferociously ambitious man, his aspirations soured with resentment at having to play second fiddle to a man he considers a dolt. "Abner Hawkins," he once said to his wife, "is a shit-kicker from one of those states beginning with a vowel."

Being a Boston Brahmin, Trent feels the highest office in the land should rightfully be his, not only on the basis of intelligence and ability, but as a kind of divine right. Hawkins' family goes back two generations to the steerage deck of an immigrant ship. Trent's ancestors span two centuries in America, and his forebears include three bishops, four college presidents, one general, an admiral, two federal judges, and a horse thief. His wife, the former Matilda Sopley Arbuthnot, is similarly well-bred.

"A challenging incident," Trent says when his aide has finished his story. "Now let me elucidate a rather enigmatic chain of events." He holds up a slender thumb. "One, you receive a puzzling phone call that, quite logically, leads us to believe that the White House is seeking a private investigator outside of official channels."

He holds up a slim forefinger. "Two, earlier today the Chief of Staff called to express regrets that he was forced to cancel our weekly luncheon. His excuse was 'press of business,' but I do not believe him."

He holds up a long middle finger. "Three, yesterday my wife received her copy of the First Lady's schedule. It stated that Mrs. Hawkins planned to spend the day at Walter Reed Hospital, visiting her ill son. Matilda decided she would join the First Lady for an hour or two, to offer what comfort and companionship she could. But when she phoned Walter Reed to ask if the First Lady had arrived, she was told that not only was Mrs. Hawkins not in attendance, but she was not expected."

"Curiouser and curiouser," Michael Oberfest says.

Then, with his thumb and two fingers still extended, the VP says, "Now, taken individually, each of these three incidents is easily explained by happenstance. But coming as they do, three strange and unusual occurrences in a twenty-four-hour period, one cannot but suspect that there is a synergism in effect. Oberfest, can you hazard a guess as to what it might portend?"

"No, sir," Michael says, "I cannot."

"Nor can I," the Vice President says. Then, curling his extended fingers, he slams a hard fist onto his desktop. "All I can predict is that, as usual, I am being kept uninformed of what well may be a significant development that might affect the country's welfare. I will not endure this deliberate neglect of my office any longer. I must know what is transpiring. It is a moral and legal obligation I owe to the citizenry of this great nation. Do I make my position clear?"

"Yes, sir," Oberfest says. "You want me to find out what the hell's going on."

"Right," Trent says. "The sooner the better."

"I'll get on it the first thing Thursday morning," his aide says. "Tomorrow the wife and I are flying up to New York to go shopping. Is there anything I can bring you, sir?"

"Thank you, no," Samuel Trent says with a grim smile. "In my view, New York is a prime example of the decline and fall of Western civilization."

"Yes, sir," Michael Oberfest says. "But the corned beef at the Carnegie Delicatessen is still good."

He returns to his own office, congratulating himself on having conjured up that New York junket so smoothly. He calls his wife to ask how she'd like an afternoon in Manhattan, dinner at their favorite Italian restaurant on East Fifty-eighth Street, and then a night flight back to D.C. Ruth is delighted.

"What's the occasion?" she says.

"Just for fun," he tells her.

So they take the shuttle to New York on Wednesday, cab in from the airport, and separate on the sidewalk outside the Plaza Hotel. They agree to meet in the Oak Bar at four o'clock. Michael watches her head uptown, then enters the hotel, finds a public phone. He makes a call.

"Yes?" a man's voice answers.

"This is Arnold," Oberfest says. "I have those two bolts of cloth you ordered."

"You've got the wrong number, buddy," the man says roughly, and hangs up.

Satisfied, Michael leaves the hotel, pauses to light a García y Vega Napoleon, then begins a slow stroll down Fifth Avenue.

When he was assigned the code name "Arnold," Oberfest asked, "As in Benedict?" And Marchuk, with his jolly smile, said, "Of course not. As in Matthew."

Leonid Y. Marchuk is a press attaché with the Soviet delegation to the United Nations. He is also Major Leonid Y. Marchuk. Of the KGB, Oberfest assumes, or another of those Russian intelligence agencies with improbable names. Michael is really not interested and has never asked.

There is no ideology involved in his treachery. In fact, he believes the political system of the USSR is destined to fail since it denies that great engine of human endeavor: self-interest. But if the shashliks are willing to pay him a thousand dollars a month for rumors and tidbits about the personal foibles of government officials—well, that's easy money, and a man would be a fool not to grab it.

He rationalizes his treason in several ways. He has never been asked to deliver copies of secret documents, and in any case, he cannot pass along classified information on military matters, space exploration, or scientific research simply because he is not privy to such matters.

He is, in fact, more gossip columnist than spy, and why on earth the comrades are willing to pay for such drivel is beyond him. But they do pay, in cash, every month. Usually, soon after his oral reports are delivered to Major Marchuk, the identical information is printed in the *Post, Times,* the newsmagazines, or perhaps in the tabloids. So what possible harm to the country could Michael Oberfest be causing?

It is a hard, tingly day in New York, temperature in the low forties, with a turquoise sky and thin scrabbles of white clouds. Bundled in his tweed Burberry, puffing his cigar, he saunters south on Fifth Avenue. As usual, he marvels at the drive and frantic energy of this city. New York is a den of hustlers in pursuit of the quick buck, and Oberfest feels right at home.

He window-shops, then stops at Saks to buy a lovely Chanel scarf for his current girlfriend. He pays for it with cash and has it sent directly to her apartment in Foggy Bottom. He also buys a cravat for himself: "power yellow" silk imprinted with tiny yin-yang symbols.

A few minutes before two o'clock, he enters the lobby of a small hotel on West Forty-sixth Street, just east of Sixth Avenue. It is a comfortably sleazy place, catering mostly to professionals in TV, the theater, and, occasionally, coke dealing.

He rides the birdcage elevator to the sixth floor, walks down the dingy corridor to Room 612, and knocks twice. The door is immediately opened by Major Leonid Y. Marchuk, who greets him with a beamy smile and a bear hug that almost cracks Michael's ribs.

"Moscow weather!" Marchuk cries after the door is closed. "Isn't it splendid? And look what I have brought to chase the chill."

He displays a bottle of Pertsovka pepper-flavored vodka, then pours each of them a full tumbler.

"My God!" Oberfest says. "I can't drink all that. I've got to meet my wife at the Plaza in two hours."

"So?" the major says, shrugging. "Drink as much as you wish. I will finish mine, and then I will finish yours. Believe me, nothing ever goes to waste."

It is a shabby hotel suite, with wallpaper of squalling parrots and an armchair and couch of brown velvet worn to an oily shine. The two men sit side by side on the lumpy couch.

"So!" Marchuk says, hoisting his glass. *"Na zdorovye!"*

"Cheers," Oberfest says. Then: "Good Lord! It's liquid dynamite."

"It will put lead in your pencil," the major says jovially.

"Who the hell wants lead in his pencil? I prefer helium."

The Russian shouts a laugh and slaps his heavy thigh. "Arnold, you are a funny, funny man. I always look forward to our little chats. Now tell me, what is the latest from Washington?"

It is all inconsequential stuff, Oberfest tells himself, and will soon be public knowledge:

—The name of the emissary being sent to Peru to negotiate the release of the hostages.

—The terms of the compromise on the trade bill being worked out with the Speaker of the House.

—The decision to appoint an economist to advise the National Security Council.

—The rumor that the Chairman of the Armed Services Committee has a fabulous collection of evening gowns and high-heeled shoes.

—The report that two members of the Supreme Court came to blows over a debate on the rights of inmates of federal prisons to sue the government.

All unimportant, Michael decides, even as he's relating it. And dull, dull, dull. But Marchuk doesn't seem bored. He sips his peppered vodka and listens intently, his broad face creased into an understanding and sympathetic smile. And he laughs easily: great, hearty laughs as if he and Arnold are partners in a delicious farce. Both know how ridiculous it all is, but they must play their roles with a smirk and a wink.

"Finally," Oberfest concludes, "something came up yesterday that's a real teaser."

He tells the major of those incidents involving the First Lady, John Tollinger, and the White House Chief of Staff.

"So now the Veep wants me to look into it," he says. "Probably all garbage."

"True," the Russian says. "But garbage smells. Capitalist garbage or Communist garbage—it all smells. That Vice President of yours—I do not like that man. He is too proud—and what does he have to be proud about? That he was not born a Hottentot? Also, he is a sworn enemy of the Soviet Union. That has advanced his political career—no? He thinks we do nothing but drink vodka, eat *kapusta,* and send people to Siberia."

And again that boomy laugh. He finishes his drink, then

takes an envelope from his jacket pocket and passes it to Oberfest.

"Invest it wisely," he advises, "and keep me informed on what you uncover in your investigation. It is—what is the English word I want? It means odd and amusing at the same time."

"Droll?" Michael suggests.

Marchuk claps him on the shoulder. "Exactly! Droll. It is a droll thing, and it will be interesting to learn how it comes out. Oh God, I love my job! I love this country! Arnold, I must tell you my greatest fear is that someday I will be transferred. To Madagascar perhaps, or Iceland. I would defect! You know, for two years I was stationed in Los Angeles. Oh, those California women! They have such *long* legs! And the tanned skin—like satin. Oh yes, I love the California women and everything else about this marvelous nation. I want to stay here for the remainder of my life."

"Lots of luck," Oberfest says, rising.

The Russian accompanies him to the door, a beefy arm heavy on Michael's shoulders. "You have memorized the emergency number?" he asks. "Just in case."

"Oh sure. I've got it."

"Good," the major says with a final loud laugh. "Now go meet your good wife and enjoy life."

After Oberfest has departed, Marchuk closes and locks the door. He bends down to retrieve the miniaturized tape recorder (made in Taiwan) from under the couch. He switches it off, removes the cassette.

He sits solidly, reflecting, occasionally tapping the tape recording against his meaty chin.

Then he reaches for Arnold's tumbler of vodka, still almost full, and starts sipping. As he told the greedy simpleton, nothing ever goes to waste.

=7=

The Family Room in the White House has been redecorated by every First Lady for the past fifty years, but certain pieces of furniture, lamps, paintings, bric-a-brac have survived the changes. The room is now an eclectic mix, composed in groupings of couches, chairs, and end tables that suggest an enormous First Family capable of making this stilted retreat hum with talk and laughter.

At the moment, the room is dimly lighted. President and Mrs. Hawkins are seated close together on a chintz couch. They seem lost in the shadows, lost in a hollow home where they own nothing. And outside in the corridor, the man in the black suit with the code case shackled to his wrist chats quietly with a Secret Service agent.

"But is he a regular minister?" the President asks his wife. "Is he ordained?"

"I don't know," Helen Hawkins admits. "I don't even know what denomination he is. But is it important, daddy?"

"Probably not. There are places in this country where you can get a certificate of ordainment for five bucks, and a degree as Doctor of Divinity for ten. All through mail order. Mommy, I don't want you to be hurt. This man may be a complete fraud."

"I know that," she says, and takes his hand in hers. "But I feel, I just *feel* that he may be the answer to our prayers. Daddy, can't we give him a chance? I do have faith in him."

He sits there brooding, knowing the risk: his political and hers spiritual, for how many times can you have your hopes destroyed before surrendering to despair? But Abner Hawkins comes from a godly family and has an ingrained respect for men of the cloth, be it silk or burlap.

"If he cannot help George," she says, "then I'll never see him again. I promise. But I want so much to do this. I think that when you meet him, you'll be as impressed as I am."

He takes a deep breath. "All right, if it means so much to you. We'll have him out to Camp David for a weekend."

"Thank you," his wife says huskily, blinking back tears. "I'll take care of everything; you won't have to do a thing."

"Be careful," he warns her. "The fewer people who know, the better."

"Of course," she cries, almost gaily, and lifts his hands to kiss his fingers.

Tollinger:

Re: Brother Kristos.

The guy's full moniker is Jacob Everard Christiansen. He was born in Bethlehem, Nebraska. (How does that grab you?) So far I've got three different dates of birth. I'll try to pin it down, but it looks like he's somewhere between thirty-eight and forty-one. No record of military service. No Social Security number under his real name. No listing at

*the National Crime Information Center—which doesn't
necessarily mean he hasn't got a rap sheet.*

*In case you're wondering how I got this stuff, I started
with the license plate of an old, rusty Ford pickup truck
he owns. He also owns the tobacco barn and ten acres
around it. He appeared about a year ago and bought everything with cash.*

*The two floozies he lives with are Agnes Brittlewaite and
Pearl Gibbs. They're half-sisters: same mother, different fathers. When Kristos showed up in Virginia, he had them
in tow. I don't know yet where or how he met them. He's
also got a flea-bitten hound that looks like a dehydrated
ghost.*

*The guy himself is big, husky, with a full mustache and
beard. Brown hair as long as a hippie's. His voice is a big
nothing, but his eyes are something else again. I mean they
glitter. Real hypnotic stare.*

*He preaches every night at eight o'clock. Then his two
playmates take up a collection. He also has private "consul-
tations"—for a fee, I assume. I don't think he's getting rich,
but he's getting by. The locals say his congregation is growing. He started with a handful of people and now, on a good
night, he might pull in as many as fifty. But he's not yet
ready for Madison Square Garden.*

*I can't find anything to indicate that he belongs to any
organized religion, but I want to keep digging into that.
Right now, I think he's winging it. He's got a reputation
in the neighborhood (blacks and whites alike) as a real faith
healer. And it's said he's able to predict the future and tell
people about happenings in their past that apparently he
couldn't have known.*

*He's also supposed to be the greatest vet for miles around.
They say he's a miracle worker when it comes to sick animals.*

*I sat in on two of his sermons. It's crazy stuff. I'm not
sure I understand it all, but I gather what he's saying is
that we're all without sin because we're created in God's*

image. But if we do feel guilty about having sinned, then just shovel it off onto Brother Kristos because he's willing to assume the sins of the world. All crap—right?

To get the full flavor of this weirdo you've got to see and hear him in action. I recommend you make the trip. It's better than the Late, Late Show.

As for me, I'm taking off for Bethlehem, Nebraska, to pick up the trail where it starts. I'm beginning to get interested.

—Lindberg

=9=

Tollinger, a lanky, loose-jointed man, folds himself behind the wheel of his black Jaguar XJ-S coupé. (Twenty-two more monthly payments, and it will *really* be his.) He gets an early start, hoping to beat the bridge traffic, but it's almost four o'clock before he's across the Potomac and heading south through Virginia.

The January thaw has finally arrived; it's a splendiferous afternoon with a cantaloupe sun, a sky freckled with clouds, and a breeze balmy enough so that he can lower the windows, breathe deeply, and believe in the afterlife.

He loves to drive: in daylight, at night, in fog or rain, snow or threatened hurricane. It's being snug, closed in, with time and distance conquered by speed. "It's your vice," Jennifer once told him. "Instead of boozing it up, whoring around, or writing haiku, you're hooked on driving."

"Maybe," he replied.

The day deepens as he goes, the sky rusting, the evening light taking on the color of Beaujolais Nouveau. He is mistrustful of gratifying sensory impressions, being the kind of man who says mournfully, "You must pay for your pleasures in this world." But even he finds this sweet twilight difficult to resist.

He locates Brother Kristos' barn with no trouble. The bare land around is crowded with parked cars, motorcycles, vans, pickups. Tollinger parks away from the jam, locks up and walks back to the barn. It is not yet eight o'clock, and cars are still arriving.

He finds a seat on one of the rough benches at the rear, figuring to make an unobtrusive exit if Kristos' sermon turns out to be a bore. He waits patiently, inspecting the congregation: a strange stew of farmers in overalls, women in furs, a few teenagers, a few blacks, a man who looks like a bank president, a woman who looks like a hooker, two gays holding hands and whispering.

Brother Kristos comes striding from the back room, the hairless hound shambling along at his heels. The preacher mounts the stage, stands before the crude pulpit, gripping it with both hands. He begins speaking without greeting or preamble.

"You are here because you are afflicted," he says. "In the flesh or in the spirit. Some of you suffer the body's decay, some the soul's despair. But all of you share a common sickness that drains away hope and turns the brightest day to blackest night.

"I speak to you of loneliness.

"It is a torment that robs you of happiness and mocks success. Oh, you may be surrounded by family and friends, but I know that in the secret corners of your heart is the corrosive acid of loneliness that eats away the healthy tissues of your life and robs the world of savor.

"Can you deny it? Deny that you feel alone and vulnerable? Your family may desert you, friends betray you, and what then is left but a loneliness that fills your spirit like some loathsome and growing tumor that devours all?

"Why must you suffer so? Loneliness is only egotism. You think yourself the center of the universe, forgetting that you are one with God. For you are created in His image. He is part of you, and you of Him. Believe in God and you are not alone."

As he speaks in his unemotional voice, Brother Kristos stares at each member of his audience. John Tollinger feels the blaze of those unblinking eyes.

"Do not weep for your loneliness," the preacher continues. "Weep for your ignorance. For God awaits you with open arms, to listen to your plaints, renew your hopes, and return tenfold the love you bring to Him.

"Listen to me with your hearts. I say to you that loneliness will continue to weaken and wear away your life until you seek God's solace. For He shall be spouse, friend, confidant, counselor, and lover. More than all that, He shall be part of you, and you part of Him if only you will bring your love to the Supreme Being.

"I speak for God. Believe in me."

He continues for another fifteen minutes, then stops abruptly and stalks from the stage, the pale hound slinking after him. The two women in white robes pass among the congregants, holding out their cigar boxes. John Tollinger contributes a dollar.

He is impressed by Brother Kristos' sermon—mostly because it wasn't the conventional "Come to Jesus and be saved" pitch he had expected. And his listeners were visibly affected.

Tollinger waits until the crowd has dispersed. Then he approaches one of the assistants.

"May I speak to Brother Kristos?" he asks. "Privately."

She inspects him, up and down. "You wait here," she says finally. "I'll go ask."

She's gone for a minute or two, then beckons Tollinger from the curtained doorway.

Brother Kristos has removed his burlap robe. He is wearing a blue denim work shirt, jeans, black motorcycle boots. He seems weary, drained, but his eyes are as fierce, his gaze as steady. Tollinger now knows what Jennifer Raye and Marvin Lindberg meant; he cannot turn away from that locked stare.

"Brother Kristos," he says, surprised by the quaver in his own voice, "I thought your sermon tonight was inspiring."

The man doesn't answer, and Tollinger plunges ahead.

"I have heard you can heal the sick. I am very ill. Cancer of the colon. The doctors want to operate. But before I go through that, I wanted to ask if you can help me."

The preacher turns away. He takes a bottle of vodka from a cupboard, uncaps it, swallows thirstily.

"You are not sick," he says to Tollinger. "You mean to test me. You are my enemy. You are an unbeliever. You have no faith in me. Or in God."

"Cut the religious bullshit," John says roughly. "So I'm a lousy actor. Give me a drink, will you? I'll pay for it."

Unexpectedly, Brother Kristos laughs. It's soundless, but he throws back his head and shows his tarnished teeth. He passes the bottle to Tollinger.

"Help yourself," he says. "I like you. Direct. No nonsense. You think me a faker—is that it?"

"That's it," Tollinger says, scalding his throat with a swallow of vodka. "I think you're gulling a lot of innocent people, and making a nice buck from it. You're a fraud."

Kristos concentrates his stare again, capturing the other man's eyes. He takes back the bottle and drinks more.

"I'm a fraud?" he says mildly. "And you're a fool. Did you think I had intended to speak of loneliness tonight? I did not. I had planned to talk of guilt. But when I came out, the first thing I saw was you sitting alone on a back bench. You looked so bereft that I decided to speak instead of the sin of loneliness. For it is a sin. You are a lonely man, and what's worse, you take pride in it."

"I'm not lonely," Tollinger protests. "I have many friends, a busy life."

Kristos gives him a sly smile. "You have lost your woman and think yourself happy in your solitude. You yearn to become a hermit. Why? You blame that on . . . on what? On your miserable childhood? Your wrangling parents?"

Tollinger is stunned, so shocked that he thrusts hands into his pockets to hide the tremor. "You're totally wrong," he says in a shaky voice.

"No," Brother Kristos says, "I am totally right. But it is not too late to change, to seek love and return it."

"God's love?"

"Or a woman's," the preacher says, shrugging. "Same thing."

"Can I have another drink?" Tollinger says hoarsely.

He has a deep swallow, then puts a fifty-dollar bill on the table. He starts to leave but turns back.

"You know," he says to Kristos, "nothing you say makes sense. I have heard that you believe we are all created in God's image and therefore are without sin. Yet you just accused me of the sin of loneliness. You tell people they are guiltless, but you offer to assume their guilt if they will only believe in you. Your beliefs are not rational. There is no logic to them."

"You think logic and reason will solve the problems of this world?" Kristos asks. "They will not. You think yourself a logical and rational man, but your problems will persist until you acknowledge the power of faith which has no logic and no reason except the love of God."

Suddenly he seems shaken. Sweat breaks out on his forehead. He leans again on the table to steady himself, and the blaze in his eyes dulls.

"Is something wrong?" Tollinger asks.

"I have seen my death," Brother Kristos says, his voice charged. "And yours. They are connected. What is your name?"

"Does it make any difference?"

"No. You are the messenger."

"What does that mean?"

Kristos doesn't answer, and again Tollinger turns to leave.

"What is the dog's name?" he asks.

"Nick," Brother Kristos says.

Tollinger drives slowly and carefully on the trip back to Washington. Not because of the vodka—he's got a hard head—but because of what Brother Kristos told him. How could the man have known those intimate things: his taste for solitude, his bickering parents, his loss of Jennifer?

He tries to account for it in rational ways but cannot. Kristos never saw him before, doesn't know his name, could not possibly have investigated his background. His ability to look into John Tollinger's life is a mystery and, for reasons Tollinger can't comprehend, he feels an almost sexual excitement.

It's almost 1:30 A.M. before he gets back to Spring Valley, but there, in his driveway, blocking the entrance to the garage, is Jennifer Raye's red Toyota.

He looks inside. She is asleep behind the wheel, her head turned to one side, mouth partly open. He raps on the window, and she rouses slowly, unlocks the door, comes staggering out.

"Where the hell you been?" she says groggily.

"Partying," he says. "Two embassy shindigs and a buffet dinner at the NAM. I must have gained five pounds. What are you doing here?"

"Beats the hell out of me," she says grumpily.

He supports her to the front door with an arm about her waist. She is a heavy woman, plenty of meat there, but Tollinger has no objection. They get rid of their coats and settle down in the den.

"I could do with a small brandy," he says. "How about you?"

"Ditto," she says.

He pours them ponies of Remy Martin and leaves the bottle on the table between the wing chairs.

"You look beat," he says.

"Not beat," she says gloomily. "Demolished. You know that thing I told you about—the First Lady having Brother Kristos out to Camp David? Well, it's on. A week from this Saturday."

"Shit," Tollinger says.

"You can say that again."

"I will. Shit."

"And I'm supposed to organize the goddamned thing. Some honor, huh? That means I've got to get the invited guests out there, coordinate with the staff at Camp David, liaise with the Secret Service men, and make sure the Mad Monk arrives on time."

"How are you going to do that?"

"I've been authorized to offer him five hundred bucks. That should do it, don't you think?"

"I'll bet on it. He'll come along quietly. Not with his two bimbos, I hope."

"Christ, no! He comes alone or it's no deal. We'll provide a chauffeured limo. That should help convince him."

"Who are the other guests?"

"The daughter of the President's General Counsel and her fiancé. The president of NOW and her hubby. And Representative Louis Gehringer and his new bride. The idea is that they're all young people and will spend the weekend tramping through the woods and won't pay too much attention to Brother Kristos."

"You blew it," Tollinger tells her. "Congressman Gehringer is from Samuel Trent's home state. The Vice President's got him in his hip pocket. If Gehringer spots Kristos, he'll be on the horn to the Veep first thing Monday morning, spilling the beans."

"Too late to worry about that," Jennifer says. "Everyone's been invited, and everyone's accepted. After all, how many chances do you get to weekend with the First Family? Now all I've got to do is make sure the hospital will release the kid for the two days. We'll probably use an ambulance to get him out there."

"With a doctor in attendance, I hope."

"At least one. And the private RN who sits with him. So that's what I've been doing for the past three days, while you've been out partying, you skunk. John, tell me this whole thing is not going to be a world-class balls-up."

"It's not going to be a world-class balls-up."

"You don't sound very confident."

"I'm not. I think it's madness. The media will find out, and then the shit will really hit the fan. Can you imagine what the reactions of the AMA are going to be?"

"Yeah," Jennifer says, "I can imagine. As I see it, I've got two choices: go along with it or resign. And I'm not going to resign. I like my job and I like Mrs. H. She may be way off base on this one, but she's a nice lady, and she needs help. I can't desert her."

"Of course you can't," Tollinger says. "Hang in there, kiddo. It may not turn out to be as bad as we think it will."

"You really believe that?"

"No," he says. "Listen, let's have another shot of that wonderful stuff and then go to bed."

"Hey," his ex says, surprised. "What's with you? Horny all of a sudden?"

"I'm entitled."

"Sure you are."

They take their second cognacs up to the master bedroom. While Jennifer is undressing, Tollinger goes into the bathroom and swabs himself off with a washcloth soaked in hot water. He's still pondering his conversation with Brother Kristos. What did the man mean by saying, "You are the messenger?"

He goes naked into the lighted bedroom. Jennifer is already between the sheets, waiting.

"Beautiful," she says, staring at him. "You could hang a wet towel on that thing."

=10=

A light snowfall has blotched the land with scurries of white and put icing on the evergreens. The guards at Camp David wear belted overcoats and earmuffs, and stamp their heavy boots on patrol. It is a keen day, the sky chiseled, a wind that cuts. Fireplaces are lighted in the main house and guest cabins.

The limousine picks up Brother Kristos early Friday morning. If the chauffeur is surprised by the appearance of his bearded passenger, he doesn't show it. Kristos is wearing his blue work shirt and jeans, cuffs tucked into his boots. A rough wooden cross is suspended from his neck on a piece of twine. He is hatless. His coat is a worn plaid mackinaw. He has no luggage, not even a toilet kit.

He will not sit in the rear of the comfortable Lincoln, but insists on taking the seat next to the chauffeur. On the long drive up to Camp David, the two men talk mostly about a home the chauffeur is building. Kristos advises him on the laying and grouting of ceramic tile.

They arrive at Camp David late on Friday afternoon. The chauffeur has a pass, but the guards on duty call the security chief in the main house to check. And before they are allowed to proceed, the Lincoln is searched and the two men asked to step through an airport-style metal detector.

Only Jennifer Raye, wearing her bulky raccoon coat, is on hand to greet Brother Kristos. She conducts him to his assigned cabin and explains, somewhat nervously, that he'll be dining alone, but the menu is extensive. If he wishes to take a walk, he should inform the security chief by phone that he's leaving the cabin. Also, because of the President's strictures, no liquor is available, but he can order coffee, tea, milk, or soft drinks at any hour of the day or night.

"The others aren't arriving until tomorrow morning," Jennifer tells him. "By helicopter. The boy is being brought out in an ambulance with his doctor and nurse."

Kristos nods, wandering around the room. There is a rack of books and another of videocassettes. The cabin is not lavishly decorated, but it's warm and cheerful, furnished in ranch-house style.

"If there is anything you need," she says, "don't be afraid to ask. I know it all looks rustic, but it's really very well organized, and the kitchen is supposed to be excellent."

"You have been here before?"

"No, this is my first visit. Mrs. Hawkins specifically asked that I do everything possible to make your stay enjoyable."

"You are here alone?" he says, staring directly at her.

"No," she says, flustered. "Well, yes, at the moment I am, but Audrey Robertson, the First Lady's Social Secretary, is coming up with her tomorrow, and she and I will be sharing a cabin."

He stares at her a moment longer, then turns his gaze away, and she is relieved. "I am hungry," he announces. "Do they have fish?"

"Fish? I'm sure they do; after all, it's Friday. How would you like it? Broiled? Sautéed?"

"In a stew," he says. "I like fish stew."

"I'll ask," she says doubtfully. "Maybe they can make it. When would you like to eat?"

He shrugs. "As soon as it's ready."

"Would you like a salad with it?"

"No. Just bread."

He stares at her again. She decides it's like facing an enormous furnace and suddenly opening the door. The heat leaps at her in a suffocating blast; breath catches in her throat.

"You will eat with me," he says, more command than request.

She hesitates. "Yes, all right," she says. "I'll have it served here. We'll have dinner, and then I'll leave you. I'm bushed; it's been a long day."

He doesn't reply. She departs to consult with the chef. When he's alone, he wanders about the cabin. He inspects the spotless bathroom, trying the hot-water tap, fingering the thick, fluffy towels. In the small bedroom, he prods at the bed, then lies down atop the satin coverlet. He grasps his wooden cross and stares at the beamed ceiling a long time.

"Thank you," he says aloud.

He rises and moves into the living room again. He's inspecting the VCR when Jennifer Raye returns. She is leading two attendants wearing white mess jackets. They're carrying stainless-steel containers zipped into quilted jackets to keep the food warm. And boxes of table linen, cutlery, and white china bearing the Presidential Seal.

"Bouillabaisse!" Jennifer sings out. "Isn't that wonderful?"

"What is it?" Brother Kristos asks.

She looks at him. "What you wanted. Fish stew."

The stewards set the table in a windowed alcove, uncover the food, and leave. Brother Kristos pulls up a chair and sits. He motions for Jennifer to join him. She pulls up her own chair, wondering if he'll say grace.

He doesn't, but immediately ladles half the pot of stew into his bowl. He rips chunks from the long loaf of hot French bread and, hunched over his food, gets to work. Jennifer helps herself to a modest portion and samples it delicately.

"Mmm," she says, "that's good, isn't it?"

"Needs pepper," he says, and begins dusting the bouillabaisse with the big shaker.

She watches him, fascinated. He eats like some great shaggy beast—a starved beast. He makes growls of satisfaction deep in his throat as he fills his mouth, chews ravenously, spits out pieces of shell. Sauce drips onto his beard. His mustache becomes slick. But he never pauses; his napkin remains neatly folded.

Jennifer tries to eat but cannot. She is more enthralled than disgusted at the sight of this grown man gorging like a famished child. He glances at her full plate, then helps himself to more from the stew pot. He devours shrimp, mussels, clams, crabmeat, lobster, fish, onions, celery, diced potatoes, carrots, garlic cloves—everything. His strong jaws work steadily as juices flow onto his beard, and the pile of spat shells and bones continues to grow.

He doesn't stop until the pot is empty, and then he wipes it clean with a piece of bread. Jennifer moves her filled bowl toward him.

"Go ahead," she says. "I'm not hungry."

He makes no protest, but finishes her dinner too. She offers him the dessert—wedges of Nesselrode pie. But he shakes his head and pushes back from the table. On impulse, she unfolds his napkin and, leaning forward, wipes his mustache and beard. He lets her do it, showing his big stained teeth in what she hopes is a smile.

"I can see you enjoyed that," she says as lightly as she can. "It was good, wasn't it?"

"All food is good," he says. "And drink. A gift."

"There's coffee. Would you like some?"

He shakes his head again, stands and stalks away from the table, leaving her sitting alone. She tries to tidy up as best she can, ashamed to have the stewards see the mess he's made when they return for the dishes.

"I think I'll have a cup of coffee," she calls. "And maybe a piece of pie. Then I'll be on my way."

There is no answer. She turns, but the living room is empty. She goes looking for him, fearing he has left the cabin without informing security. The door to the darkened bathroom is open; he is not in there. But she finds him in the bedroom. He is kneeling at the bed, his head bowed. She hears him muttering and assumes he is praying.

She returns to the table and has a cup of coffee, lukewarm now, that does nothing to calm her agitation.

Leave, she tells herself. Leave!

But she stays.

She finishes the coffee and returns to the bedroom. Brother Kristos is standing at the knotty-pine dresser, staring at himself in the framed mirror.

"I think I'll leave now," she says, shocked by the timidity in her voice. "I'm sure you'll be all right. Sleep as late as you like."

He turns slowly then and comes close to her. The fire flares up in his eyes, and the hands he puts on her shoulders are heavy and hot.

"Stay with me," he says.

"No," she says, "I've got to go."

"There is no sin," he tells her. "So there can be no guilt. Do not heed your mind. That is nothing. Obey only your will. Do you believe in me?"

"Well, I—I'm not sure what—the things you say . . ."

She cannot turn her gaze from that scintillant stare. It burns.

"What do you see?" she asks breathlessly.

"Fear," he replies. "Not of me but of life. You pretend to be strong, but you question. You dream of monsters."

"I don't—" she says, then chokes on her own words.

He draws her to the bed. "I am no monster," he says. "I am the brother of Christ, brought to earth to show you the one truth."

"You're—" she begins, but cannot finish.

When they are naked, he reverts to the savagery she saw

at the table. She is a big-boned woman, well-padded, but he handles her like a toy, flipping her this way and that. She feels herself lost and gone, as raw and primitive as he.

His body is rude; there is no grace to it. His skin is scarred and torn, rough and hairy. He is as clumsy as a bear that has learned tricks. But the brute strength is there, animal cries, and a sour, primeval scent to his flesh.

He ravages her, his passion insensate, gnawing, clawing, until she is weeping, but from pain or bliss she cannot tell. The wooden cross hanging from his neck falls onto her face, and she puts it into her mouth, biting down on it and hearing his howls.

=11=

The helicopter arrives shortly before ten A.M., bringing the First Family, their entourage and guests. Everyone is transported to the compound by golf carts, and there's a lot of laughing confusion until luggage is sorted out, visitors get settled in their assigned cabins, and the kitchen can begin taking orders for lunch.

A little after eleven A.M. the ambulance arrives with George Powell Hawkins, his doctor and nurse. The boy loves Camp David and is allowed carefully supervised walks along the trails and visits to the security posts, where he has made friends with the guards and Secret Service agents on duty.

At 11:45 A.M. the President and First Lady leave the main house and walk to the cabin assigned to Brother Kristos. He has been alerted to their coming by Jennifer

Raye, and though they are accompanied by the usual Secret Service contingent, the couple enters the cabin alone.

If he is awed by the status of his visitors, he gives no indication. The President and his wife sit side by side on a couch while Kristos slumps negligently in an armchair. Throughout the interview he combs his beard slowly with his blunt fingers, moving those burning eyes from one to the other as they speak.

"My wife has told me about you, Brother Kristos," the President says, "but there are a few questions I'd like to ask if it's all right with you."

"Yes, father," Kristos says.

"Why do you call me 'father'?" Hawkins says with a wan smile. "Washington was Father of Our Country, not me."

"You are father of all the people and must care for us as if we are your children."

"Well, yes, I suppose so," Hawkins says doubtfully. "The first thing I want to ask is this: Are you a member of any organized religion or church?"

"There is only one religion, one church, just as there is only one God, no matter what name He is given."

"Have you been ordained?"

"Only by God. I am His apostle on earth, the brother of Christ."

"How long have you been preaching?"

"I spoke of the glory of God as a child. But only in the past several years has it become my mission."

"You talk like an educated man, Brother Kristos," the First Lady says. "Did you attend college?"

"No, mother. Nor did I finish high school. Whatever learning I may possess has been gained through reading and listening to those I thought wise."

"My wife tells me you have unusual gifts," the President says. "That you can heal the sick. Is that true?"

"If their faith is strong enough."

"Faith in God or faith in you?"

"It is the same thing," Brother Kristos says.

"Can you divine the future?" Mrs. Hawkins asks.

"Sometimes I see things that will happen."

"And the past?" she says, almost breathlessly. "You can see into the past. When we first met, you told me something that occurred in my life that only my husband and I knew about."

Kristos doesn't answer, but turns his stare to the President. That stocky man shifts uncomfortably, but does not look away. There is silence a moment, then the preacher says in his flat voice:

"I see a time in your life, father, when you came to love God. It was at night, following a battle in which many of your friends died. But you did not seek God from fear of what the morning held. You came to Him in thanksgiving, vowing that if you were killed on the morrow you would accept that with your love for Him undiminished, and if you were spared, your love would endure and grow."

"Yes," Hawkins says, his face ashen. "That is what happened."

"That faith sustained you, and you resolved it would never weaken. But then, caught up in your career, your faith became a thing of rote, a Sunday-morning habit that lost the passion you first felt in combat. Now, fervor gone, your faith is being sorely tried. The sickness of your son corrodes your spirit. You wonder how you have sinned to deserve such punishment. But you have not sinned nor should you feel guilt. It is your faith that has withered, and God has sent you this sorrow to strengthen your faith."

"Yes," the President says fervently. "Oh yes."

"Belief in God is a muscle of the will," the Brother concludes, "and must be exercised constantly if it is to remain healthy and hard. Listen to what I say, for I bring you His word."

"Please, Brother Kristos," Helen Hawkins begs, "will

you come visit our son? He's having his lunch now, and then he must have his nap. But when he's awake, can we send for you and will you meet with him?"

"If you wish," Kristos says.

Shortly after 2:30 P.M., Jennifer arrives to escort the preacher to the main house. En route they pass a group of guests who stare at the bearded man curiously, but Jennifer makes no effort to introduce him.

The First Lady is waiting and conducts Brother Kristos to a small bedroom decorated with bright posters of cartoon characters on the walls. Toys are scattered about, but the bed is the hospital type, and in one corner is a locked cabinet of glass and white enamel. It contains medicines and drugs; the lower half is refrigerated.

A doctor and nurse are in attendance, but Mrs. Hawkins speaks to them quietly, and they withdraw as the President enters. Then the First Family and Brother Kristos are alone in the room. George is lying in bed, covered to his waist with a sheet and light blanket. He follows all the activity with widened eyes.

The President and Mrs. Hawkins stand against the wall, watching. Brother Kristos approaches the bed slowly. He looks down at the thin, bleached face. Suddenly he waggles his beard at George, flipping it up and down. The lad bursts out laughing, and Kristos laughs along with him. Then he gets down on his knees alongside the bed and takes one of the frail hands in his.

"Who are you?" the boy says. "Santa Claus?"

"No," Kristos says, "I am your brother."

"I don't have a brother."

"I want to be. May I?"

"All right," George says, "if you want. Are you a doctor?"

"A special kind of doctor. Tell me, brother, have you been taught about God?"

"Oh sure. I know what He looks like. He's got a big beard like yours, but His is white and He's got white hair."

"And what does God do?"

"He runs heaven."

"Yes," Kristos says. "He runs heaven and this earth and all the stars. Do you know how to pray, brother?"

"Oh sure. But sometimes I fall asleep before I finish."

"I know. But God understands."

"What's your name?"

"Brother Kristos."

"Where do you live?"

"Far from here. I live in a barn."

"A barn? With animals?"

"Only a dog."

"I like dogs," George says, "but I'm not allowed to play with them. They might bite."

"My dog wouldn't bite you. He'd like you."

"Would he?" the boys says eagerly. "Then I'd like him right back. What's his name?"

"Nick."

"Nick? That's a funny name for a dog."

"Well, he's a funny kind of dog. Have you learned to write?"

"Oh sure, I can write."

"Why don't you write Nick a letter? He can't read, but I'll read it to him and he'll understand."

"No kidding? He'll really understand what you're saying?"

"He is a very smart dog."

"All right," George says, "I'll write him a letter. What should I put in it?"

"Whatever you like. How you're feeling, what you've been doing, things you'd like to do."

The lad giggles. "That's funny, writing to a dog. But I'll do it. Will he answer?"

"Of course," Brother Kristos says. "He'll bark and yap, but I'll know what he means and write it out for him."

"Gee, a letter from a dog!"

Kristos gets to his feet. He leans over the bed, and holding his beard with one hand so it doesn't fall onto George's face, he kisses the boy's brow.

"God be with you, brother," he says tenderly and turns away.

Outside the bedroom, the First Lady grips his forearm tightly and looks into his eyes.

"He likes you," she says. "We could tell."

"He is a beautiful boy."

"Speak honestly," the President says. "Will he live?"

The focus of Kristos' eyes changes; the stare becomes deeper, darker, as if he is searching within himself.

"For many years," he says finally. "A happy life."

"Thank you," Helen says, beginning to weep.

Jennifer escorts Kristos back to his cabin.

"Will you stay with me?" he asks her.

"No," she says sharply. Then adds lamely: "I'm going to be busy with the guests. Have you ordered dinner yet?"

"No."

"They don't have fish stew tonight. But you can have lobster salad, breaded veal cutlet, or steak poivre."

"What's that—that last?"

"Steak poivre? It's a boneless sirloin with a hot pepper sauce."

"I'll have that. Two of them."

"Vegetables? Salad?"

He shrugs. "Whatever they have. And bread."

She tarries at the door of his cabin. "How did it go with George?"

"All right." He stares at her. "I will see him again. Very soon."

Then he enters the cabin, leaving her standing there, frightened for reasons she cannot understand.

He undresses and goes into the bathroom. It is completely equipped for guests: perfumed soap, shampoo, toothpaste and a new brush sealed in plastic, a sealed comb, bubble bath, cologne, a manicure set. Kristos inspects this assortment, sniffing the soap and cologne.

He fills the tub with water so hot it steams. He dumps in some of the bubble bath and watches the soapy foam rise. He eases into the searing water, his skin turning red. Finally he is immersed up to his chin. His beard floats in the suds. He closes his eyes, feeling his body dissolve.

He soaks in the tub for almost a half-hour. Then, the water cooled, he stands and drains the tub. He makes no effort to scrub himself with the bar soap or a washcloth—he does not touch himself—but simply turns on the shower and rinses. He uses two thick towels to dry his body and beard, dropping the damp towels to the floor.

He is fully dressed when a steward appears with his dinner and begins setting the table. The attendant is a roly-poly man with a mustache that looks as if it was drawn on his upper lip with an eyebrow pencil. He moves slowly, indolently.

"Will there be anything else, sir?" he finally asks.

"Yes," Brother Kristos says, looking at him. "I want something to drink."

The steward blinks. "I brought you coffee, sir. Would you prefer tea, milk, or a cola?"

"Vodka. I'd prefer vodka."

"Oh no, sir," the man says virtuously. "The President and his missus don't allow any hard stuff on the premises."

"I know," Kristos says. He reaches into his pocket, pulls out bills, counts off fifty dollars.

"Vodka," he repeats. "Any brand."

"It'll mean my job if anyone finds out," the man says, taking the money. "They're very strict. Why, just last month one of the security guards . . ." His voice trails off when he sees Kristos' glare. "Be right back," he says.

By the time he returns, ten minutes later, the bottle concealed in a food container, the Brother has devoured one of the steaks, picking it out of the peppercorn sauce with his fingers and ripping it to shreds between his big teeth.

He uncaps the vodka bottle, drinks deeply, and starts on the second steak, pausing occasionally for a bite of baked potato or a handful of string beans. He drinks more vodka, finishes the small loaf of crusty rye bread, using the heel to sop up the remaining steak sauce.

He leaves the table to sit in an armchair. A different steward appears to clear away the dishes, and if he thinks it strange that the cutlery hasn't been used, he doesn't show it. Nor does he speak to the bearded man.

By midnight the bottle is empty, and Brother Kristos lets it fall to the floor. He goes into the bedroom and lies down on the satin coverlet, not even removing his boots. He is asleep almost instantly, a dreamless slumber during which he never turns nor twitches but lies as slack and silent as a corpse.

At about 2:40 A.M. he is awakened by a pounding on the outside door. He rises immediately and goes into the lighted living room. He pulls open the door. It is Jennifer. The hem of a nightgown hangs below her raccoon coat.

"It's George," she says tensely. "I think he's having a hemorrhage. They want you right away."

He says nothing but walks beside her to the main house. It is an icy night, clear, the black sky spangled with stars. A steady west wind knifes, and their footfalls crunch on patchy snow.

"You should have worn your coat," she says.

Again he doesn't reply, but grabs the wooden cross hanging from his neck and looks up at the glittering heaven. There is a brilliant wildness to the night, the dark dome above seeming to whirl, and the bright stars descending, as if to crush and burn.

There are three Secret Service agents standing outside the main house, hands thrust into their overcoat pockets. They draw silently aside to let Jennifer and Brother Kristos pass. Abner Hawkins is there when they push open the door. The President's face is gaunt.

"It's George," he says dully. "He's bleeding, and they can't stop it. Apparently he threw his leg over the edge of the bed in his sleep and cut it on the steel cranking mechanism. Not a deep cut, but deep enough. They've used compresses, coagulants, and an injection of that new clotting stuff, but nothing helps. The doctor wants to call for an emergency transfusion team, but I don't know if they can get here in time. The boy's lost a lot of blood."

"Is he conscious?" Kristos asks.

"Oh yes, he knows what's happening; he's been through this before. Is there anything you can do, Brother Kristos?"

"Take me to him."

They all crowd into the cheerful bedroom with posters of Mickey Mouse and Donald Duck on the walls. The bed has been cranked up, and the doctor and nurse are working on George's leg. The bandages, towels, sheet have all been soaked through with bright, shiny blood.

The doctor looks up as they enter. "Please, Mr. President," he says angrily, "let me call the hospital for a trauma team."

Hawkins looks to Kristos, and the Brother nods.

"Yes," the President says, "go make your call. And tell them, for God's sake, to hurry."

The First Lady is standing against the wall, a knuckle between her teeth. Brother Kristos goes to her, takes her arm, talks quietly a moment. She nods dazedly.

"Please leave us alone," she says to the nurse. "And, Jennifer, would you also leave."

The nurse begins to object, but Mrs. Hawkins waves her out. Then the First Family and Brother Kristos are alone. He goes over to the bed.

"George," he calls softly.

The boy opens his eyes. "Hi," he says faintly. "Am I going to die?"

Kristos bends over him. "You told me that you know about God."

"Oh sure."

"Do you believe in God, brother?"

The lad nods.

"Of course you do. Well, God has sent me to bring you His love and make you well."

"God knows about me?"

"Of course. Now I want you to pray."

"What should I say?"

"Say, 'I believe in you, God, and I love you.'"

"I believe in you, God," George says in a piping voice, "and I love you."

"Good. Now say, 'I believe in you, Brother Kristos, and I love you.'"

"I believe in you, Brother Kristos," the boy repeats obediently, "and I love you."

"God likes that," the preacher says. "He has heard your prayer and will stop your bleeding."

"He will?"

"Close your eyes and think only of your love of God and your faith in me."

George closes his eyes. Brother Kristos places his hands on the boy's leg, one above and one below the wound. The President and his wife have fallen to their knees and, hands clasped, they watch with fearful eyes.

Kristos' blunt fingers dig into the bloody bandages. His eyes close, his body is shaken by tremors. Sweat breaks out on his brow. His lips move but there is no sound.

The four in the room seem frozen, caught in postures of silent supplication. It is almost five minutes before Brother Kristos straightens up. He withdraws his hands slowly from the soaked wrappings. Then, with infinite care, he peels away the sodden towels, the bandages, the pads. He bends again to look down at the wound, then lifts the wooden cross to his lips with a bloodied hand.

He turns to Abner Hawkins and his wife.

"Father, mother," he calls, "come witness the glory of God."

They rise, rush forward, stare down at their son. The bleeding has stopped.

"A miracle!" the President cries, and embraces Brother Kristos.

=12=

The Chief of Staff is leaning forward, elbows on his desk, head clamped between his palms.

"You got all this from Jennifer?" he asks.

"Yes, sir," John Tollinger says. "She drove back yesterday afternoon and stopped at my place to tell me. She was practically hysterical."

"I don't blame her," Henry Folsom says. "*I'm* practically hysterical."

"Look, Chief, there's a very rational explanation for what happened. The doctor treated the boy's hemorrhage with coagulants and a clotting agent. While they're working, Brother Kristos comes along, recites some mumbo jumbo, and the bleeding stops. It probably would have stopped if he had been a hundred miles away, but he gets the credit."

"You know that and I know that, but try telling it to the Boss. What was it he called it—The Miracle of Camp David?"

"I think Mrs. Hawkins used the phrase first, but the President picked up on it."

"Who knows about this?"

"The President, First Lady, George, Kristos, the doctor and nurse, and Jennifer for sure. Maybe some of the security people and guests heard what happened."

"They probably did," Folsom says, sighing. "Well, where do we go from here?"

"Chief, are you sure you don't want to alert the President's counsel and the National Security Adviser? If there's a firestorm of publicity about this, we'll all want to put the same spin on it."

"No," Folsom says, "not yet. But let's tell the Press Secretary. We might be able to put the lid on it by saying the First Family has the right of privacy when it comes to their religious beliefs."

"I don't think that'd work," Tollinger says doubtfully. "There's something I haven't told you yet."

"Oh God," the Chief says, groaning. "More good news? All right, let's have it."

"Well, according to Jennifer, the Boss and his wife decided they want Kristos closer at hand in case George has another hemorrhage. They persuaded him to move to D.C. They'll pick up the tab for a place for him in the city."

"Wonderful," Folsom says bitterly. "Where are they going to put him—in a two-bedroom suite in the Watergate Complex? And is he going to bring along the tramps in the white sheets?"

"The details haven't been worked out yet," Tollinger says. "Right now, Jennifer is out scouting for a place for the guy to live. I did do one thing: I told her that no way, *no* way, is the President going to put his name on a lease. If he insists on paying Brother Kristos' rent, then the smart way to do it would be to give the guy cash. We can always claim it's a charitable contribution to an organized religion."

"Yeah," Folsom says, "but some snoop will find out where Kristos' cash is coming from. Have you learned any more about him?"

"Not since that first letter I showed you. Lindberg is out in Nebraska, probably freezing his ass off; they had a blizzard the other day. I expect to hear from him this week."

"Well, let me know as soon as you do. The sooner we

can put Brother Kristos down, the better." The Chief of Staff lifts his head and looks up. "Chopper coming in," he says. "That'll be the Boss. Let's go out with the glad hand. And not a word to him about what we know. If he wants to tell us, he will. And if we get a chance this after-noon, let's get together with the Press Secretary."

"Yes, sir," John Tollinger says.

At the same time White House officials are greeting the First Family, Samuel Trent is in his office listening to an intriguing phone call and occasionally saying, "Really? . . . Remarkable. . . . I find it difficult to lend credence to that." The caller, as Tollinger had predicted, is Representative Louis Gehringer.

The call concludes with Trent's verbose thanks and a vow to do everything he can to further a projected VA hospital in Gehringer's home district. Then the Vice President rings for Michael Oberfest and, while waiting for the aide to arrive, Trent swings slowly back and forth in his swivel chair, never taking his eyes from an oil painting on the opposite wall. It is a Copley portrait of one of Trent's ancestors: the admiral, not the horse thief.

When Oberfest has taken up a position of attention be-fore his desk, the VP asks sharply, "What progress has been made in your investigation of that curious matter we discussed last week?"

"Very little, sir," the aide admits. "I can't find out what's going down."

"Well, *I* have," Trent says with satisfaction. He then relates the gist of his phone conversation with Congress-man Gehringer.

"Good God!" Michael says. "The President is consult-ing a faith healer?"

"Not consulting," the Vice President says, holding up an admonishing finger. "Apparently employing him, though the White House would prefer to keep it a secret. According to Gehringer, the man's a pretty scruffy char-acter."

"I can't get over it," Oberfest says, shaking his head. "If this gets out, can you imagine what—"

"I can indeed," Trent says loudly. "Allow me to explicate for a moment on the possible consequences should this matter become public knowledge.

"One: The President of the United States of America will be branded a fool by every right-thinking voter for disregarding the latest advances of medical science and opting for the services of a bearded faker who uses prayer to cure an ingrown toenail.

"Two: Our friends overseas will be shocked and dismayed by this latest evidence of the President's incapacity for logical, rational thought.

"Three: Our enemies, particularly the Soviets, will greet the news with enormous glee, publicizing it as added proof of the superstitious ignorance of capitalist societies.

"Four: The medical establishment in this country—indeed the entire scientific community—will be outraged at this rejection of their profession.

"Five: The Congress, already aware of Hawkins' regrettable tendency to oversimplify complex problems, will seize upon this incident as confirmation that the man is a dolt and not to be trusted with significant matters of state.

"Now it is true that a certain class of voters will sympathize with Hawkins' action and see nothing unnatural in asking assistance from a religious quack. But these people—fundamentalists, evangelicals, charismatics—are, for the most part, strictly non-U. I assure you, the majority of the upper-drawer voters in this great nation will consider Hawkins' conduct an insult to their intelligence. The midterm elections are already heating up, and I tell you this blunder makes me weep for the future of our party."

Oberfest hesitates a moment, not certain if the Veep has finished his oration. Finally: "Well, sir, what you say is very true, and all the things you foresee might happen.

But only if it becomes a matter of public knowledge. What if the White House is able to keep a lid on it?"

The Vice President resumes swinging back and forth in the swivel chair. "Oberfest," he says, "you have a contact at *The New York Times,* do you not?"

"Yes, sir. An old classmate."

"Then why don't you give him a call?" says Trent softly. "I think he might be interested."

=13=

Tollinger:

Re: Brother Kristos.

If all goes well, I expect to mail this from Omaha, where I hope to get a plane south. I've just spent three days in Bethlehem, Nebr., not because I wanted to but because I got snowed in. They've finally 'dozed the roads, and I should be able to leave tomorrow morning early in my rental car, heading for Omaha.

Incidentally, I'm charging everything on my plastic, so expect to be clobbered with a heavy tab (itemized) when I return to D.C.

Bethlehem is more than a crossroad town—but not by much. Population right now is about 2,800. Twenty years ago it was 11,000—which will give you an idea of what's happened to it. No bank anymore, no movie house, no hotel. But a lot of boarded-up stores. And mostly older people. What few kids are left have to be bused twelve miles to a high school.

I stayed at a grungy motel (the only one in the area)

called Hillcrest and took all my meals at the Ace-High Café. I'll never be able to look at a fried pork chop again. But I'm proud of myself; I didn't hit the bottle, and if I can endure being snowed in for three days in Bethlehem without getting whacked, I figure I can stay sober anywhere, anytime.

Now to business. . . . Here's what I've been able to dig up:

Jacob Everard is the third son of the Christiansen family (four sons, three daughters) that owned a 400-acre farm just west of Bethlehem. Mostly wheat, but also a herd of dairy cows, hogs, and chickens. The farm was sold and is broken up now into smaller plots. The mother and father died, and all the grown children moved away. I don't blame them. This is harsh country.

Anyway, the Christiansen family had a good reputation as farmers. They worked hard (including the kids), and their milk, cream, and butter were supposed to be the best. Ditto hogs and chickens. They paid in cash for what they bought, never went into debt, and had a small nest egg at the local bank (now closed). When the parents died, the kids decided to sell out and split.

That was their reputation as farmers. As neighbors and good citizens, they didn't do so well. Apparently they were a clannish, suspicious lot, never went to town meetings, never joined local activities, never visited or invited anyone over—including the kids' friends (if they had any).

But what really made Bethlehem treat them like pariahs was their religion. This area is mostly Lutheran. As a matter of fact, I got most of this poop from the local Lutheran pastor, who is one year younger than God and likes to talk.

The Christiansens belonged to a radical sect that was an offshoot of the Swedenborgians, a legit religion that says divinity is infinite love. But the sect the Christiansens belonged to went overboard on that and claimed that only through love (especially sex) could the teachings of Jesus Christ be followed.

(There were a lot of these wild sects and cults in the Midwest during the nineteenth and early twentieth centuries, but most of them have just faded away.)

The religion the Christiansens followed was called the Christers by the locals, and there was a lot of outraged gossip about what they actually did in their services and rituals. About five or six families in this area belonged, and they all got together on weekends at one of the members' farms on a rotating basis.

It was said that men and women (not married) slept together to prove that sex was not sinful, since we are all created in God's image, and He is without sin. Sound familiar? Also, there was talk of whippings of shy members who refused to join in the fun and games. And rumors of incestuous relations.

As far as Jacob Everard goes, apparently he was a handsome kid, a hard worker and a good student at the local school. He seems to have attracted a lot of attention from farmgirls, and more than one informant told me that Jacob had a lot of girlfriends but no pals amongst boys his own age.

He was supposed to have a ferocious temper—always getting in fights—and even as a child had developed the wild stare I mentioned in my first letter. He was also a very articulate boy and won several oratorical contests. They said that, if he wanted to, he could speechify a bird out of a tree, but used his talents as a glib salesman mostly to persuade girlfriends to join him in the hayloft for a session of "You show me yours, and I'll show you mine."

Jacob was eighteen and a senior in high school when he allegedly got a local girl "in trouble." Reportedly, the girl's father and brother were coming after him with a shotgun when he did what any other respectable red-blooded American boy in similar circumstances would do: he flew the coop.

Apparently he hitched a ride to a nearby town (New Castle). At the time, there was a carnival playing, and the story is that Jacob wangled a job. When the carnival left town a few days later, he went along with it. This is all hearsay, of course, but I believe every word of it.

So I phoned the New Castle sheriff, identified myself as an FBI agent (just a small lie), and asked if he'd be kind enough to check his files and tell me what carnival was playing at the fairgrounds on the date in question. The sheriff said he didn't have to check his files; there was only one traveling show that had played in New Castle in the past forty years: the Ryan-Goldfarb All-Thrill Monster Extravaganza. Love that name!

My next call was to a contact I've got at Billboard *magazine. He promised to check it out and get back to me— which he did in a couple of hours. Turns out the Ryan-Goldfarb carnival is still in business and winters in Sarasota, Florida. So that's where I'm heading as soon as I get out of this icebox. It'll be great to thaw out amongst the palm trees.*

The picture I get so far of Jacob Everard Christiansen is of a strong, obstreperous lad with the gift of gab—an apprentice womanizer. He had a strict, religious upbringing but that doesn't mean much if all the gossip I heard about the Christers is true. Everyone says he had a talent for healing sick animals, and if his success with the local farmgirls is any indication, he must be hung like a horse.

One final note: From the tender age of fourteen it was generally known that he had a taste for the grape—only in this case it was Bethlehem's homemade applejack, supposedly a potent brew. Our Jacob was seen completely smashed on several occasions. Even I didn't start that young!

Next letter from Florida. . . .

—Lindberg

=14=

They're having dinner at a corner table at Chez Belle in Georgetown. Their heads are close together, they keep their voices low, and their smiles are carved. "What an attractive couple," other diners might comment, never realizing that Jennifer and John are cutting each other to shreds.

"How many times do I have to explain it to you?" he demands. "The doctor treated the boy with coagulants and a clotting agent. While they're taking effect, Brother Kristos shambles in, mumbles a prayer, and the hemorrhage stops. He had nothing to do with it. The drugs did what they were supposed to do. No miracle. Sorry."

"Bull*shit!*" she says. "You weren't there and you don't know what happened. Well, I was, and I do, and I tell you Brother Kristos stopped the bleeding. Listen, the doctor was calling in an emergency trauma team to give George a transfusion. Would he have done that if he thought the drugs would work?"

"Come on, Jennifer, I know you've got a brain; try to use it. The doctor was just covering his ass, that's all. More wine?"

"Damned right," she says, helping herself. "All right, so you don't believe in faith healing. Well, I do."

"I didn't say I don't believe in faith healing. A lot of sick people feel better when they're given a placebo if they're convinced it's a wonder drug. Religion has nothing to do with it."

"No?" she challenges. "Well, what if a devout person who's sick is persuaded that God will make him well if his faith is strong enough? He prays, and gets well. Now is that psychotherapy or religion?"

"Eat your chop," Tollinger says.

"Another thing," Jennifer goes on. "I told you that Brother Kristos knew things about me at our first meeting that there was no way he could have known. Mrs. Hawkins told me he did the same thing with her. And Katherine Downley and Lenore Mattingly said the same thing. So if he doesn't have special powers, how could he know those things?"

"Easy. They're tricks used by every palm reader, crystal-ball gazer, tea-leaf reader, and fake medium in the world. Look, I set myself up as a fortune-teller. A stranger comes in, and I say things like, 'You have had a great sadness in your life. A close friend or member of your family has recently died. Many people have betrayed you.' Now some of that rubbish is true of ninety-nine percent of the population, but the stupid mark says, 'Gee, this fortune-teller is really good; he knows everything about me.' And that's how Brother Kristos hoodwinks the suckers."

"Well, for your information, wise guy, Brother Kristos hasn't pulled any of that stuff. He's much more specific. He knew I had left my husband. He knew Kate Downley had arthritis in her knees and that Lenore Mattingly suffered from migraine headaches. How did he know those things?"

"Most older women have arthritis or headaches. And I've told you how he might have guessed you were recently divorced. I've already proved he's not a faith healer. Now you're claiming he's clairvoyant. This guy has really gotten to you, hasn't he?"

Jennifer puts aside her fork. "Too much food," she says faintly. "I can't finish. Let's have black coffee and a brandy. Okay?"

"Sure," he says, looking at her. "My God, you're pale. Feeling all right?"

"I'll survive," she says with a wan smile.

He gives their order to the waiter, then turns back to her. "How are you coming along on finding a place for Brother Kristos to live?"

Jennifer becomes animated again. "Bingo!" she says. "I couldn't find an apartment in a good neighborhood at a decent rent. My God, the prices they're getting these days! Then I remembered Lenore Mattingly owns a house on Eighteenth Street. She's a widow and lives with Emily, her unmarried daughter, in a big, ugly elephant of a house, three stories high. I went to see her, swore her to secrecy, and asked if she'd be willing to rent a room to Brother Kristos. Just him, not his assistants. She was practically ecstatic. Said the top floor is vacant, and he can have that. Big study, bedroom, bathroom. No kitchen of course, but Lenore said he can take his meals with her and Emily. No extra work since she has a live-in housekeeper. It sounds like the perfect solution."

"It might be at that," Tollinger says thoughtfully. "When will Brother Kristos be moving in?"

"Probably in a week or so. The First Lady is delighted, of course. She's talking about inviting him to the White House to conduct one of their prayer breakfasts."

"Oh God," John says despairingly.

"I know you think he's a fake," Jennifer says, gulping her brandy. "But you're wrong. He happens to be a very superior person with very superior talents."

He stares at her. "If you say so," he says.

They finish their coffee in silence. Tollinger pays the bill, they reclaim their coats, and exit onto the sidewalk.

"I'd ask you up," Jennifer says, "but Martha is working her computer, and the place is a mess."

"That's all right," he says. "Want to come out to Spring Valley for a nightcap?"

"I'll take a rain check."

"Suit yourself," Tollinger says.

=15=

To his wife and close friends, Vice President Samuel Landon Trent is fond of remarking, "Remember, I am only a heartbeat away from the presidency."

With that in mind, and determined to persevere until the brass ring is his, Trent has worked hard to establish a national network of sympathetic party leaders and campaign contributors. Most of the big-money men are in Manhattan, and Oberfest is frequently dispatched to New York to arrange speeches by the VP to trade associations, investment bankers, and other corporation executives.

It is on one of these trips that Oberfest finds time to make his enigmatic phone call. Three hours later he is closeted with Major Leonid Y. Marchuk in that grubby hotel suite on West Forty-sixth Street.

The Russian is at his jovial best, telling Michael scandalous anecdotes about his colleagues at the United Nations, roaring with laughter and frequently slapping his meaty thigh with glee. But finally he sobers.

"Well now, Arnold," he says, "what do you have for me?"

The Veep's personal aide relates some tidbits of Washington gossip: the drug problem of a Cabinet member's wife, the probable passage of a new Medicare bill, the disagreement in the National Security Council over the sending of military matériel to Swaziland, the soon-to-be-revealed peculations of a Federal Appeals Court judge.

Nothing Oberfest reveals is of world-shaking import and nothing, he tells himself, affects the national security of the U.S. But the major listens without interrupting, smiling, nodding, apparently delighted to learn of this trivia.

"And that's about it," Michael concludes.

"Oh?" Marchuk says. "What about the matter we discussed the last time we met? Has anything come of that?"

The American had hoped the major had forgotten. Talking about it makes him uncomfortable. Perhaps, he decides, because his own role in the affair has been rather ignoble. But there is no reason the Russian shouldn't know; the whole thing is sure to become public.

So he tells Marchuk the whole story, not omitting Trent's suggestion to him to leak the details to his friend on the *Times.*

"I imagine it'll be a media circus," he finishes. "Lots of interviews, editorials, cartoons, and TV talk shows—the whole enchilada."

"Enchilada?" the Russian says, puzzled. "That is a Mexican food—no?"

"Yes, but it's slang for the entire thing, the whole schmear, the big picture."

Marchuk sighs. "Sometimes I doubt if I will ever fully understand the American language. But this enchilada I find of great interest. First of all, faith healers I know about. We have them in my country too. But only ignorant, superstitious peasants believe. It is to me amazing that your President would seek help from such a—swindler? Is that the right word?"

"It'll do," Oberfest says.

"Second," the major goes on, "I do not understand the motives of your Vice President in making this matter public. He wishes to harm President Hawkins?"

"Not harm him exactly," Michael says hesitantly. "But he wouldn't object if Hawkins became a laughingstock. My boss is a very political animal. I'm not revealing any secrets when I tell you that he's already looking ahead to the next presidential election. More than one columnist has hinted that if Hawkins does a lousy job, Trent is waiting in the wings."

"So he feels that if the President makes a public fool of himself, all the better?"

"Something like that."

Marchuk nods. "We have men like that in the Soviet Union. Very ambitious. Thinking only of their personal glory. Their power. And to achieve what they believe is rightfully theirs, they will do anything, act in many devious, underhanded, and sometimes criminal ways."

"Hey, wait a minute," the aide protests. "Trent is no criminal. But as someone once said, politics ain't beanbag. The Veep plays hardball."

"Beanbag? Hardball? Explain please."

"Politics isn't a game for children. Trent plays it forcefully. He's an end-justifies-the-means type of guy."

"A dangerous man," the major observes.

"Oh no, I don't think so. In spite of the way he talks, he's got a good brain. He's really very sharp. Always one step ahead of the opposition."

"One step ahead of the President?"

"Well, Hawkins is as well-meaning a man as a politician can be and survive. But he's almost totally without guile. Why do you think he was nominated? Because his honesty and sincerity came across on TV, and the party bigwigs knew he could be scammed and manipulated. And that's just the way it's turned out. He's loyal to his friends—too loyal—even to the crooks."

The KGB man ponders that awhile. Finally: "Tell me, Arnold, if, as Trent hopes, the President becomes a laughingstock, will it end his chances of reelection?"

"Oh, I doubt that," Oberfest says. "The election is almost three years down the road, and Americans have a notoriously short attention span. No, I think that no matter how much the faith healer embarrasses the White

House, it'll all blow over and some other scandal will grab the headlines."

"But if it doesn't blow over? If, aided by the efforts of your boss, it becomes worse, is it possible that three years from now the Vice President might become President?"

"In our politics anything is possible. As a matter of fact, if you're looking for a worst-case scenario, Hawkins' reputation and ability to govern might be damaged to the extent where he'd resign, and then Trent would take over before the next election."

"I would not like that," the Russian says.

"I didn't think you would," Oberfest says with a smug smile. "Right now you people have a pal in the Oval Office. Hawkins is a real peace freak. But Trent is another breed of cat entirely. You get him in the White House, and it'll be the cold war all over again."

"And you approve of that, Arnold?" Marchuk asks curiously.

"I don't approve or disapprove. Look, I don't make policy, I just help implement it."

"Me too," the major says seriously. "We are both apparatchiks. Let the ruler have the final responsibility—correct?"

"Sure. President Truman had a sign on his desk: 'The buck stops here.' "

Marchuk laughs uproariously. "But in my government, the buck *never* stops!"

After Michael Oberfest departs, the white envelope tucked into his pocket, the Soviet agent retrieves the tape recording from under the couch and sits a few moments, pondering. The first law in his business is self-preservation or, as the Americans say, "Cover your ass." He decides he better get a dispatch off immediately. Let the men in Moscow decide what he should do next.

TWO

=1=

The home of Lenore Mattingly on Eighteenth Street N.W. is, as Jennifer Raye described it, a real elephant. Built of weathered gray limestone, it has unexpected bay windows, an arched entrance five steps up from the street, and a turret atop the roof that serves no purpose at all. This house was built during the administration of President Harding, and it is said to have served as residence for his Secretary of War.

If the outside is gloomy, the interior offers little more cheer. The sash-hung windows are draped with brown velvet. The massive furniture, mostly with carved frames and upholstery fabric in a fern design, looks so ponderous as to be immovable—which it almost is. As a result, the carpeting has faded over the years, but beneath each heavy couch and armchair is a puddle of the rug's original colors—bright and sparkling, if they could only be seen.

The living room (originally called the parlor) is on the first floor, just off the hallway. Sliding doors of dark walnut lead to the dining room and a smallish chamber that was once a paneled library but has been converted by Mrs. Mattingly into a sprightlier sitting room decorated with white wicker furniture, chintz floral upholstery, and framed Audubon reproductions.

Also on the main floor are the kitchen and pantry, a lavatory, and a tiny storeroom crammed with forty years' copies of the *National Geographic*. There are three bedrooms on the second floor, occupied by Mrs. Mattingly, daughter Emily, and housekeeper Brenna O'Gara.

The third floor, to be rented by Brother Kristos, provides a large study, bedroom, and bathroom. As in the rest of the house, illumination is provided mostly by chandeliers of tarnished brass. The light from these overhead fixtures (the ceilings are eleven feet high) is dim and ocherous. The entire home, even during the day, seems to have the color of aged parchment and the fusty smell of a disused library.

The arrangements made by Jennifer Raye for the housing of Brother Kristos are these:

He is to occupy the third floor by himself, with his own front-door key. If he wishes, he may take his meals with the Mattingly household, at no additional cost. He will pay five hundred dollars a month for his apartment, with one month's security paid in advance.

It is understood that he will spend Friday night and all of Saturday at the Virginia tobacco barn, returning to Washington, D.C., on Sunday morning. This last is the cause of another argument between Jennifer and John Tollinger.

"You can't blame him for not deserting his church," she says. "After all, his flock needs him."

"His *flock?*" Tollinger says with a cold laugh. "You make the guy sound like a sheepherder. You know why he wants to go back to that dump every week? It's the money, honey. He's got a good thing going there with his two woodland sprites taking up a collection in those crazy cigar boxes. Plus whatever he gets from private meetings with the sick and disturbed people he cons. He's not about to give up that income by moving to D.C. full-time. This way he's got the best of both worlds: he can continue to gull the country suckers on weekends, and he can scam Mrs. Mattingly and her rich friends during the week. Kristos is going to make out like the thief he is."

"How can you be so cynical?" she says hotly. "Just because you don't believe in him doesn't mean other people don't. They depend on him, and he feels he has a responsibility to continue preaching."

"Did he tell you that?"

"As a matter of fact, he did."

"Uh-huh," Tollinger says, looking at her thoughtfully. "Of course another explanation might be that he wants to return to the barn on weekends so he can get his rocks off with his two disciples."

"You're disgusting!" she cries.

Brother Kristos arrives at the house on Eighteenth Street N.W. just before noon on a Monday, having been driven to the nation's capital by Pearl Gibbs in the Ford pickup truck. She follows his command to drop him two blocks from his destination. So he makes his appearance on foot, carrying a scuffed and battered leather valise tied with a scrap of rope.

He is greeted warmly by Mrs. Mattingly, a corpulent matron. She is flanked by Emily and Brenna O'Gara, both tall and thin, so that the three women in line look like the number 181. Daughter and housekeeper are introduced, Kristos' plaid mackinaw is taken from him and hung on an oak coatrack.

He is conducted to his apartment by O'Gara, a woman of at least three score years who bounds up the steep, carpeted stairway with the verve of a teenager. She shows him about his new home with a rat-a-tat of comments:

"Fresh bed linen and towels every week. There's an extra blanket on the closet shelf if you need it. Put the curtain inside the tub when you shower. The bottom drawer of the dresser is stuck. We're having a phone put in for you. The number will be different from ours, so you must pay for it. Breakfast at eight o'clock, lunch at twelve-thirty, dinner at seven. If you wish to eat with us, be prompt; we won't wait for you. Are you hungry now?"

"No," he says, looking about slowly.

"We're all in bed by twelve, so if you come in later, do

try to be quiet. Mail is usually delivered by noon. It's an old house, but snug. The furnace is in the basement. The missus likes it warm, so we keep the heat up, night and day. If you want it cooler, you can close the hot-air vents or open a window. Are you handy?"

"Handy?"

"With tools. Do you know about plumbing and electricity and such?"

"Some."

"Good. The wall outlet over the kitchen sink doesn't work."

"I'll fix it," he promises.

"And the faucet in your tub drips. Needs a new washer, I expect. Maybe you can do that too."

He nods. He is wearing a freshly laundered white shirt. The cuffs of his jeans are tucked into his boots. There is a heavy gold chain about his neck. A massive gold cross hangs from it—a gift from the First Lady in gratitude for The Miracle of Camp David.

"I must tell you," Brenna O'Gara says determinedly, "I am a Roman Catholic and don't hold with your religion."

"We are all God's children," he says.

"Not all," she says sharply. "I've known some that were the devil's. Now I've got to go downstairs and put lunch on. Fresh fruit salad with cottage cheese. Will you be joining us?"

"No," he says. "Thank you."

"I'll be leaving you then. If there is anything you need, you can let me know later. Before three o'clock. I take my nap then. There's a bolt on the inside of your hallway door if you want to use it. If you buy some snacks, you can keep them in the refrigerator. You'll have to make arrangements for your own laundry; I won't do it."

He nods again.

She stares at his beard, hanging halfway down his chest.

"My father had a beard, God rest his soul," she says. "How long have you had that thing?"

"Since last Friday," he says, expressionless.

Her eyes widen. Then: "Oh, you're a joker, are you? Well, I can give as good as I get. The missus is always bragging on you—curing her headaches and all—so I hope you like it here and behave yourself."

"I will," he says.

Finally, finally, she leaves, and he closes the bolt on the hallway door. He puts his old suitcase on the bed and unties the rope. There's a fresh bottle of vodka wrapped in his underwear. He uncaps it, takes a deep swallow and, carrying the bottle, inspects the apartment.

The high, beamed ceiling needs painting, and the wainscoting in the study could use cleaning and waxing. But the old bathroom is spotless, and the bedroom is neat, even if it seems to have been furnished with castoffs from the rest of the house.

There is a matched set of mission furniture in the study: big table, couch, two armchairs, an empty bookcase, four straight chairs, and a cabinet—all dark stuff with cracked black leather on couch and chairs. The brass chandelier hardly lights the corners of the dim room; the windows have been closed with drapes of rough brown linen.

Brother Kristos sits at the table, drinking slowly and running his fingertips over the solid oak top. The room is warm, almost hot, but he appreciates it as only one can who has known the frightening bite of hard cold.

He has finished almost half the vodka when there is a tentative tap on his outside door. He moves slowly to open it, making no effort to hide the liquor bottle. It is Emily Mattingly, carrying a plate covered with a napkin.

"I'm sorry to interrupt, Brother Kristos," she says breathlessly. "Brenna said you didn't want any lunch, but mother thought you might enjoy a slice of our dessert. It's cherry pie. I made it."

He takes the plate from her outstretched hands.

"Thank you," he says in his flat voice. Suddenly his eyes flare, and she takes a hesitant step backward.

"I hope you like it," she says faintly, unable to look away. Then, with a small nervous laugh: "Why are you staring at me so? What do you see?"

"Loneliness," he says.

She makes a sound deep in her throat, a cry, then turns and flees.

He rebolts the door, carries the plate over to the table, tosses aside napkin and fork. Hunched over, he shovels the wide wedge of cherry pie into his mouth, cramming it in, chewing and swallowing frantically. Syrup drips from his lips onto his beard. Some of the red juice splatters the tabletop, glistening there like drops of blood.

=2=

Media coverage of the affair begins in a low-key fashion. The first public notice of Brother Kristos appears in a short report (three paragraphs) on the "Washington Talk" page of *The New York Times.* It states only that the First Family invited Kristos to spend a weekend at Camp David, and mentions that the "itinerant preacher" is reputed to be a faith healer and clairvoyant. Nothing is said of The Miracle of Camp David.

The *Times* story is picked up by several newspapers around the country. Most treat it in a gingerly fashion; there is no editorial comment, no questioning of why the President of the United States wishes to associate with a so-called seer. The television networks make no mention at all of Brother Kristos.

Vice President Samuel Trent is incensed by what he considers a lack of media initiative and enterprise.

"This is a biggie," he fumes to his wife. "It's a disaster waiting to happen. I cannot understand why the press and particularly the TV news programs are pussyfooting. It's a disgrace."

"Why don't you call them, dear?" she says placidly, knitting away at an enormous afghan. "Just a hint, you know. Tom Watkins is a good friend. Doesn't he have something to do with television?"

"That loudmouth?" the Veep says grumpily. "Not much. He's an outside director on a network board."

"Still," Matilda Trent says, looking up at her husband, "he might put a flea in someone's ear."

"That may be in the realm of the possible," the VP says slowly. "Worth a try. I'll tell him how concerned I am that network news programs will cover the story, since it may damage the public esteem in which the President is presently held. I'll ask Tom to utilize what influence he possesses to keep Brother Kristos off the tube."

"Yes, dear," Matilda says with a hard smile. "I think that would be the best way to handle it."

The initial response of the media to the Chief Executive's relationship with Brother Kristos is also a matter of concern to certain members of the White House staff—but for different reasons.

"The cat's out of the bag," Chief of Staff Folsom says grimly, "and no way are we going to jam that fucking tabby back in again."

He is meeting in the Situation Room with John Tollinger and Press Secretary Pete K. Umbaugh.

"Pete," he says, "can you find out who leaked it to the *Times*?"

"I tried," says Umbaugh, a porcine man who wears pretied bow ties and parts his hair in the middle. "All I got was the usual 'protection of confidential sources' bullshit."

"That figures," the COS says. "John, you have any thoughts on the subject?"

"A crazy idea," Tollinger says. "I see Trent's fine Italian hand there."

"Not so crazy," Folsom says. "I think the bastard leaked. It wouldn't be the first time. And then he wonders why we don't keep him up to speed."

"Look," Umbaugh says, "sooner or later I'm going to be questioned on this at the briefings. How do we spin it?"

"Like we discussed," the Chief says. "Very serious, very solemn. The President's religious and spiritual beliefs are a highly personal matter and not a proper subject for inquiry."

"That might fly if Brother Kristos was an Anglican bishop," the Press Secretary says. "But as I get it, he's a one-man church who also tells fortunes. It's going to be tough talking about him and the sanctity of the Boss's spiritual beliefs in the same breath."

"Do your best," Folsom says. "At least the TV networks aren't onto it yet."

"Just a question of time," Umbaugh says. "I cringe every time I think of seeing that bearded mug on the tube."

"That's not the worst of it," the Chief of Staff says. "Now the Boss wants to have a prayer breakfast in the White House with Brother Kristos conducting the service."

"Oh God!" Umbaugh cries.

"John, did you know about that?"

"Jennifer mentioned something about it, but I hoped it would just go away."

"Well, it hasn't. The Boss wanted a big affair with the Cabinet, congressmen, diplomats—everyone and his sister Sue. But I think I persuaded him to keep it small. I suggested that guests be limited to the White House staff.

Make the first introduction of Brother Kristos an intimate family affair. He went for that. John, do you know Audrey Robertson, Mrs. Hawkins' Social Secretary?"

"Sure, I know her. Sharp lady."

"Well, will you liaise with her? Explain the problem. Try to keep the guest list to a minimum. And just White House staffers."

"Will do."

"No photographers on this, Pete, unless Mrs. Hawkins insists. Let's treat the whole thing like a family get-together."

"It's not going to work," Umbaugh says gloomily. "It'll be all over town an hour after Kristos says, 'Amen.' "

Folsom shrugs. "It's what the Boss wants. You know, the screwy thing is that I've never seen him looking better. Since meeting Brother Kristos he's full of piss and vinegar, on top of things the way he used to be. He's whizzing through his paperwork and making all the tough decisions."

"Chief," Tollinger says, "does he have any idea of what his association with Brother Kristos could do to his political career?"

"No," Folsom says shortly. "I don't think he's even considered it. It's like he's under a spell."

After the meeting breaks up, Tollinger goes looking for Audrey Robertson. He's worked in the White House for more than a year now, but he still gets lost in the rambling place. Just to make things more difficult, staffers seem caught up in a perpetual game of musical chairs. Offices, desks, and nameplates are constantly being shuffled, and last week's directory is already obsolete.

He finally finds the Social Secretary tucked away in a cubbyhole, just room enough for a standard-issue desk, swivel chair, armchair, and file cabinet. The door is open, Robertson is behind her desk talking on the phone. She's a diminutive woman wearing a hat that belongs at a garden party. She sees John standing there, waves him in, points to the armchair.

"Of course, darl," she's saying, "I understand perfectly. But it's a diplomatic reception, you see, and I just cannot get you on the list. Believe me, you'd be bored stiff, darl. All those stuffed shirts. But we do have a fun thing coming up in March: a formal evening musicale with some yummy people onstage. I'll definitely put you down for that—okay, darl? Now you keep in touch, y'hear?"

She hangs up and wrinkles her nose at Tollinger. "Mrs. Edith Todd. You know her?"

He shakes his head.

"A nut," Audrey says. "Not just eccentric but completely insane. Certifiable. She calls at least three times a week, trying to get her name on the list for *everything*. She'd barge in on Cabinet meetings if she could."

"Why do you put up with that nonsense?" he asks.

"Money, darl, strictly money. She's had four husbands and collected from all of them. They paid up gladly to get loose. She's one of the largest individual contributors to the party, so I have to treat her gently. Now what's on your mind?"

He explains about the prayer breakfast, and how the Chief of Staff wants to limit it to White House staffers with no publicity, no photographers.

"Let's try to keep it very small," he urges. "We're not flacks for Brother Kristos."

"Look," Audrey says, "I heard all about it from Mrs. Hawkins, and I'm on your side, darl. I think the whole idea is crazy, but ours is not to reason why. I figure to invite no more than twenty or thirty. I plan to have the breakfast first, so a lot of freeloaders will take off before the service begins."

"Good thinking," Tollinger says admiringly. "Will you pick up Brother Kristos and make sure he gets here on time?"

"Not me. That guy gives me the creeps. Jennifer volunteered to fetch him. Those two seems to be *muy simpá-tico.*"

"What?"

The Social Secretary stares at him a moment. "Listen, darl," she says, "you don't suppose they're having an affair, do you?"

"I wouldn't know," Tollinger says.

He returns to his office and works late into the evening, reading the day's stack of memoranda and interoffice communications that have nothing to do with Brother Kristos. Most of the bumf he handles himself; only a dozen or so documents are put aside for action by the Chief of Staff.

On the drive home he stops at a fast-food joint for a cup of chowder, hamburger, french fries, two black coffees, and a piece of apple pie. It's the first solid food he's had all day, but everything tastes like dreck and does nothing to help him unwind.

Back in his den, he pours himself a tot of Glenfiddich, but even that doesn't help. He sits, he rises, he wanders about, takes a copy of *A Tale of Two Cities* from the bookcase, tries to read, gives up and replaces the volume, finishes his drink, pours another, and decides to confront what's making him so antsy.

It's that final question from Audrey Robertson: "You don't suppose they're having an affair, do you?"

The suggestion did not come as a complete shock to John Tollinger because the possibility of Jennifer getting it off with Brother Kristos had already occurred to him. A lot of things added up: her impassioned defense of the preacher, when her initial response to the man had been as skeptical as his; her delight in finding a place in D.C. for Kristos to live; her recent unwillingness to share Tollinger's bed.

So? he asks himself. He is divorced; he has no claims on the woman; she can shack up with the entire House of Representatives (including pages) if that's what turns her on. He acknowledges all that, but her possible affair with Brother Kristos offends him. Any other man, okay; he could accept that. But not Kristos.

He tries to analyze why he finds the idea so unpleasant, almost painful. Not because of Jennifer's infidelity; she owes him nothing. So his resentment must be triggered by the man. What is it about that shabby character that alarms Tollinger so?

It takes a third noggin of the single malt before he admits the truth. Despite his frequently expressed scorn of Brother Kristos as a fraud, a worm of fear gnaws that perhaps the man may actually possess supernatural powers. How did he guess so many people's secrets? What made him ascribe Tollinger's loneliness to an unhappy boyhood and venomously argumentative parents?

How many times can John utter a derisive "Lucky guess." Evidence, admittedly all anecdoctal, is steadily accumulating that this seedy shaman has an uncanny ability to peer into the past, foretell the future, and maybe, just maybe, cure the physical ills of others by the strength of his faith and that of his patients.

Even admitting the possibility of all that without totally believing it leaves him shaken. For if Kristos is right, then he himself is wrong, and his ordered world of thought, logic, and rationality is but *one* world. There is another that exists beyond Tollinger's ken, a world of faith, demonic will, and spiritual authority that can cure the sick and, for all he knows, raise the dead.

Tollinger suddenly remembers an old story about a renowned and respected physicist who is visited in his laboratory by a stranger.

"I can levitate," the stranger says.

"Oh?" the scientist says, much amused. "Demonstrate."

So, with a little push of his toes, the visitor floats slowly upward, braking himself with palms against the ceiling. The physicist, staring, knows his world is crashing about him, for where now are his laws, theories, equations, proofs—all the bone, muscle, flesh, and blood of his existence? All denied and brought to naught.

That's the way John Tollinger feels, an empty whiskey glass gripped in his fingers, staring upward and seeing Brother Kristos floating above him.

=3=

With Kristos' permission, Mrs. Mattingly has invited three close friends to have afternoon tea with him, during which he has promised to answer questions concerning sin, prayer, and redemption.

The party is organized by Emily, but it is Brenna O'Gara who does the work. She makes four trips up the stairs to Kristos' study, carrying table linen, china, cutlery, a hot plate, teapot, lemon, sugar, cream, a tin of Fortnum & Mason's tea, and a cheesecake tastefully displayed atop a paper doily.

On her last trip, after the big table has been set, chairs arranged, and water put on to boil, Brenna steps back to inspect her handiwork.

"I hope you're satisfied," she says snappishly.

"Yes," Brother Kristos says, eyeing the table. Cloth and napkins are pink linen. "Very nice."

She looks at him with a twisted grin. "Too bad you'll have to drink tea," she says, "and not that stuff you keep hidden beneath your bed."

He is not at all discomfited. "Help yourself whenever you like," he says.

"Not me," she says tartly. "I know what strong drink does to people."

"Oh? What does it do?"

"It makes them crazy," she says.

He steps close to her. She is a plain, rawboned woman, all teeth, elbows, and knees. Brother Kristos puts a hand on her neck, slides it slowly down her bony back. She quivers once, then jerks away.

"You devil!" she says. "A fine man of the cloth you are. You keep your dirty hands to yourself or I'll tell the missus what you're up to. Satan's spawn!"

She slams out of the apartment. He stands a moment, not moving, then goes into the bedroom. He retrieves a bottle of vodka from under the bed and drinks deeply. Then he recaps it, slides it back out of sight, and stands before the dresser mirror, inspecting himself. He takes a small comb from the hip pocket of his black whipcord slacks and combs hair, mustache, beard, all scented with a musky cologne given to him by Jennifer Raye.

His shirt is dark maroon silk cut cossack style: buttoned high on the neck, with ballooning sleeves and tight cuffs. It has a long tail worn outside his trousers. It is cinched with a wide belt of black calfskin, closed with a silver filigree buckle. The shirt is a gift from Mrs. Katherine Downley. Emily Mattingly gave him the belt and buckle.

And Emily is the first to arrive, bringing a bowl of pink sweetheart roses arranged with maidenhead fern. She places it in the center of the table.

"There," she says. "Isn't that lovely?"

"Yes. Very nice."

"The other guests have already arrived and will be up soon. I think you've met Kate Downley."

He nods.

"The other two ladies are Mrs. Edith Todd and Mrs. Cynthia Jorgenson. Both are very active on the Washington social scene. They're so anxious to meet you, especially after that newspaper story about Camp David. My,

I had no idea how famous you are. Have you seen the President recently?"

He is saved from answering by the arrival of the other guests. They come filing into the room led by Mrs. Mattingly. All four women are remarkably similar: middle-aged matrons, thick-bodied and corseted, wearing plain black costumes they believe suitable for an audience with a religious sage.

Introductions are made, everyone is seated. Brother Kristos is at the head of the table. With his long hair, full mustache and beard, his direct stare, he appears a man of authority and stern resolve. He is younger than the women, except for Emily, but all defer to him, leaning forward in postures of obeisance.

Emily serves the tea and slices of cheesecake. Nothing is said until all have been helped, and she takes her place at the foot of the table.

"Brother Kristos," Mrs. Todd says breathlessly, "I just can't tell you what a thrill it is to meet you in person."

He inclines his head gravely.

"It is said," she continues with a smile, "that you can see into a person's past. Is that true?"

"Yes," Kristos says. "But I reveal such things only in private with the person concerned, never in the presence of others."

"Oh, come on," she says girlishly. "I've done nothing in my life I'm ashamed of. You can say anything about me, and I won't be embarrassed."

He stares at her, and a small flame leaps in his eyes. He sits in silence a moment, the others waiting breathlessly.

"You wish everyone to know?" he asks finally in his toneless voice. "That incident in your childhood which may or may not have been repeated. And the guilt you felt at not telling your parents. You want these ladies to know about that?"

Suddenly Mrs. Edith Todd begins sobbing, raising a

pink linen napkin to her face. "Please," she wails, "no more, no more!"

The others look at her in astonishment, then busy themselves with their tea and cake.

"That was the error of a child," Kristos tells the weeping woman. "God has forgiven you."

"And will God forgive all of us our sins, Brother Kristos?" Cynthia Jorgenson asks.

"Sin does not exist," he says, and they gasp.

"But surely," Mrs. Downley says, "when we do something we know is wrong, something against God's commandments, then that is a sin."

"Yes," Mrs. Mattingly says, "like murder. God says, 'Thou shalt not kill.' So murder is a sin, is it not?"

"Murder is not a sin, but a crime against God. It is lack of faith."

"What about thought?" Emily says in a low voice. "Sometimes thoughts can be sinful, can't they?"

Kristos stares at her. "Your hidden desires, unfulfilled lusts—these things are suppressed because of guilt. But ask yourself: Where do these so-called evil yearnings come from? The answer is from God; whatever we are comes from His hands."

"Then we may do anything?" Mrs. Jorgenson asks. "Lie, cheat, and steal because God has given us those desires?"

"No. Like murder, those things are crimes against God and demonstrate insufficient belief in the omnipotence of the Supreme Being. To be without guilt, one must strive for total faith. Then we become part of God's everlasting love, and our lives are then part of the godhead."

Mrs. Todd, who has recovered from her weeping fit, turns to Kristos. "What about sex?" she asks boldly. "With someone you're not married to. Is that a crime against God?"

"It is not," Brother Kristos says. "Love is part of divinity, and that includes physical love."

"Brother Kristos," Mrs. Downley says, "if that is true, then why does sex outside marriage make so many people unhappy?"

"Guilt," he answers. "The punishment of those unfaithful to God."

The discussion continues for another hour. Finally the ladies rise to leave and, after much fumbling in their handbags, leave folded bills beneath their plates. "For your church," they murmur. He accepts their contributions gracefully and embraces each woman before she leaves. "Go with God," he says. Then he collects their donations and stuffs the cash in his pocket.

Emily stays behind to clear the table, stack the dishes.

"Can't Brenna do that?" he asks her.

"Oh, she's taking her nap now," Emily says gaily. "I don't mind. Goodness, you didn't eat or drink a thing. Weren't you hungry?"

"No," he says, slumping wearily in his armchair, watching her move about the room.

"I can't tell you how much I enjoyed this afternoon," she tells him. "*So* inspiring. Thank you for sharing your faith with us."

He doesn't reply. Finally, everything straightened, she looks around the room.

"Well, that's better," she says brightly. "Now I suppose I better go. I'm sure you want to be alone for a while."

He rises, goes over to her. He picks up one of her long, thin hands, kisses the palm.

"You agree with the things I said?" he asks her.

"Oh yes," she says fervently. "I do, I really do. It was all so—so enlightening."

"You have no fears of a world without sin?"

She shakes her head.

"Say to me, 'I believe in you, Brother Kristos.' "

"I believe in you, Brother Kristos," she repeats in a small voice.

He leads her toward the bedroom, and she follows along willingly.

=4=

Tollinger:

Re: Brother Kristos.

Well, "sunny Florida" turned out to be overcast, windy, and rainy, but at least I'm getting thawed out even though I have yet to see a single bikini. Sarasota is on the west coast, the Gulf, and that water out there looks mean and choppy.

I finally located the winter quarters of the Ryan-Goldfarb All-Thrill Monster Extravaganza. There is no longer a Mr. Ryan or a Mr. Goldfarb; both gentlemen went to the great midway in the sky several years ago. It's now owned by a youngish yuppie type, Simon K. Masilla, strictly a bottom-line character who has a total of six traveling shows and runs them all with computers.

Masilla bought the Ryan-Goldfarb carnival about eight years ago and knows nothing about Jacob Everard Christiansen. But he had the name and address of the former road manager, now retired and living in Sarasota. The guy's name—are you ready for this?—is Billy Feinschmecker. If my German serves me, Feinschmecker means wine-taster or something like that.

I located Billy in a retirement home. It was raining too hard to play shuffleboard so he was happy to sit and tell me about the young Brother Kristos. I've boiled down his story because he talked a blue streak for almost three hours. He walks with a limp and has tremors in his right hand, but there's nothing wrong with his memory or vocal cords.

He remembers Jacob Everard Christiansen very well. When the kid came around looking for a job with the carnival in New Castle, Nebr., back in the late 60's, Billy grabbed him because he was always losing workers in every town they played.

Anyway, according to Billy, he put Jake to work as a kind of apprentice roustabout, guessing that he was underage and had run away from home, but not caring. The kid was strong, willing to work, and learned fast.

Billy says he was a quiet, moody lad who did what he was told and didn't get into any serious trouble. But he did like the sauce, although he learned to handle it as well as carnies twice his age. He also earned quite a reputation as a Don Juan. Billy claims the kid screwed every woman traveling with the Ryan-Goldfarb All-Thrill Monster Extravaganza, including the Fat Lady (more than five hundred pounds) and the Siamese Twins (both of them).

He stayed with the carnival for almost ten years, signing up early in the spring and leaving late in the fall. I asked Billy what Jake did in the winter, and he shrugged and said, "A beach bum. Lived off women mostly. From Naples to Tampa. I never heard of him getting a winter job."

Some other interesting things Billy told me:

Young Jake was an eager reader—and mostly heavy stuff: religion and philosophy.

He got in a lot of fights (usually by coming on to other guys' girlfriends) and won most of them. Very good with his fists and feet. But the husband of the contortionist sliced open Jake's belly with a shiv before the kid decked him.

No matter what town they were playing, Jake always went to a local church on Sunday. The denomination didn't seem to matter to him.

I asked Feinschmecker (every time I write that name I start laughing) if Jake had any close friends in the carnival. He said only women, no men.

One of the women he cozied up to was Madame Olga, real name Lorna Burgoos. A lot of the booths on a carnival *midway are concessions, and Madame Olga leased one of them: a small tent in which she told fortunes with cards—not tarot but a regular deck. Jake spent a lot of time with the Madame.*

"Was he sleeping with her?" I asked.

Billy looked at me as if I was the village idiot. "Of course," he said. "She was old enough to be his mother, but Jake didn't discriminate because of age, color, creed, or physical handicaps."

The former road manager figures it would have been Jake's eleventh year with the carnival, when he didn't come around to sign up. Billy hunted him down, but Jake told him he was quitting. He had raised enough money to buy a second-hand pickup truck, and as soon as the weather warmed up, he was going to start touring the Bible Belt, selling his own brand of religion. Billy wished him the best of luck, and that was that.

It seemed to be the end of the road for me, but just for the hell of it I asked him if Madame Olga was still alive. He said sure she was, probably in her late seventies by now, and living in Fort Myers. He and Lorna Burgoos exchange Christmas cards every year, so he was able to give me her address. Fort Myers is not too far from here. I'm on my way.

The craziest thing about my interview with Billy was that never once did he ask me why I wanted to know about Jacob Everard Christiansen. I had a scam all prepared—that Jake had applied for a job with the FBI, and I was checking him out—but I never had a chance to use it. I guess he was too happy to yak about old times. I'll try the same con on Madame Olga, if necessary, and find out how good a seer she is.

—Lindberg

=5=

Five tables, each seating six, are set in the East Room of the White House. The President and First Lady are at the head table with Brother Kristos. Vice President Trent and his wife preside over another table, and Chief of Staff Folsom a third.

The other guests are mostly second-echelon White House staffers, including John Tollinger, Jennifer Raye, Audrey Robertson, Michael Oberfest, Dr. Stemple, and Press Secretary Umbaugh. Officials *not* present include Cabinet members, the director of the Central Intelligence Agency, and the director of the Federal Bureau of Investigation.

There is a subdued drone of conversation, most of it concerning the guest of honor. He sits upright between the President and Mrs. Hawkins, conversing quietly.

It is noted, with some scorn, that he wears a black silk Nehru jacket. The gold cross swings brightly on its chain. With his long hair, wild mustache and beard, he makes a striking if somewhat unkempt figure. The staffers may smile at his costume, but most are curiously aware of his physical presence.

"He looks like a muzhik," Tollinger says to Jennifer.

"What's a muzhik?"

"Something like Muzak but without the music."

"Idiot," she says. "I think he looks romantic."

"Uh-huh. Do you think he's going to say grace?"

"No," she says promptly. "He never says grace. He

thinks it's prayer by rote. He doesn't believe in mechanical worship. Like rituals. He says they are the trappings of religion without the spirit and soul."

"Oh my," Tollinger says snidely. "The faith of Brother Kristos according to Sister Jennifer."

She is so offended that she ignores him for the remainder of the morning.

While everyone is breakfasting hungrily on honeydew melon, scrambled eggs, smoked kippers, and home fries, Brother Kristos drinks a cup of tea.

"Maybe he's fasting," Michael Oberfest says to Pete Umbaugh. "Or he's too nervous to eat."

"Nervous he ain't," the Press Secretary says. "That I guarantee. You meet him yet?"

"Nope."

"Quite an experience. Doesn't offer to shake hands. Just left me standing there with my paw out. But he stared at me as if he could read my mind. Quite an experience. If you get a chance, introduce yourself to him."

"I think I will. He's supposed to be able to predict the future. Maybe he can give me some stock tips."

The guests finish their tea or coffee, and wait for the President to rise, signaling the end of the meal.

"We'll all be moving to the Cabinet Room soon," Audrey Robertson tells Dr. Stemple. "If you want to cut out, I'll understand, darl."

"Not me," Stemple says. "I want to hear his sermon. The man fascinates me. You'd think he'd be awed, breaking bread with the President of the United States. But he doesn't look like he thinks it's any big deal. Notice the way he slowly strokes his beard? Like an Old Testament prophet. I've got to meet the guy. Will you introduce me?"

"If you say so, darl," the Social Secretary says. "Isn't *anyone* going to sneak out?"

No one does.

In the Cabinet Room, the guest of honor is seated in what would ordinarily be the President's chair, halfway down one side of the long polished table. Senior officials occupy the other chairs around the table; lower ranks take the uncomfortable seats against the walls, usually occupied by aides to Cabinet members. When all those chairs have been filled, several guests are left to stand. Audrey Robertson, making a quick count, realizes dolefully that her scheme has failed; everyone has stayed.

The room gradually quiets. Brother Kristos stands. For the first time, the staffers become aware of the intensity of his gaze. A few fidget, lower their eyes.

"Look at me, all of you," he commands. "I am Kristos, brother of Christ, an apostle sent by God to bring you salvation."

A shocked exhalation whispers through the room.

"You ask yourself, 'Who is this man who dares to claim divinity?' Look into my eyes. What you see is the holy fire of faith.

"You are all educated, I know. You believe yourselves to be rational. And your logic cannot accept my godliness, for you see before you a human being like yourselves, flesh and blood, and so you reason I must be as you—but I am not. I have no logic but the power of faith.

"I say to you that faith and logic are two different languages, and neither can be translated into the other. Today I ask you to put aside your formal, disciplined principles of reasoning and enter into a world in which faith, not thought, is the mover, and love of God the only allegiance you need know."

He has them now, and they lean forward, craning to follow his message. He speaks with such deeply felt conviction that no one can laugh, and even doubt seems facile and cheap.

"Is faith so difficult to comprehend and embrace? You awoke this morning with faith that the sun would rise. You traveled to this magnificent home with faith that you would arrive safely. In a hundred ways, you act with faith. Your present and your future depend upon faith. Is it impossible then to recognize its power and wonder if it might also be your road to a happiness that logic and rational thought cannot offer?

"So I ask you to listen to what I have to say now with belief in your hearts. My message is short. It is said that this country is a nation of laws, not of men. But men make the laws; they are the result of human effort and subject to human error. There was a time in this nation when men and women were sold into slavery, legally. When little children labored in factories and mines, legally. And think how many legal wrongs exist today.

"Laws made by humans are chaff on the wind, doomed to perish unless they are created with total faith in God. Our laws, our human laws, are fallible and mortal. Only God's law is infallible and forever. And His law is love."

Brother Kristos sits down abruptly. His rapt listeners, caught in postures of strained attention, are shocked by the sudden finish of the sermon. Then they begin to stir, look at each other nervously, not certain the service is over. But President Hawkins stands.

"Thank you, Brother Kristos," he says huskily, looking down at the seated preacher. "You have given us much to ponder." Then he addresses the assembled staffers: "Thank you for coming. I ask you all to reflect on Brother Kristos' message and discuss with one another how we may better serve our country by following the faith he has so eloquently expressed."

"Let's get out of here," Vice President Trent says to his wife as soon as the Hawkinses have left. He jerks his chin toward Brother Kristos, now surrounded by eager questioners. "The man is insane!" Trent says wrathfully. "Practically a Communist. It's a disgrace that he was allowed to spout such drivel in the White House."

"I hear he drinks a great deal," Matilda Trent says mildly. "Do you suppose he's drunk now?"

"No excuse," the VP growls.

"Will you get him home, darl?" Audrey Robertson asks Jennifer Raye.

"Sure. No problem. Wasn't his sermon just wonderful?"

"Marvy," Audrey says. "You think you could get him to shave off the beaver?"

"I doubt it."

"Well, maybe it's for the best. Men who have beards are supposed to have very weak chins. Does he, darl?"

"How would I know?" Jennifer says stiffly.

"Extremely interesting," Dr. R. Judd Stemple says to Pete Umbaugh. "There's monomania there; no doubt about it."

"He sounded sincere to me," the Press Secretary says.

"Oh, he is, he is—and so is anyone who thinks he's Napoleon or Peter Pan. What impressed me was his fluency. He'd make one helluva used-car salesman."

"I wish he was," Umbaugh says dismally. "I've got a feeling he's going to be trouble with a capital T."

The guests gradually disperse; only a few remain. Folsom draws Brother Kristos over to a corner of the Cabinet Room. The two men stand close, and Kristos seems to be doing most of the talking.

"I apologize," Tollinger says to Jennifer Raye. "I didn't mean to be a smart-ass."

"You're forgiven," she says brightly. "Just give the guy a chance, will you?"

"Sure."

"What did you think of his sermon?"

"Impressive. He obviously believes every word he said."

"Of course he does. He's not a hypocrite, you know. Oh-oh, looks like his confab with Folsom is breaking up. I've got to drive him home."

"Call you later?" he asks.

She hesitates a moment. "All right," she says finally. "Late tonight would be best."

She takes Brother Kristos in tow. On their way out, Kristos stops to stare at Tollinger.

"I enjoyed your sermon," John says. "For a man who sneers at logic, it was organized very logically."

The preacher shows his big teeth. Someone has persuaded him to see a dentist; they are white and glistening.

"You are going to say that my reasoning was excellent," Kristos says, "but my original premise is faulty."

"Yes, that's what I was going to say."

"You and I must have a long talk."

"I'd like that," Tollinger says, surprised that he really means it.

Then only he and Folsom remain. The Chief of Staff is sitting slumped in one of the armchairs at the big table.

"Quite a morning, Chief," Tollinger says lightly, and then is shocked at Folsom's appearance. The man is badly shaken: face drawn, eyes glazed.

"Are you all right?" John asks sharply.

Folsom looks up. "I took him aside," he says in a low voice. "And I told him I thought he was just a cheap trickster. I said he was supposed to be able to see things in people's past, so, come on, tell me some deep, dark secret in *my* past."

"And?"

The Chief looks up, his mouth twisted into an ugly grin. "He did. He stared at me with those crazy eyes and told me something that happened years ago, something I'm not proud of. And I swear as sure as I'm sitting here that no one alive today knows about it. No one could possibly know, but Brother Kristos did."

"I'm not going to ask you what it was," Tollinger says, "but are you absolutely sure you never told anyone?"

Folsom shakes his head. "And the other people involved are dead. Died when it happened."

Tollinger is silent. It would be fatuous to comment, "Lucky guess."

The Chief of Staff looks up at him fearfully. "John," he says, "the man is dangerous."

=6=

Pearl Gibbs is waiting for Kristos in the pickup truck.

"Don't you look spiffy," she says.

He is wearing a black leather trench coat, creakingly new.

"You like it?" he says, climbing in beside her.

"Very nice. Must have cost a mint."

"You'll get yours," he says shortly. "Just drive."

Friday-afternoon traffic is heavy. It's stop-and-go until they're out of the city and heading south through Virginia.

"How's Agnes?" he asks.

"She's okay. Jake, how come we can't live with you?"

"I'm working on it. And Nick—how's he?"

She laughs. "You won't believe it, but that dog got a letter yesterday from some kid."

"That kid is the President's son. I hope you kept the letter."

"Oh sure. It's cute."

"I've got to answer it. The kid's my passport."

"Yeah? To where?"

He doesn't reply, and she knows better than to repeat her question.

"Jake," she says, "now that you're in the bucks, don't you think we ought to fix up the barn?"

"No," he says. "People come because it doesn't look like a church. It looks like the stable where Christ was born."

"Hey, did you ever realize you have the same initials as Jesus Christ—J.C.?"

"The thought had occurred to me," he says dryly. "That barn is just right the way it is. Proves that you can find salvation in a dump; you don't need a cathedral."

"Well, since you got that newspaper story, we've had a lot of people coming around asking when you're going to preach. At least we can get some more benches."

"No," he says. "Let them stand. What's for dinner tonight?"

"Fish stew. It's all made. Just needs heating up. Plenty of pepper."

"Good," he says.

"Jake, if you don't want to fix up the barn, how about getting a new truck or car? This heap costs more for repairs than it's worth."

"I'm working on that too," he says.

"What sermon are you going to give tomorrow night?"

"I haven't thought about it."

"Why don't you do that one about sex being God's will. I like that one."

"I know," he says. "Can't we go any faster?"

That night, before they eat, he gives money to Agnes and Pearl.

"Buy some clothes," he tells them. "Plain stuff. Long skirts and high in front. If you move to D.C., I don't want you looking like hookers."

"When?" Pearl says. "When are we moving?"

"I told you I'm working on it."

"What about the barn?" Agnes asks. "Are you going to keep it?"

"Yes. This will still be my church. Though I may walk with the mighty, I shall never neglect the poor, the meek, the lonely who seek the word of God. Heat up the stew."

The women set to work. Kristos leaves by the rear door, the pale hound slinking along at his heels. A half-hour later, Agnes goes looking for him. He is out in the barren field behind the barn, on his knees, head bowed, hands clasped.

"Jake!" she yells at him. "Come eat!"

They sit around the table, ladling stew onto their tin plates. The vodka bottle is passed. Brother Kristos gorges ravenously, hunched over his food. The women tell him all the neighborhood gossip, but he says nothing.

Finally he wipes his mouth and takes a fresh bottle of vodka from the cupboard.

"Good food," he says. "That's what I miss most in the city."

"Don't you miss more than that?" Agnes says.

His grin is feral. "Remind me," he says. "Put on a show."

Giggling, the two women start to undress.

"Jake, were you telling the truth about us coming to D.C.?" Pearl asks.

He nods.

"You wouldn't leave us, would you?" Agnes says.

"No," Brother Kristos says, moving toward them. "I can't leave you. You're my hell."

Late in February, George Hawkins is released from Walter Reed Hospital and moves back to his own bedroom. Adjoining chambers are occupied by his nurse and his personal bodyguard, a huge Marine sergeant named Dennis McShane who frequently carries the frail lad about on his shoulders.

The presence of the boy leavens the mood of the entire White House. He receives so many toys from well-wishers that regular deliveries of the overflow are made to orphanages and children's hospitals in the Washington area— with George making the presentations personally.

"Really super photo opportunities," enthuses Peter Umbaugh.

The boy is tutored privately—lessons four days a week—but as often as possible the First Lady takes him on outings to government buildings, monuments, nearby military bases, and—not infrequently—to visit Brother Kristos in his apartment on Eighteenth Street N.W.

It is on one of these trips, early in March, that Kristos gives George a gift that instantly becomes the boy's favorite. It is a boxed set of magic tricks and puzzles.

Brother Kristos has pulled aside the brown linen drapes, and the usually gloomy study is flooded with pale afternoon light. Brenna O'Gara has brought up tea for Mrs. Hawkins, a glass of milk for George, and a plate of homemade oatmeal cookies. Then she has returned to her kitchen to continue gossiping with Sergeant McShane.

The First Lady is seated in one of the armchairs, sipping her tea and watching George and Brother Kristos at the big table. She marvels at the rapport between the two: the boy fair-haired and slight, the man dark and massive. They play together, laugh together; George pulls the preacher's beard, and Kristos gently tweaks the lad's nose.

The brother of Christ is showing the boy how to operate the Marvelous Money Machine from the magic set. A sheet of blank paper is fed into a miniature printing press, a little crank is turned, and lo! a genuine dollar bill emerges from the other side. George is fascinated but, after he understands how it is accomplished, puts it aside to try to solve a puzzle of five interlocking metal rings.

Brother Kristos tousles the lad's hair, then comes over to Helen. He sits on a worn leather hassock close to the First Lady and clasps her bony hands between his.

"Mother, you are happy," he says, staring at her. "Having the boy home and healthy has brightened your life. I see it in your face."

"My husband and I have you to thank for that," she says. "How can we ever repay you?"

"You have already repaid me many times over. Your generosity has enabled me to continue bringing the word of God to those in need, and for that I thank you. I pray for you and your family every night."

"Thank you," she says faintly. "And you are always in our prayers, Brother Kristos."

He smiles stiffly. "And the President? I hope he is well."

She sighs. "He's healthy, thank God, but working so very hard. People pull at him constantly, you know, everyone wants something. Everyone has different ideas on what should be done."

Brother Kristos nods gravely. "He must listen to all. But then, in the end, he must do what he *feels* is right. He need only listen to the voice within him, for it is the voice of God."

"I believe that," she says, "I really do. But Ab has so many responsibilities. The decisions he's called on to make are tremendous."

"Yes, yes," Kristos says. "But his power is tremendous too."

"Are you saying you think he should assert himself more? I've often thought that myself."

Kristos releases her hands. "The President has enormous power," he says. "But power is a muscle and must be used constantly if it is not to wither. Do you think your husband realizes the full extent of his power?"

"No," she says finally, "I don't believe he does. And because of that, some people take advantage of him."

"There is so much he could do. So much!"

"Like what?" she challenges. "Tell me, Brother Kristos, what would *you* do if you were President?"

He shakes his head. "I know nothing about politics and how government works."

"But you know about people, and that's more important. Please, I'd like to know: If you had the President's power, what would you do?"

He rises and stalks about the room. He pauses at George's side, takes the puzzle from the boy's fumbling fingers, and in a trice has the five metal rings separated.

"Now put them together again, brother," he tells the lad.

He returns to Mrs. Hawkins, stands in front of her and stares down.

"If I was President?" he says. "I would do as I urge your husband to do: Obey God's will."

"But politics are so complicated!" she cries. "How can Ab be certain he is obeying God's will?"

The eyes of Brother Kristos widen and flame. "I am God's apostle on earth," he says.

He leaves her then and goes over to sit beside George again.

"Brother, did you get a letter from my dog?" he asks the boy.

George laughs delightedly. "Oh sure. It was such a funny letter. Did Nick really say those things?"

"Of course he did, with yips and barks and little howls. And I wrote it all down. Don't you believe a dog can understand things and talk in his own language?"

"I suppose so."

"Well, he can. And I understand him. You believe me, don't you?"

"Oh sure."

"Good," Brother Kristos says. And then in a louder voice so that the First Lady will be sure to hear: "If you believe, truly believe, all things are possible."

=8=

There are a few follow-up stories in newspapers and weekly newsmagazines, and one television network runs a short clip of Brother Kristos visiting the Lincoln Memorial, but generally media coverage of the "itinerant preacher" and his relationship with the First Family is brief and cautious. Vice President Samuel Trent is incensed.

"This could be a bigger scandal than Watergate or the Iran-Contra mess," he fumes. "I cannot for the life of me understand why the media—who are supposed to be the watchdogs of our most precious liberties—have not thoroughly investigated that scoundrel."

"Perhaps, sir," Oberfest suggests diffidently, "they feel the President's spiritual beliefs are not a proper concern of the press. After all, Hawkins is entitled to *some* privacy."

"Rubbish!" the VP says. "A President's life, even his religion, should be an open book. Mine certainly is. The electorate deserves no less. Well, I am not going to allow this outrage to fester and possibly damage the party in the midterm elections. I intend to cast the harsh glare of publicity on this whole distressing affair, and if Hawkins suffers in the court of public opinion, so be it."

As usual, Trent seeks the counsel of his wife. That austere woman has read widely, including *The Prince,* and offers excellent advice.

"First of all, dear," she says, knitting away, "your own

motives in taking action must be beyond reproach. You haven't told anyone how you feel about this, have you?"

"Not actually," he says, beginning to worry. "I did mention to Mike Oberfest that the President's friendship with Brother Kristos might hurt the party. . . ."

"But Michael knows nothing about what's on your mind?"

Trent is uncomfortable, trying to recall exactly how much he revealed to his aide. "All I remember is telling him how this scandal may affect the party's future. Of course I did ask him to call a newspaper contact to leak the story of Kristos' visit to Camp David. But that was only to alert the media to what was happening. Then public opinion might force Hawkins to rid himself of this charlatan."

Matilda Trent sighs. "Sam, you are playing a very dangerous game. I think it is a game worth playing, but it must be done cleverly and with discretion. On the one hand you want to publicize the close association of the President and Brother Kristos, believing, as I do, that their relationship can only end in a political disaster for Hawkins. On the other hand, you are telling people that publicity about their relationship will hurt the party."

"I hadn't thought of it quite that way," he confesses. "What should I do, Matilda?"

She goes back to her knitting. "The two policies are not necessarily incompatible," she tells him. "But one must be pursued publicly and the other privately. In conversations with party leaders and contributors, you may discreetly suggest that you are worried about Brother Kristos because, if he is proved a fraud, it will harm the President and, by extension, the party."

"Yes, I can do that."

"But in secret, you can continue to focus attention on the President's relationship with Kristos."

"But how can I do that?" he argues. "I can hardly call in my media adviser and say, 'Here's what I want.' "

"No," Matilda says calmly, "of course you can't do that. The fewer people who are aware of your private activities, the better. Do you trust Michael Oberfest?"

"Oh, I trust him well enough, but he's not the brainiest man who ever came down the pike. He was graduated from a state university, you know, and I'm afraid it shows."

"Then he may be exactly the man you want to handle this. You certainly don't want anyone intelligent enough to question your motives. Will Oberfest obey orders?"

"Oh yes, he's good at that."

"Then use him. Tell him what you want—in private, of course—and leave the details to him. If he succeeds, fine. If he doesn't, replace him."

"Yes," Trent says, "I think that's wise."

"And, in a way, he can serve as your cut-out. If the Kristos scandal does become public knowledge, you can deny any involvement. It will be your word against Oberfest's. Just make certain there are no written or taped instructions."

"Excellent advice," the Veep says. "I do believe you have a taste for intrigue, Matilda."

"Of course I do," she says gruffly. "Keeps my brain from turning to mush. All right, Sam, you do your part, and I'll do mine. I understand that Brother Kristos is living in an apartment in Lenore Mattingly's home. I've known her for years. Can't stand the woman, but that's neither here nor there. I think I'll ask her for lunch and see what I can find out about her tenant. Perhaps she'll invite me to meet him. I'm curious about the man."

"Do that, dear," Trent says, rising. "Pick up all the gossip you can. Coming to bed now?"

"Not just yet," his wife says. "I want to knit awhile."

The next morning the Vice President summons Michael Oberfest into his private office.

"Sit down, Mike," he says genially, which so shocks the aide that he's convinced he's about to be terminated.

"Mike," Trent says, "I know you have never repeated anything you have heard within these walls. I trust you fully or you wouldn't be sitting here today. I have absolutely no doubts about your loyalty."

"Thank you, sir."

"But what I am about to tell you is of such a sensitive nature that I must ask for your complete and utter secrecy. Do I have your word on that?"

"Of course, sir."

"Excellent. Mike, as you know, I have been deeply troubled by the President's association with Brother Kristos, that religious fraud, and how their relationship might affect the party's future. I have decided my best course of action would be to exacerbate the scandal so that, as quickly as possible, party leaders can bring pressure to bear on Hawkins to convince him that his continued friendship with that swindler represents a clear and present danger. Do you follow me?"

"Oh yes, sir."

"And you agree with me?"

"Absolutely."

"What I wish to do, in effect, is to lance the boil, bring this entire distressing matter to the attention of the public. Then, after Kristos is taken out of the picture, the party's campaign can sail ahead unencumbered by an embarrassment that could well spell disaster for the administration if allowed to fester. The good of the party is our sole concern. Do you concur?"

"Oh yes, sir," Oberfest says, completely dazed by this bombast.

"Glad to hear it," Trent says heartily. "Because I want you to handle it. You alone, and no one else. I am to be kept out of it, of course, because of the prestige of my office. But I am depending on you to make certain the truth about Brother Kristos and his association with the First Family is exposed as soon as possible for all the world to know. Then, when Hawkins is forced to rid himself of this leech, the party can look forward to the upcoming elections with confidence. How you accomplish this task is up to you. I have selected Michael Oberfest from all the members of my staff for this critical assignment because I respect your judgment, admire your intelligence, and envy your initiative and can-do enthusiasm. What do you say—will you accept this important challenge?"

"I'll do my best, sir," the aide says, just beginning to get a glimmer of what's going on.

"Marvelous!" Samuel Trent says, rising and extending his hand. "Your best is good enough for me, I do assure you."

Oberfest goes back to his office and sits behind his desk in shock until he gets it all sorted out. Then he has nothing but admiration for the intensity of the Veep's ambition to be President.

Five minutes after that comes the pleased realization that at last he is a player in a genuine conspiracy.

=9=

The door to the hallway is bolted. In addition, he has closed the door to the bedroom. He sits on the rumpled bed, counting his money. On the floor at his feet is a fresh bottle of vodka, recently opened.

He counts almost six thousand dollars, mostly in small bills: donations at his Virginia church, gifts from the President, contributions by the ladies he has met at what Mrs. Mattingly now calls his "sermonettes."

The cash makes a thick wad, and he binds it with a rubber band, then slips it into the foot of a wool sock in the bottom drawer of the dresser. He is reaching for the bottle when his new phone rings on the bedside table. He sits again on the bed, and answers.

"Yes?"

"Brother Kristos?"

"Yes."

"President Hawkins is calling. Just a moment, sir."

He has time for a small gulp of vodka before the President comes on the line.

"Brother Kristos?"

"Yes, father, I am here."

"I had hoped to have a talk with you before this, but things keep coming up."

"I understand."

"Right now I'm on my way to a birthday party for the Speaker of the House. It'll probably go on till the small hours, but I plan to break away early. Would eleven o'clock be too late to meet with you?"

"Eleven will be fine."

"What I suggest is this: When I leave the party I'll stop in front of your house. I won't come in because the Secret Service agents would insist on first conducting a search. It would be less trouble if you could come down and we could talk in my car for a while. Would you be willing to do that?"

"Of course, father. I'll be waiting on the sidewalk at eleven o'clock."

"Thank you. It will be good to see you again."

Kristos carries his vodka into the study and sets it at the head of the big table. Then he returns to the bedroom. He has placed a package of salted herring to chill on the windowsill. He brings the fish back to the study. Then he fetches a new Bible, a gift from Mrs. Cynthia Jorgenson. It is a handsome leather-bound volume, the pages edged with gilt.

He uses the scarlet ribbon page marker to open the Bible

to the Psalms. Sipping vodka, nibbling salted herring, Brother Kristos reads avidly, enthralled by the sublime harmonies, the divine poetry. It moves him as nothing else can—not drink, not food, not the naked bodies of complaisant women.

Finally he puts the book away and brings out a fat folder of correspondence. When his preaching was limited to the barn, occasionally he would receive a letter from a congregant requesting advice on spiritual, family, or financial problems. Or sometimes just asking for his blessing. Invariably these letters contained cash or a check. Not a lot; just a few dollars. But Kristos answered them all.

Now, since the newspaper articles and his appearance on network television, his mail has increased to a flood. Some letters are sent to the White House and forwarded to him. Some come directly to the Mattingly home. One that he cherishes was addressed simply "Brother Kristos, Washington, D.C.," but somehow it got to him.

Most of the recent letters also contain cash, checks or, in a few cases, coins taped to a piece of cardboard. Many of them plead that he apply his healing talents to their ailments, ranging from acne to cancer. All assure him of their complete faith in his power to restore them to perfect health.

He replies with brief adjurations to the writers to put their faith in God and pray daily. He signs: "Yours in Christ, Brother Kristos."

He sets to work to answer the latest batch. He has mentioned his heavy mail to Emily Mattingly, and she has suggested he have a form letter printed that need only be addressed and signed. She has volunteered to take over the task of addressing and stamping the envelopes, and he thinks now he will accept her offer.

He writes out fourteen letters, and then puts the correspondence aside. He finishes the herring, swallows more vodka to wash it down. Then he rinses his mouth, sucks on a Tic Tac, rubs his mustache and beard with cologne.

He dons a new leather windbreaker and goes down to the street to await the President of the United States.

A few minutes after eleven, a three-car cortege pulls up, a black limousine in the middle. Kristos walks toward the Cadillac, but a Secret Service agent steps in his path.

"Sorry, padre," he says. "Orders." And he pats the preacher down so swiftly and expertly that Kristos is hardly aware of what's happening.

Then he climbs into the back of the car and shakes hands with Abner Hawkins. The President presses a button on his armrest; a glass window rises silently to isolate the chauffeur.

Kristos leans close to peer at Hawkins in the gloom. "Father, you look tired."

"I *am* tired. The work and worries never seem to end. Mrs. Hawkins and I keep talking about a vacation, but we keep putting it off; always a new crisis. Well, I guess it comes with the territory. But it does bother me that I have to spend so much of my time dealing with events beyond my control. I had hoped for a more active administration."

"You can still achieve much."

"Well, that's what I wanted to talk to you about. My wife told me of the conversation she had with you about the power of the presidency and how I might accomplish more. Interesting. Very interesting."

"Father, as I told Mrs. Hawkins, I know little about politics. But I do agree that at the moment you seem to be a prisoner of events, unable to plan and carry out policies you know would benefit your children."

"Exactly!" the President says, clapping his palms together. "I want to be an innovative Chief Executive. But I just can't seem to find the time."

"Delegate more authority on routine matters," Brother Kristos advises. "I know you have good people working for you who share your aims. Let them do more; it is not necessary that you oversee every detail. You must make the final decisions, of course, but try to give yourself a chance to dream about the future."

"I can't tell you how much I enjoy talking with you," Hawkins says. "All right, assuming I achieve the balanced management style you recommend—what then? There are many things I want to do, but obviously I can't ride off in all directions. I'll need a system of priorities, a method of selecting those policies that are most important and have a reasonable chance of succeeding."

"Father, with all due respect, I believe you need a lodestar, a standard by which all your projects should be judged. Do not overly concern yourself with whether or not a plan may succeed or fail. More important is that it conform to your guiding light."

"Which should be?"

"The commandment of God. That is the one true test by which to judge the fitness and righteousness of your actions."

"There are many unbelievers out there, Brother Kristos—and not a few in the Congress."

"I know that. The way I suggest is not an easy path. But I believe there is a great hunger in this land for a transcendent faith. I believe the majority seeks a belief that will give meaning to the present and promise for the future. Father, I know my words may sound foolish, perhaps even crazy, but I truly believe that if you undertake a great religious crusade to make our government conform to God's will, you will find millions of disciples who will follow you."

The President is silent, sitting with bowed head. Finally he stirs, turns sideways so he can look directly at Brother Kristos.

"You ask a great deal," he says in a low voice. "The risks are enormous."

"There is no risk for you," Kristos says sternly. "Even if you fail, you will be filled with the beatitude of doing

God's work on earth. And it is not I who ask this of you. I bring you God's message."

"If I do set out to remake the government in the manner you describe, what, specifically, do you suggest as a first step?"

Brother Kristos speaks fluently for almost five minutes. When he finishes, Hawkins takes a deep breath.

"I don't know how that could be done," he says. "Or if it could be done at all. But I cannot give you an answer now. It would be a tremendous undertaking, and I need to discuss it with my wife."

"Of course," Kristos says. "Do not make your decision lightly, for what God demands is absolute faith and total dedication."

The President nods. "The most important decision of my life," he says solemnly. "Before we part, may we pray together, Brother Kristos?"

"Let us," the preacher says, and clasps Hawkins' hands in his. "Praise the Lord! Praise Him, the mighty and those in high places! The kings and rulers of the earth, praise the Lord! Those of wealth and power, all kneel and praise the Lord!

"Praise the Lord!"

=10=

"Now listen," Tollinger says, "there is no such thing as The Miracle of Camp David and never was."

"You don't know," Jennifer says stiffly. "You weren't there."

"But I've been doing some reading about hemophilia, and I have a pretty good idea what happened."

"I don't want to hear it."

"Will you just listen a minute, for God's sake?" he says angrily. "It's not true that hemophiliacs die from a simple cut or scrape. Their skin heals normally. Sure, there's bleeding, just as if you or I cut ourselves. But with the usual first-aid treatment, the bleeding stops, the wound closes and heals."

"But it didn't stop," Jennifer says. "George was bleeding, and bleeding a lot. I saw it."

"So his parents panicked," Tollinger goes on. "That's understandable; who wants to see their kid bleed? But they should have known there was little danger from a surface cut. The big problem for hemophiliacs is internal bleeding; they lack the clotting agents to stop the hemorrhage. But George didn't have any internal injury; he just had a simple skin cut. So don't talk about The Miracle of Camp David. Brother Kristos just used a minor accident to hoodwink the President and First Lady."

"I don't have to convince you," she says. "I believe there was a miracle, the Hawkinses believe it, and so do a lot of other people. You should take a look at the mail that's coming in."

"But that doesn't make it true. My God, Jen, you of all people should know the difference between reality and perception. You and I spend half our working hours trying to put a spin on events so they'll be perceived by the public in a favorable light. In other words, we twist the truth. Well, that might be okay in politics, but I don't like seeing you do it in your private life. Just try to get it through your head that The Miracle of Camp David is a mirage. It just doesn't exist in real life."

"I didn't expect you to believe," she says scornfully. "You don't believe in anything."

"I have one belief," Tollinger says. "It's that ninety-eight percent of the human race are fucking idiots, and this whole brouhaha over Brother Kristos proves it. People who should know better are treating him like the holy man of the Capital Beltway. I saw him on his way into the Oval Office the other day, and supposedly intelligent and sophisticated staffers were stopping him in the hallway to beg for his autograph. Disgusting!"

She looks at him thoughtfully. "I think you're jealous."

"Jealous? Why in hell should I be jealous of that faker?"

"Because he's not a faker; he sincerely believes in what he says. And that faith is what makes you jealous."

"You're talking rubbish!" he says furiously. "The man's an out-and-out fraud with an eye for the quick buck. Look at the way he's dressing these days: leather coats, silk shirts, fur hats. What do you think he's using to buy those things? Donations from the suckers he's conned with his garbage about there being no sin if you just have faith. Have *you* given him money?"

"I made a contribution to his church," she says defensively.

"I hope it was enough for a case of vodka," Tollinger says, "because that's probably where it went." Then, casually: "Have you been seeing him lately?"

"What business is it of yours?"

"We were married once—remember? And I like to think we're still good friends. I know how you feel about Kristos, and I just don't want to see you getting hurt."

"Oh-oh," she says, staring at him. "Not only are you envious of Brother Kristos because of his capacity to believe, but you're jealous of his friendship with your ex. It never occurred to you that I might find a man superior to you. And I mean superior in *every* way."

He looks at her, his face twisted. "So you're another of his converts. Jen, for God's sake, haven't you heard the gossip? The man has the reputation of a satyr."

"I don't care about the gossip. It's not going to affect my relationship with Brother Kristos in the least. All I know is that he makes me feel alive—more alive than I've ever been in my life. And what he says about faith is absolutely true. It's given me a new way of looking at things. I've never been so happy, so filled with the sheer joy of being alive and able to obey God's command. And I owe it all to Brother Kristos."

"You're lost," John Tollinger says despairingly. "Lost and gone."

=11=

In the labyrinthine halls of the Capitol there are many labeled doors leading to the offices of legislators. There are fewer doors, unmarked, giving access to small hideaways. Congressmen fortunate enough to possess them by virtue of seniority may relax from the cares of state, free of the importuning of constituents and lobbyists.

Actually, much of the business of government takes place in these sanctums. Rumors are repeated, gossip exchanged, votes traded, compromises arranged, and a great deal of bourbon and branch water consumed.

It is in one of these secluded chambers that an informal meeting is held that participants later recall in such portentous terms as "the writing on the wall" or "the shape of things to come."

Seated in captain's chairs around a scarred pine table are the Speaker of the House of Representatives, the Majority Leader of the Senate, Henry Folsom, and the President's congressional liaison, Luther Dunkirk, familiarly known to almost everyone on Capitol Hill as the Deacon, or Deac.

The Speaker, who "owns" the hideaway, makes certain each man has a full glass at his elbow, and then gets down to business.

"Hank," he says to the Chief of Staff, "just what the hell is the President up to on this food-giveaway plan?"

Folsom takes a gulp of his drink, then shakes his head. "Don't know what you're talking about, sir," he says.

"Deacon?"

"I pass. It's news to me."

The Majority Leader, a big man with three chins and a tomato nose, moves his bulk irritably. "Let's not pussy-foot around," he says testily. "My spy at Agriculture tells me the President asked for a report on how much powdered milk, butter, cheese, and other eatables the government has in storage, where it's located, the condition it's in, and how long it would take to ship it out to the poor and hungry. He wants a contingency plan for emptying the warehouses and distributing surplus food."

"And I heard," the Speaker adds, "that he's asked his General Counsel to research whether he can give the food away by presidential edict or if he'll need special legislation. Come on, you two—what gives? We like to know about calamities before they happen."

The President's men look at each other. "Deac, you take it," Folsom says.

"Well," Dunkirk says cautiously, "the President did mention something about it, but it's still in the talking stage; no decision has been made. It's my guess that the whole thing will just fade away."

"It damn well better," the Leader says. "Do you know what a giveaway of all the government's food would do to market prices? Instant disaster."

"In spades," the Speaker says. "And we'd have ten thousand farmers crowding onto the Beltway ready to hammer in our heads. What in God's name is Hawkins thinking about—if he's thinking at all?"

"Now wait a minute," Folsom says. "It's been done before, you know. In Reagan's administration, I think."

"Sure," the Leader says. "A limited handout of cheese. But Hawkins is talking about handing out everything from soup to nuts. What that'll do to the commodity markets, I hate to think. Who the hell is supposed to get all these freebies?"

"Senator," the Chief of Staff says, "there are an awful lot of hungry people in this country. I'm not saying they're starving to death, but they're just not getting enough to eat."

"There have always been hungry people," the Speaker says roughly, "and always will be. What happens after the government's surplus is eaten up? What then? You still have a lot of hungry people like you had before. So they had full bellies for a couple of days. Giving away free food isn't going to solve the problem of the poor and hungry. Only jobs will do that."

"Chief," the Leader says, looking directly at Folsom, "how do you feel about it? Forget your loyalty to Hawkins and give us your personal opinion. You know it won't go beyond these walls."

"What do I really think about it?" the Chief of Staff says. "I think it's strictly from Nutsville."

"I'll go along with that," the Deacon says. "It sucks."

"Well," the Leader says, "can't the two of you convince the President that the idea just won't fly? If he brings it up to the Hill, he's going to lose what little clout he's got left."

"Now wait a minute," Dunkirk says. "Supposing Hawkins decides to push this and gets on the tube with pictures of people sleeping on subway grates and shuffling along in breadlines. He'll get tremendous support from every church group and bleeding-heart liberal in the country. And he can make a good pitch on economic grounds too. You know how much it's costing us to keep buying up surplus food, and how much it costs to store it. Eliminate those outlays and you make a nice dent in the budget deficit. Then what arguments have you guys got left? Objecting to feeding hungry Americans is like being against the flag, mom, and apple pie. You'll end up looking like a bunch of Scrooges. Is that what you want?"

The two congressmen stare at him, expressionless. Folsom drains his drink and leans forward.

"Look," he says earnestly, "what Deac says is right, but it doesn't begin to address the real problem. I know I shouldn't wash dirty linen in public, but I'm going to level with you: It wasn't Hawkins' idea; he got it from Brother Kristos. You've heard about the guy?"

"Yeah, I've heard about him," the Leader says grimly. "The so-called holy man."

"And you mean to tell us," the Speaker says incredulously, "the President of the United States is following the advice of this self-appointed messiah?"

Folsom nods glumly. "You know how devout the Boss is. He and the First Lady are convinced the preacher saved their son."

"My God, Hank," the Leader says, "can't you talk any sense into Hawkins?"

"I've tried," Folsom says miserably, "but he doesn't want to hear it. He really believes Kristos is the brother of Christ, come to earth to bring us the Lord's message."

"That's heavy stuff," the Speaker says. "Isn't there anything you can do to eliminate the guy?"

"I've got a detective searching his background, and I'm hoping he'll turn up evidence of a criminal record or *something* I can use to persuade the Boss that this man is a fake."

"But you've discovered nothing yet?" the Speaker asks.

Folsom shakes his head. "Not yet."

"Hank, you believe the guy is a fraud, don't you?"

Folsom hesitates a beat. "I don't know what to believe," he says finally in a low voice.

"I don't like this, gentlemen," the Leader booms, slapping the table with a meaty palm. "Politics and religion are a lethal combination. Oh, I know we've got 'In God We Trust' on our money, and we open congressional sessions with a prayer. But once we start passing laws because we think it's God's wish, we're in deep shit."

"And it would tear the nation apart," the Speaker adds. "We've got more religions in this country than baseball teams, and a lot of them have diametrically opposing beliefs. So mixing religion and politics is a no-win situation."

"You think I don't know all that?" Folsom says hotly. "I want to get rid of Brother Kristos as much as you do. But *how?*"

No one has an answer, and the four men sit in silence a moment, heads bowed, until the Leader speaks.

"Maybe," he says with a sour smile, "just maybe we should pray."

On the trip back to the White House, Folsom says to Dunkirk, "Those guys are really worried. Well, they should be. Are you getting much political flak on Brother Kristos?"

"Plenty," the Deacon says. "Calls from the party's national chairman, state chairmen, big contributors."

"What do you tell them?"

"As little as possible. Yes, the President knows Brother Kristos. Yes, he meets with him in the Oval Office occasionally. Yes, he contributes to the preacher's church. But, no, Brother Kristos is not about to be appointed to a new Cabinet post. No, he is not running the White House. And, no, the First Lady is not sleeping with him. Now where the hell did those crazy rumors come from?"

"I'll tell you where," Folsom says wrathfully. "There's some son of a bitch, high up in the government, who wants to see this thing become a world-class scandal. I don't know who's doing it or why, but if I ever catch the bastard, I'll cut his balls off."

"Now, now," the Deacon says. "There are faith, hope, and charity, and the greatest of these is charity."

"Screw charity," the Chief of Staff growls. "I want blood!"

=12=

Brenna O'Gara, that pious, acidic woman, comes up to Kristos' apartment to change bedroom and bathroom linen, to dust and clean, and at least once a week to prepare for one of his sermonettes, delivered to a small coterie invited by Lenore Mattingly.

The tart-tongued housekeeper is scornful of Brother Kristos' faith.

"You're the brother of Christ?" she scoffs. "And I'm Queen of the May!"

"And so you might be," he says, staring at her. But she stares back just as determinedly.

She finds his soiled towels on the bathroom floor. "You're a filthy animal," she tells him.

"And you're a sour drudge," he says, and reaches out to touch her. She jerks angrily away.

But he persists and laughs at her fury. "How much money did you send the Pope this week?" he jeers. He tastes the food she has prepared and pushes his plate aside disgustedly. "Swill!"

She has learned to move warily about him, for his hands are too free. "Keep your dirty paws to yourself," she yells at him. "I'm going to tell the missus."

"You do that," he says. "She won't believe you."

So she does, and he is right: the missus will listen to

no derogatory reports about the man of God who has helped so many people—and brought Mrs. Mattingly new popularity and made her home famous.

"Are you still a virgin?" he asks Brenna O'Gara.

She begins weeping.

"Use it or lose it," he advises.

She prays nightly that he might be destroyed by a thunderbolt from heaven. But he flourishes in silk shirts the ladies have embroidered for him, his hair pomaded, beard scented. She is convinced he has sold his soul to the devil.

One morning, early in April, she sees him leave the house. She climbs the stairs to his apartment to change the linen. She is bending over his bed when her thin hips are strongly clasped. He has returned silently, and now he is grinding his groin against her bony buttocks, saying things so awful she could never repeat them in the confessional.

She pulls away and he lunges after her. She flees, out of the bedroom, through the door, down the stairs, running and stumbling, sobbing.

Several hours later he goes downstairs to find Mrs. Mattingly and Emily deep in nervous conversation in the sitting room.

"Oh, Brother Kristos," Lenore wails, "something dreadful has happened. Brenna has quit!"

"She just packed up and left," Emily says wonderingly, "and wouldn't tell us why. We just can't understand her acting like that."

"A very disturbed woman," Kristos says. "The poor thing."

"She's been with us so many years," Mrs. Mattingly mourns. "Now whatever shall we do? We absolutely need a cook and housekeeper."

Brother Kristos nods sympathetically.

"I may be able to help," he says.

=13=

Michael Oberfest never dreamed conspiracy could be so much *fun*. And what's more, he discovers he has a talent for it. Following Vice President Trent's instructions, he has devised a campaign to inflate President Hawkins' association with Brother Kristos into a *scandale majeur*.

He sends anonymous letters to the press. He phones the television networks, giving fake names and addresses. And he calls all his contacts in the capital: "Have you heard the latest? Don't quote me, but I understand that . . ."

In a city that thrives on false reports—the more outlandish, the better—Michael's rumormongering is a big success. He is amused at how swiftly his lies spread and are reported back to him.

One morning, at 10:45, he phones an acquaintance at the Pentagon.

"Have you heard the latest, lieutenant?" Oberfest asks. "A woman who works at Commerce just called me and says she heard the First Lady is balling Brother Kristos."

"No kidding?" the lieutenant says.

And at 11:33, Michael gets a call from Fred Hechett at the FBI.

"Hear the latest?" Fred asks. "It seems that Helen Hawkins and Brother Kristos are doing their praying together—in bed."

"No kidding?" Oberfest says.

So that particular falsehood had a Rumor Return Rate of forty-eight minutes—not bad.

The Veep seems pleased with his aide's progress. Twice he's winked at Oberfest, twice he's clapped his shoulder, and once he's given him a whispered, "Well done!" Michael envisions a promotion, a raise and—if Trent's ambitions are realized—a future that seems unlimited.

One Thursday night, late in April, he calls his wife to say he'll be working late and probably won't be home much before midnight.

"Oh Mike," Ruth says, "again? What is it this time?"

"Planning the VP's itinerary on that upcoming trip to South America. Trent's handed me the whole job."

"He works you so hard. You should tell him you need another secretary."

"Good idea," Michael says. "Maybe I'll do that."

So he picks up a jumbo pizza with all the toppings, a bottle of Chianti Classico, and drives to the apartment of his consenting adult in Foggy Bottom. He also brings her a tennis bracelet, a circle of very small diamonds he brought back from his most recent trip to New York.

Oberfest, a soft, plumpish man who has a facial and manicure once a month, is hardly the answer to a maiden's prayer. But so severe is the shortage of eligible males in the nation's capital that the hordes of female government employees must find companionship where they can.

"Beggars can't be choosers," Shirley Bowker, Michael's girlfriend, once remarked to a confidante. "Remember, half a loaf is better than none. And if you ever saw Mike naked, you'd know exactly what I mean by half a loaf."

Shirley is taller than Michael, younger, and a great deal cannier. She works as secretary for the President's Council of Economic Advisers and is an accomplished guitarist with a fondness for folk songs. Her affair with Oberfest has lasted almost a year now and, despite his gifts, she's thinking seriously of giving him the broom. There's a young stud at her health club who's been sniffing around, and if anything comes of that, it's ta-ta, Mike.

They eat pizza, drink the wine, and then hop between

the sheets with little ceremony and less passion. Michael, who dotes on X-rated videocassettes, is inclined to be somewhat kinky. As Shirley tells her best friend: "He knows the words but he hasn't got the tune."

Afterward, Shirley plays the guitar for him naked. He likes that because as she strums, one large breast rests on the instrument and jiggles as chords are struck. Some of the happiest moments of his life have been spent watching that vibrating gland and listening to her sing "Old Folks at Home."

The mini-concert finished, Michael showers, dresses, and gives Shirley the tennis bracelet. Her eyes widen when she sees the diamonds, and she figures she'll stall the health-club stud a little longer.

Oberfest leaves, takes the elevator down, and exits into a gloomy night. He walks around to the parking lot of the apartment complex. He's reaching for his cigar case when a burly man steps out of the shadows and startles him.

"Hello, Arnold," says Major Leonid Y. Marchuk.

It is some time before Michael can respond. "What are you doing here?" he finally manages.

"Let us talk in your car," the Russian says, clamping a heavy hand on his arm. "It's the green Eldorado, is it not?"

Oberfest drops the cigar case, bends to pick it up. His eyeglass case slips from his breast pocket onto the tarmac, and he retrieves that. When they get to the Eldorado, he loses control of the car keys and they fall.

"Arnold, Arnold!" Marchuk says with his hearty laugh. "Calm, calm! It is not the end of the world."

He motions, and Michael gets into the car first, sliding over behind the wheel. Then the major climbs in awkwardly, carrying a bulky package. He slams the door.

"Nice troika," he says, stroking the leather upholstery. "I drive a Lincoln, but it's a company car."

The aide is getting his nerve back. "What are you doing here?" he repeats.

"Why, I've been transferred to our embassy in Washington," Marchuk says with great satisfaction. "Isn't that nice? Now you and I can see a lot more of each other."

"But how did you know I'd be *here?* In Foggy Bottom? In this parking lot?"

"Oh, Arnold," the KGB man says, laying a meaty hand on Michael's thigh, "I try to know everything about my boys. That Shirley Bowker—she looks like a very friendly lady. Long legs. Is she from California?"

"No."

"Well, I think she is an attractive woman, and I approve of your taste and envy your good fortune. But I didn't come to discuss your sweetheart; you and I have something more serious to talk about."

"She is not my sweetheart."

"If you say so. Arnold, this business of your President and the man who claims to be a faith healer is very worrisome to us. We admire Mr. President Hawkins and wish him well. We would not like to see anything endanger his administration and perhaps threaten his election to a second term."

"Because you think he's a patsy you can manipulate," Oberfest says boldly.

"Oh no," Marchuk says, sounding shocked. "But Hawkins is a reasonable man; we can do business with him. Your Vice President Trent, on the other hand, is a narrow-minded bigot with an almost pathological hatred of the Soviet Union. Wouldn't you agree?"

"Well . . ." Michael says, "he doesn't have much admiration for Communism, that's for sure."

"So you can understand why we wish to prevent Hawkins' downfall and the elevation of Trent to the White House."

"From your point of view, I suppose that makes sense."

"Not just from our point of view. Trent's hostility toward the Russian people represents a threat to world peace. I say these things to you because I know you are

an intelligent man and can appreciate the tragic consequences of your President's infatuation with this so-called
holy man."

Oberfest is silent.

"Now from what you have told me, Arnold, and from
what I read in your newspapers and see on your television,
I get the feeling that this is becoming a cause célèbre.
When you first told me about it, I thought it was just a . . .
a—what is the expression I want meaning a big stir about
very little?"

"A tempest in a teapot?"

"Yes, thank you, a tempest in a teapot. That is what
I thought it was at first. But now everyone is talking about
it. There have even been comments in the European press.
Now why do you suppose it is getting so much public notice?"

"I wouldn't know," Oberfest says.

The major booms a laugh and squeezes Michael's thigh
painfully. "Of course you do. Someone has launched a secret campaign to . . . to—now I need another expression.
It means to enlarge something very small to something
very large."

"Making a mountain out of a molehill?"

"Exactly! Someone is making a mountain out of a molehill. And we know who that someone is, don't we?"

Oberfest says nothing.

"I don't blame you, Arnold," Marchuk says, almost
tenderly. "As you told me, you do not make policy, you
just obey orders. I am in the same position. But surely,
after what I have just told you, it must be obvious to you
that your Vice President's ambitions represent a real
threat, not only to the future security of the Soviet Union
but to the future of the entire world."

"Now I think you're the one who's making a mountain
out of a molehill."

"I believe you are wrong. The people for whom I work

like to look ahead. We would not care to see Samuel Trent leading your great nation."

"It's a free country," Michael says, shrugging. "With free elections. There's not much you can do about it."

"Come now," the major says sharply, "you're talking like a child. Of course there is something we can do about it. Our first step is to eliminate or at least cripple the campaign to vilify Hawkins. His association with this Brother Kristos cannot be allowed to weaken his prestige to such an extent that he becomes a one-term president or, even worse, is forced to resign."

"And what do you propose to do?"

"Why, Arnold, I thought you would have guessed by now. You, my boy, are going to be the key player in our efforts to sabotage Trent's malicious campaign. You are going to help us make certain that your boss's ambitions are thwarted."

"Oh no," Oberfest says. "I couldn't do that. First of all, you overestimate my power. I'm just a hired hand. There is no way I can influence the Vice President."

"I think you are more than just a hired hand. You are Trent's personal aide. You know his plans, and how he intends to implement them. And we are not asking you to influence him. I think that would be impossible. But you are in a position to frustrate his plans. And those you cannot stop, you can tell us about in advance so we may find other means to checkmate him."

"No," Oberfest says, "I just can't do it."

"Your monthly reward would be increased, of course," Marchuk says.

"No," the aide repeats, "it's out of the question. I'd be endangering my career, my reputation—everything. I can't do it."

The KGB man sighs. "Well," he says, "I have tried to speak to you in a forthright and reasonable manner. But the carrot has not succeeded. Now I must apply the stick. Do you own a tape recorder and a VCR?"

"What?"

"Do you own machines that will play back audio- and videocassettes?"

"Sure. I've got a tape player right here under the dash. Why do you ask?"

The major thrusts his package onto Michael's lap. "When you get home tonight, unwrap that. I suggest you do it privately. I don't think you would care to have your wife—what is her name? Ruth?—I don't think you would care to have Ruth hear or see."

Oberfest hefts the package nervously. "What is it?"

"Four audiotapes of our conversations in that dreadful hotel room in New York. And two videotapes of you entering and leaving the hotel, and entering and leaving Room 612."

"Jesus Christ!" Oberfest cries.

"You may destroy the tapes if you wish," Marchuk goes on, talking rapidly, as if it's a set speech he has delivered many times before. "These are only copies. We are holding the originals, of course. And it would be our painful duty, if you persist in your refusal to cooperate, to deliver another set of these tapes to your Federal Bureau of Investigation. Naturally, I'd be out of the country before we did that. The only one who would suffer would be you. Do think it over carefully. Inside the package you will find a telephone number you can call to contact me. Merely say it's Arnold and hang up. I'll get back to you. I'll expect your call by midnight tomorrow. If not . . ."

The major pats Michael's shoulder and climbs out of the car. Before he closes the door, he leans back inside. "I like you, Arnold," he says, "I really do. So I hope you will act in a responsible manner. It would hurt me to lose you."

Then he slams the door and is gone. Michael sits there in the darkness, staring down at the package on his lap as if it were a time bomb.

Suddenly conspiracies aren't fun anymore.

=14=

Matilda Trent entertains Lenore Mattingly at lunch, and
finds her guest so stuffed with self-importance as to be
well-nigh unendurable. All because Brother Kristos re-
sides in *her* home, and *she* controls the guest list for the
prophet's weekly sermonettes.

"He is a great, great man," Lenore proclaims. "*So* talented. Literally a gift from God. He has cured my mi-
graines completely, and Emily no longer has her nervous
rash. I'm sure that if you're suffering, my dear, he could
do wonders for you."

"I am quite well, thank you," Matilda says stiffly. "But
I would like to meet the man and hear him preach."

"Oh my, that might be difficult," Lenore says. "He's
so busy, you know. I have a full house this week, but I
might be able to fit you in next Tuesday."

"Please do," the Vice President's wife says. "Does he
take up a collection?"

"Oh no," Mrs. Mattingly says, horrified. "But it is cus-
tomary to leave a donation under your plate. For his
church, you know. Of course, if you wish a private audience, you must make your own arrangements. I've introduced so many troubled women to him, and everyone has
been completely satisfied. The man is a wonder."

On the following Tuesday, the last day of April, Ma-
tilda joins a group of matrons in Brother Kristos' study.
Folding chairs have been brought in and arranged in rows.
There are more than twenty congregants, and Matilda rec-

ognizes most of them: government executives, senators' wives, a journalist, a museum curator, the black ambassadress from a tiny country in West Africa.

The ladies are served tea and slices of pound cake by two young women clad in white silk robes. Pearl Gibbs passes the paper plates of cake, and Agnes Brittlewaite pours strong tea into Styrofoam cups. Then the two acolytes take up positions on both sides of the closed bedroom door, standing with bowed heads and clasped hands.

Matilda expects a dramatic entrance, but Brother Kristos comes almost tentatively into the study from the bedroom. He pauses a long moment, head turning slowly as he surveys his audience. Except for black boots, he is clad entirely in white. The heavy gold cross hangs low on his chest, below his full beard.

He moves to the empty armchair at the head of the table, but he does not sit; he stands so all can see him, big hands gripping the chair back. Again his head turns as he stares at each guest. He holds them in expectant silence.

He is, Matilda decides, handsomer than she had previously thought. Not classically handsome, but with a strong appeal, his skin weathered and creased, lips full. She cannot deny his animal magnetism. He is so *sure*. And his eyes are as impressive as remembered from the White House prayer breakfast; that luminous stare penetrates and disturbs.

He begins speaking almost in a monotone, and later Matilda is to wonder again how such a flat voice can convey such fervor.

"Today," Brother Kristos says, "I shall preach to you of the millions who live in desperation. Not only the desolation of the hungry and the homeless, but the despair of people much like you who may reap the material blessings of wealth and yet find their lives hollow and without joy.

"When I entered this room a moment ago, I sensed the presence of one amongst you who suffers this misery in its most virulent form. And yet is so inured to her unhappiness that she can no longer conceive of a life of delight and everlasting hope. It is to that woman I speak, so she may know that she is not alone and her life is not lost."

He pauses then, and once again directs his ardent stare at each woman in turn. All feel themselves singled out, selected for Brother Kristos' special understanding and sympathy.

"You say to yourself," Kristos goes on, " 'Is this all there is?' For your days are so empty that you question the very purpose of your existence. Were you brought into this world merely to endure a lifetime of boredom, wearied by the smallness of all things?

"Where is the grand passion? Where is the great love? Your waking hours are spent on meaningless tasks. Your sleep is fretful and your dreams blank. All you know is a vague longing, unable to believe that you were born merely to shuffle to the grave never having felt passion, never having known a love so great that it conquers you, and by so doing, allows you to triumph.

"I say to you that passion and love await you. I speak of the glory of unquestioning faith, the bliss that you will know through total obedience to God's commands."

Listening closely to this intense man, Matilda feels he is speaking to her alone; he knows her secret, understands her anomie, and offers salvation. As he continues, she recognizes the magnitude of what he is asking and, as if reading her mind, he says:

"It is no small thing I ask. The risk is enormous, for God demands that you remake your life. When you have yielded to God's will, new duties will devolve upon you. But in return, you will be granted a happiness that will lift up your soul and bring you singing into a new world."

Kristos' voice holds such power, with its promise of a rebirth, that her reserve melts, and she begins to believe that she might shed her stultifying existence and, like a butterfly from a cocoon, emerge young and brilliant, borne on the wind.

Brother Kristos continues speaking for another ten minutes, his audience enthralled. He concludes abruptly, and before the guests can come clustering about, some bearing fancily wrapped gifts, he retires to the bedroom and closes the door.

Matilda remains seated in the uncomfortable chair as the others drift away. She keeps her head lowered, staring down at her hands, turning her wedding ring around and around. She wonders if she dares, fears if she does, fears even more a lifetime of regret if she does not.

Finally she rises and approaches one of the young women in a white robe.

"May I see Brother Kristos?" she says. "Privately."

Agnes Brittlewaite stares at her a moment. "I'll ask," she says, moves to the bedroom door, knocks once and enters.

"A woman wants to see you," she reports. "Fifty-five to sixty. Lots of diamonds. The real stuff."

"Mink stole?" Brother Kristos asks. "Gray hair cut short? Black suit?"

"That's the one."

"The Vice President's wife. Lenore mentioned that she'd be here today. Bring her in. Make sure everyone is gone, then you and Pearl take off."

Matilda comes hesitatingly into the bedroom. Kristos is standing at the dresser, slowly combing fingers through his beard.

"Thank you for seeing me," she says in a voice so faint she hardly recognizes it as her own. "I wanted to tell you how greatly I was affected by your sermon."

He inclines his head gravely.

"I am the woman you were talking to," she says earnestly. "Am I not?"

"Yes," he says. "You are the one."

"I knew it!" she cries. "When you spoke of a drab life and empty days, you were describing my existence exactly."

He gestures toward the only chair, a plain wooden ladder-back. Matilda sits down, letting her stole slip to the floor. She looks about the sparsely furnished room curiously. On the dresser top is a crystal decanter filled with a colorless liquid. Alongside are two glasses.

"Is that something to drink?" she asks with a nervous laugh.

"Vodka."

"Would you think me bold if I asked for a little? Your sermon left me shaken. I need something for my nerves."

He pours the two glasses full and hands her one.

"Too much," she protests. "I can never drink all that."

"Have as much as you like," he says, shrugging.

He sits on the bed facing her. Their knees are almost touching. He waits until she sips, then he gulps from his glass.

Matilda takes a deep breath. "That's better," she says. "I really felt wrung-out." She pauses a moment; then: "May I ask you something?"

He nods. "Whatever you wish."

"When you spoke of making a new life, you never said how it is to be done. Gradually? By reading and learning? Or by a sudden conversion?"

He raises his eyes to her, and she cannot look away. She imagines she sees flame in his eyes, something hot and flickering.

"In your life," he tells her, "you have always admired those able to create. Painters, sculptors, composers, poets. You have envied their magic because you feel yourself bursting with creative energy but unable to channel it into works of art."

"Yes, yes," she says eagerly, "that is so. How did you know?"

"Your life, too, can become a work of art," he continues. "A masterpiece that no one can create but you. If you are sincere in loving God and being loved in return, you will look upon your life as a unique achievement, as glorious as any painting, symphony, or poem. But only through total belief may that splendor be found. And your faith will be tested. Many times."

She finally looks away and takes another swallow of vodka. "I don't know if I have the courage," she confesses.

"Let me lead you. Do you believe what I said to you today?"

"Yes. Oh yes!"

"Then you have faith in me?"

"Yes, I have faith in you, Brother Kristos. I never thought I'd be saying those words, but it is the truth."

"I am the brother of Christ and God's apostle on earth. I am less than He, but to believe in me is to believe in Him, to follow me is to follow Him. Let me bring you to a new life."

He rises, moves behind her chair. He puts his strong hands on her neck, massages her shoulders.

"A new life," he repeats. "A bright, sinless world of faith and love. Give yourself to the Lord. With your devotion you will create meaning and purpose, and find joy in your duties."

His litany continues, but all she knows is the pressure of his hands, the scent of his beard as he leans to kiss her neck.

"Surrender yourself," he intones. "For only by yielding completely can you know the bliss that faith brings to the children of God."

She undresses with fumbling fingers, and when she is naked, he urges her to unbutton his shirt, open his trousers, remove his boots, socks, underpants. He leads her by the hand into the bathroom. He makes her wash his private parts and his feet with a wet cloth, telling her it is a test, that she is entering a world without sin, and by washing him she proves the strength of her faith.

He leads her back to the bed, murmuring continually of duty, sacrifice, obedience, and total submission to God's will.

His hard body lies atop her, his powerful hands grip her, his rough skin abrades her. She gives herself to his commands and, through him, to God's, thinking thereby to gain the shining kingdom. Faith turns to frenzy, and she matches his passion with hers, both lost in a paroxysm of ecstasy.

And later, when they are slack and depleted, drinking more vodka, she rolls onto her side and tugs gently at his beard.

"Let me give you a gift, Brother Kristos," she whispers. "To thank you."

"All right."

"What would you like?"

"A car," he says. "For my church."

=15=

Tollinger:

Re: Brother Kristos

Sorry I haven't written sooner, but I've been laid up awhile with the flu. Can you imagine catching a bad cold in sunny Florida? Well, I did, and it knocked me for a loop. But I'm okay now and on the road again.

I went down to Fort Myers to interview Lorna Burgoos, formerly known as Madame Olga. She's an old woman now—but she's spryer than I am, and she's got all her marbles. I found her in her garden setting out a flat of ruby bromeliads. I told her I'd like to talk about Jacob Christiansen, and she took me into her home. I guess Madame

Olga saved the bucks from the days when she was telling fortunes on the carnival circuit.

She uncorked a bottle of dark rum that poured like molasses. I declined, and she brought herself a waterglassful—and I mean full! That old lady could really put away the sauce, but as far as I could see, it didn't have the slightest effect on her.

Anyway, she asked why I wanted to know about Jacob, and I gave her that scam about him applying for a job with the FBI and me checking him out. She laughed so hard she almost lost her upper plate.

"Bullshit!" she said. "Jake would never apply to the FBI in a million years. What's the real story?"

So I winged it. I told her Jake wanted to marry my daughter, and I was trying to get some background on the guy.

"That's a lie too," she said. "Jake's never been married and never wants to be. Why buy a cow when milk's so cheap? He's not in any trouble, is he?"

I told her that as far as I knew, he wasn't in trouble with the law or anyone else. But he was getting buddy-buddy with the President, and Hawkins' political opponents wanted to dig up the skinny on him—good, bad, or indifferent. That's pretty close to the truth.

"Yeah," she said, "I read that in the paper. Jacob calls himself Brother Kristos now, and he's got a beard, but I recognized him right away. I guess he's doing all right. I always knew he would; that man's got the luck of the devil."

I asked her a lot of questions, and she answered readily enough. I think she was telling me the truth—or at least the truth as she remembered it.

She said she and Jake got to be good friends during their travels. "He never had any other close friends. Just women." Jake would set up her booth on the midway, and when the show closed for the night, he'd usually come around and they'd drink and talk for a few hours.

"And if you're wondering if he fucked me," Madame

Olga said, "he did—many, many times, God bless him. And I'm here to tell you that he is the world's greatest lover, bar none."

Over a period of years, she taught Jake all the tricks of fortune-telling—at his insistence. The first thing she taught him was how to make educated guesses about customers from their appearance and way of speaking.

"For instance," Lorna Burgoos said to me, "I make you as an alkie who's off the booze right now. I figure you're a widower or divorced man, and you used to be some kind of a cop. And you were born in New England, probably Maine."

Bingo! I told her she was right on every detail and asked her how she knew. But she just smiled, drank her rum, and said, "Tricks of the trade."

After Jake learned how to analyze customers, she taught him the "fortunes" he could predict—mostly what people wanted to hear. Men would get a better job or raise. Women would find a new love. Sick people would get well. Pregnant women would have a boy. Young girls would get married within a year. And everyone would come into an unexpected inheritance. After a while, she said, Jake had the patter down perfectly and would fill in for her at the fortune-telling booth when she wanted some time off.

"He had the gift of gab," she marveled. "We charged fifty cents for five minutes, a dollar for ten. But Jake got tips! Can you imagine that? I never got a tip in my life, but he'd usually get an extra two bits. He was good. Always turned the tips over to me, of course; I'll say that for him."

Then, Madame Olga told me, something strange began happening: Jake started telling customers things about their past that he couldn't have guessed from their appearance. He'd tell them secrets they swore no one else knew. And sometimes he'd predict things in their future that scared them. But when the tips dried up, he stopped.

I asked Lorna how he did it, but she just shook her head.

"Wouldn't tell me," she said. *"I kept after him about it, but all he'd do was laugh and say, 'Tricks of the trade.'"*

I asked if she thought it was possible Jake had supernatural powers. But she just grinned and wouldn't answer.

She said that during the winter before Jake left the carnival, he told her he was going to tour the Bible Belt with his own religious tent show. She always knew he had the hots for the Bible—*"I swear he had it by heart"*—but she couldn't see how he could do the revival bit by himself and make any bucks. But she wished him well.

I asked if she ever heard from him after that, and she said yes, for two or three years he had sent her postcards from little towns throughout the Deep South, Texas, Oklahoma, Arkansas—towns she had never heard of before.

"He didn't say much on the postcards," she told me. *"Just that he was doing okay and hoped I was too. Once he wrote that when the carnival played Bear Junction, South Dakota, I shouldn't open my booth. I thought he was kidding and opened as usual. The last night we were there, some crumb waltzed into my tent waving a shooter and picked me clean—the bastard!"*

I asked her how Jake knew something bad would happen to her in Bear Junction. She shrugged and said, *"Just a guess. But I should have believed him."*

Then I asked if she still had the postcards Brother Kristos sent her, and she said sure, she never threw anything away—including liquor-store receipts from fifty years ago!

She wouldn't give me the postcards, but she let me make a list of the postmarks. So I rented a car, and now I'm on the road tracing Jake's wanderings through the Bible Belt—which accounts for this letter being mailed from Boaz, Alabama.

I left Madame Olga dreaming of the world's greatest lover, bar none.

As for me, I'm now convinced that Kristos is a fake, a fraud, and a con man.

—Lindberg

=16=

After the shattering meeting with Marchuk and after reviewing the tapes the major dumped in his lap, Michael Oberfest expects to spend at least one sleepless night pondering his predicament.

But in less than an hour he decides he has no real options. If he sabotages Trent's campaign, Oberfest risks the loss of his job and all those delightful perks concomitant with being personal aide to the Vice President.

But if he goes public with the Veep's secret conspiracy, the man will be irretrievably hurt, ambitions doused, career down the drain. So, in effect, Trent and Oberfest have each other by the short hair. If the VP threatens retribution because he learns that Michael has switched sides, Oberfest has enough ammunition to blow Samuel Landon Trent out of the water.

Marchuk, on the other hand, represents a much more dangerous problem. Michael has no doubts whatsoever that the Russian is capable of doing exactly what he threatens: informing the FBI of Oberfest's relationship with a foreign government.

If that becomes a matter of public record, the aide will not only lose his job, but his reputation will be ruined and future employment doubtful. And if the FBI wants to press the case, criminal prosecution and a jail term are not unlikely.

So, within an hour, Michael Oberfest realizes his only

choice is to cooperate with the KGB. He salves his conscience by reflecting that his working for the Soviet Union
will have no effect on national security. He is not selling
military secrets or anything like that. And it is quite possible that by aiding the Russians he will end up on the side
of the angels.

He contacts Marchuk, and a meeting is arranged at a
crowded shopping mall near Bowie, Maryland. Oberfest
is given his orders:

He is to cease immediately all his personal efforts to
publicize the association of President Hawkins and
Brother Kristos.

He is to thwart all surreptitious initiatives by Trent to
ballyhoo the influence of the so-called faith healer on the
President and First Lady.

He is to report weekly—more frequently, if necessary—
on any new plots by the Vice President to damage Hawkins' credibility and prestige.

He is to assist any individuals or agencies in the administration that are seeking to protect Hawkins' reputation
by minimizing the role Brother Kristos is playing in the
formation of White House policies.

"There!" Major Marchuk says with a kindly smile.
"Now that's not so bad, is it, Arnold?"

Michael Oberfest has to admit it isn't. And besides, the
pay is good.

He calls Tollinger the next day, intending to invite the
Chief of Staff's executive assistant to lunch. It is not a
meeting he anticipates with pleasure. He has heard that
Tollinger once referred to him as "a lightweight." And
on his part, he considers John a cold fish.

"Sorry," Tollinger says shortly, "can't make it today.
Up to my eyeballs in bumf."

"Listen," Michael says, "this is important. I think we
better get together as soon as possible."

"Oh? What's it about?"

"I'd rather not spell it out on the phone, but it concerns the preacher."

Silence from Tollinger.

"Look," Oberfest goes on, "if you can't get out, how about coming over here? I can call down for a pizza."

"You come over here," Tollinger says, "and I'll call down for a pizza. One o'clock."

"Suits me," Michael says.

Tollinger hangs up, wondering what the little nerd has on his mind—if anything. He and Folsom have their suspicions on the role the Vice President is playing in spreading rumors. Now Trent's personal aide wants to share a pizza. Tollinger decides to play it very, very cool.

He calls Domino's and orders a large Extravaganza, a pie with everything on it. He's unwilling to ask his secretary to perform the chore, so at 12:45 he makes the long walk from the West Wing to the guardhouse on Pennsylvania Avenue to pick up the pizza in its bright red insulated case.

"Smells good," the guard says.

"And it's all no-cal," Tollinger tells him.

"Oh sure," the guard says. "Just like spaghetti and meatballs."

Oberfest arrives on time, bringing a cold six-pack of Diet Coke. They start on the pizza, spreading paper napkins on Tollinger's desk to catch the drippings.

"I haven't got much time, Mike," Tollinger says. "You better get on with it—whatever it is."

"Your office wouldn't be miked, would it?" Oberfest says, laughing nervously. "This is sensitive stuff."

John looks at him. "Don't be an idiot. Of course it isn't bugged. Want to search?"

"No, no! I'll take your word for it. Well, listen, I know how concerned you people must be about Brother Kristos."

"Concerned? Why should we be concerned? The President is entitled to seek religious guidance from whomever he chooses."

"Yeah, I know. But all this publicity can't be helping. The rumors going around . . ."

Tollinger shrugs. "There will always be rumors—you know that. Nothing you can do but ignore them. Denials make them seem important—which they're not."

"What about the columnists?" Oberfest argues. "They're hinting that this two-bit preacher is becoming the power behind the throne."

"Garbage," Tollinger says, popping a can of cola. "Believe me, the Boss is still running the show. He's never been more on top of things."

"So you say. But the talk around town is that he's taking political advice from Kristos. A lot of people don't like it."

"Screw 'em," the EA says calmly. "They don't know what they're talking about. Is that why you came over—to warn me that people are gossiping?"

"Not exactly," Oberfest says, realizing he's getting nowhere. "I just wanted to let you know that if there's anything I can do to help you keep a lid on this situation, I'll be happy to do it."

Tollinger stares at him. "What situation?" he asks.

The man's equanimity infuriates Michael. "Listen," he sputters, "you think I don't know what's going on? This business of giving away all the surplus food—it's causing a holy ruckus up on the Hill. The political fallout could be disastrous."

"And that's why you're volunteering your help. You're worried about the midterm elections?"

"Well, sure. I don't want to see the party take a fall just because of this faith healer—or whatever the hell he claims to be."

Tollinger starts on another slice of pizza. "You're full

of shit," he says equably. "Your boss would probably be delighted to see the party lose the midterms. That would give him a leg up if he decides to go for the Oval Office. Did he tell you to call me for lunch?"

"No, he knows nothing about it."

"If you're telling the truth, it means you're volunteering on your own. That makes me wonder what your motive could possibly be."

"I told you: I don't want to see the party—"

"Oh, cut the crap!" Tollinger says, finally getting angry. "You're insulting my intelligence. Either tell me what the hell you're doing here or get out. I don't have time for penny-ante mysteries."

"All right," Oberfest says hastily, "I'll tell you the truth. I'm here because I don't like what Trent's been doing. It sickens me so much I've decided to risk my job by offering to help you any way I can."

Then he recounts details of the Vice President's plot to discredit Hawkins.

Tollinger listens intently, sitting silently a moment after Oberfest finishes. Finally . . .

"And you're telling me all this, Mike, because suddenly you've become a man of high moral rectitude—right? You just can't stand to see someone as good and decent as Abner Hawkins get the shaft. Correct?"

"That's it," Oberfest says happily. "That's why I'm here."

"You'll have to do better than that," Tollinger says. "Like proving your conversion by admitting your part in Trent's nasty little scheme."

"I was just following orders," the aide says in a low voice.

"Now where have I heard that before? You leaked to the press?"

"Some."

"You spread vicious rumors?"

"Maybe a few."

"In fact, you did everything you could to aid and abet Trent's rotten campaign until you suddenly saw the light. Is that how it was?"

"Don't you think I'm sincere?" Michael cries.

"Oh sure, you're sincere. Unless Trent sent you over to play the spy and find out what's going on."

"I swear that's not true! I told you, he doesn't even know I'm talking to you."

Tollinger stares at him somberly. "I don't know why, but now I think you're telling the truth. Not *all* the truth; you just don't make it as a reformed sinner. I believe you when you say Trent didn't send you, but I don't believe that you're doing it because you've suddenly decided to become a Boy Scout. You've got some other reason. But that's neither here nor there."

"Then you'll let me help you?" Oberfest says eagerly. "I can tell you everything Trent is up to."

"I'll think about it," Tollinger says. "Now take off and let me get back to my paperwork. I've had enough melodrama for one day."

But after Oberfest leaves (taking the remaining cans of his Diet Coke with him), Tollinger doesn't touch his In basket. He leaves his office and seeks out the Chief of Staff to report on his bizarre lunch meeting.

=17=

George Hawkins has been allowed to stay up late to play with Brother Kristos. Kristos is down on his hands and knees, and George is astride his back, digging his heels into the preacher's ribs. The President and his wife look on benignly.

"Giddyap, horsey!" the lad shouts gleefully, and away they go with the horse swaying and bucking as the rider hangs on to his collar and screams with joy.

Then the two collapse onto the rug, hugging each other and laughing.

"I hope he wasn't too heavy for you," Helen Hawkins says.

"George heavy?" Brother Kristos says, climbing to his feet. "Why, George is a bag of feathers." He reaches down, lifts the boy high in the air and swings him back and forth. "You're a bag of feathers, that's what you are!" Then he deposits the lad gently on the couch between his parents.

"To tell you the truth," the preacher says, smiling, "our hero *is* putting on weight. We won't be able to play horsey much longer. Come on, brother, show me your muscle."

Obediently George bends his thin little arm, and Kristos feels the bicep.

"Wow!" he says. "That's getting big. I don't want to wrestle with you anymore."

"I bet I could make you say 'Uncle,' " the boy boasts.

"I bet you could," Brother Kristos says, stroking the lad's cheek. "You're getting too strong for me."

President Hawkins glances at the ormolu clock on the mantel. "Long past your bedtime, young fellow," he says to his son. "Helen, will you ring for McShane?"

The sergeant, waiting outside in the hallway, comes in smiling. He's wearing his dress blues, and George never tires of hearing the name of each of the Marine's ribbons and how it was earned.

The boy kisses his mother and father, then solemnly offers his hand to Kristos, who shakes it just as gravely.

"Don't forget your prayers, brother," he says, "and sleep well."

Dennis McShane leads the lad out of the room and closes the door softly.

"He's putting on a little weight," the President agrees, "but I wish it was more. I'm afraid he's not going to be a big man."

"Perhaps not in physical size," the preacher says, "but I promise you his spirit will be powerful. You will be proud of him. Do you wish him to follow you into public service?"

"It's a rocky road," Hawkins says doubtfully. "How do you feel about it, mommy?"

"Oh, it's much too early to decide," Helen says. "Sometimes he wants to be a fireman, or a pilot, or a policeman. Today he told me he's going to be a Marine just like Dennis McShane."

"He could do a lot worse," her husband says. "At least he's thinking about his future."

"And we have Brother Kristos to thank," the First Lady says. "That George will *have* a future. We can never repay you for the help you gave us at Camp David."

The preacher shakes his head. "It was God's help," he says, "not mine."

"Amen," the President says. "But now I need your advice on a more temporal matter. Brother Kristos, one of the reasons I asked you over tonight was to report on our surplus food plan. The people at Agriculture are devising a distribution program involving personnel from churches, organized charities, and poverty groups. How do you feel about that?"

"I think it is wise."

"I've also asked the Office of the General Counsel to provide a legal opinion on whether I can give away the food by presidential decree or if I'll need legislation."

"I am happy to hear the project is going forward."

"But so slowly!" Hawkins complains. "You know, it's easy for a President to issue an order, but I've learned that I must follow it up continually until it's actually carried out. I was hoping you might be able to suggest some way we can give the program the importance it deserves."

Brother Kristos reflects a moment. "As I have told you, father, I know little of politics. But it seems to me you would do well to forget about convincing government officials and take your plan directly to the people. I am certain your children will approve. Perhaps you could appear on television and explain it in your own words. Show breadlines and soup kitchens, with lines of good people waiting for a handout from strangers, their pride conquered by their hunger."

The President turns to his wife. "What do you think, mommy?"

"Oh yes," she says. "You look so handsome on television."

"But not in the flesh?" he teases. "Well, it's a viable option, Brother Kristos, but I'll have to think about it."

"By going directly to the public," Kristos says, "and getting their approval and support, you bring pressure to bear on the bureaucrats who are dragging their feet in obeying your orders."

Hawkins smiles. "I think you know more about politics than you admit."

"Not politics, but I know people and how difficult it is

to prod them to action, especially when that action involves change. That is why I suggest marshaling the moral force of your people with a television address."

"I might be able to bring it off," Hawkins says thoughtfully. "I think we could get, say, a half-hour of prime time on the networks if I tell them it will concern a news announcement of national importance. I'll have to talk to my media people about that. Would you be willing to appear on the program, Brother Kristos? I'm sure your words would have a very special appeal."

"Oh no, father, I could not do that. First of all, I have no desire for publicity. The food giveaway must be presented as your idea. And I would not care to give your enemies ammunition by sharing your TV presentation. They would then claim I have influenced you."

Abner Hawkins looks at him keenly. "There is not much that escapes you, is there? I understand there has already been talk along those lines. All right, if you won't appear on the show, will you at least be willing to work with my speech writers to give the script a religious eloquence? I want to emphasize that what I am proposing is morally right."

"Of course. I will be happy to help any way I can."

The President considers a moment. "I think," he says finally, "that before I request TV time I will have a confidential poll taken. Let's find out exactly what percentage of the public would be in favor of the giveaway. After all, that surplus food actually belongs to the American people."

Brother Kristos stares directly at Abner Hawkins, his eyes blazing with fervor. "I tell you now," he says in his flat voice, "that more than two-thirds of your children will endorse the plan."

"Two-thirds?" the First Lady says. "Isn't that wonderful!"

"First let's see how accurate Brother Kristos is. The poll shouldn't take more than a day or two. And if the results are as favorable as we hope, we'll go along with the television program."

They spend almost two hours discussing the proposed TV presentation: what film clips should be included; which theatrical star might narrate; and whether or not scenes of expensive banquets and elegant restaurants should be used for contrast—or would that be overkill?

Finally, after midnight, Hawkins says, "I think we better bring this to a close. I have a heavy schedule tomorrow, and I also want to get that opinion poll organized. Brother Kristos, once again I thank you for your assistance. As usual, everything you advise makes good sense and yet is still an expression of God's will."

"I don't like the idea of Brother Kristos driving home alone at this hour," Helen says.

The President turns smiling to the preacher. "How would you like to sleep in the Lincoln Bedroom?" he asks.

=18=

Henry Folsom looks up in wonderment. "He called it right on the button," he says. "Brother Kristos said two-thirds of the public would approve, and the poll shows 65.4, with three points either way. Now how in hell did he do that?"

"I don't know," Tollinger says.

"I tell you, John, in spite of what Lindberg wrote in his last letter, I'm beginning to think the guy is more than just a trickster. Do you think he's got some kind of weird power?"

"I've stopped trying to figure it out."

"No, you haven't," the Chief says. "This is just the kind of intellectual riddle you love. Anyway, after that poll came in, the Boss decided to go full speed ahead with the television show."

"Was that his idea or Brother Kristos'?"

"Who knows? These days it's hard to tell where Hawkins leaves off and Kristos begins. The flak is so thick you could walk on it. I had a long confab with the party power brokers last night. Heggerman flew in from Minneapolis, Olson from Kansas City, Planey from Denver, and Leibowitz from L.A. We had a six-hour session in a Baltimore motel."

"And?"

"And that's where you come in."

"Oh-oh."

"Yeah. The consensus was this: Hawkins might get the approval of all the bleeding-hearts for his giveaway, but the food producers are going to kill him. And that includes the farmers, processors, distributors, commodity traders, and all the supermarkets and grocery stores in the country. If this goes through, we can kiss the Midwest good-bye in the fall elections."

"You said this is where I come in."

"Well, everyone agreed the key to the problem was Brother Kristos. If we could get rid of that psalm-singing bastard there wouldn't *be* a problem. So I was authorized to ask if you'd take on a job for us. We want to offer Brother Kristos a nice hunk of cash, all in small unmarked bills, if he'll just fade away. We'd like him to get out of the country—go toast his priestly ass on the French Riviera, for God's sake!—but if he won't do that, at least get out of Washington and promise not to contact the President again."

"How much are you going to offer him?"

"We decided a million is the absolute top, but naturally we hope he'll take a lot less. Look, the guy is still scrounging for nickels and dimes in that church of his. We're offering him more money than he's ever seen before in his life. He'd be a dummy if he didn't jump at it, and I don't think he's a dummy."

"Neither do I," Tollinger says slowly, "but I'm not sure he'll jump."

"But you'll give it a try? If anyone can swing it, you can."

"All right. I'll do what I can."

"Thank you, John. I knew I could depend on you. Make it as soon as possible—okay?"

"Sure. Maybe I'll invite him out to my place; that's private enough."

"Good idea. Listen, have you heard anything more from Mike Oberfest?"

"Yes, he keeps feeding me tidbits, but not much we don't already know. Trent is still calling his party contacts all over the country and telling them Hawkins has become a zombie."

"Oh, that slimy son of a bitch! Well, if we can bribe Brother Kristos to disappear, it'll cut Trent off at the knees. He'll be lucky to be nominated for dogcatcher of Skunk Hollow. Good luck, John. And try to keep it under a million if you can."

The executive assistant goes back to his office, not as optimistic as Folsom about the bribe attempt, but determined to give it his best shot. He gets Brother Kristos' phone number from Audrey Robertson.

"Why do you want his number, darl?" the First Lady's Social Secretary asks. "Feel the need to confess your sins?"

"What sins?" John says. "I'm clean as a whistle. You know what that means, don't you?"

"Sure, darl," she says. "Shrill and full of spit."

But he gets no answer to his repeated phone calls until almost four o'clock that afternoon. Then, finally, Brother Kristos picks up, and Tollinger identifies himself.

"Yes, I remember you," the preacher says. "The cynic."

"Not exactly. More skeptical than cynical. Anyway, when you were here at the White House for that prayer breakfast, you said that you and I might have a talk one day."

"I recall."

"I was hoping we could make it tonight. Could you come to my home in Spring Valley? We'll have a few drinks and maybe get to know each other better."

"Maybe," Kristos says. "What time?"

"Around nine." Then Tollinger gives the preacher his address and directions how to get there. "Unless you need transportation," he adds. "I'll be happy to pick you up."

"That won't be necessary," Brother Kristos says. "I have a car. A new car."

"Oh? What did you buy?"

"A Scorpio. A silver four-door."

On the way home that night, Tollinger stops to buy a bottle of Glenfiddich for himself and a liter of Absolut vodka for Kristos. Then, amused, he also buys a bottle of pepper-flavored vodka. He's determined to test those rumors about the faith healer being a drunk. And even if they're not true, the booze might help convince Brother Kristos to accept a fat bundle of lucre to get lost.

The preacher arrives promptly at nine P.M. He's wearing a belted tunic of black silk over wide-legged silk slacks, the cuffs flapping outside his boots. The costume looks like lounging pajamas to Tollinger, but he makes no comment. He gets his guest settled into an armchair in the den.

"Thank you for coming on such short notice," he says. "I've been wanting to have a talk with you."

Brother Kristos smiles but doesn't reply.

"I have beer, wine, Scotch, vodka, gin, and I can mix a martini if you like. What's your preference?"

"Vodka, please."

"With ice? Water?"

"Just plain."

"I came across something unusual," Tollinger says. He hands Kristos the bottle of pepper vodka. "I took a sip. Very spicy. Would you like to try it?"

The preacher inspects the bottle. He uncaps it, raises it to his lips, takes a swallow. "Very nice," he says.

Tollinger gives him a six-ounce glass, and Kristos fills it while John pours himself a shot of single malt Scotch.

"Your health," he says, raising his drink. He takes a small sip. When he looks up, he sees the preacher is holding an empty glass.

"Where did that go?" Tollinger says, astonished. "Well, help yourself; the night is young."

"Why did you ask me to come here tonight?" Brother Kristos says, filling his glass again.

"Just to get better acquainted. I really didn't think you'd accept. I know how busy you must be with your— what are they called? Sermonettes?"

"Other people call them that, but I do not. A sermon is a sermon. Some of the best are very short. The most powerful sermon in the Scriptures consists of two words: 'Jesus wept.' "

"From the Gospel According to John," Tollinger says.

"You know the Bible?"

"Only John," Tollinger says, laughing. "Because it's my name. Yours is Jacob, isn't it?"

"Yes."

"Well, that's a good biblical name."

"And that's why you invited me here tonight?" Brother Kristos says. "To talk about names?"

"Not really. I wanted to get your ideas on the relationship between government and religion."

"It's in the Pledge of Allegiance: 'One nation under God.' "

"I know that," Tollinger says, "and I suppose only atheists would object to official recognition of a Supreme Being. But what influence do you feel religion should have on the day-to-day operations of the government?"

"I believe obedience to God's commands should be the lodestar of all government activities."

"Ah, but that's where you run into trouble. There are dozens of religions and hundreds of sects in this country. Their translations of God's commands are sometimes contradictory. How is a president to know the correct interpretation of divine will? It would be easy if we had one national religion, but the wise men who wrote our constitution saw the danger of that and prohibited it."

"Faith cannot be prohibited, and you are seeing problems where none exist. Belief in a beneficent Creator is universal. The contradictions in the doctrines of different religions are mostly minor matters of ritual and ceremonies of worship."

"Those so-called 'minor matters' have been the cause of an awful lot of religious wars."

Brother Kristos stares at Tollinger a moment, then takes a gulp of vodka, drinking directly from the bottle. "There are many false prophets. Killing is not one of God's commands."

"Then if our legislators truly believe in the Almighty's message of peace on earth, they should adopt unilateral disarmament. Is that what you are saying?"

"No, that is not what I am saying. In a perfect world, disarmament is sensible. But in an imperfect and dangerous world, it is only prudent to prepare a defense."

Tollinger pours himself another tot of Glenfiddich. "I was hoping you'd say that. In an imperfect world, weapons of war are necessary even if they contravene the Lord's will. Faith in God cannot be the sole guide for politicians or statesmen. The world is too complex. There is no one solution. Instead, there is pulling and shoving, debates and shouting. Compromise is the only way to get anything done."

"You speak from the head," the preacher says, "and I speak from the heart. Compromise may be justified in temporal matters, but not in matters of faith, for that is a rock that cannot be split."

John is amazed to see that the bottle of pepper vodka is empty. Yet Brother Kristos still sits erect in the armchair and speaks fluently and eloquently. Tollinger brings him the liter of Absolut, reflecting that if he himself had consumed that much eighty-proof, the paramedics would be carting him off to intensive care.

"Brother Kristos," he says casually, "let me give you a specific example of a proposed policy that would undoubtedly meet your high standard of godliness but would be politically inexpedient. I'm sure you've heard talk of the President's plan to give surplus food to the needy."

Kristos smiles, uncaps the bottle of Absolut, takes a deep swallow. "Ah," he says, "now I know why you invited me here tonight."

Tollinger ignores that. "While the *aim* of the program is certainly responsive to God's commands, the *result* may well be horrendous. I'm talking about enormous damage to the income of farmers and everyone else engaged in the production and sale of food. Do you really believe they will endure their personal loss without objection simply because it's the Christian thing to do?"

"If they have faith," Kristos says, "they will endure gladly, knowing their individual sacrifices will benefit many."

John Tollinger sighs. "Was the food giveaway the President's idea," he asks suddenly, "or yours?"

"It arose during a discussion we had on how the government might become more obedient to God's wishes."

"Uh-huh. But do you agree it might have the harmful results I just mentioned?"

Brother Kristos smiles. "And harmful also to the President's political party?"

"Of course," Tollinger says. "That goes without saying. It happens to be, in my opinion, a political party that has greatly benefited the country and will accomplish even more if allowed to keep control of the White House. But now that control is threatened by the intrusion of religion into what should be a purely secular administration. Do you realize what you have done?"

"Tell me—what have I done?"

"You've aroused anger and divisiveness on the eve of the midterm elections. If you continue on your present course, the party leaders see nothing ahead but defeat."

"So?"

"So they want you out. They want you to leave Washington and end your association with the First Family."

Brother Kristos looks at him with the sly shrewdness of a horse trader. "Do you also want this?"

"Yes," Tollinger says definitely, "I do. My objections are more philosophical than political. I think your close association with the President represents a dangerous intrusion of religion in the business of government. That is Caesar's world—and rightly so."

The prophet is silent for several moments, looking at Tollinger with broody eyes. As he ruminates, he drinks steadily.

"How much?" he says finally.

"A lot of money," John says. "A quarter of a million. Cash. Small bills."

Kristos gives him a mocking grin.

"They may be persuaded to go higher," Tollinger admits.

"How much higher?"

"Half a million."

The preacher shakes his head.

Ashamed of this vulgar haggling, Tollinger says rapidly, "I am authorized to offer a million. No more. That's it."

"No," Brother Kristos says, and now his eyes are almost shut. "Not a million, not five, not ten, not any amount."

John finishes his drink, pours another, bolts that, and leaves his glass empty.

"Not any amount?" he repeats. "Then what *do* you want?"

The other man doesn't answer.

Tollinger leans forward. "I know what it is," he says in a voice tight with anger. "You want power."

Brother Kristos lurches to his feet, brandishes the vodka bottle high over his head.

"God's power!" he roars. *"God's power!"*

THREE

=1=

"And now . . . the President of the United States."

The Presidential Seal fades from the screen. Abner Hawkins comes on, seated behind his desk in the Oval Office, flanked by flags. He is dressed soberly in a dark suit. His hands are clasped on the desktop, and he speaks firmly in his midwestern twang.

"My fellow Americans," he begins, "thank you for inviting me into your home. Tonight I want to discuss with you a problem that affects everyone in our national family. I speak to you of hunger in America."

The President then states the estimated numbers of children, women, and men being fed in soup kitchens operated by religious organizations, poverty groups, and private charities.

"They do their best, but their funds are limited, and the ranks of the hungry grow daily. Those they feed are good people—your brothers and sisters, mothers and fathers, your children and grandparents—but through misfortune they are forced to surrender their dignity and self-respect and accept handouts to keep body and soul together.

"Let me show you some of the soup kitchens that are doing their best, however modest, to provide meals for the poor and needy. I warn you, these are sorrowful and harrowing scenes, but please do not turn away or switch off your television set. You owe it to yourself and to your country to see how some members of our nation are forced to exist."

The screen then shows a long line of people in New York City, shuffling forward so each may receive a thin sandwich and an apple; a church basement in Los Angeles where the needy are given unsalable food donated by supermarkets and restaurants; a garage in Chicago where damaged cans and rotting produce are distributed twice a week.

"And now," Hawkins continues, "I'd like you to meet some of your fellow Americans to whom starvation is a very real threat."

The screen then shows brief taped interviews with an unemployed Pittsburgh steel worker; a carpenter in Ohio who can no longer work because of arthritis; a young Florida woman with three children, deserted by her husband; an old couple in Colorado whose Social Security payments are not sufficient to cover their rent, medical expenses, and an adequate diet.

"Food stamps are not the answer," President Hawkins says. "They help, certainly, but the problem of hunger in America has become so pervasive that our existing programs cannot cope with the crisis—and I use that word deliberately, for it is a crisis.

"Well, what is to be done? Why should anyone go hungry in this abundant land? The problem is not one of production but of distribution.

"And where is the food to feed all these hungry Americans? It exists stored in government warehouses. And who owns all this bounty? *You* do! Let me show you."

Then, with the aid of charts, the President displays how many hundreds of tons of foodstuff are U.S. property. The charts are followed by film clips showing silos and warehouses of grains, butter, cheese, sugar, powdered milk, fruits, vegetables, nuts, canned fish—foods of all kinds.

"There is *your* larder," Hawkins says, "*your* national pantry. It exists while hungry Americans search through garbage cans or beg for a second helping of watery stew."

The President then proposes to give away the tons of

surplus foods in the government's possession. Distribution will be by churches and other public and private charities. No one will profit financially from the program; only the hungry will benefit.

"By giving our surplus food to the needy," he says earnestly, "we are affirming our existence as one nation, indivisible, and one family in which each is responsible for the other. We will show the whole world that we will not allow our children to cry for food while our granaries and warehouses are overflowing."

The President then takes a deep breath, clasps his hands tighter, and leans forward.

"But there is another reason to feed our hungry," he says solemnly, "other than just national pride." He then delivers a conclusion written with the assistance of Brother Kristos.

"This nation was created by men and women with an abiding faith in a Supreme Being. Our history illustrates our belief in God and our obedience to His commands.

"That is why we must go forward with this plan to feed the hungry. To paraphrase the Good Book: Whoever has this world's goods, and sees his brother in need, and shuts compassion from him, how can the love of God be in him?

"I believe the love of God dwells in the hearts of all Americans. Tonight I ask you to prove that love by approving the gift of life to your brothers and sisters in need.

"Good night and God bless you."

The image of the President has scarcely faded from the screen when the phones start ringing at the White House switchboard.

=2=

Life has changed for Lenore Mattingly. She has become the mistress of what one society columnist referred to as the Little White House. Her phone never stops ringing. She is besieged by reporters, magazine writers, photographers, even the clergy.

Sermonettes are now delivered four afternoons a week in Brother Kristos' study, and the demand to hear the preacher has grown to such an extent that reservations must be made weeks in advance.

Mrs. Mattingly finds herself much sought for lunches and teas. Everyone wants to know about Brother Kristos. What kind of a man *is* he? Can he really see into a person's past, predict the future, heal the sick? Is it true that he drinks a great deal, and fornicates frequently and without guilt?

Mrs. Mattingly defends Brother Kristos with stern resolution. He is, she tells the curious, a man of God, genuinely, deeply religious, with rare powers.

There are, of course, a few drawbacks to having a saint reside in her home, though Lenore would never mention them to anyone, not even Emily. For instance:

That smelly dog sleeps under the kitchen sink and must be frequently let out into the small backyard, where he has already killed most of the rhododendrons.

The two young women who serve as cook and housekeeper dress decently enough, but there is no gainsaying that they both have slatternly habits. Pearl Gibbs is an indifferent housekeeper; she simply doesn't know *how* to dust. And the meals prepared by Agnes Brittlewaite are overspiced.

But her strongest resentment, never voiced, involves Brother Kristos himself. The man has become a social lion. Not only does he attend functions at the White House, but he is invited to embassy dinners, performances at Kennedy Center, and openings of exhibitions at the Smithsonian.

And not once, not *once,* has he asked Lenore to accompany him. She is hurt by his inattention and seeming lack of gratitude for all she has done for him. But she comforts herself with the thought that he means to protect his reputation by not squiring her around. After all, he *is* a man of God and must strive always to convey a public impression of celibacy and spirituality.

One of the social events Lenore desperately wishes to attend, but to which she is not invited, is a cocktail party at the Italian embassy in honor of Marcello Mastroianni. Brother Kristos attends, and attracts almost as much attention as the movie star.

Kristos, dressed completely in black, is surrounded by politicians, all eager to discuss the President's controversial food-giveaway program and discover, if possible, what role the preacher played in planning it.

He answers their questions as briefly as possible, claiming no credit for Hawkins' performance other than providing the biblical words used in the President's concluding remarks.

Someone standing at his elbow speaks up. "From the First Epistle of John," she says, and then quotes: " 'Little children, let us not love in words or speech but in deed and in truth.' "

He turns slowly to look at her. She is a slight black woman with hair a battleship gray. She is wearing steel-rimmed spectacles and a shapeless dress of mauve silk.

"Yes," Kristos says, "you are correct."

"And do you love in deed and in truth, Brother Kristos?" she asks, her voice hard.

"God will judge me," he says.

"Not in this world," she replies, and a few people laugh.

The political chitchat continues, and after a while Kristos excuses himself and finds the men's room. There he dawdles a few moments, combing his hair, mustache, beard. When he exits, the little black woman is waiting for him in the carpeted corridor. She is holding a filled champagne glass and a hunk of powdered pastry.

"Would you like some?" she asks.

"Thank you, no."

"Could you and I have a talk?"

He stares at her. She has a brisk, no-nonsense manner, as if she is more accustomed to talking than listening and won't put up with any sass.

"I was about to leave," he tells her.

"Won't take but a minute," she says decisively, and leads the way down the corridor to two ornate armchairs.

"My name is Lu-Anne Schlossel," she says. "Representative from Georgia, Twelfth District. I'm in my fourth term and expect to get reelected in November. I serve on several House committees, but Hunger is my baby. Up to now, we've had no help from the administration at all, and I figured Hawkins for a real do-nothing. Then out of the blue, he makes that speech. It's what I've been shouting about in Congress for years. Now, with the White House behind us, we might be able to get something done. I wanted to thank you personally."

"It was completely Hawkins' idea," Brother Kristos says.

"That's a good line," she says, "and you stick to it. It wouldn't do if word got around that a conjureman is coaching the President."

"Conjureman?"

"That's what we called guys like you in the backwoods of Georgia. Look, I don't know what your angle is, and I don't want to know. Maybe you're really on the up-and-up, but I've been around this town long enough to take everything people say with a grain of salt. But what is important is that you're on my side. I figure we can do each other some good. Apparently you've got the President's ear, and I've got a little clout myself—on the Hunger Committee and in the Black Caucus. People call me the Ebony Gadfly—which I take as a compliment. So, what do you say? You can use at least one friend up on Capitol Hill, can't you?"

"Yes."

"Then we can work together?"

He nods.

"Good. Let's meet as often as we can and trade ideas. If Hawkins asks Congress for legislation on this, he'll have a real donnybrook on his hands. It's going to take a lot of organizing to get this thing through."

"Why should anyone object to a food giveaway?"

"Parson, you might know a lot about preaching, but you know nothing about politics. The first thing you've got to do is stop calling it a 'giveaway.' No one likes the idea of giving away government property. It just sounds dumb. But if you call it 'food sharing,' people will accept it."

"Yes," he says seriously, "you are right."

"Okay," she says, rising, "so we'll be partners on this. I'm glad you're a practical man." She finishes her piece of pastry, wipes her fingers on the hip of her silk dress, holds out her hand to him. "Thanks for the talk, Brother Kristos. I'll be in touch."

He shakes her hand, but doesn't release it immediately. Instead, he gazes deeply into her eyes, and she is conscious of the hot intensity of his stare.

"Oh my," she says mockingly, "now you're giving me that conjureman look."

"Just because the one you loved married another," he says, "is no reason to give up on all men."

She jerks her hand away as if it has suddenly been burned.

"You son of a bitch!" she says furiously.

Tollinger:

Re: Brother Kristos.

This could be called "Through the Bible Belt with Gun and Camera"—only I didn't have a camera. Anyway, I've covered eight states and more towns, villages, and one-horse burgs than I want to remember. I think now I've got a good idea of how B.K. operated before he showed up at that Virginia tobacco barn, and I'm ready to pack up and return to D.C.

It's obvious he stuck to the back roads and sold his religious snake oil in small farm communities with populations of a couple of hundred to twenty thousand tops. He seems to have avoided larger cities, probably because he figured the citizens were too sophisticated to fall for his line of bunkum.

He'd pull into a town, set up his tent, and plaster bills on telephone poles and fenceposts. They all had his picture and an announcement that the Reverend Jacob Christiansen had arrived and would preach at evening meetings on sin, temptation, and God's love. But he was smart enough to check in first with the county sheriff and shake pinkies with the ministers of the local churches. If there was a quid pro quo here, with Jake promising to share his take, no one would admit it. I'd guess he paid off.

Everyone seems to remember his sermons, mostly because of his main theme: you could go out and screw until you fainted because we are all made in God's image, and He is without sin. This was great stuff to the yokels, who were mostly hard-shell Baptists.

Before the actual sermon, to get the attention of his audience, he'd pick out a few farmers and tell them things about their past they swore that he, a stranger, couldn't possibly know. He also was said to "work wonders" with sick farm animals.

All the people I spoke to seemed impressed by the reverend, while admitting there was something weird about him. Everybody mentioned his wild stare. A lot of women got breathless when they talked about him, so I reckon Jake did okay in the Love 'Em and Leave 'Em Department.

About two years before he quit the Bible Belt circuit to settle down in Virginia, he changed his name to Brother Kristos, let his hair grow, and sprouted a mustache and long beard. Also, his repertoire of sermons had grown, and now included claims to be the brother of Christ and God's advance man on earth. A Baptist minister I talked to in Arkansas always went to hear him when he came to town. He claimed Kristos could "preach up a storm" and convince his congregation he really was a holy man. The Baptist said he doubted that, but Brother Kristos had a God-given gift of gab and also allegedly cured the minister's impotence.

He picked up a sick hound named Nick in Tennessee, nursed it back to health, and took it along in the truck. It was in Traviston, Miss., that B.K. met up with the half-sisters Agnes Brittlewaite and Pearl Gibbs. Agnes was slinging hash at a local diner (the Waldorf—"Where the Elite Meet to Eat"), and Pearl was selling tickets at the movie house, the Bijou. But reportedly both girls were turning tricks after working hours. When Brother Kristos left town, *they went along with him, and started taking up the collection at his tent shows.*

Sorry to report I was unable to find any record of criminal activity, other than a few minor pinches that B.K. talked his way out of. As far as I could find out, he was never convicted of anything. Cops don't like to arrest "men of the cloth," even when they're out-and-out hustlers.

But as I followed B.K.'s trail, I came to the conclusion that he was guilty as hell—but not of anything you could charge him with. He was like these TV evangelists who wheedle the Social Security money from poor old farm ladies and then go out and buy BMW's and lizardskin shoes. Brother Kristos was and is doing the same thing: making bucks by taking advantage of people's religious faith and their love of God. That sucks. I'd have more respect for him if he held up a bank or cracked a safe. I'm really beginning to hate the guy.

I want to talk to you more about this when I get back to Washington.

—Lindberg

After declining several invitations, Jennifer Raye finally agrees to have dinner, and John Tollinger is so delighted that he makes a reservation at Maison Blanche, not too far from the White House. He imagines a secluded table, candlelight, champagne cocktails to start, perhaps veal cordon bleu, cognac for dessert—and then home to Spring Valley for a sweaty romp.

But when Jennifer shows up, only twenty minutes late, she is wearing a sack dress of black linen that completely conceals her zaftig figure. And hanging from her neck is a silver crucifix.

"What's this?" Tollinger says, holding a chair for her. "Get thee to a nunnery time?"

"Now don't start that," she says sharply.

"Start what? I was just making a lighthearted comment on your virginal costume. I'm having a champagne cocktail. Okay for you?"

"I'd prefer a Perrier with a wedge of lime."

His vision of how the evening will end begins to fade.

"So," he says, sitting across the table from her, "what have you been up to lately? Busy?"

"Very," she says.

"Are you involved in this food giveaway?"

"Some," she says.

"You *are* allowed to make more than one-word replies."

"Sorry," she says, trying a small smile, "but I've got a lot on my mind."

"That's what I'm trying to find out," he says patiently. "What have you got on your mind?"

"It *is* the surplus-food program, but don't call it a giveaway. We refer to it as food sharing."

"Semantics is a wonderful thing. Was it your idea to call it food sharing?"

"No."

"Let me guess: Brother Kristos suggested it."

"What's wrong with that?" she says hotly.

He holds up a palm. "Nothing, nothing! I think it's a good marketing gimmick. What's your job?"

"We're trying to plan a schedule for the First Lady. She wants to travel all over the country, visit soup kitchens, talk to the hungry. She's going to do everything she can to push the program."

"Good idea. Television coverage. Lots of photo opportunities. Her sitting next to a derelict slurping a bowl of gruel."

"Now you're being snotty," Jennifer says. "As usual."

"It comes with the territory," he says. "Maybe I've been in politics too long. Everything begins to smell of hype."

Their veal is served.

"Looks awfully rich," she says doubtfully. "I'm on a diet."

"Sackcloth and ashes?" he says, and she glares at him.

They eat slowly and in silence.

"You believe in the food-sharing program, don't you?" she says finally.

"Not this food," he says, eyeing his plate. "It's too good. But yes, I believe in the basic idea. Get rid of the surplus; it's costing us a fortune to store. But the concept is too simplistic. Not all the results will be beneficial. The farmers will suffer, and the food processors."

"So what?" she says angrily. "It's the hungry who need help most. Whose side are you on?"

"Yours," he says. "I'm just trying to suggest that sometimes generosity has unforeseen and disastrous consequences."

"Must you analyze everything? If you give a bum a dollar, that's an act of charity, isn't it? If he wants to spend it on cheap wine, that's his responsibility. But it doesn't change the fact that you did something good."

"I'm not so sure of that," he says slowly. "For instance, if you know or suspect that the bum is a drug addict, is giving him money really an act of Christian charity?"

"Well, the starving aren't addicts; they're just *hungry*. So you don't have to worry about the horrendous results of giving them free food."

"I wish it was that simple," he says, "but it's not. There's going to be the goddamnedest political brannigan over this that you've ever seen."

"Try not to *think* about it so much," she advises, "and try to *feel* about it more."

"Now where have I heard that?" he says. "It couldn't have been from Brother Kristos, could it? At the White House prayer breakfast?"

"You should try it once," she says furiously. "If you only let yourself *feel*, you'd discover there's more to life than playing games with words."

"What's that," he says, "the Gospel according to Saint Kristos?"

"I feel sorry for you," she says. "You think you're so superior, and you're really a small, small man. How I ever put up with you for three years I'll never know."

"Surely it had its moments," he says.

"Few and far between," she says snappishly.

"Ah, go to hell," he says. "Or worse, go back to that hairy huckster of holiness and pretend there's no such thing as sin."

"You're despicable!" she spits at him, rises, gathers up purse and gloves, stalks away.

"Shall I serve the brandy now, sir?" the waiter asks.

"Yeah," Tollinger says. "Both of them."

Later, he drives home alone, ashamed of the way he acted, the things he said to Jennifer. And bewildered, too, because he has always been proud of keeping a tight rein on his passions.

It was, he admits ruefully, a triumph of glands over common sense. He could not endure Jennifer's religiosity, but most of all he could not bear the thought of her in the embrace of that hokey messiah. And so he ran off at the mouth and said things with a mean animosity he knows she will never forgive.

He groans with frustration. He never feared the competition of any male for Jennifer's love. But how do you compete with a self-proclaimed man of God?

=5=

Early in June, the President sends a bill up to Capitol Hill which, if approved, would authorize the Chief Executive "or those he may delegate" to dispose of all stores of food "deemed surplus" that are presently the property of the United States.

The introduction of the food-sharing legislation touches off a greater political commotion than Hawkins' television presentation. Members of Congress are quick to react, with impassioned opinions for and against.

In the House of Representatives, the bill is referred to the Select Committee on Hunger, where the first battle will be waged. Representative Lu-Anne Schlossel becomes the champion of the new legislation. She is able to schedule hearings that will include testimony from the clergy, farmers, executives of charitable organizations, nutritionists, and several witnesses claiming to be authentically hungry. Representative Schlossel also prevails upon the Black Caucus to pass a resolution approving food sharing.

In the Senate, the bill is sent to the Standing Committee on Agriculture, Nutrition and Forestry—for want of a better place to send it. The chairman, the senior senator from Kansas, vows to bottle it up in committee or, if that proves impossible, to filibuster it to death on the Senate floor.

While the lines are being drawn in Congress, a more rancorous public debate is developing. An ad hoc coalition of liberal groups is formed to lobby for the President's bill on Capitol Hill and to organize a publicity campaign to persuade the citizenry that food sharing (with no expenditure of public funds required) is both fiscally sound and morally right.

Although the opposition is initially civil, it is not long before Hawkins' religious motives are publicly questioned and Brother Kristos' influence scathingly condemned.

It is this last development that is the subject of discussion when Michael Oberfest meets with Major Marchuk at that shopping mall in Maryland.

"Now look," Oberfest says, "I did what you asked, didn't I? I mean I really tried to put a lid on the Hawkins-Kristos connection. But it's hopeless. Last night I saw a stand-up TV comic do an impersonation of Brother Kristos. He had the guy down to a T. His patter was all about how he got the idea of helping the poor and needy while sleeping in the Lincoln Bedroom and eating in the East Room of the White House. If comedians are doing shticks on it, you know it's too late."

"Shticks?" Marchuk says. "What are shticks?"

"Show-business talk for doing a set routine."

"Well, yes," the major says regretfully, "I think you are right; we can no longer hope to keep the affair quiet. I suppose Vice President Trent is happy about what is happening?"

"You bet he is. He's convinced that even if Hawkins gets the bill passed, he's going to make so many enemies that the party will dump him."

"You think he's correct?"

"Could be. Did you see where a farmers' union is planning a march on Washington? Hawkins carried the Midwest in the last election; he'll never do that again, and the party leaders know it."

"So they may turn to Trent?"

"A very real possibility."

The major pulls thoughtfully at his lower lip. "It is a setback certainly," he says, "but the war is not lost."

"Yeah, well," Michael says, "I'm out of it—right? I mean, I did a job for you: the best I could. But there's nothing more I can do."

"Oh no, Arnold," Marchuk says. "You are very valuable to us. We still need confidential information on Trent's plans. You are in a unique position to supply that intelligence."

"Hey, come on," Oberfest says. "How long is this going to go on?"

"As long as necessary. My boy, you are making history—don't you realize that? You are playing a very important role in affairs of state. It should make you proud."

"Well, it doesn't make me proud. It scares the hell out of me. I'm no hero. If the VP finds out what I'm doing, he'll crucify me."

"If you are clever," the KGB man says, "he won't find out." Then he adds significantly, "And neither will anyone else."

"All right," Michael says, sighing, "I get the message."

=6=

Pearl drives, and Agnes sits beside her. Brother Kristos lolls in the back, the pale hound sleeping at his feet. They sing ribald songs on the trip down to the Virginia tobacco barn. It's like the old days in the pickup truck, but now they're in a fine new car with leather upholstery.

It's late June, and the air conditioning purrs away. Passing a jug of chilled vodka back and forth, they are flushed with content, knowing it's no more than they deserve after all the lean years.

On Saturday night, the crowd begins gathering well before the scheduled eight P.M. sermon. There are limousines in the parking lot now, and even a chartered bus that has brought a group from Richmond. All the wooden benches are packed, and standees jam the back of the hall. Latecomers listen at the open door and windows.

Brother Kristos wears his old burlap robe, and preaches in his bare feet with his hair and beard artfully disarrayed. He has insisted the barn remain as it was, lighted by kerosene lanterns and devoid of religious ornamentation.

"Tonight," he says, staring at his parishioners, "I shall preach to you of the divinity of love, infinite love which is pleasing to God. He commands us to love one another, for only by loving each other can we learn to love God truly and earn His love in return.

"Love is expressed in many forms: devotion, sacrifice, duty, affection, obedience, patriotism, tenderness, passion. All forms of love are divine, but the rapture of physical pleasure between a man and a woman is a holy prayer to the Supreme Being."

Brother Kristos embroiders this theme for almost twenty minutes. His language is eloquent, but his audience knows full well that he is talking about fucking, and they lean forward raptly, anxious not to miss a word.

The collection is particularly heavy that night.

The crowd is dispersing when Pearl Gibbs is approached by a short dumpling of a man. He's almost totally bald, with a thick unlighted cigar clamped between yellowed teeth.

"I want to see the reverend," he says.

Pearl inspects him. The plaid suit is hand-tailored, the tasseled moccasins shined to a high gloss. His jacket is unbuttoned, and she spots the monogram on his shirt pocket: LBT.

"What's it about?" Pearl asks.

"A private matter," the man says, his voice raspy. "Tell him I know Billy Feinschmecker down in Florida."

Pearl goes into the back room and reports.

"Billy Feinschmecker?" Brother Kristos says, smiling. "Is he still alive? What does this man look like?"

"I think he's in the game," she says. "He's got hustler written all over him. But he must be in the chips; he's wearing a gold Rolex."

"All right," Kristos says, "bring him in. If he's not out in fifteen minutes, you come in to remind me of a meeting I have scheduled."

"Got it," she says.

The bald man is ushered in. He thrusts a business card at the preacher.

"Lamar B. Tumulty," he announces. "Personal representative."

"What is a personal representative?" Brother Kristos asks. "An agent?"

"Something like that, reverend. But more."

"You know Billy Feinschmecker?"

"Sure. Whenever I'm down his way, I stop in for a game of pinochle and to chew the fat."

"How is he doing?"

"Surviving. Walks with a limp, and he's got the shakes, but he still talks a blue streak."

"Yes," Kristos says, "that's Billy. What can I do for you, Mr. Tumulty?"

"It's what I can do for *you*. Could we sit down for a minute?"

"All right, but not for long. I have a meeting scheduled."

"Sure you do. Mind if I light up the stogie?"

"Yes," Kristos says, "I mind."

"Okay," the agent says equably, "I won't. Got anything to drink in this palace?"

"Pepper vodka."

"That's a new one on me, but I'm game."

Brother Kristos offers him the uncapped bottle. Tumulty takes a swallow and blinks his watery eyes. "You sure it ain't battery acid?" But he takes another swallow before he sets the bottle back on the table.

"Here's the deal, reverend: I represent clients, mostly in show biz, and teach 'em how to haul in the real money. Right now I got three singers, a punk rock group, two exotic dancers, a juggling team, and an Olympic gymnast. I only take comers, and I work closely with them. I get thirty percent of the gross, not negotiable, but it's worth it to them because I've never handled an act that didn't double its gross after I took 'em on. I can do the same for you."

Brother Kristos takes a swig from the vodka bottle. "Thank you," he says, "but I'm not interested."

"You should be, reverend. I can make you a millionaire."

"And how would you do that?"

"It'd start with this shithouse you call a church. I suppose you think it's quaint. Like the stable where Jesus was born—right? Forget it! People come to a dump, they donate what they think the dump is worth. They go to St. Patrick's and see all that gilt, they're embarrassed not to come up with folding money. You need a nice place. Maybe not like St. Pat's, but attractive and comfortable, where the marks don't have to worry about rats and roaches. And air-conditioned. I sweated bullets out there tonight. By the way, that was one helluva sermon you preached. It all sounded strictly legit, and the pigeons loved it. You really killed 'em."

"Thank you," Kristos says.

"You're welcome. But this is a rinky-dink operation you're running here. The fields were jammed with cars parked every which way. If you put in a blacktop and installed parking meters, you'd have a gold mine. And why don't you write a book? Something like *Brother Kristos' Prayers for All Occasions*. It doesn't have to be long, but bind it in fake red leather and you could sell it at the door for a fin, maybe a sawbuck."

"Smart ideas," the preacher says, nodding.

"See the way I work?" Tumulty says, reaching for the bottle. "And those gimmicks are just off the top of my head. The main thing you gotta do is give your church a name. Whatever you like; it doesn't make any difference. Something with 'Holy' in the title; people go for that. Then you get the church chartered and registered as a nonprofit organization. No taxes: that's how you become a millionaire. You got a diploma or some piece of paper from a divinity school? Well, it's not important. I know half a dozen mills in California that'll sell you a framed parchment for fifty bucks."

"I can see you've given this a lot of thought."

"I've worked on it. Reverend, I'm not a flimflam artist. I deliver the goods for my thirty percent. But listen; the best is yet to come. Once we've got you set up in a decent church, everything legal and aboveboard, with county, state, and federal licenses, then we start you on the local radio. For free. Maybe once a week on Sunday morning. I'm betting you'll build up an audience. Then we start syndicating *The Brother Kristos Hour*. That's where the big take is—in syndication. If that goes good, we put you on TV. You start a television ministry, and I don't have to tell you how much money there is in *that*. We'll have to hire a crew just to open the mail and take the checks to the bank. Now how does all that sound?"

"Have another drink," Kristos says, moving the jug toward Tumulty, and then watching the bald man gulp thirstily.

"Well?" the agent says, wiping his mouth with the back

of his hand. "What do you say? Want me to start you on the road to fame and fortune?"

"Mr. Tumulty," Brother Kristos says slowly and carefully, "I have no doubt that you are capable of doing exactly what you propose. You have some very exciting visions, and I think all of them are practicable—except for one thing."

"Oh? What's that?"

The preacher leans forward, stares directly into the other man's eyes. "You may find this difficult to believe, but I have absolutely no interest in accumulating wealth. I am perfectly satisfied with my life just the way it is. Yes, this is a mean, shabby church, but the people who come to listen to me don't expect or desire fine surroundings. They come to hear the words of God's apostle on earth. I try to teach them love, faith, and understanding of God's will. It is a small flock, but I have no wish to increase it for personal gain. Money means nothing to me. I have enough to eat, to drink, to wear. Each morning I awake happy that I have been given another day to do God's work. No, Mr. Tumulty, I do not want fame and fortune. All I seek is to be worthy of God's love."

The agent stands abruptly. "You're good," he says. "You're really good. Well, Billy Feinschmecker told me you were, and now I believe it. You've got my card, reverend. If you should change your mind, drop me a line or give me a call. You and I could do big things together."

After he leaves, Pearl and Agnes come in, and the three of them finish the pepper vodka and start on another bottle while they count the night's take. It's slightly over six hundred dollars.

Then they unwrap the whole barbecued chickens they have brought, and eat, drink, and roister into the small hours of the morning. They start the trip back to Washington shortly after noon on Sunday, with Brother Kristos driving, Nick curled up in the passenger seat, the two women snoozing in back.

That evening in his study, Brother Kristos sits sprawled in his armchair, legs spread. Emily Mattingly kneels before him, lowered head between his thighs.

"Dear," he says, stroking her hair softly, "on the drive back from the church today, I pondered on how I might be with my flock when I cannot speak to them in person. I thought I might write a book. Something small and tasteful. Perhaps a red leather cover and gilt on the page edges. I could call it *Brother Kristos' Prayers for All Occasions.* Would you contact printers tomorrow and get some idea of what such a book would cost to produce?"

Emily nods, and he gasps and holds her head more firmly.

"Also," he says, "would you see if there's any company in the area that sells parking meters."

=7=

During that summer the debate on the President's food-sharing plan becomes louder and angrier. Nothing, foreign observers agree, has so fragmented American public opinion since the war in Vietnam.

As expected, most supporters of the President's program are blacks, Hispanics, Asian immigrants, union members, the organized poor and homeless, and more affluent voters with liberal political convictions. But to the surprise of many, the ranks of the left are swollen by millions of fundamentalists.

These deeply religious folk are ordinarily a mainstay of the right, with conservative views on everything from abortion to prayer in the public schools. But Hawkins' appeal for food sharing has galvanized the devout.

More than one columnist has noted what strange political bedfellows the food-sharing plan has produced. It has even been suggested that if this coalition of liberal and fundamentalist endures, it could have a profound effect on the upcoming midterm elections.

This is a possibility much on the mind of Vice President Samuel Trent.

"The pinkos holding hands with the Holy Rollers," he says disgustedly to his wife. "That's all this great nation needs."

"Yes, dear," she says placidly, knitting away, "but I'm sure they're just joining together on this one issue."

"Don't be so certain of that. They could become a voting bloc to be reckoned with." He looks up frowning. "What's that you're working on?"

"A cashmere muffler," she says, holding it up. "Like it?"

"Very nice. But you know I never wear a muffler. It looks so wimpy."

"Then it'll be a Christmas present," she says, smiling secretly. "For someone. Samuel, I feel like having a sip of something."

"Splendid idea. Brandy?"

"Oh, I forgot to tell you; the liquor store had a special on something new: pepper vodka. So I bought a bottle."

"Vodka?" he cries, aghast. "From Russia?"

"I'm afraid so, dear. But it's very tasty. Would you like to try it?"

"No, thank you," he says firmly. "I'll stick to good old California brandy."

He brings their drinks, then takes up a position alongside the cold fireplace, leaning on the marble mantelpiece, his ankles crossed.

"Matilda," he says portentously, "I have been giving a great deal of thought to my political future."

"I'm sure you have, Samuel."

"I think my efforts to bring the relationship between Hawkins and Kristos to the attention of the American public have been crowned with notable success."

"They certainly have."

"Of course, Oberfest made a considerable contribution—I am man enough to give credit where credit is due—but I engineered the whole thing and drove it through to a satisfying conclusion. Now the entire country—the world!—is aware of the pernicious influence this religious fanatic has on White House policy-making."

"Samuel," his wife says, looking up, "I think the President's bill is going to be passed and signed into law."

"Matilda," he says sternly, "I must tell you in all honesty that in this case I believe your judgment is flawed. The food-giveaway bill will *not* be passed. The farm lobby will kill it."

"I still don't think it would be wise for you to oppose it."

"I don't intend to," he says. "Notice that I have made no public comment on it whatsoever. But what concerns me most is the effect it may have on the future of the party. 'Now is the time for all good men to come to the aid of the party' is as true today as when it was first spoken."

"I don't believe anyone actually *said* it," Matilda says, sipping her vodka. "It's just a sentence used to teach typewriting."

"Well, you know what I mean. I've been considering the possibility of meeting with a small group of state chairmen and contributors to discuss the problem. There are still enough right-thinking men who recognize the danger Brother Kristos presents."

"I think you're exaggerating his influence."

"I am *not* exaggerating," the Vice President says hotly. "I *never* exaggerate. I tell you that unshaved lunatic is practically in command of domestic policy in the White House. He can twist Hawkins around his little finger. If we let this situation continue, the midterms may be lost, and the party will suffer damage that'll take twenty years to repair. All because of a so-called holy man who claims to have a hot line to God."

She stares at him a long moment. "I told you I met him at Lenore Mattingly's. He impressed me as being a very sincere man."

"Bushwa! And so was Jack the Ripper sincere, thinking to rid the world of prostitutes."

She puts her knitting aside, rises, walks over to the wet bar. She adds more pepper vodka to her glass, plops in a few ice cubes.

"I don't understand you," she says severely. "Your original aim was to publicize the activities of Brother Kristos in order to discredit Hawkins. Well, you certainly helped bring Kristos to the attention of the public, but now you seem to resent his association with the President because you fear it may damage the party. If that happens, won't a defeat at the polls enhance your own political future?"

"Not if the party is taken over by the crazies. I refuse to sit idly by while the party is captured by the great unwashed, led by a two-bit seer who may very well be getting his orders from the Kremlin."

"Now you're talking rubbish," she says.

They glare at each other. Both are well-bred and have never raised their voices. But now they realize they are having a disagreement, almost an argument. Their heightened passions come as a shock, almost a thrill.

"Let me repeat," he says stonily, "so there can be no possibility of your misunderstanding the course I intend to pursue. I have spent my entire career with firm and loyal adherence to the platforms and beliefs of the political party I judge best suited to govern this great nation. Now that organization is being threatened by an influx of half-witted rabble, riffraff, and come-to-Jesus nuts. I will not accept that without a fight. I will not allow the party to which I have pledged my life, my fortune, and my sacred honor to become a haven for slum-dwellers, white trash, and the dregs of society who lack the intelligence, pedigree, and noble courage to steer the ship of state safely through the shoals of a complex and frequently hostile world."

"Oh, you're full of beans," says Matilda Trent, and then the squabble really begins.

During her next tryst with Brother Kristos, Mrs. Trent reports on her husband's plans.

A bloated sun is blaring in the cellophane sky, but the wind cools with a briny tang, and sweaters are needed at noon. That stretch of Maine coast is a jumble of humongous boulders, and the sea comes dashing. Farther out, it seems unrippled, fading to a smoky horizon.

The big gray house is built on the cliff, a floating dream of turrets, minarets, bay windows, and a widow's walk large enough to accommodate chairs, lounges, a long table, and a small weathered dinghy filled with earth and planted with geraniums.

This summer home belongs to the U.S. Ambassador to the United Kingdom, but the First Family has borrowed it for a two-week vacation, beginning with the Labor Day holiday. In attendance are the President's personal staff and a perimeter guard of Maine state troopers.

The President and Mrs. Hawkins occupy the master bedroom. George shares a smaller room with Sergeant

Dennis McShane. Others are doubled up in even tinier sleeping chambers. But most of the entourage, including pool reporters and press photographers, have taken over the only motel in Bear's Head, the nearest town.

On Tuesday morning, an hour before luncheon is to be served on the lawn at the leeward side of the house, George and his bodyguard go exploring. There are acres of woods shelving down from the cliff to the road, and the boy is fascinated by this wilderness of gnarled trees, tangled undergrowth, and unexpected sprinklings of wildflowers and berry bushes.

Sergeant McShane is wearing camouflage dungarees with a web belt and combat boots. George wears a miniature version of the same uniform, plus a plastic helmet in olive drab. He also has a rubber hunting knife strapped to his waist, and carries a toy rifle that shoots sparks every time the trigger is pulled.

They move slowly along a faintly marked dirt path, the Marine explaining the fine points of reconnoitering a wooded environment: avoid stepping on twigs, do not let branches scrape your clothing, keep your eyes moving, and stand motionless every few minutes to listen for suspicious sounds.

George leads the way, his rifle gripped at the ready. They proceed cautiously for almost ten minutes, the forest closing in about them, the house invisible, the sounds of the sea muted. Suddenly a fat squirrel leaps madly across the path. The boy raises his weapon and squeezes off two bursts of sparks.

The animal darts into the undergrowth and, before McShane can intervene, the lad plunges after him. He's out of sight within seconds, and the startled bodyguard goes after him, yelling, "George! George, come back!" He crashes through a snarl of saplings, vines, and shrubs, tripping over fallen logs, his face whipped and cut by low branches.

"George! George!" Dennis shouts with growing desperation. But he cannot catch a glimpse of the boy. He stops abruptly to listen. Nothing. Then he continues his frantic search, fearing the worst and imagining a court-martial for dereliction of duty if the "worst" becomes a reality.

Still screaming the lad's name, he bursts through a thick stand of young maples and catches himself just before he falls. He's teetering on the edge of a rock-studded ravine. And at the bottom, lying faceup, is the crumpled form of the President's son.

Cursing viciously, McShane scrambles down and bends over the lad's body. He sees no bleeding, but George's eyes are closed and he's quite still. At least his chest is rising and falling, and his arms and legs appear sound.

"George?" the Marine says, but there is no response.

Without touching the body, Dennis climbs out of the ravine and fights his way back to the dirt path. He takes off his web belt and leaves it dangling from a branch to mark the way. Then he starts running back to the house to spread the alarm.

Things move quickly after that.

An ambulance is summoned from Bear's Head.

The President's helicopter, parked at the Bangor airfield, is ordered to Bear's Head, to land on the high-school football field.

Sergeant McShane returns to the ravine with the President's personal physician and two Secret Service agents.

The reporters are told the President's son has been hurt in an accident, the extent of his injuries not yet known.

George has not regained consciousness, but blood is flowing steadily from the corner of his mouth. The doctor fears internal bleeding, treats the boy for shock, and prepares a clotting injection.

McShane organizes a crew of the strongest men he can find. Equipped with hatchets, axes, shovels, and machetes, they begin clearing a passage through the forest from the ravine to the dirt path.

A Bangor hospital is alerted to expect the arrival of a "prominent" trauma patient.

George's personal physician and favorite nurse at Walter Reed in Washington are hustled to Andrews Air Force Base and put aboard a plane for Bangor.

The President's son, still unconscious, is placed on a stretcher, covered with blankets, and carefully lifted out of the ravine and carried down to the ambulance. His mother and father ride with him to the helicopter.

The copter is met at the Bangor airport by another ambulance, and the boy is rushed to the hospital.

Closer examination confirms the initial diagnosis: though bruised by his fall, George has suffered no broken bones. But he apparently has internal injuries and is hemorrhaging badly. The doctors are considering surgery.

At 9:46 P.M. on Tuesday, the President places a call to Brother Kristos.

When the phone rings, the preacher is sprawled naked in a half-drunken stupor on his rumpled bed. An empty vodka bottle lies on the floor. The room smells of stale sex. He rouses groggily, picks up the phone.

"Brother Kristos?"

"Yes."

"Just a moment, please, sir. The President is calling."

"Brother Kristos?"

"Yes, father, I am here."

Hawkins tells him what has happened. "They can't give us assurance that the bleeding will stop. They think perhaps they should operate."

"No," Kristos says, "don't let them do that."

"Will my son recover without surgery?"

"Yes," Kristos says. "The bleeding will stop and the boy will recover."

"Thank you," the President says huskily. "We have complete faith in you. My wife sends her eternal thanks."

Brother Kristos hangs up. He stands shakily, stumbles over to the dresser mirror, examines his visage. Hair, mustache, and beard are matted. Lips are parched. His skin is rancid with dried sweat. There are reddish bite marks on the insides of his thighs.

He finds his twill trousers and with shaking hands pulls the wide leather belt from the loops. He wraps the belt around and around his hand until, when he clenches his fingers, a length of the leather swings free, ending with the silver buckle.

He stands before the mirror again, flaming eyes locked with those of his image. He begins to whip himself, swinging the belt over each shoulder in turn. The buckle thuds into the flesh of his back. But not hard enough. Not half enough.

His blows become faster, more frantic. Leather slaps and metal cuts. Finally, finally, he feels blood beginning to flow, and almost joyously he scourges himself. His arm rises, falls, rises, falls. The buckle bites deeper; he knows the penitential ecstasy of pain.

He whips himself silently, lips drawn back in a wolfish grimace. He will not gasp or cry aloud but continues in a steady rhythm: right shoulder, left, right, left. His torn back is a soaked shroud now, skin torn and lacerated. Still he flogs himself until his arm is too weary to lift again, and his legs tremble.

Finally he falls to his knees at the bedside, clasps his hands on the stained sheets, bows his head. He prays, not asking forgiveness or mercy or any bounty from God other than the boy's survival.

=9=

Tollinger has never seen the Chief of Staff in a more savage mood.

"That tears it," Folsom says furiously. "Listen, I'm happy George is getting better. Everyone is. But the Boss swears it's all due to Brother Kristos, even though George was in Maine and Kristos was in D.C. How the hell do you figure it? Long-distance faith healing?"

"Chief," John says, "if you accept the viability of faith healing, then I suppose you've got to believe it could be done at a distance."

"But you don't accept it?"

"No, I don't. I think George is one lucky boy who wasn't injured too seriously and would have healed without surgery and without the prayers of Brother Kristos."

"Don't try telling the Boss that," Folsom says bitterly. "He'll throw your ass out the window. He's absolutely convinced—and his wife is too—that their son owes his life to Brother Kristos. And there's not a goddamn thing anyone can say to convince them otherwise. So right now my best bet, as I see it, is to try to ignore Brother Kristos and plan damage control on the food-sharing bill."

"It's not going to make it, is it?"

"No, it's not going to make it," the Chief says disgustedly. "The Deacon and I were up on the Hill this afternoon counting noses, and it hasn't got a chance. The farm states will kill it. Rather than suffer the embarrassment of a defeat, the Boss should just pass the word to let it

die in committee. But he insists on bringing it to the floor
for a vote. Maybe he figures if Brother Kristos mumbles
a prayer, the bill will sail through without a fight. Fat
fucking chance!"

Tollinger goes back to his office, despondent at what
he's heard. Always an introspective man, he now finds he
cannot marshal his thoughts about Brother Kristos. What
began as fury at the preacher for having "converted" Jennifer has become an infinitely more complex emotion. And
one of the ingredients, he ashamedly admits, is fear.

There is a message on Tollinger's desk. Marvin Lindberg has called and left an Alexandria number. Tollinger
stares at the note, wondering what urgency would make
the ex-FBI man call him at the White House. But when
Lindberg comes on the phone, he doesn't sound urgent
at all.

"I've been back in town a few weeks," he reports,
"cleaning up my mail and getting the hayseeds out of my
hair. I was wondering if we can get together. At your con-
venience. Nothing important, just to talk."

"Sure, we could do that," Tollinger says slowly. "Listen, it's supposed to be a mild night. Suppose you come
out to my place, and I'll throw a couple of steaks on the
grill. I'm not a great cook, but I don't burn steaks."

"Sounds good to me," Lindberg says. "Around eight
o'clock or so?"

"Just right. What are you drinking these days?"

"Seltzer."

"Good for you," Tollinger says.

On the way home he stops at the market to buy two
thick New York strips, a container of mixed greens from
the salad bar, a large can of shoestring potatoes (ready to
eat), a six-pack of seltzer for Lindberg, and one of Molson's ale for himself. Shopping cheers him, and he finds
himself looking forward to playing the host.

The first thing he does in Spring Valley is concoct a double martini, which further improves his mood. He takes

off his suit and gets into chinos and a black cotton turtle-neck. Then he starts his preparations.

There's a tiled patio at the rear of the house, leading onto a small lawn. John opens the grill, gets a heap of charcoal briquettes lighted, and lets them grow a gray crust. He dusts the steaks with garlic powder, empties salad and potatoes into glass bowls, and sets the table. By that time his martini is gone, but he doesn't mix another.

Lindberg shows up just a few minutes late. The investigator looks scrawny, with a sallow complexion and hollows in his cheeks. But his eyes are bright and lively enough, and he slumps into a patio chair with a sigh of content. He watches Tollinger fork the steaks onto the grill.

"Man," he says. "If I told you what I've eaten the last few months, you'd upchuck. Grits? I've got 'em coming out my ears. I sure gave my taste buds some cruel and unusual punishment."

"Whatever happened to good old down-home southern cooking?"

"Must be a lost art; I couldn't find any."

"Medium-rare okay on the steak?"

"That'll do me fine. You don't mind if I nibble on these shoestrings while we're waiting, do you?"

"Of course not. And help yourself to more seltzer and ice when you're ready. It's all in the bucket. Nice night."

And so it is. Balmy, with just enough breeze to keep the bugs away, and a fat moon sailing through a cloudless sky. The odors of garlic and broiling steaks don't hurt either.

"You got the money okay?" Tollinger asks.

"No problem. That was quite a chase. I was really enjoying it until the end."

"Let's talk about it while we're demolishing all that red meat. I'm going to have an ale. That won't bother you, will it?"

"Sure, it'll bother me," Lindberg says. "Watching

someone else drink and remembering what it tastes like. But I've learned to live with it. One day at a time. Go ahead, have your ale. Just try not to smack your lips too much."

John remembers to bring the plates to the steaks and not vice versa. Once he had a big porterhouse slip off his barbecue fork while trying to convey it to the table. He serves them both, then uncaps and pours his Molson's.

"You still going to Alcoholics Anonymous?" he asks casually.

"Oh yeah," the ex-FBI man says, slicing into his meat. "While I was on the road, whenever I hit a town that had a group, I'd stop by for a meeting. Hey, this is great."

"Would you like A-1 or anything else?"

"Nah, this is fine. Listen, I'm sorry I couldn't get the goods on Brother Kristos. I really tried, but like I told you in my last letter, he seems to be clean as far as the law goes. So you spent a lot of money for nothing."

"Not so," Tollinger says. "Your reports told us much we didn't know. Good background stuff. Helps us understand what makes the man tick."

"Uh-huh," the investigator says, taking a fistful of potatoes. "He's really moving up in the world, isn't he?"

"Yes."

"Buddy-buddy with the President, visits to the Oval Office, advising on White House policy. Pretty good for a carny hustler who got his start reading the cards in Madame Olga's tent—wouldn't you say?"

"He's come a long way."

"Too long, as far as I'm concerned," Lindberg says. "Someone should really lower the boom on that guy."

"Who? And how?"

"There's got to be a way. I guess I'm off the case—right?"

"I'm afraid so. You did an excellent job, but there's not much point in further investigation. He's got enough reporters on his tail now. It's hard to pick up a paper or newsmagazine without reading something about him."

"Yeah," Lindberg says. "But maybe I'll still keep tabs on him."

Tollinger looks at him curiously. "Why would you want to do that?"

"Oh . . . just for the fun of it."

They finish their meal and push back from the table.

"I've got some ice cream," John says. "Heavenly Hash. Interested?"

"No, thanks. But I could do with some coffee."

"Instant okay?"

"Sure, that's all I drink."

"Would you like it iced?"

"Hey, that's a great idea. Black and strong."

Tollinger goes into the kitchen, dissolves some instant coffee in two highball glasses under the hot-water tap. Then fills the glasses with ice cubes and cold water. At the last minute he takes a gulp of his, then adds a wallop of cognac. He brings the iced coffees out to the patio.

Lindberg takes a swallow. "All *right!*" he says. "That'll put lead in my pencil. You added a brandy to yours, didn't you?"

"How did you know?"

"I can smell it. Brandy is pungent stuff, and since I knocked off booze and cigarettes, my sense of smell has improved a hundred percent."

They lounge quietly in the darkness, enjoying the calm night. There's a sudden burst of laughter from a neighbor's yard; life is going on and someone's enjoying it.

"I'm interested in why you want to keep digging at Brother Kristos," Tollinger says.

"I'm not trying to promote a job," Lindberg says. "Don't get me wrong. I'll do it on my own."

"But *why?*"

"Long story."

"I've got all night."

"It goes back years. I was a field agent working out of the Wichita office. A guy kidnapped a six-year-old girl. He took her through four states, raping her as he went. Then he strangled her, cut her body into pieces he wrapped in old newspapers. He left the bundles in trash-cans in Little Rock. We caught up with him in an abandoned barn not too far from Memphis. We told him to toss out his gun—he was packing a Luger—and come out with his hands up. He did as he was told, and I blasted him. It was good shooting. I put three in his chest in a pattern you could cover with the ace of spades. All the other guys, FBI and locals, swore he had pointed the Luger at me, so that was that."

Tollinger stirs uncomfortably. "Ever regret it?" he asks.

"Never," Marvin Lindberg says. "There were other cases after that, some worse. I came to the conclusion that everyone may be equal under the law, but some people are just plain rotten. Heredity and environment have nothing to do with it. They're born rotten, live rotten, and die rotten."

"Original sin?"

"Maybe. Anyway, I decided some people just don't deserve to live; it was as simple as that."

"Is that when you started drinking?" John asks quietly.

Lindberg stares at him. "Sometimes you're too damned smart," he says. "Actually I started serious boozing after my wife died. But that's neither here nor there. So, eventually, the FBI gave me the boot. One night I woke up in a Baltimore gutter. I was filthy and had been rolled, of course. They even took my shoes. I knew I was killing myself with the sauce, and that scared me. So the next night I went to Alcoholics Anonymous, and I've been dry ever since. Romantic story?"

"Not very," Tollinger says. "More grim than romantic."

"You know anything about AA?"

"Not a great deal."

"Well, it's got a strong religious foundation. You've got to believe in a Power *greater than yourself* if you really want to beat the bottle. AA isn't linked to any particular creed or sect, but it does ask you to believe in God *as you understand Him.* That probably sounds like a lot of bullshit to you, but all I can tell you is that it's working for me."

"That's the bottom line," Tollinger says.

Lindberg finishes his iced coffee and starts crunching the ice cubes. "The reason I'm boring you with this confession is so you'll understand how I feel about Brother Kristos. Acknowledging the reality of God has saved my life, and I don't take kindly to a bozo who trades on the idea to hustle a buck."

"Before you go on," John says, "I should tell you I'm a card-carrying agnostic."

"Different strokes for different folks," Lindberg says equably. "But when I finished tracing Kristos I realized that this guy is a world-class sleaze. He's taking the most precious thing in life, which is faith, and using it to make money, buy booze, and screw women. To him, religion's just another rigged game on a carnival midway to con the rubes."

"Wow," Tollinger says. "You really feel strongly about him, don't you?"

"Hate his guts. And that's why I'm going to keep walking up his heels for a while. Until I can expose him for the devil he is."

"Oh? And how do you propose to do that?"

The investigator is silent for so long that Tollinger wonders if he's going to answer. Finally Lindberg uncaps another bottle of seltzer, takes a swallow, then bends forward, forearms on his thighs.

"You trusted me to keep my mouth shut," he says. "I guess I can trust you to keep this under your hat. So here's another story for you. I wasn't personally involved in this, but I heard about it from an agent who was working in the San Diego office. The perps were a con man and his wife, both in their late thirties. Good-looking, well-dressed people. They made a nice living selling phony oil stock to widows and running crooked card games on cruise ships.

"They had a daughter who, according to my pal, was a real looker. She was only fifteen, but she was tall, had a body that didn't end, and when she put on the right makeup and an elegant evening gown, she could pass for a young woman of twenty-one. So they worked out this variation of the old badger game.

"The family would check into a hotel where there was a convention. The daughter would cruise the cocktail bar and try to promote a middle-aged geezer who was half in the bag and wanted to prove what a demon lover he was. The daughter would give the signal to mommy when she had landed a fish, and then go up to the guy's hotel room.

"Her parents would give her maybe ten minutes to strip down and for the guy to drop his pants. Then they'd start pounding on the hotel-room door, threatening to break it down. Inside, mommy would flash the daughter's birth certificate, and daddy would make like a cop, with a phony badge and fake ID. The conventioneer would be charged with trying to bang a female minor.

"After all the hysteria, the sucker was usually eager to pay off with all the cash he was carrying or could borrow. The scam went like silk, and the take per victim ranged from a couple of hundred to more than three thousand in one case. The family moved up and down the west coast, following the convention circuit. They had a nice thing going for more than a year."

"But they were caught?" Tollinger says.

"Eventually. Enough patsies had the gumption to file complaints after they sobered up, and gradually the Bureau built up a file with descriptions of the unholy threesome. The next time they hit San Diego, the man the daughter picked up in the cocktail bar was the guy who told me the story, the FBI agent."

"Fascinating," Tollinger says, "but what's it got to do with Brother Kristos?"

Lindberg stares at him. "That's how I'm going to cut him off at the knees," he says. "I'm going to con the con man. Look, I've given this a lot of thought. Kristos has three weaknesses: greed for money, thirst for vodka, and lust for women. I can't do much with the first two, but I think I can nail him on the third. From what I've heard, he just can't keep his zipper closed. So I'm going to sucker him with an underage piece of tail. I think he'll take the bait. Only he won't escape by paying off like the conventioneers. The mother will take the attempted statutory-rape charge to the newspapers. It will bring Brother Kristos down with a crash."

Lindberg sits back and gulps thirstily, finishing his seltzer. "Well?" he says. "What do you think?"

"Tawdry," John says, "but effective—if it works."

"Oh, it'll work," Lindberg says confidently. "Some of the details have to be ironed out, but I've already got a mother and daughter lined up to play the game. They're perfect for the parts. Central Casting couldn't do better."

"They want payment for going along?"

"Of course."

"And that's why you're telling me about the scheme. You want me to bankroll it."

"Not you personally. The people you represent."

"How much will it cost?"

"Two thousand in advance. Mother and daughter get to keep that even if the scam flops. Another five grand if it succeeds. Nothing for me. Except satisfaction."

"I think I need another brandy," Tollinger says.

He goes into the kitchen, pours a heavy shot of cognac into his empty iced coffee glass, and drinks it off. He realizes his ebullient mood has vanished. He wonders if the melancholy is due to his corruption from a man of thought to a man of action.

He returns to the patio.

"All right," he says. "Let's do it."

=10=

They meet in Mrs. Mattingly's sitting room, with Brother Kristos seated in the largest wicker armchair, regarding the others with his implacable stare.

The First Lady is present, with Jennifer Raye on her right. Lu-Anne Schlossel fidgets on a chintz-covered couch alongside Lenore Mattingly. Emily Mattingly perches on a wicker hassock padded with a bright corduroy cushion.

Kristos eats and drinks nothing, but the ladies are served tea and ginger cookies by Agnes Brittlewaite with surly indifference.

Lu-Anne waits until Agnes has left the room before resuming her discourse.

"I hate to be the bearer of bad news, Mrs. Hawkins," she says, "but you can tell the President that the food-sharing bill is in deep trouble. We'll approve it in committee, but it'll lose if it's brought to the House floor. In the Senate, from what I hear, it'll never get out of committee."

"My husband will be disappointed," Mrs. Hawkins says sadly. "As I am. Is there no way to save it? So many hungry people are in need."

"Granted," Schlossel says, "but the farm lobby has dumped on us."

"They've mounted an enormously well-organized and well-financed campaign," Raye adds. "I'm sure you've all seen the newspaper ads and TV commercials. Their pitch is that the bill must be defeated to preserve the family farm. They never mention that these days most food is produced by multimillion-dollar conglomerates that are afraid food sharing will cut into their profits."

"It's not fair!" Emily bursts out. "I see those pictures of families with little children waiting on line at a soup kitchen to get some watery stew and a piece of bread, and I just want to cry."

"We do what we can personally," her mother says, "and I'm sure all our friends contribute as well. But private charities can only do so much. I read the other day that there are now twenty million hungry people in the country. Can you imagine? Twenty million!"

"Brother Kristos," the First Lady says, "is there anything you can suggest that might help get the bill passed? After all, the polls show that the majority of the people are in favor of it."

The ladies look at him expectantly, and he slowly closes his eyes. They wait silently, thinking he may be praying. When he opens his eyes, they see that his stare has intensified.

"The bill will pass, sisters," he pronounces in his toneless voice. "The hungry will be fed. That is my vow to you."

The mood lightens; the ladies look at each other with relieved smiles.

"May I tell my husband that?" Mrs. Hawkins asks.

"Yes," Brother Kristos says. "Tell the father that he will succeed, and his act of mercy shall be blessed."

He stands abruptly. He is wearing his black silk cossack shirt, gold cross, diamond ring, a bracelet of linked gold ankh emblems.

"It is the Divine Will," he says, "and the Eternal Preserver shall feed his children. Trust in God, and your faith shall be rewarded. Now I must leave you, for I have much to do to further the Lord's commands. Representative Schlossel, will you accompany me, please?"

Startled, Lu-Anne rises, gathers up her coat and handbag, and hurries out of the room after the preacher. She follows him up the stairs to his apartment. He gestures toward the big table in the study, then bolts the door. He goes into the bedroom, returns with the crystal decanter of vodka and two glasses.

"Is this how you further the Lord's commands, parson?" she asks mockingly.

"It helps," he says, not smiling.

"Just a little for me," she says. "The House has a night session scheduled."

He pours a bit into her glass, then fills his. He pulls his armchair closer.

"That stuff you told us downstairs," she says, "about the food-sharing bill being passed—do you really believe that or was it just mumbo jumbo to give hope to the faithful?"

"It will be passed."

She takes a sip of her drink. "And after you get it passed, are you going to take a walk on the Potomac River?"

He ignores that. "I wish to speak to you of something else. You have worked long and hard on the President's bill, and you deserve to know. Vice President Trent is my sworn enemy. He thinks I have an unholy influence on Hawkins."

"That's no secret. I've been hearing rumors about Trent for months."

"What you haven't heard is that Trent is planning to meet with top party leaders to destroy me."

"Yeah," she says, looking at him curiously. "And how did you learn that—a voice from on high?"

He takes a deep swallow of vodka. "From what the reporters would call 'an unimpeachable source.' Trent doesn't like what is happening to the party. He thinks it is being taken over by the minorities and what he calls the 'crazies.' "

"He means people who work for a living. He inherited his money."

"Well, the purpose of the meeting is to persuade party big shots to desert Hawkins and support Trent as candidate in the presidential election."

Schlossel abruptly drains her drink.

"He's got more ambition than brains," she says. "But in this case I must admit that he's got something going for him. If the party takes a bath in the midterm elections—and all the experts are predicting it will—everyone will be looking for a scapegoat, and Abner Hawkins is a natural."

"There's more," Brother Kristos says, refilling his own glass. "If Trent gets a go-ahead from the money men, he may very well resign immediately. Then he'll blast Hawkins for being my puppet and betraying the party's traditions by catering to special-interest groups."

Schlossel looks at him in astonishment. "You really are a conjureman," she says. "Trent resign? Are you sure?"

"It's a good possibility."

She ponders a moment. "Yeah," she says finally, "it makes sense from Trent's point of view. He'll use you as a whipping boy. And when the food-sharing bill is defeated, Trent will be in an even stronger position."

"But the bill will not be defeated."

"So you say. But how do you figure to get it passed?"

"After the elections, I will wait a few months, and then I will suggest to the President that he withdraw his original food-sharing bill and submit a new one to Congress. The second bill will have the same provisions as the first, but it will also include increased farm-support prices."

Schlossel's eyes widen. Then she leaps to her feet, embraces Brother Kristos, and kisses him on the lips.

"Oh, you genius!" she cries. "What a great idea! The

bill will just sail through. How can the farmers object to something that'll put more loot in their pockets?"

"I come from a farming family," the preacher says stolidly. "I am in favor of giving away the government's surplus food, but it should not hurt the prices farmers get for what they sweat to produce. That is not right."

"I'll buy that," Lu-Anne says, nodding. "Listen, if you ever decide to run for public office, let me know first. Beautiful, parson. Just beautiful! But tell me something: Why do you want to wait until after the elections to get Hawkins to amend his bill? If he does it immediately, the party stands a good chance of sweeping the vote."

"Because the party's fate does not concern me," Brother Kristos says coldly. "I *want* it to lose the elections. Because I want Samuel Trent to resign as Vice President. *Then* Hawkins will submit his revised bill, and it will be passed. Hawkins will become the party's nominee again."

"In other words you want to smash Trent?"

"I do. The man is not godly."

She whoops with delight. "Not godly? That's the best reason I've ever heard for screwing a politician. I'm glad I'm your friend and not your enemy. I *am* your friend, am I not?"

"Yes," he says with his lupine grin. "A valuable friend."

"Then what the hell are we waiting for?" she says, rising, grabbing his hand, pulling him toward the bedroom. "Let's go seal our friendship. I hear you're a holy terror in the sack."

Her small body is all bone, tendon, muscle. She has strength, and her skin is black velvet.

"Flat tits and flat ass," she tells him, "but I've got juice. Be as rough as you like; I bend but I don't break."

She wraps herself around him, exploring his flesh.

"What's this?" she asks, stroking the scar across his belly.

"Knife fight."

"And these?" she demands, touching the scabbed wounds on his back. "Looks to me like you got a whupping."

"Yes."

"Some man of God you are," she scoffs. "Well, come on, conjureman, show me some magic."

She meets him, rut for rut. Their demonic exertions roll them off the bed onto the floor. She takes his weight with grunts of joy, pulling on his hair, beard, furred shoulders, to bring him closer, tighter.

"Lordy!" she gasps once, and then takes his furious pounding with bared teeth and closed eyes.

Until, raw and spent, exhausted and dulled, they lie without moving.

She opens her eyes, lifts his head to stare at him.

"The Lord is my shepherd," she whispers. "I shall not want."

"Amen," says Brother Kristos.

=11=

On the flight to New York, Trent asks for the third time, "Have all the arrangements been made?"

"Yes, sir," Oberfest says patiently. "A limo will meet us at the airport and take us directly to the Bedlington. A suite has been reserved in my name. It will be stocked with liquor, mixes, ice, cigars, cigarettes."

"Maybe we should have provided dinner," Trent says worriedly.

"I don't think so, sir," his personal aide says. "Eating would just be a distraction. And you said yourself that the meeting shouldn't last more than two or three hours."

"Yes, that's right. That should be enough time for me to convince them, eh?"

"Yes, sir."

"Will you serve as bartender? These men are accustomed to being waited on."

"Yes, sir."

"And don't speak unless you are asked a direct question."

"Yes, sir."

The suite at the Hotel Bedlington is not lavish, but it's comfortable enough. Trent decides it's overheated and has Oberfest open a window. He inspects the bar that's been wheeled in and is gratified by the variety of bottles. And the vodka is American. He also checks to make certain a fresh roll of toilet paper has been provided in the bathroom.

"It's the little things that count," he tells Michael.

The four men who arrive singly during the next half-hour may not be the wealthiest party members, but they are rich enough, active in party affairs, and wield a great deal of influence on party policy and organization. All self-made millionaires, they recognized a long time ago that power unused is power denied.

They all know each other, of course, and after Oberfest has supplied them with drinks and cigars, there is ribald joshing amongst the four that Trent feels would be more suitable in the locker room of a country club than at an important political conference.

The men are Weisbard, Nugent, Packinhouse, and Whitman, all chief executive officers of large corporations. When their raucous jollity ebbs, he stands and waits until he has their attention. Then he launches into the speech he has rehearsed twice, once in the presence of Matilda, whose reaction was, "Are you sure you know what you're doing?"

"First, I wish to thank you for coming," he says. "I am fully aware of how busy each and every one of you is. But the matter I wish to discuss with you is of such importance that I felt a confidential meeting was essential."

He then relates what they already know: the most recent polls indicate that in the November elections the party will lose control of the Senate, and its majority in the House of Representatives will be reduced by ten to fifteen members. In addition, it is predicted the party will lose three or four governorships and myriad other state and local offices.

"This sorry state of affairs," Trent says, beginning to thunder, "is the fault of one individual: Abner Randolph Hawkins, the so-called President of the United States."

"Whoa, Sam," Nugent says. "That's pretty strong talk."

"The times demand nothing else," Trent says forcibly. "If no one else will say it, I shall: Abner Hawkins is destroying the party. Unless energetic actions are taken now, we face a continuing erosion of public support, a debacle from which it may take us twenty years to recover."

There is no response from his listeners, their faces set in the masklike rigidity of poker players holding a pair of twos.

"Are there hungry people in this great nation?" Trent goes on. "Of course there are. Always have been. But this ill-considered plan is no way to solve the problem. An enlarged food-stamp program would have more beneficial effects over a longer period without the disastrous political fallout."

Trent then states that it is common knowledge that the President has become a pawn manipulated by an alleged faith healer, a man widely reported to be a drunk and a womanizer, who now, in effect, dictates the domestic policies of the administration.

"This Brother Kristos," Trent says, almost choking with anger, "is a fraud, a faker, a charlatan, a *thief!* And yet he has ready access to the Oval Office and has slept in the Lincoln Bedroom. Eventually the entire country will realize that we have a devil in the White House."

"You've got a point there, Sam," Packinhouse says, relighting his cold cigar. "At my club, all they talk about is whether or not Brother Kristos is banging the First Lady."

"And talk of that nature will continue," Trent says, "until this administration becomes a laughingstock. I know that as Vice President it is my duty to provide enthusiastic support for the policies of our Chief Executive. But one of the reasons I have called you here today is to tell you honestly that I can no longer provide that support."

There is a pause then while Oberfest refills glasses and passes around fresh cigars. Trent has his first drink, a brandy and soda, but only takes a small sip.

"Sam," Nugent says, looking at him thoughtfully, "you paint a gloomy picture. I'm not saying you're totally wrong, but I don't think things are as bad as you say. Perhaps some of us could talk to Hawkins, get him to straighten up and fly right."

"Impossible," the VP says definitely. "He and his wife are totally convinced that Brother Kristos twice saved their son's life. They won't listen to a word against him."

"All right," Packinhouse says, "I think we agree we've got a serious problem. What's your solution?"

Samuel Trent takes a deep breath. This is it.

"When you suffer from a malignant tumor," he says, "your only hope of survival is surgery. I suggest the party excise Abner Hawkins as quickly and painlessly as possible. We must have the courage to face facts, gentlemen: Hawkins' is strictly a one-term presidency. It is not too early to begin seeking a more attractive candidate for the presidential election two short years from now."

"You, for instance?" Weisbard says.

"Yes, me," Samuel Trent says with much dignity. "I shall not attempt to delude you with false modesty. I consider myself a rational man with many years of experience at all levels of public service. In addition, I have been a loyal party member since arriving at voting age. My contributions to the party, in money, time, and energy, have been considerable. I have a large and faithful personal following, particularly in Boston. And I need hardly remind you that I have sufficient personal wealth to enable me to finance a large part of my precampaign costs on my own."

The four men look at each other.

"All I ask of you," Trent continues, "is tacit approval of the course I have set for myself. I freely admit that I cannot succeed without that approval. But I must also add that I intend to persevere no matter what. I feel so strongly about what I have said to you here that I am seriously considering resigning as Vice President of the United States."

His words have the desired dramatic effect. His four listeners drain their drinks.

"Are you serious, Sam?" Nugent says.

"I have never been more serious in my life. My enemies have accused me of many things, but never of being a hypocrite. I cannot continue to defend and support an administration in which I no longer have faith or respect."

"Who knows about this?" Packinhouse asks.

"Only my wife. And now you gentlemen and my personal aide."

"Sam," Weisbard says kindly, "on my way into the hotel I noticed a quiet cocktail lounge just off the lobby. I wonder if we could ask you and your aide to leave us and spend about a half-hour down there. It'll give us a chance to have a little private confab here, discuss what you've told us, and decide what our reactions should be. I hope you won't be offended."

"Of course not," Samuel Trent says, immediately offended. "I understand perfectly. Michael, come with me, please."

After the two have left the suite, the four men rise, open the window wider to rid the room of cigar smoke.

"Cut the bullshit," Weisbard says, "and he makes a lot of sense."

"But can he be a winner?" Nugent asks. "I'd rather go with a penniless winner than a rich loser."

"The man is a fucking idiot," Packinhouse says.

"Yeah," Whitman says, speaking for the first time, "but he's *our* fucking idiot."

=12=

Oberfest slumps in the front seat of Marchuk's car, glaring balefully at the radio in the walnut dash. He is certain it contains a recorder, and every word he has reported on Trent's meeting in New York is now on tape.

"Finish your story," the Russian says impatiently. "Surely there is more."

"Well, when we came back up from the cocktail lounge, they gave Trent their decision. It wasn't an out-and-out okay, but it wasn't a turndown either. They told him to do what he felt he had to do. They were very honest about it. They said they didn't want to pledge their support until they know definitely how the elections turn out. Then, if the party took a shellacking, and Trent resigned and announced his hat was in the ring for—"

"Hat in the ring?" the KGB man says. "What means that?"

"That he's a candidate for president. If he does that, and public reaction is favorable, the four men as much as promised Trent that he can count on their cooperation."

"I see," the major says. "In other words, they will desert President Hawkins and aid that despicable Vice President."

"You've got it."

"Very discouraging."

"Well, the Veep made a strong presentation, and the idea of a preacher advising the President really turns them off. That's why they're willing to see how far and how fast Trent can run."

"I don't like it," Marchuk says fretfully. "Trent is sure to appeal to all the Red-bashers in your country. I had hoped those days had ended."

"Well, they haven't," Oberfest says with some satisfaction. "And when Hawkins' food-sharing bill is defeated, that'll be another plus for Trent. He'll inherit the farm vote."

"You believe he deliberately intends to turn the party to the right?"

"You better believe it."

The Russian takes a deep breath. "I shall report all this and let the great brains in Moscow puzzle it out. They will decide what our reaction should be. Meanwhile, keep me informed on Trent's plans. Are you maintaining contact with John Tollinger in the White House?"

"Yep. I figured I'd drop by his office tomorrow and repeat what I've told you."

"Good. The President's men should know of Trent's treachery."

"Believe me, it will come as no surprise."

=13=

A late October wind comes moaning in from the northwest, and the afternoon is brazen with a weakling sun and a scum of scudding clouds. Not much traffic on the road, and Marvin Lindberg pushes his battered Buick with insouciant disregard of balding tires and thumping trunk lid loosely tied with a piece of twine.

"I think it's time you put this clunker out to pasture," Tollinger tells him. "It's a menace to you and everyone else."

"And buy a Mercedes or BMW?" Lindberg says. "Don't I wish it. Brother Kristos can afford a new Scorpio; not me."

Tollinger, fully realizing what a sordid escapade he has approved and is helping to finance, is tempted to leave it all to the ex-FBI man. But he concludes that would be cowardly, and besides, if the scheme succeeds, he wants to be a witness to Kristos' downfall.

Seated in the back of the car are Mrs. Tessie Lapchick and her daughter, Judy. The mother, an overblown woman with a raddled face and a beehive of hennaed hair, assured John during their introduction that she would have no objection at all if he calls her Babe. In return, she promised, she will address him as Jack. It is a name he loathes.

It is difficult to believe that daughter Judy is only fifteen years old, even though Mrs. Lapchick has produced a birth certificate to prove it. Tollinger guesses she is five feet, eight inches tall and weighs perhaps 120 pounds, most of it in her bust and behind. She has straight wheaten hair down to her bum, and her rather sharp features are a curious and exciting mixture of childish innocence and adult guile.

John has no doubt that the girl can easily pass as a young woman of twenty or so. The dress she is wearing adds to the impression of knowing sophistication. It has long sleeves and a high neck, but clings to her body like a second skin, ending three inches above dimpled knees. Her legs are bare, shapely, and shaved smooth.

Mrs. Lapchick's costume for her role as avenging mother is a rusty black dress, loose-fitting and adorned with a tarnished brass pin in the shape of a leaping dolphin. She wears a light coat of soiled tan poplin, but Judy has nothing over her revealing dress and, Tollinger reckons, nothing under. She carries a large suede shoulder bag.

During most of the drive down to Brother Kristos' church, Lindberg directs a final run-through of the parts both women are to play. He has obviously rehearsed them well, and John is surprised at how natural and believable their dialogue sounds. He becomes increasingly confident that Brother Kristos will be unable to resist the trap being set for him.

They arrive at the tobacco barn at the same time other vehicles are pulling up and discharging congregants. The fields around have been blacktopped, and lines painted to delineate parking spaces.

"Look at that," Marvin says, almost admiringly. "He's installed parking meters. That guy doesn't miss a trick."

He parks and reaches out his window to slip two quarters into the meter. Then he turns and lifts Judy's shoulder bag into the front seat. He takes two electronic devices from the glove compartment and shows them to Tollinger.

"This small one is a combination microphone and transmitter. Range about three hundred yards. Battery-powered. On-off switch. Volume control. This is the receiver-recorder. With loudspeaker. Also battery-powered. Enough tape for ninety minutes. I've checked them out a dozen times, and they do the job. Good reception and not too much interference. Made in Japan, of course."

He places the receiver-recorder on the front seat, and tucks the microphone-transmitter into Judy's bag.

"Don't touch the volume control, honey," he tells her. "After the sermon is over, just reach in and flip the switch to On. Then you try to have a private meeting with Brother Kristos, and take it from there."

"Sure," Judy says in a bored voice. "I know what to do."

"Of course you do. We'll be listening out here, and if the guy gets physical, we'll come in like gangbusters, so there's nothing to be scared about."

"Who's scared?" she says. "I can handle the guy."

"Sure you can," Lindberg says. "Okay, in you go. Remember, don't turn on the mike until the sermon is finished. The batteries are fresh, but we don't want them to run down."

The girl gets out of the car, tugs her skirt down, slings the bag over her shoulder.

"Ma," she says, "you think we'll get home in time to catch the *Gilligan's Island* reruns?"

"I put the VCR on timed record," Mrs. Lapchick says. "So even if we're late, you won't miss anything."

They watch the young girl sashay away. She joins the throng of worshipers entering the church and disappears inside.

"His sermons usually last about twenty minutes," Lindberg says. "Half-hour at the most. So we got some time to kill."

"I think I'll take a stroll around and smoke a pipe," Tollinger says.

"Take your time," the investigator says. "Babe and I will stay here and lie to each other about our love affairs."

"Oh you!" she says.

John wanders beyond the parking area to an empty field with a dried stubble of mown grass. He is not wearing a coat, but there is a tad of winter in that northwest wind, and as he paces slowly up and down, pipe clamped between his teeth, he turns up the collar of his jacket and shoves his hands into his trouser pockets.

He marvels again at the absurdity of life. Never, in the nuttiest of fantasies, could he conceive of spending an evening like this one: waiting to entrap a religious crazy by offering him the ripe body of an underage sexpot. A new form of pimpery, he reflects mordantly, and not one to buttress self-esteem.

But he has chosen public service as a career, and no one ever promised it was a sanitary profession. And he learned a long time ago that debating whether or not the end justifies the means is as futile as arguing how many angels can rumba on the head of a pin.

Public service is practically an oxymoron. Too often the good of the many takes second place to the gain of the few. Not because all public servants and politicians are venal; they are not. They are simply human.

Engrossed with these melancholy reflections, he is scarcely aware of time's passage. But then his pipe, smoked out, gurgles noisily, and he taps out the dottle on the heel of his hand and hurries back to the Buick.

They wait almost five minutes in the car, watching the door of the church. Then it opens, parishioners begin to stream out.

"Here we go," Lindberg says tensely. He switches on the receiver-recorder. Cassette reels under the clear plastic lid begin to revolve slowly.

Silence for another moment or two, then the miniature loudspeaker crackles with static.

"She's turned on the mike," Lindberg says. "Good girl."

They hear the confused sound of many voices, the

scrape of wooden benches, then, unexpectedly sharp and clear, Judy saying, "Excuse me, but could I see Brother Kristos for a few minutes? In private. I've really got to talk to him."

Pause. A woman says, "You wait here. I'll see if he's available."

They wait silently in the car, trying to visualize the action inside the barn.

Judy stands patiently, spine straight, head erect. She's wearing high-heeled pumps, and her feet are beginning to hurt. Pearl Gibbs finally returns.

"Brother Kristos can see you now," she says. "Try to keep it short. He has a very important meeting scheduled."

"It won't take long," Judy promises.

Inside the back room, the preacher is standing, one hand propped on the wooden table. He is still wearing his burlap robe. The pale hound is crouched at his feet.

"Brother Kristos," the girl says breathlessly, "I wanted to tell you that your sermon tonight was the most important thing that ever happened to me in my life."

He nods, inspecting her closely, and then begins combing his fingers slowly through his beard.

"I have a personal problem," Judy goes on, "and I thought a man like you who's so sympathetic and understanding and all could tell me what to do."

He nods again and gestures toward one of the chairs. She lowers the shoulder bag to the floor, then sits down and crosses her bare legs; the short skirt hikes up. Brother Kristos pulls another chair close and sits facing her.

"What is your problem, daughter?" he asks.

She looks down at her hands, twists her fingers. "It's embarrassing to talk about," she says with a nervous giggle. "You'll probably laugh at me."

"I shall not laugh."

"Well, I'm twenty years old—will be next month anyway—and, uh, I've never been with a man, if you know what I mean."

"You are a virgin?"

"Yes, I am. I know a lot of men, some of them very nice, and I date a lot. But most of the men I go out with want to go to bed with me. You know? I'm not old-fashioned about sex or anything like that, but it frightens me. I mean it's a big step for me to take. All my girlfriends do it and think I'm silly to feel the way I do. I tell them I want to wait until I'm married, but the real reason is that the whole idea of sex scares me. I know the way I feel isn't normal, and I was hoping there was something you could do so I could get rid of my fear. Like you said tonight, what happens between a man and a woman is pleasing to God."

Brother Kristos leans forward and reaches to take her soft hands in his.

Outside in the car they have listened to this dialogue breathlessly. Lindberg raises the volume slightly.

"She's doing a fine job," Tollinger says in a low voice.

"Just the way we rehearsed," Lindberg says.

"My daughter is one smart cookie," Mrs. Lapchick says proudly.

Then they are quiet, straining to hear the voices coming from the little black box.

Kristos: "You are wrong when you say the fear you feel is not normal, daughter. Everyone, man and woman, has that same fear. And though it may diminish with experience, it never totally disappears."

Judy: "I'm not sure I understand what you mean."

"Now he's going to make his pitch," Lindberg says.

Kristos: "Physical intimacy between man and woman is a religious experience. And so it is part mystery. It is natural that we feel terror of the unknown. But our fears should not prevent our seeking the pathway to spiritual bliss."

"Spiritual bliss?" Lindberg says incredulously. "A

bang? What's he talking about? Why doesn't he get on with it?"

Judy: "So you think I should do it?"

Kristos: "Whatever is in your heart, daughter."

Judy: "Just the idea of sex sends shivers up my spine. Maybe if I could be sure the man would be gentle and loving and not hurt me . . ."

"Great line," Tollinger says. "That should turn him on."

Kristos: "You are a beautiful young woman. It is a gift from God, and you must cherish it. Do not seek the ecstasy of which I spoke until you are certain the man is right for you. Your body is a temple. It is a holy place, and only by loving in the service of God can you find joy."

"We just lost him," Tollinger says, trying to control his anger and not succeeding.

Kristos: "Go forth, child, and seek a man with whom you may share the glory of God. And resolve to conquer your fears and discover the oneness with the Almighty that only physical love can bring."

"Shit!" Lindberg says furiously. "He made her for a shill. Notice how he called her *child.* Now how did he know that?"

Kristos: "And now you must leave me, for I have God's work to do. Go with my blessing and find the happiness you deserve."

Judy (faintly): "Thank you, Brother Kristos."

There are scrapings, the click of Judy's high heels on the barn floor. The investigator turns off the receiver, and they wait in gloomy silence.

The young girl comes out of the church and skips over to the car. She's carrying a slim book, and displays it before she slides into the Buick.

"Look what he gave me," she says. *"Brother Kristos' Prayers for All Occasions.* Isn't that nice? He's a real doll."

"Oh yeah," Marvin Lindberg says. "The son of a bitch!"

=14=

On election night three television sets are wheeled into the Oval Office, plugged in, and switched to the three national networks. Soft drinks, pretzels, and salted peanuts are set on a sideboard, and tally sheets are available for anyone who wants to keep a record as the results come in.

The chamber gradually fills with the President's senior aides. There are not enough chairs for everyone but no one complains because no one expects to stay past midnight. "After all," Chief of Staff Folsom says, "how long can an execution take?"

The President is seated behind his big desk, listening to the banter with a fixed smile but saying very little. Occasionally he glances across the room to where Brother Kristos, clad in black, stands with his back against the wall. The preacher observes the activity in the Oval Office, but makes no effort to talk to the President's men.

Early on, it becomes evident that the preelection polls were accurate: the party is going to suffer a major defeat.

By ten P.M. the Senate and three governorships are lost, and the party's majority in the House of Representatives reduced by twelve, with predictions of five more when the western count is completed. In addition, four state legislatures, mayoralties in several large cities, and many elective judicial offices are won by the opposition. It is not a complete rout, but certainly a serious setback.

The lighthearted banter has long since turned to gallows humor, and because all the drinks on the sideboard are nonalcoholic, the room slowly empties as staffers drift away.

Last to leave is Henry Folsom. "Better times are coming, Mr. President!" Stewards wheel away the television sets and remove the scarcely touched refreshments from the sideboard. Then Hawkins and Kristos are left alone. The President beckons and the preacher takes the armchair alongside the desk.

"The Lord gave," Hawkins says with a strained smile, "and the Lord hath taken away."

"Yes, father," Kristos says. "And the remainder of that verse is 'Blessed be the name of the Lord.'"

The President rubs his forehead wearily. "I expected a midterm defeat, but this is heavy." He rises and moves about the office turning off lamps. "Saving the taxpayers' money," he says wryly, then slumps back into his leather swivel chair. "I'm afraid the loss of the Senate means the food-sharing bill is dead. I know you told my wife it will be passed, but now I don't believe it has a chance."

"It will be passed," Brother Kristos says. "All in good time."

"I wish I had your confidence."

They sit silently in the gloom, the President gazing down at the desktop, nervous fingers twirling a pencil with a broken point.

"Father," Brother Kristos says calmly, "this is a temporary disappointment, nothing more. You are a man of faith, of courage and resolve, I know that. You must not allow this bad news to depress you. There is much good work still to be done. I believe in you, as all your children do. You are not a man to falter. You have the power of righteousness."

The President straightens in his chair, looks directly at the other man. "Thank you. And you are right, as usual. I cannot let this setback slow me down. My enemies in Congress and the media will say I have lost clout, that I no longer can produce results. But I intend to stick to my guns and go on fighting. This office is still the nation's command post."

Brother Kristos leans forward intently. "Repeat your continued support of the food-sharing bill," he advises. "Travel around the country. Talk to the hungry just as your wife has done. Bring home to every American the condition of these poor people. At the same time, announce in another television speech your intention to seek legislation that will enable the federal government to build thousands of units of low-income housing. And finally, appoint a commission to study the best way to repair and restore the nation's bridges and roads and dams and waterways and all the physical things that keep our system functioning."

"The infrastructure."

"Yes. I have traveled much, and I can tell you the country needs new sources of fresh water, new ways to dispose of waste. Only you can move the people to demand a cleaner, safer, healthier land."

"Brother Kristos, I agree with everything you say, but I can think of a dozen reasons why what you suggest is politically impractical. You may believe that faith can move mountains. Not in government! The first reaction of every politician will be: Where is the money coming from? And how do I answer that? With higher taxes? That's political suicide."

"Father, if your faith is strong enough, and you can communicate that faith to the nation, the money will be found."

"You are an idealist."

"No!" Brother Kristos says sharply. "I am a realist, for I know these things can be accomplished. They have not been tried because of greed, indifference, and lack of faith. Oh, father, what a fortunate man you are! For you have the power of igniting a renaissance."

The President is silent. Kristos stands and moves slowly toward the door.

"You ask a great deal," Hawkins calls after him.

The preacher turns to look at him sternly. "It is not I who ask. It is God who commands."

=15=

Samuel Trent has a long talk with Oberfest, planning the press conference at which Trent intends to announce his resignation.

"I don't think you should hold it in the auditorium or anywhere else on government property," Oberfest says. "It'll look strange if you use official facilities to say you're leaving the administration."

"A hotel ballroom?" the VP suggests.

"I don't think so, sir. All the gilt and crystal chandeliers—they'd give the wrong impression. You want someplace plain, down-home: a background to make you look like a man of the people."

Finally Michael comes up with an idea that the Veep approves: The press conference will be held outdoors, in the graveled driveway of the Trents' enormous old house near Chevy Chase Circle.

"If it rains," the aide says, "we can move it indoors. And if it's very cold, it'll cut down on the questions; everyone will want to get the story and split as soon as possible."

"Good thinking," Trent says. "Should my wife be standing at my side when I make my announcement?"

"I don't recommend it, sir. She'd just be a distraction. We want to keep you the center of interest."

"Of course. What do you suggest I wear?"

"Three-piece navy-blue suit, light blue shirt for the TV cameras, perhaps a maroon or regimental striped tie. I think it will be okay if you read your statement, but you want to come across as a man of principle."

"A man of principle," Trent repeats thoughtfully. "Yes, I can do that."

The morning of November ninth is raw, cold, overcast. But by noon the clouds have shredded away, the sky is a washed blue, and an orangy sun is warming a puffy breeze. Trent takes it as a good omen.

Oberfest has done his best to ensure media attention, assuring the press that the Vice President is going to make an announcement that will stun the world.

"Is he pregnant?" one editor asks.

About twenty reporters and two TV camera crews crowd onto the driveway, and precisely at 12:30, Trent marches from his front door. He is almost immediately surrounded by reporters thrusting tape recorders in his face. He is later reported to appear "grim" or "angry."

"First I have a brief statement to read," he says. "Then I shall answer your questions as honestly as I can. Copies of the statement will be available later."

He then begins reading:

"This morning I personally delivered to President Abner Hawkins my letter of resignation as Vice President of the United States."

There is a gasp, and the mob presses closer.

"Since I am no longer able to support and defend the policies of this administration, I decided that the only honorable course I could take would be to resign, effective immediately. That I have done, with sorrow and yet with relief that I will now be able to convey to the American public my own independent views on the serious problems that confront us."

There is such a clamor that Trent is forced to hold up his palms.

"Please," he says, "this is too important a matter to become a circus. One question at a time."

"When did you deliver your letter of resignation?"

"This morning, at approximately nine-thirty."

"Did you hand it to the President personally?"

"Yes."

"Where?"

"In the Oval Office."

"Who else was present?"

"Chief of Staff Henry Folsom."

"What was the President's reaction?"

"He read my letter and asked if I was certain in my own mind that I wanted to do this. I told him I was."

"Did he try to talk you out of it?"

"No."

"How did he seem to you? Angry? Disappointed? Sad?"

"You'll have to ask him that."

"You said you're resigning because you're no longer able to support and defend the policies of this administration. Was the President aware of how you felt?"

"I'm sure he was."

"What were your disagreements with him?"

"There were many."

"Such as?"

"The food-sharing bill, for one."

"Anything else?"

"The polarization that bill has caused in the party. I am totally convinced that the President is moving the party to the left. I happen to believe that its future lies in the middle of the road, making its appeal to all intelligent voters of this great nation who are not radicals of either the right or the left."

"What about Brother Kristos?"

"What about him?"

"It is said he influences White House policy. Do you object to that?"

"Of course I do. It will be a tragedy for this great nation

if religion and politics become inextricably entwined. Read your Constitution, young man. The first words of the Bill of Rights—the very *first*—are 'Congress shall make no law respecting an establishment of religion . . .' Our wise and far-seeing Founding Fathers knew very well the dangers of religion intruding on government. Of course I object to the reported influence of Brother Kristos, just as I would object to the representative of any religion dictating government policy."

"Sir, does your resignation mean you are retiring from politics?"

"By no means. In fact, I look upon it as the start of a new career in public service."

"So it's possible you may run for public office again?"

"Very possible."

"For President?"

"It's too early to speak of that."

"But you don't rule it out?"

"I refuse to foreclose on any option. Now, ladies and gentlemen, I think we have covered all important matters. Thank you for your attention."

Trent marches back into his house. Oberfest stays behind to hand out copies of the one-sentence letter of resignation and the written press statement.

"Well!" Trent says brightly to his wife. "I believe it went excellently."

"I'm sorry I wasn't able to hear it."

"I'm sure you'll see the whole thing on television. Matilda, I am going to start planning my campaign immediately. I intend to do a lot of traveling. The only thing that bothers me is that I shall be forced to leave you alone a lot. I hope you won't be lonely."

"I'll try to cope, dear," she says, smiling sweetly.

=16=

It's the first snowfall of the season, but doesn't amount to much—just a light sifting of powder that will surely melt under the morning sun. But while it lasts, the trees wear a gauzy dress and the cold black earth is dappled with white.

The presidential helicopter arrives at Camp David late Friday afternoon, bringing the First Family, several of the President's aides, Jennifer Raye—who has been promoted to Helen's executive assistant—and Brother Kristos. The arrival of the preacher prompts the chef to start preparing a caldron of fish stew, plenty of pepper.

Kristos goes directly to his cabin. It now has a large driftwood cross affixed to the living-room wall and a handsome prie-dieu installed in the bedroom. He unpacks his new pigskin suitcase, which contains clothing changes for the weekend and three liters of vodka carefully wrapped.

He and Jennifer dine with the First Family, an occasion enlivened by George's seemingly inexhaustible supply of riddles. ("Why does a turkey cross the road? Because he thinks he's a chicken!") Before dessert is served, the President excuses himself to start on his paperwork. After the lemon ice and pralines are finished, George is sent off with Sergeant McShane to prepare for bed.

Helen, Jennifer, and Kristos move to the living room, where the ladies are served a second cup of coffee.

When the steward leaves the room, Kristos turns to Helen. "You seem subdued, anxious. Is it the President?"

"Yes," she says, trying a small smile. "He's been so depressed since Trent resigned. He says it's just politics, but I know he's taken it personally."

"Trent is a fool," Jennifer says roughly. "He's blinded by ambition. The man has dreams of being elected President. Never, never, never!"

Kristos stares at her. "Sometimes fools can be dangerous," he says. "The media have called him a man of principle because he resigned rather than continue serving an administration he can't support."

"His good publicity won't last long," she predicts. "The man is a dodo. Mrs. Hawkins, I think the President is better off without him."

"I don't know," she says doubtfully. "Ab feels that Trent could do a lot of damage, stirring up hostility between the haves and have-nots. My husband has always believed in consensus politics, even though there are certain fundamental beliefs he will never surrender."

"Your husband is a godly man," Brother Kristos tells her. "He tries to persuade by appealing to the best in people. Trent exploits their dark side, their fears, prejudices, greed, and cruelty. The President is right to be concerned about such a man, for he sets brother against brother and ignores the harmony God demands."

"At least," Jennifer says, "Trent's resignation will enable the President to nominate someone in tune with his beliefs."

"I know Ab has a list of twenty possible candidates," Helen says. "Brother Kristos, do you have a suggestion? Is there anyone in particular you'd like to see as our next Vice President?"

If this question surprises him, he doesn't show it. His expression is unchanged; his only movement is the slow combing of fingers through his beard.

"Yes," he says, "I would like to suggest someone for the father's consideration, someone both you ladies know. Representative Lu-Anne Schlossel."

They look at him in astonishment.

"I have thought much about this," Kristos goes on, "and have prayed to God for guidance. Before you give me your opinions, let me tell you the way I feel.

"First, I think Congress would confirm her appointment. She is black and has just been reelected by a large majority. Not only does Congress tend to support their more popular members, but many southern senators and representatives owe their elections to the black voters of their states. They would not care to risk their political future by offending those voters. In addition, she would receive enormous support from black and feminist organizations outside the government.

"As to Lu-Anne's qualifications, she is an experienced congresswoman whose many years on Capitol Hill have given her an insider's knowledge of how government works. She could be of invaluable aid in getting the President's legislation passed.

"Finally, Lu-Anne is a devout, caring woman who has never forgotten her past. She is one with the poor, the hungry, the homeless. Her entire political career has been devoted to helping the underdog."

There is a moment of silence. Then Jennifer says excitedly, "I think that's the best idea I've heard in my life! Lu-Anne Schlossel! Of course! I wish I had thought of her! Ma'am, don't you think she'd make a marvelous Vice President?"

"I don't know," Helen Hawkins says hesitantly. "She is very talented and capable, granted, but is the country ready for a woman *and* a black Vice President?"

"If not now," Brother Kristos says, "when?"

"It *is* an interesting idea," the First Lady says, "but wouldn't it split the party even further than it is now?"

"I believe that in this case your husband will think only of what is good for the country, not what is good for the party."

"Well, I certainly think Ab should know of your suggestion. Will you tell him, Brother Kristos?"

He replies in the magisterial manner he has recently adopted. "In all conscience," he says, "I do not believe I should. After all, I am not employed in public service, not a member of his administration, and I know so little about politics. Better the suggestion should come from you; I know how much your husband depends on your wise and loving counsel. Would you be willing to present Lu-Anne's name to the President as your own idea? I'm certain your recommendation would carry more weight than mine."

Mrs. Hawkins considers that a moment. "Very well," she says finally, "if that's the way you think it should be handled. And I'll try to be as enthusiastic about Lu-Anne as you and Jennifer are. But you must realize, the final decision is Ab's."

"Of course," Brother Kristos says gravely. "I would never attempt to influence the President."

A short time later he leaves the two women and returns to his own cabin. He uncaps one of the vodka bottles and fills a tumbler. He sips that as he undresses. He hangs his new cashmere Norfolk jacket carefully away in the closet and counts the money in his wallet before removing his Black Watch tartan trews. He slips the wallet beneath the mattress.

He takes off his tie and gray flannel shirt. He is wearing no undershirt, but his drawers are knitted silk long johns. He leaves those on and sits on the bed, the glass of vodka on the floor at his feet. He slides a file of correspondence from a hidden compartment in his suitcase.

Following the visit of Lamar B. Tumulty, and after the parking meters were installed and the prayer book published, Brother Kristos approached a small AM radio station that covers most of Virginia and part of the Carolinas, Tennessee, Kentucky, and West Virginia. He signed a contract to purchase six half-hours of radio broadcast time (five hundred dollars per half-hour) beginning at 8:30 A.M. on Sundays.

The program is called *Brother Kristos' Prayertime* and consists of a sermon, a prayer, and an appeal for contributions to keep the program on the air. The preacher tapes each *Prayertime* in advance, so it is not necessary for him to be present in the radio studio on Sunday morning.

After listening to the first tape submitted, the station's sound engineer said, "He sounds like a constipated duck." But by the wizardry of modern electronics, the technician is able to give Kristos' voice timbre and resonance. The voice radio listeners hear is totally unlike that heard by congregants at the tobacco-barn church.

Whether it is due to the preacher's new sonorities or to the problematic content of his sermons, *Brother Kristos' Prayertime* is a success. Contributions (mailed to a post-office box) average about eighteen hundred dollars a week, and the radio station receives a heavy volume of enthusiastic mail.

The general manager of the station has written Brother Kristos suggesting the preacher buy an hour of airtime every Sunday morning (one thousand dollars per hour) and enlarge the format. It could, the manager suggests, be called *Brother Kristos' Family Hour,* and include a choir, gospel singers, and a segment in which the preacher would offer spiritual advice on personal problems submitted by listeners.

Sitting in his silk drawers and sipping warm vodka, Brother Kristos rereads the station manager's letter and decides his suggestion has a great deal of merit. But before he produces an hour-long radio show, the preacher realizes he would be wise to appropriate more of Tumulty's ideas: give a formal name to his church, have it properly chartered and registered as a nonprofit religious organization, make certain his sermons and prayers are copyrighted, look into the possibilities of going nationwide with *Brother Kristos' Family Hour.*

All that requires the establishment of a functioning business, with an office, payroll, record-keeping, and so forth—matters in which Kristos has no expertise. He has always run a one-man operation, and now he acknowledges he will require legal and financial assistance if he hopes to take advantage of his current good fortune. He wonders ruefully if he has been smart to fob off Lamar B. Tumulty.

He is still ruminating on how he might best plan his future, when he becomes aware of a faint but persistent tapping at the outside door. He pads into the darkened living room on his bare feet and stands to one side of the door.

"Yes?" he says.

"Jennifer," she says in a low voice.

He opens the door just wide enough for her to slip through, then closes it and locks it behind her.

"Were you sleeping?" she asks.

"No."

"I brought some ice cubes," she says, holding up a plastic bag. "How about buying a thirsty girl a drink?"

They go into the bedroom. He mixes her an iced vodka and water, but keeps his drink neat and warm.

They sit on the bed, and she notices the file folder of correspondence. "Were you working?" she says. "I'm sorry I interrupted you."

"Nothing important. The radio station in Virginia wants me to increase my Sunday-morning prayer service to a full hour."

"That's wonderful! How can you say it isn't important? I should think you'd be happy and excited."

He shrugs. "I learned a long time ago what is important. Food on the table and a roof over your head. Those are basic things and meaningful. Money, possessions, fame, power—they mean nothing. 'Lay not up for yourselves treasures upon earth, where moth and rust doth corrupt, and where thieves break through and steal: But lay up for yourselves treasures in heaven.' "

"I think you get your greatest happiness in helping people," she says. "Like you did for Lu-Anne Schlossel tonight."

He looks at her, thinking of other things. "Do you have a lawyer?" he asks her.

"Just the man who handled my divorce."

"Does he do other things—business contracts, tax matters?"

"I suppose he does, but his specialty is divorces."

"I don't think he's for me. I'll find someone."

"Why don't you ask the President's general counsel? I'm sure he could give you some names."

"A woman," Brother Kristos says. "I would prefer a smart woman attorney."

Jennifer makes a moue. "You don't have any close men friends, do you? Every time I see you, you're surrounded by women. Don't you like men?"

"Of course. Some. But I have rarely found a man I can trust."

"You trust women?"

"Yes."

"Do you trust me?"

He stares at her, takes her free hand, places it on his genitals. Her fingertips stroke the smooth silk.

"You're making a tent," she says.

"Come into my tent."

"Do you want me to wash you?"

"Yes," Brother Kristos says. "Make me clean."

=17=

They no longer meet at the Maryland shopping mall.

"In this business," says Major Marchuk, "you do not establish routines. Patterns are death."

So they drive separately toward Annapolis, turn off the highway, and meet on a dirt road the Russian deems sufficiently dark and deserted for a midnight meeting.

It's a surprisingly warm night for mid-December, and they're able to get out of their cars and stroll up and down the lonely lane while Michael brings the KGB man up-to-date on the activities of Samuel Trent.

"He's rented a suite at the Madison," he reports, "and is in the process of organizing what is really a skeleton campaign staff. I mean he's interviewing people for media adviser and press secretary."

"But you will continue to serve as his personal aide?"

"Oh sure. I even got a small raise to compensate for the perks I lost when I left government service."

"Tell me, Arnold," the major says, "is Trent rich enough to pay all these expenses?"

Michael laughs. "He's got money he hasn't even counted yet. The last time I saw a published estimate of his net worth it was almost fifty million. It's probably more than that now. No one has ever accused him of being a big-time spender. Did I ever tell you he saves his tea bags? Uses them two or three times before he throws them away. Isn't that a hoot?"

"I do the same thing," the Russian says.

"Oh," Oberfest says.

They saunter in silence a few moments, walking up and down, never getting too far from their parked cars.

"You have been traveling with him?" Marchuk finally asks.

"I sure have. Detroit, Chicago, Denver, San Francisco—you name it."

"And tell me, what kind of reception does he receive?"

"I hate to disappoint you, but so far he's been a smash hit. He's got a new speech writer who's a real whiz—an ex-professor of English from Bowdoin. He's persuaded Trent to cut out the blather, try to use words of one or two syllables, and to stop saying 'great nation' like it's one word. Anyway, he gets a good reaction wherever he speaks. I've even seen some 'Trent for Prexy' buttons and bumper stickers."

"I don't like that," the Russian says.

"Didn't think you would," Oberfest says cheerfully.

"But what does he *say* that makes people like him?"

"At first it was the usual craperoo—you know, the old 'Get the country moving again' and 'This nation has a rendezvous with destiny' and 'Our greatest danger is lack of courage.' And of course he's been lambasting the Soviet Union. So far he's called your country the biggest prison in the world, a wicked wilderness, and an insane asylum run by the inmates. He refers to your leader as the Red Napoleon."

"We expected that," the major says gloomily. "The man is obsessed with hatred of all things Russian."

"Well, if it'll make you feel any better, his Commie-bashing doesn't get the biggest applause. That comes when he slams President Hawkins for taking advice from Brother Kristos."

"Yes, we have been aware of his nasty references to the faith healer. His audiences respond to that?"

"They love it! Trent is hanging Brother Kristos around Hawkins' neck like an albatross."

"That is the feeling of my superiors in Moscow," Marchuk agrees. "It is their belief that if we hope to see Hawkins reelected, we must do all we can to end his association with this so-called holy man."

"So what do you propose to do?"

"Buy him off," the Russian says promptly. "Every man has his price, and I think that itinerant preacher will find a generous offer of cash very tempting."

"And what does he have to do for it—get lost?"

"Exactly! Leave Washington, say good-bye to the President."

"How much were you thinking of giving him?"

"I have been authorized to go as high as a hundred thousand dollars."

"A nice neat number," Oberfest says slowly. "It just might work. Who's going to make the offer?"

Marchuk stops walking, waits until the other man has stopped. Then the major faces him directly. "Why, I thought you would have guessed, Arnold," he says gently. "You are going to bribe Brother Kristos."

"Me? But I don't even know the guy!"

The Russian claps a heavy hand on Michael's shoulder. "Do what you can," he says. Then, smiling, he takes a white envelope from his inside coat pocket and hands it over. "This is not Kristos' money; it's yours, with a little extra added for Christmas."

"Thanks," Oberfest says. "But about Kristos, I don't think I—"

"I have great faith in you," the KGB man interrupts. "I would not care to be disappointed."

"You don't understand," Michael says desperately. "Why would he listen to me? He doesn't know me from Adam."

The hand on Oberfest's shoulder tightens. "We have a saying: 'The bear dances, but the bear has claws.' Don't make me show you the claws, Arnold."

"Are you threatening me?" Michael asks weakly.

"Yes," Major Marchuk says. "Now do the job you are being paid for. Failure is unacceptable."

Oberfest, driving back to Washington alone, lights a cigar with trembling hands. But it tastes like straw, so he lowers the window and tosses it away.

His mind is a jumble of possible scenarios: leave his wife and take off for Hong Kong; go to the FBI and Confess All; tell Marchuk he made the bribe attempt and struck out. That last seems the most attractive until he recalls the Russian's cold warning: "Failure is unacceptable." He begins laughing hysterically.

But within an hour after he arrives home, Ruth already asleep and snoring, he has decided how he's going to handle the bribe: he's not; John Tollinger is.

By this time, Michael reasons, the President's staff must be desperate to get rid of Brother Kristos. He is certain John will be happy to approach the preacher. Having determined that, Michael begins dreaming up ways to explain the source of the bribe.

He calls the White House early the next morning, but Tollinger is in a staff meeting. He calls again around noon, but the meeting is still going on. Finally, at two o'clock, Tollinger is back in his office. He doesn't sound too happy to hear from Oberfest.

"What are you doing in town?" he asks. "I thought you and your boss would be in Oshkosh spreading your slime."

"It's not *my* slime," Michael protests, "it's *his*. Listen, I've got to talk to you."

"You *are* talking."

"I mean in private."

"About what?"

"About that slime you say Trent is spreading. I know how it can be stopped."

"Oh? How?"

"Do we meet?"

"All right," John says resignedly. "Come out to my place tonight at nine o'clock."

"I'll be there," Oberfest says happily, figuring he's got Tollinger hooked.

But that night, sitting in John's den, Michael discovers it's not going to be easy to con this cool, reserved man. But at least he's had the decency to provide his guest with first-rate Scotch.

Oberfest starts by telling John of Samuel Trent's current efforts to organize a campaign staff. He thinks this revelation will prove his sincerity, but Tollinger listens with no apparent interest.

"Get to the point," he tells Michael. "I brought a lot of work home with me, and I want to start on it."

"Look," Oberfest says earnestly, "I know what you must think of me. I work for a guy who's giving your boss the shaft. Granted. But to me it's just a job; it doesn't mean I approve of what he's doing."

"But you take his money."

"Sure I do. And you work for the Chief of Staff. Does that mean you agree with everything he does?"

"No," Tollinger admits grudgingly. "We have our occasional differences. But they're usually about matters of style, not basic policy. From what you're telling me, you disagree with Trent's entire rationale."

Oberfest takes a gulp of his drink. "That's right," he says. "And if you knew how many times I've been able to detoxify Trent's more poisonous speeches on Hawkins and Kristos, you wouldn't be so ready to condemn me. In fact, I'm in close personal contact with a group of men who sympathize with President Hawkins."

Tollinger shrugs. "A lot of people sympathize with Hawkins. That's how he got elected."

"But these men I'm talking about are something special. They're liberals and want to see Hawkins move farther to the left. For instance, they're all in favor of his food-sharing bill, and they're doing their best to lobby for it—not as an organized front but as individuals. John, these are big executives, publishers, columnists, high church dignitaries. They don't want any publicity about their activities. They think they can be more effective by working quietly behind the scenes."

Tollinger is interested. He pours them more Scotch. "Are these men members of the party?" he asks.

"Some are, some aren't. But they are all concerned about all the publicity Brother Kristos is getting. They think he may ruin Hawkins' chances of getting any social legislation passed."

"They're right. And Trent isn't helping."

"So they've come up with a painless way of solving the problem. They believe Kristos will accept a bribe to get out of town, and they all contributed to come up with a nice package of money. What do you think of that?"

Tollinger, expressionless, takes another sip of his Glenfiddich. "And why are you telling me all this?"

"Because these men are convinced that you're the one to negotiate with Kristos. You know the guy and, more important, you know the damage he's doing to Hawkins' reputation."

"I see," John says. "And how much were they thinking of offering the preacher?"

"They'll go as high as a hundred thousand dollars."

Tollinger can't take any more of this. He throws back his head and shouts laughter.

Oberfest watches this display with astonishment.

Finally Tollinger quiets down, wiping his eyes.

"What's so funny?" Michael asks.

"You're more than a day late and a dollar short," John tells him. "A bribe has already been tried. Brother Kristos was offered a cool million to vamoose, and he turned it down. Sorry."

He figures Oberfest will be chagrined, but is shocked when the plump little man suddenly begins crying, tears streaming down his cheeks.

"Hey," Tollinger says, "take it easy. It's not your fault. It was a good idea, but Kristos just isn't interested."

Then Oberfest leans forward, face in his hands, his body still racked with sobs.

Tollinger stands, puts a hand on the other man's shoulder. "Calm down," he says gently. "Have another drink."

Gradually the violent paroxysm diminishes. Oberfest is able to raise his tearstained face. John hands him his glass and watches as Michael gulps greedily.

"What brought that on, Mike?" he asks quietly. "Surely the group of men you represent will realize it wasn't your fault."

"There's no group," Oberfest says dully. "I lied. It was all a swindle."

"Oh?" John says. "Then where was the hundred thousand dollars coming from?"

Michael inhales deeply. He begins talking, faster and faster, words tumbling out. He tells Tollinger all about Major Marchuk, how he got involved with the KGB, why the Russians are so anxious to see Samuel Trent defeated.

Tollinger listens with incredulity and disgust. And when Oberfest finishes, he blurts out, "You stupid shithead!"

"I know," Michael says mournfully. "But when it started, it seemed like a game."

"A *game?*" Tollinger cries. "Oh my God! He suckered you. Mike, was it the money?"

"Well, sure, that was part of it. The market has been killing me lately. But I swear, John, I just didn't think what I was doing was all that important."

"It sure as hell is now. You better get yourself to the FBI as fast as you can. Tell them exactly what you've told me. The FBI will get Marchuk kicked out of the country, but I don't think they'll rack you up. You weren't exactly treasonous—just dumb, dumb, dumb!"

Oberfest shakes his head. "I can't go to the FBI. Even if there's no criminal prosecution, I'll be ruined. You know what this town is like. And I need an income."

"Then go on the lecture circuit. Write a book."

"About what? If I had sold blueprints of our new cruise missile, maybe the public would care. But all I peddled was silly scandal. There's no book in that."

"You've got a point there," Tollinger says. "Then do the obvious: go back to this Major Marchuk, tell him you tried to bribe Brother Kristos and failed. What's he going to do—kill you?"

"Yes," Michael says, staring at the other man, "that's exactly what he's going to do."

"You're kidding."

"I swear he'll do it—or have it done. My failure would be his failure and he won't accept that. I'd pay for it."

They are silent then, both sipping their drinks slowly.

"All right," John Tollinger says finally, "let me think about it. I don't know why I should get involved—you've been such an idiot—but I don't like the idea of the Soviets trying to finagle our presidential elections. My God, we don't try to influence their choice of General Secretary."

"But what should I *do?*"

"For the time being, stall. Tell Marchuk you're trying to meet Brother Kristos informally, at a diplomatic reception or cocktail party. Tell him anything, but keep putting him off. Give me some time to see what I can come up with."

"John, you really think you can save my ass?"

"Maybe," Tollinger says, looking at him strangely.

=18=

Four days before Christmas Henry Folsom holds an open house for members of his staff. It's a catered party held in the Chief of Staff's big Watergate apartment. It starts at five P.M., and goes on and on. Plenty of booze is available, and the food (baked ham, roast beef, Cajun fried chicken) is solid enough to keep anyone from getting too smacked.

More than a hundred guests show up, not all at the same time, since there are many other parties going on in Washington during Christmas week. But the crowd is always thick enough to require shouted conversation and a certain amount of jostling at the bar.

John Tollinger arrives early and has every intention of leaving soon, but not before he's had a few slices of rare roast beef, some green salad, and just enough to drink so that he mellows out. He's not good at parties, and knows it. Small talk bores him, and he sees no reason to laugh at feeble jokes. It's not so much that he's unsocial, but every time he finds himself at a noisy bash like this, he thinks of how contented he'd be at home alone with a pipe, a book, and his own brand of Scotch.

But he gamely sticks it out for almost an hour, talks to a few people, has his beef and salad, and is about to slip quietly away when the host pops out of the mob and grabs his arm.

"Not yet, John," the Chief of Staff says. "I want to talk with you."

"Here?" Tollinger says, looking round at the chattering throng. "Why not the Kennedy Center?"

"I know just the place. Follow me."

He dives back into the crowd, shouldering his way through, and Tollinger slides along in his wake. They make their way to the rear of the apartment, through a bedroom with twin beds piled high with coats and hats, and into a white-tiled bathroom. Folsom locks the door. He sits down heavily on the closed toilet seat. John remains standing, leaning against the sink.

"Good party, Chief," he says.

"Is it?" Folsom says. "I wish I could enjoy it, but I can't. The Boss ruined it for me this afternoon. He told me who he wants to nominate for Vice President. Want to guess? Ah, what am I asking you that for; you'd never come up with such a dumb idea—Representative Lu-Anne Schlossel."

"The black woman?"

"You've got it. Two minorities for the price of one."

Tollinger sits down on the edge of the tub. "Who suggested her?"

"Who? Who the hell do you think? It had to be Brother Kristos. No politician would ever throw the Boss a curve like that. Goddammit, it's going to splinter the party."

"I'm not so sure of that," John says slowly. "I think she'll be confirmed. Congress will believe they have no moral alternative."

"Oh Jesus! John, morals come and go, but politics go on forever. Do you think anyone on the Hill will be happy being handed a *moral* choice? That's the one thing every politician tries to avoid. Sure, Schlossel will be confirmed, because voting against her would be like voting against the Declaration of Independence, the Constitution, and Old Glory. But Congress will never forgive Hawkins for sending her name up. It's forcing them to do something that in their heart of hearts they don't want to do: confirm a woman, a *black* woman, to an office that's a heartbeat away from the presidency."

"I'm not certain your assessment is correct, Chief. I think a lot of congressmen will welcome the choice and vote for her because she's capable and experienced, and because they really do believe it's time for a woman to have that job."

"Bullshit!" There's a tentative rapping at the bathroom door; someone rattles the knob. "Occupied!" Folsom yells. "Go pee somewhere else! Look, John, you think Schlossel will be confirmed, and I do too. But let me ask you this: If Congress voted by secret ballot—just Yes or No scribbled on a piece of paper with no name attached—do you still think she'd be confirmed?"

Tollinger ponders that a long moment. "No," he says finally.

"You bet your sweet ass No!" the Chief of Staff says explosively. "So much for your moral choice. John, this is a middle-of-the-road electorate we've got. And I'm telling you that Hawkins will lose them the moment he sends Schlossel's name up to the Hill. People will say that they're not prejudiced and that anyone—woman, black, Jew, whatever—should have a chance to be President. But when they get in the privacy of that polling booth, do you think they vote what they *say?* Like hell they do! They vote what they *feel,* which is that yeah, maybe, someday, a woman, a black, or a Jew can be President. But not yet, not yet. That's why I'm telling you the Boss is going to crack the party wide open. He'll never be nominated again. He's handed Trent the nomination on a silver platter. All because he's listening to that asshole guru, Brother Kristos."

Tollinger starts to speak, then thinks better of it and shuts his mouth.

"John, you're a certified intellectual; tell me something . . . I know the Boss listens to Kristos because he thinks the guy saved his son's life. And also the preacher is supposedly a man of God, and you know how devout Hawkins is. But is it possible to be *too* devout, to have *too* much faith in God?"

"Of course," Tollinger says. "Then you become a zealot and start planning a sequel to the Spanish Inquisition. But I don't think the President is a zealot. He's simply a very religious man who trusts his spiritual adviser."

"Yeah," Folsom says gloomily, "even if it means smashing the party to smithereens and ruining his political future. Listen, you know everything—who was that old king who wanted to get rid of a preacher?"

John thinks a moment. "You're probably referring to Henry the Second. He was having his troubles with Thomas à Becket, the Archbishop of Canterbury, and is supposed to have said to his knights, 'Who will free me from this turbulent priest?' They did."

"Right on, Hank baby," Folsom says. "I wish I had a couple of knights available. You know, John, I've been thinking—maybe it's time I pulled a Trent and resigned."

"Oh no," Tollinger says. "You don't want to do that. The Boss needs you."

"What the hell for?" the chief says bitterly. "He's got Brother Kristos, hasn't he?"

They leave the bathroom to find a queue of jigging guests waiting to get in. It takes Tollinger twenty minutes to find his hat and coat, work his way through the crush, and depart just as another clutch of boisterous partygoers is arriving.

It's an almost physical pleasure to be alone in his Jaguar, driving home to his empty house. The solitude gives him a chance to replay that disturbing conversation with the Chief of Staff. He wonders what his own future will be if Folsom is serious about resigning.

Finally, finally, he has his pipe and pony of Glenfiddich, with a case of books awaiting. But the contentment he expected remains elusive. Instead, his brain churns, and even

he can recognize his own thinking as feverish and so flexu-
ous that he can come to no conclusion, make no decision.

By a determined effort of will, akin to squaring his
shoulders and straightening his spine, he forces himself
to think logically and linearly, to untangle his feelings
about Brother Kristos and put them in a meaningful
order.

Sexual: He resents the swami because he has seduced
Jennifer Raye and put the quietus to any hope Tollinger
might have had of a reconciliation.

Religious: As Marvin Lindberg angrily asserts, the
preacher has perverted faith in a Supreme Being for the
sake of private profit and his own reportedly insatiable
physical desires.

Political: Although Kristos' belief in social legislation
is no more radical than that of many other liberals, the
way he has attempted to convert his tenets into law has
fractured the party and probably doomed Abner Hawkins
to a one-term presidency.

Philosophical: Here Brother Kristos has offended in
many ways. By ignoring the traditional and, Tollinger believes, essential separation of church and state. By confusing his followers with gobbledygook that conceals the true
meaning and significance of faith, sin, and redemption.

And, most important, this strange man has, by his inex-
plicable acts of divination, cast into doubt the entire
corpus of rational thought, and made John question the
logical and reasonable principles in which he believes and
by which he lives.

In his dogged way, Tollinger reviews this bill of indictment several times, and with each reiteration the crimes
of which Brother Kristos is guilty seem more horrendous.
He rises and moves to his bookshelves to find a particular
volume.

He locates the book he seeks and brings it under the

FOUR

=1=

"I suppose I shouldn't care," Matilda Trent says, "but I do. Betraying him like this. What bothers me most is that my treachery doesn't bother me. I've seen women in my own circle kick over the traces—leave their husbands and run off to Brazil with a flautist, or something like that—and I'd wonder what they were thinking about. But now here I am spying on my own husband."

"God's spy," Brother Kristos says. "Sister, what you are doing is right and good."

"Keep telling me that," Mrs. Trent says with a mournful smile. "I can't help thinking that my conduct is what Samuel would call 'totally infra dig.' "

They're sitting close together at the big table in Kristos' study, and he is holding her hand. Around his wrist is a bracelet of heavy platinum links, her Christmas gift. From it dangles a small disk engraved *Amor vincit omnia*.

"Go on with what you were telling me," he says softly. "Your husband has hired a media adviser?"

"Yes, a very experienced man who's been through several presidential campaigns. He's convinced Samuel that it would be counterproductive to attack you personally. He insists it is better for Sam to keep harping on the traditional separation of church and state. People don't like the idea of their government being too closely linked with religion."

Brother Kristos releases her hand. He begins to comb his fingers slowly through his oiled and scented beard.

"I have seen your husband on television. He seems to be attracting large crowds."

"His speech writer has done wonders for him," Matilda says. "Made him cut down on the garbage he usually spouts. And he's let his hair grow a bit, and dresses more youthfully. All image-making, you know. And of course he does have an alarming message to deliver: that you, an unordained minister, practically a mystic, are telling the President how to run the country."

Kristos stirs restlessly. "As for being unordained, I have already taken steps to remedy that. I now have an attorney, and soon I will have the proper documentation from a small church in California."

"How did you manage that?"

He shows his teeth. "With a generous contribution to their good works. In addition, for the past few months I have visited many of the established church leaders in Washington. I have made some excellent contacts; they are sympathetic to what I am trying to do."

"Of course. And the fact that you have frequent meetings with the President impresses them."

"I am attempting to blunt your husband's accusations by letting my suggestions to Hawkins be offered by his other advisers."

"What a clever man you are!"

"The President is a good and decent man. If he asks for my advice, I give it freely. But I would rather have recommendations for policy decisions be presented to him by others. You can't own people. I am not Svengali, and he is certainly not my Trilby."

She looks at him a long moment. "No," she says, "*I* am your Trilby—am I not?"

"If you are, it is only because you wish to be."

"Yes," she says in a low voice, "I wish it."

The drapes are open, but it is the last week of December, and the afternoon light flooding the room is thin and colorless as ether. As usual, the apartment is overheated, the air bloated and steamy. Brother Kristos has unbuttoned his shirt; the gold cross hangs in a tangle of chest hair.

"Do you have any vodka?" Matilda Trent asks. "The peppered kind? I would like a drink."

He nods, rises, moves to the bedroom. But when he turns, she is directly behind him, following. She comes up close, looks into his eyes.

"Love me," she says.

He begins to open his belt, unzip his trousers.

" 'Never hide yourself from those in need,' " he says. "Isaiah."

She has become addicted to him, and there is nothing he asks that she will not do. This proud, austere woman has indeed, as he promised, remade her life. She has found a world of joy and color, of such intensity that when she is in his arms she feels her entire being thrumming, as if she has found a new music, new harmony.

It is not simply a physical delight, but a molting of the soul. She sees herself as young, slender, naked, the years dropped away, laughter and fleetness restored.

The pale light is waning in the bedroom when she takes a comb to his hair, mustache, beard. He submits to these ministrations docilely, a hand stroking her bare back.

"I think I shall divorce Samuel," she tells him suddenly. "I have been thinking about it a long time, and I've decided I must do it. What do you think?"

"Whatever is in your heart, sister."

"You've made me realize how narrow and stifling my life has been. I need to break out."

He catches her hand and stills it.

"This will injure your husband's political career," he says. "You realize that?"

"Of course! But for once in my life I want to be completely selfish. Is that so awful?"

"It is honest to end a loveless marriage. Have you spoken of this to your husband?"

"No, not yet," Matilda says. "He's on a tour of the West right now. I'll talk to him when he gets back."

"Wait awhile," Brother Kristos urges. "Timing is everything, and the moment is not yet right. Will you wait?"

"If you tell me to. But you do approve of my getting a divorce, don't you?"

"Yes, I approve."

"Will you tell me when?"

He nods and rises from the bed. He enfolds her in his arms, and she strains forward. His strength surrounds her, hard fingers press into her softness. She puts her head down on his shoulder and sighs contentedly.

"Here is the gospel according to Saint Matilda," she says. "A hug is as good as a hump."

=2=

They sit on a bench in Lafayette Park, hands deep in overcoat pockets, collars turned up against the numbing wind. They can see the White House gleaming in the pellucid morning light. It is as perfect and still as a stage set, erected as a backdrop for the capital's dramas: comedy, tragedy, farce, epic.

"The son of a bitch," Lindberg says bitterly. "He's doing exactly what I figured he'd do. Listen to this . . . He's expanding that cockamamy radio show of his to a full hour on Sunday mornings. *Brother Kristos' Family Hour.* How does that grab you? And he's got a producer working on a format for a TV ministry. If that's not enough, he's been cozying up to every influential bishop, rabbi, and reverend inside the Beltway, making sure no Holy Joe is going to dump on him."

"How do you find out all these things?" Tollinger marvels.

"Come on, you know there are no secrets in this town. Anyway, Jacob Everard Christiansen is off and running. More suckers to con, more pigeons to pluck, more bucks from the true believers. Believe you me, he'll be opening a Swiss bank account one of these days. The only part of the Good Book he believes in is 'Seek and ye shall find.' Ahh, you'll have to excuse me, but I blow my stack every time I start talking about that gonif."

"Actually," Tollinger says, "that's why I asked you to meet me—to talk about Brother Kristos."

"Oh? What's up?"

"Well, those men who financed your travels around the country had hoped you'd find something in his past that would bring an end to his friendship with the President. When that didn't pan out, they authorized me to offer Brother Kristos a hefty bribe to get out of town. He turned it down."

"Of course," Lindberg says angrily. "His connection with Hawkins is going to make him a multimillionaire."

"So now," John goes on, speaking slowly and deliberately, "they've come up with a new idea they want me to investigate."

"And what might that be?"

"These men honestly believe that Kristos represents a clear and present danger to constitutional government."

He is silent then, for such a long time that the ex-FBI man finally says, "Go on."

Tollinger gets it out in a rush: "They want me to explore the possibility of having Brother Kristos put down."

Lindberg turns to stare at him. Then his lips purse in a silent whistle. "That's heavy stuff."

"The heaviest," Tollinger agrees. "But they've run out of options. Anyway, I agreed to look into it. You're the first one I've told about it. Not only do I trust your discretion, but you've got the experience we need—if you're willing to help."

"Help how? By telling you how to plan the perfect crime?"

"I didn't think there was such a thing."

Lindberg gives him a crooked grin. "There are plenty of perfect crimes committed. They're the ones you never hear about."

"Well?" John says. "What do you say? If your answer is no, I'll understand completely, and I'll deny this conversation ever took place. If you agree, then we can discuss ways and means. You'll be well-paid, of course."

"What are you talking about?" Lindberg says, aggrieved. "I'm not a professional hit man. If I get involved it'll be because I *want* to be, not for a payoff. That would make me worse than Brother Kristos."

They are silent again, watching the bustle of traffic along Pennsylvania Avenue. A protest group of some sort, equipped with banners and placards, is gathering outside the White House fence. A man with a bullhorn is directing, but they cannot hear what he is shouting.

"You still on the wagon?" Tollinger asks absently.

"What?" Marvin says. "Oh yeah, I'm still dry. Look, let me think about this. It's not something I want to rush into. You can understand that, can't you?"

"Of course. When can I expect an answer? Tomorrow?"

"Tomorrow is New Year's Eve—remember?"

"Oh, that's right," Tollinger says. "Believe it or not, I forgot all about it. Too much on my mind, I guess. Are you partying?"

"Yeah, with my AA group. We'll have soda pop and chocolate-chip cookies. But that's all right; we'll have a few laughs. What about you?"

"I'm staying home," John says. "Maybe I'll have a glass of champagne at midnight."

"That's smart. Stay off the streets, and you'll live to see

the new year. Maybe I'll give you a call on New Year's Day. Satisfactory?"

"Fine. At least you're not turning me down immediately."

Both men rise, shake hands. Lindberg lumbers away with the stride of a much heavier man. Tollinger watches him go, then pulls his black homburg down snugly and heads for the West Gate.

Walking up the driveway, he pauses a moment to stare at the Executive Mansion. It is so finely proportioned, so *serene,* that seen from outside it is difficult to remember what a beehive of chaotic activity it is.

He does routine work for the remainder of that day, and the same until noon on New Year's Eve. Folsom is at Camp David with the First Family, and Tollinger can guess how frustrated the Chief must be, taking part in a nonalcoholic celebration.

He drives to Duke Zeibert's for a late lunch, and polishes off enough pickles, onion rolls, corned beef, and home fries to last him the remainder of the day. On the way home to Spring Valley he stops to treat himself to a bottle of Dom Perignon, and wonders wryly if he should also buy one noisemaker, one funny hat, one streamer, and a small packet of confetti for his own lonely end-of-the-year ceremony.

By eight o'clock that evening he has consumed half the Dom Perignon, drinking it from a tumbler because Jennifer took the champagne flutes as part of her divorce settlement. He starts phoning her every half-hour, just to wish her a Happy New Year—the civil thing to do, he tells himself—but there is no answer. He gives up at eleven, trying not to imagine where she might be. He finishes the bubbly, and pours himself a tot of cognac.

He is in bed before midnight. Sleep comes quickly. His last thought is a question: Why did he tell Marvin Lindberg that the plot to murder Brother Kristos was initiated by a group of VIP's and not admit the proposal was his alone? Was it an act of cowardice or merely a prudent move by a man developing a taste and talent for conspiracy?

He awakens New Year's Day with no hangover, but with a vague feeling of anomie, a disorientation as disturbing as a persistent fever. But he fixes a big breakfast, wolfs that down, and gets started on two months' accumulation of magazines. By noon, his uncertainty has evaporated, and he celebrates with his first drink of the new year: a mild Scotch and soda.

Lindberg calls, wishes him a Happy New Year, and says he can come over about three o'clock. John tells him to come ahead, and checks to make certain he has enough seltzer in the fridge. He doesn't even think of what he'll do if Lindberg turns him down.

The ex-FBI man is in a brisk, no-nonsense mood.

"Listen," he says, "when you threw this thing at me, I hope you didn't figure I'd volunteer to pop the guy myself."

"Of course not," Tollinger says. "I just wanted to take advantage of your expertise."

"Pick my brains?"

"That's about it."

"All right," Lindberg says, "I'll go along with that. But if not me, then who? Who's going to do the dirty deed?"

"Me," Tollinger says.

Marvin stares at him. "You got the balls for it?" he demands.

"I think I do. I've never done it before, so I can't be absolutely certain. But yes, I believe I can do it, provided the plan has a reasonable chance of success. I have no desire to spend the rest of my life behind bars."

"You shouldn't have to, but you can't pull it off by yourself. It'll take at least two. Three would be better, but we might be able to manage with two."

"You said 'we,'" John says. "Does that mean you're in?"

Lindberg ignores the question. "Let me tell you something about homicide," he says. "I worked a lot of cases, talked to agents who handled more, and I've read a lot of files. The best way to get away with murder is if the body is never found. It just disappears."

"How?" Tollinger asks. "Burn it?"

"Nah. Attracts too much attention. Someone might see the fire or smoke. Or smell it. And the bones and teeth would probably be left."

"Throw the body in the ocean, a lake, a river?"

"It might come up eventually. Even with weights. Too chancy."

"Chop it up into little pieces and scatter them?"

"Where do you do the chopping? And how? Are you a trained butcher or surgeon? And would you like to take on a job like that? I wouldn't. No, the best solution is burial. Six feet down in some deserted place. The grave carefully concealed to look like the surrounding ground."

Tollinger nods thoughtfully. This is his delight: an intellectual challenge, a problem to be solved by logic.

"Y'see," Lindberg goes on, sipping his seltzer, "a successful homicide has to be worked backwards. How to dispose of the body: that should be the first concern. The finding of a stiff alerts the cops, and everything else follows from that: identification, murder weapon, means, opportunity, motive. The law doesn't consider a missing-person inquiry as important or urgent as a homicide investigation."

"All right," John says, tasting his highball, "assuming you devise a way to bury the victim, what comes next?"

"Transportation. The body has to be transported to some remote area for burial—right? I mean, you're not going to dig a pit in the Mall, are you? That means a car or a truck, and that determines your choice of weapon. Use a gun or knife, and that sucker is going to bleed, with maybe bits of tissue and bone in addition to blood. How are you going to keep that stuff out of your car or truck?

Use a big plastic garbage bag? It might leak, and jamming a corpse into a trash bag is not a job I'd recommend to anyone. Also, if slugs are left in the body, the cops will be able to determine the caliber of gun used and maybe trace it from ballistics files. Even slashes and puncture wounds will tell them what kind of a knife was used to ace the victim. Why are you looking at me so funny?"

"I just realized that we keep talking about the victim, the body, the corpse. Not once have you or I used his name. We're speaking about killing Brother Kristos—remember?"

"Yeah, well, I'm talking like a cop. It's always the victim, the perpetrator, the assailant or attacker, the body or corpse or remains. Cops rarely use names; that personalizes it too much. You've got to keep your cool, and one way you do it is by using legalese. If you call a bloody massacre a multiple homicide, it's easier to handle."

"I guess so," Tollinger says, sighing. "All right, I gather you've ruled out a gun or a knife. What does that leave?"

"Poison," Marvin Lindberg says promptly. "They've got stuff today that's odorless, colorless, and is almost impossible to detect, especially if the body's been in the ground for a long time and the worms have done their duty. A few drops do the job. But even the best poison has its drawbacks. Like how do you get it into the target?"

Tollinger considers that a moment. "It shouldn't be too difficult," he says. "Brother Kristos has been here before. Sitting exactly where you're sitting right now."

"You think you could get him here again?"

"I think I could. He likes pepper vodka."

"Then that leaves only one problem: Where do we get the poison?"

Tollinger ponders, rises, pours himself more whiskey, sits down again. "I think I can get the poison," he says.

"Yeah?" Lindberg says. "Where?"

It's a long recital, and Marvin has finished another seltzer and John his highball by the time it's ended.

"Uh-huh," Lindberg says, "it just might work. And it'll give us the third guy. Look, you get started on the poison, and meanwhile I'll drive around and see if I can find a good place for a grave. Maybe in western Maryland. There's some wild country out there. It would be a long drive carting a clunk in the backseat, but it might be worth it if we could find the perfect spot. I remember there's a place near the West Virginia border called Backbone Mountain."

"Significant name," Tollinger says.

"You're right," the other man says. "If we're going to do it, then let's *do* it."

After Lindberg leaves, John sits for almost ten minutes, turning his empty glass in his fingers, musing on their conversation. He realizes he is becoming an intrigant, and wonders if, had it happened sooner, he might have risen farther in the Byzantine world of national politics.

Then he picks up the phone and calls Michael Oberfest.

=3=

Frantic gyrations concluded, they shower together, laughing when they compare the length and girth of their thighs, hers so slight and smooth, his so massive and matted with curly hair. Then she dresses, and Brother Kristos pulls on a white cashmere robe, a gift from Jennifer Raye.

"Listen, preacher," Lu-Anne Schlossel says, "this is the last time I'm going to visit this love nest. Mrs. Mattingly saw me come in, and she's a mouthy old broad. My confirmation is coming up for a vote, and I've got to behave."

He nods. "That would be wise. We can talk on the phone, and after you are confirmed, we'll make arrangements to meet somewhere else."

"You talk like my confirmation is a sure thing."

"It is."

"Is that one of your conjureman predictions?"

He doesn't answer, but leads the way into the study. She takes his big armchair at the head of the table, but he doesn't object.

"I never have thanked you properly," she says.

"For what?"

"For leaning on Hawkins to nominate me for Vice President."

"I didn't. Mrs. Hawkins did."

"And who suggested it to her? When are you going to advise the President to submit a new food-sharing bill— one with increased farm subsidies?"

"I'm not; you are. Suggest it to him after you are confirmed. You will get credit for the idea, and there will be less talk of how I influence the White House."

"You think of everything," she says, shaking her head. "And after we help the hungry, how about doing something about the homeless? The lack of low-income housing in this country is a disgrace."

"I have already spoken to the President about that. I outlined a complete program of social change, including low-income housing and a plan to upgrade the nation's bridges, tunnels, and highways. That would create a lot of jobs."

"My God," she says admiringly, "you think big, you do. And where is the money for all this coming from?"

He shrugs. "Higher taxes, bond issues. If the will is there, it can be done. But I recognize these things take time. That is why I am trying to downplay my influence on President Hawkins. I don't wish to endanger his chances for reelection."

"I'm not sure Sam Trent will let the country forget that you sleep in the Lincoln Bedroom."

"Only once," he says with his feral grin. "And I have taken steps to cripple Trent's public career. The man is my enemy, and I am his. The new food-sharing bill will weaken him, and there are other things that will contribute to his early political death."

She gives a mock shiver. "I'm glad you're not my enemy," she says. "How about a shot before I take off."

He brings the decanter from the bedroom and pours them drinks. She takes a sip, then stares at him over the rim of her glass.

"I hear you've been visiting all the churches in the D.C. area," she says. "Making friends?"

"Something like that," he admits. "I want to persuade the religious community to support the President's program for social change. Eventually I want to see a nationwide campaign by the devout to feed the hungry, house the homeless, and provide jobs for everyone capable of working."

She straightens up in her chair. "Whoa, preacher man," she says. "You're getting the churches too closely involved in the affairs of government. I don't much like that."

"There is nothing to fear," he assures her. "I merely want to speak to the people of moral values and spiritual needs."

"You wouldn't be trying to bamboozle me, would you? If your pious constituency wants to feed the hungry and house the homeless, all well and good. But if you want prayers in the schools and legislation against abortion, then you and I part company."

"No, no, sister," he says. "I merely wish for social change to make this a more equitable society."

"Uh-huh," she says. "I wish I could believe you, but I can't. Sometimes you scare me. There are days when I think you're a messiah come to comfort the poor, and there are times when I think you've got delusions of grandeur, with ambitions as big as all outdoors."

"I am what you see: a simple man trying to do as God commands."

"Maybe," she says, "and maybe you're the king of the hypocrites. I'm going to keep a close eye on you, conjureman. When you get on the pulpit, you're too good to be true. You've done a lot for me, and I appreciate it. But if I decide you're going over the line with your religious crusade, I'm going to lower the boom on you. Just stick to helping the poor and needy, and leave the government to the politicians elected to run it. Okay?"

"I must answer to a higher power," he says, eyes blazing.

"That's what worries me," she says. "Is the higher power God in heaven, or is it your greed for money and power? Don't mess with me, preacher; I wouldn't enjoy putting the whammy on you. But here's something the Bible doesn't say: 'Fuck not, lest ye be fucked.' "

John Tollinger is beginning to see the conspiracy as an edifice, something made of closely fitted stones. It is pyramidal in shape. At the apex is the assassination of Brother Kristos. Below are the motives of the conspirators and the planning and intrigue that must offer support strong enough to withstand chance and accident.

He even draws a rough diagram of this murderous structure, making notes of the "stones" that will provide the foundation: weapon (poison), transportation, timing, preparations to be made by the assassins, possible reactions of the victim, the burial, alibis, etc.

Reducing the plot to coherence converts it from a madcap scheme to an assignment in Logic 101–102, an intellectual exercise requiring rigorous thought. It also rids the killing of emotional baggage that would only serve to confuse and weaken the resolve of the killers.

It is ironic, Tollinger acknowledges, that the key role in the slaying of Brother Kristos must be played by an individual who, to John's knowledge, has no reason to desire the preacher's death.

So he spends a great deal of time planning how to convince Michael Oberfest, a man Tollinger considers a mindless weakling, to take part in a homicide. He finally devises a plot which, though admittedly ignoble, should prove effective. He checks it out with Marvin Lindberg, gets his approval and promise of cooperation.

He starts by inviting Oberfest out to Spring Valley for dinner. As he anticipates, Michael eagerly accepts.

"Do you have something?" he asks. "You know—about my problem."

"We'll talk about it at dinner," John says.

But when Oberfest arrives, Tollinger keeps saying, "Later, later," and during their meal of baked chicken, cheese tortellini, and salad, speaks only of Trent's speeches and the success he's having in undermining the President's popularity.

It is only after they have moved into the den for black coffee and brandy that John remarks casually, "I think I've come up with a ploy that may get you off the hook with the KGB."

Michael's pudgy features wrinkle into a happy smile. "Thank God for that," he says, "and thank you. I was praying you'd come through for me. Marchuk is getting surly. He's convinced I'm stalling. What's your idea?"

"You may think it overly dramatic," Tollinger says calmly. "Even outlandish. But you must realize that an agent in the major's position is used to complex plots and convoluted schemes. I believe he'll accept it."

"What *is* it?" Oberfest cries.

"I think you should go to the Russian and tell him you've made personal contact with Brother Kristos, and that he turned down the bribe."

"My God, John, Marchuk will be furious. I don't know what he'll do—probably deliver my tapes to the FBI immediately."

"Just listen," Tollinger says patiently. "There's more to it than that. After you tell him Brother Kristos won't take a bribe, you suggest another option. If the Soviets are serious about getting rid of Kristos to protect the political future of Abner Hawkins, then the best way is to *really* get rid of him. Why don't they have him killed?"

"What? What are you saying?"

"You heard me. You suggest to Major Marchuk that the Russians have Brother Kristos terminated."

"Oh Jesus, I can't do that!"

"Will you just let me finish? Drink your brandy and listen."

Tollinger pauses a long time, knowing he's got a lot to throw at Oberfest in one session, and willing to go slowly so this dimwit can absorb it all.

"Now, Mike, just hear me out and try not to get upset until you learn how it ends. All right, now you've told the major that Brother Kristos should be put down; what do you think the Russian's reaction will be?"

"I don't know," the other man says, biting nervously at his thumbnail. "I guess he won't say yes or no right away. He'll probably tell me he's got to buck the proposal to Moscow for a decision."

"Of course," Tollinger says approvingly, "that's exactly

what he'll say—and do. We all have a boss, including a KGB major. After he tells you he'll consult his superiors, you add a little sweetener. You say that if they want Kristos eliminated, you're willing to do the job."

"Come on, John, that's crazy!"

"Will you just *listen?* You tell Marchuk you're willing to do the job provided he hands over all your tapes."

Oberfest sits up in the armchair, stares at Tollinger. "I'm beginning to get it," he says. "I tell the Russian I'll snuff Brother Kristos, but I don't really do it—right?"

"Right. But there's more to it than that. You tell Marchuk that you'll murder Kristos—but only if the Russians supply the weapon. Mike, do you know anything about guns?"

"Of course not. How would I know anything about guns?"

"That's too bad," Tollinger says smoothly, "but it's not essential. Poison will do just as well. Tell the major you'll kill the preacher if the KGB provides the poison. That should be no problem; those cloak-and-dagger types have access to all kinds of exotic drugs. So tell Marchuk if he supplies the poison, you'll visit Kristos or invite him for a drink and slip the stuff into his vodka."

"Hey, John," Oberfest says, "what kind of a solution to my problem is that? If Marchuk's bosses okay the killing, and he gives me the poison, and then I don't go through with it—which I won't—he'll feed *me* the poison."

Tollinger leans forward and stares at the other man intently. "No, he won't," he says, "because you'll have him by the short hair. When you go to pick up the poison, you'll be wired. You understand? You'll have a miniaturized microphone and transmitter strapped to your shin. And I'll be within broadcast distance with a receiver and a tape recorder. You get the Russian to talk about the poison he's handing over and how Brother Kristos will never know what hit him. And I'll be making an audiotape of your entire conversation. Are you beginning to get it now?"

"Jesus!" Michael says. "I get it, I get it! He'll have the tapes of me, but I'll have a tape of him that'll cook his goose!"

"Of course it will. And he'll do anything you demand to get that tape back. My God, can you imagine what an international flap there would be if you went to the CIA or FBI. All your past sins would be forgiven if you hand them evidence that the Soviets are plotting to assassinate a close friend of the President of the United States. You realize what the media would do with *that* story? And I assure you, Marchuk will realize the same thing. He'll give you your tapes, never fear, just to recover the incriminating tape you have of him."

Oberfest begins to gnaw his thumbnail again. "But what if we make the trade," he says worriedly, "and then he has me terminated because I double-crossed him?"

"Not to worry," Tollinger says lightly, "because you'll make a copy of that tape before you hand it over. And you'll make sure he knows you've got the copy in a safe place, to be delivered to the authorities if anything happens to you. That's your insurance. Believe me, you'll have nothing to worry about."

"I don't know," Oberfest says nervously. "So many things could go wrong. What if the electronic stuff doesn't work?"

"It will. I know a very good technician who can supply the equipment."

"But what if Marchuk sees you lurking around and wonders what you're doing there?"

"He won't see me if you give me enough advance notice of where you're meeting him."

"He might search me and discover the mike."

"He's never searched you before, has he?"

"What if he keeps copies of the tapes he has of me?"

"What if he does? You'll have a copy of your tape of him, won't you? It'll be a Mexican standoff."

"What if—"

"Forget it!" Tollinger explodes. "Just forget the whole damned thing! I tried to help you, and all you can do is raise stupid objections. Let's just let the whole thing drop. I don't think you've got the balls for it anyway."

"I do!" Michael cries despairingly. "I really do! It's a very clever scheme, John, honest it is. I want to do it."

"No," Tollinger says coldly, "I think you better forget it. I wash my hands of the whole affair. It's your problem; you figure out how to solve it."

"Please, John, please let me do it. I know it'll work. I appreciate your trouble and your volunteering and all. I really want to do it."

"You're sure?"

"Absolutely. Positively."

"All right," Tollinger says. "I'm not saying it's totally without risk, but I think it's do-able. Now let's go over the whole scenario again to get the sequence straight. Then we'll rehearse the dialogue between you and Major Marchuk so you'll be ready for any questions he may throw at you."

"Whatever you want, John," Michael Oberfest says humbly.

=5=

On the evening of January 14, a musicale is held in the East Room of the White House. More than a hundred guests attend, including prominent churchmen of all faiths from the District of Columbia and distinguished ecclesiastics from all over the country.

The program, planned by Brother Kristos, features singers, instrumentalists, and choirs that have auditioned for his hour-long radio show and projected television ministry. There are gospel singers (traditional, jazz, country-western, and rock), guitar-plucking balladeers, and choristers of spirituals, hymns, prayers, and psalms.

It is a joyous evening, sparked by foot-pounding and rhythmic hand-clapping by the assembled clergymen, with frequent shouts of "Amen!" and "Hallelujah!" The program concludes with the entire audience standing, holding hands, and singing "Amazing Grace." It is, as Brother Kristos proclaims, a "glorious jubilee!"

The entire ninety-minute program (without commercials) is telecast live on all the networks and garners the highest ratings in television history. The public response is enthusiastic, with a tremendous outpouring of phone calls and letters of approval to the White House.

In the days to come, more sober and analytical commentaries appear. The question most frequently posed is whether the White House is a proper setting for what is termed a "revival meeting." To all such criticism, President Abner Hawkins replies that "the evening was a celebration of faith and the human spirit."

A few hours after the musicale has ended, Brother Kristos relaxes in the Family Room with the President, the First Lady, and their son.

"That will be a hard act to top," Hawkins says. "Perhaps we might consider making it an annual event."

"I think the people would love it," his wife agrees. "It was really very moving."

"And impressive," the President adds. "To get representatives of all creeds together to share their music. Now that's what I call real ecumenism!"

"There are men and women of goodwill in all religions," Brother Kristos says mildly. "For there is only one true religion—and that is faith. Once that is understood, then the rites, rituals, and ceremonies of all the various beliefs become unimportant. What remains and endures is the universal love for the Almighty."

"Amen!" George pipes up, and the President, laughing, embraces his son.

Soon after, Mrs. Hawkins and the boy say good night, and she takes him off to bed.

"Can you stay awhile?" Hawkins asks the preacher. "You and I haven't had a quiet talk in a long time."

"Of course, father," Brother Kristos says. "For as long as you wish."

The President leads the way, and the two men, trailed by Secret Service agents and the man carrying the code case, go down to the small study adjoining the Oval Office. It is a secluded chamber with four armchairs, a single telephone.

"There are a few things you should know about," Hawkins says after the door is closed. "First of all, we've counted heads, and it looks like we'll have the votes to confirm Lu-Anne Schlossel as Vice President."

"I am happy to hear that," Kristos says. "She is a fine woman, a valuable asset to your administration."

"I'll want her to work mostly on our relations with Congress. She knows the machinery of legislating—which is exactly what we need. Second, I wanted to talk over some of the programs you mentioned on election night. Do you remember?"

"Yes, father. I suggested a program of social change: feeding the hungry, housing the homeless, organizing work programs to provide jobs."

"I've been thinking about all that," the President says somberly. "As a practical politician, I know what a blue-sky project it is. The obstacles are enormous. But as you said, no matter how idealistic the vision may be, it must be attempted. God wills it. So I have organized a sort of ad hoc commission to draw up an overall plan to cure our public ills. The people I have approached from the business community, universities, labor unions, human-rights organizations, and so forth are all eager to help and willing to work without pay. They promise a complete report to me within three months. Not only *what* should be done, but *how* it may be done."

"My prayers have been answered," Brother Kristos says. "Just one additional suggestion, if I may make it, father."

"Of course."

"We both know that such an enormous and radical program must first win the hearts and minds of the American people. To do that, it will need a catchy name—something similar to the New Frontier or the Great Society—and a cleverly designed campaign to sell its benefits to *all* the people. I do not think it is too soon to enlist the efforts of the best media advisers and advertising experts willing to volunteer."

"Excellent idea!" the President says heartily. "I'll start the wheels turning on that as soon as possible."

They sit in comfortable silence then, the preacher combing his fingers slowly through his beard, the President staring down as he turns his wedding band around and around.

"I would like to devote more time to domestic matters," Hawkins says, almost as if talking to himself, "but lately most of my schedule has been taken up by foreign affairs. If you think there are many national problems crying for solution, there are double that number in our relations with other countries."

"I believe that, father."

"It is so difficult to form a consensus," the President says, sighing, "even amongst our friends. Every nation acts out of self-interest, of course—that's understand-able—but sometimes sacrifices have to be made for the common good. Then diplomacy becomes about as elevat-ing as horse trading."

Brother Kristos stares off into space. "I have long felt," he says, "that governments come between the people of one country and those of another. Yet all human beings are essentially the same the world over. We all want peace, food, a home, a job, family. More important, we are all inspired by a common faith in a Divine Being, no matter what we may call Him."

"But the peoples of the world can't deal with one an-other. They need governments to represent them."

The preacher lowers his eyes to stare at the President. "They need only the government of God, and His repre-sentatives."

Hawkins is puzzled. "What are you saying? That we should concentrate our diplomatic efforts on the religious leaders of foreign countries rather than on their elected representatives?"

"I am saying that if you neglect the universal religion of faith, you will never win the lasting support of the peo-ple of those countries. And without the support of the people, gaining the cooperation of their leaders will be a hollow victory."

The President leans forward. "Would you be willing to

outline your ideas to an audience of high-level diplomats at the State Department?"

"I would. To urge them to work closely with the religious leaders in the countries to which they are assigned. If we are to influence the future of the world, it must be done from the pulpit."

"I warn you, they are a hard-nosed group. In all negotiations, the first rule is to demand more than you can reasonably expect to receive. Then, when the haggling is ended, you settle for the most you can get."

Brother Kristos smiles sadly. "God does the same thing," he says.

=6=

Michael Oberfest has always thought of Tollinger as a cold man, stiff, upright and aloof, just too fucking superior. But here is that same prig, that heartless intellectual, showing a warm and sympathetic nature.

They spend three evenings together in Tollinger's Spring Valley home, going over and over the scenario for the duping of Major Leonid Y. Marchuk of the KGB. John's patience never dwindles as he leads Michael slowly through the role he is to play, his dialogue, and how he is to handle accidents of stagecraft.

Tollinger acts the part of Marchuk, shooting hard questions at Oberfest, then gently correcting him when he screws up. By the end of the three rehearsals Michael's brain is fuzzy with all the cues and replies that have been drilled into him. But Tollinger seems satisfied with their final run-through, and pats Michael's shoulder before sending him off to his opening performance.

Finally Oberfest calls the contact number, and a meeting is arranged at the shopping mall near Bowie, Maryland, a rendezvous they haven't used in weeks. Marchuk shows up wearing an astrakhan greatcoat and a fur hat.

"So," the Russian says when they are seated in the front of his Lincoln, "what do you have to report? Good news, I hope."

"Nyet," Oberfest says with a high-pitched whinny. "Brother Kristos won't take a bribe. I met with him four times. Once in his apartment, twice in his church down in Virginia, once at my home. We've become real drinking buddies, and I gave it to him straight: a hundred thousand dollars if he'll get lost."

"And?"

"He laughed. Then he said not even for a million. Can you blame him? He's got a good thing going: pals with the President, his own radio show, and now he's planning to start a TV ministry. A hundred grand is chicken feed compared to what he stands to make. Listen, I tried, I really did, but it's no soap."

Marchuk sucks his teeth. "I do not like that," he says. "And my bosses won't like it. They are liable to transfer me to Mozambique. No more California women."

This is the opening Tollinger instructed Michael to watch for. "But there may be a very simple solution," he tells the major. "Crude, but simple."

"Oh? And what is that?"

"If you guys are serious about taking the preacher out of the political picture, why don't you just terminate him?"

The KGB man turns his head slowly to stare.

"Look," Oberfest says, "it's an option, isn't it? And don't tell me your outfit hasn't used it before. When you can't persuade and can't blackmail and can't bribe, you eliminate—correct?"

"And who do you suggest might eliminate Brother Kristos?"

Michael shrugs. "You've probably got a stable of trained professionals who could bring it off."

Marchuk shakes his head. "Too risky," he says. "If something goes wrong, and your CIA links the assassin to us, our problem becomes even bigger."

Michael shrugs again. "Then forget it. It was just a suggestion."

"It is not a *bad* suggestion, Arnold," the major admits. "Not an *impossible* suggestion. But if it is done, it must be planned so there is no trail to us."

"And where are you going to get a killer like that—hire some hophead off the street?"

This, Tollinger has pointed out, will be the moment of truth. Either the Russian rises to the bait or the whole plan self-destructs.

"No," Marchuk says seriously, "we never employ freelancers we cannot control." He puts a heavy hand on Michael's knee. "But there is one man who could do this job for us."

"Yeah? And who might that be?"

"You, m'boy," the major says softly.

Got him! Oberfest thinks, and is shocked by his own surge of joy.

"Me?" he cries indignantly. "Are you out of your mind? I'm no killer, in any way, shape, or form. I've never fired a gun in my life—wouldn't know how—and as for a knife, forget it! I'm just not the assassin type."

The KGB man is silent for a moment, and Michael fears they may have lost him. But then: "There are many methods, Arnold; not only gun and knife. There are modern, sophisticated ways. Easy but effective. Simple ways but, as you Americans say, satisfaction guaranteed. Are you still friends with this faith healer?"

"Oh sure."

"You say that the two of you have become drinking buddies?"

"That's right."

"What does he like to drink?"

"He's got a taste for peppered vodka."

"Excellent!" Marchuk says with a boomy laugh. "At least we have taught something to the capitalists. It is Russian vodka?"

"Yep."

"Better and better! It will be a good joke. Does the holy father ever get drunk on peppered Russian vodka?"

"Well, not falling-down drunk, you understand, but feeling no pain. Why do you ask?"

"Because I see a method of terminating Brother Kristos that even you could handle."

"Hey," Oberfest says angrily, "I told you to leave me out of it. A killer I ain't."

(Protest, Tollinger instructed. But not *too* much.)

"Arnold," the major says softly, "*everyone* is a killer if the circumstances warrant it. Let me tell you what I am thinking. There are poisons available: colorless, odorless, tasteless. Only a few drops are needed. The formula can be adjusted to paralyze the nervous system at any time from seconds to several hours. Then it hits like a massive coronary and is almost impossible to detect in an autopsy. Now would it be so difficult for you to pour a few drops into Brother Kristos' vodka when he is, as you say, feeling no pain?"

"But *why* should I do it?" Michael asks. "What's in it for me?"

"Ah," Marchuk says, "what is in it for me: America's national motto. I shall tell you what is in it for you—those incriminating tapes of our early meetings?"

Oberfest is silent. Play it cool, Tollinger urged. Make him believe you hadn't thought of that before, and now that it's been suggested, you're seeing the murder of Brother Kristos in a new light.

"The original tapes," Marchuk goes on, voice seductive, "and all the copies. Your nightmare ended. Is that not tempting?"

"Let me think about it," Michael says hesitantly. "I don't know. I'm not sure."

"Of course," the major says heartily. "Think about it, but not too long. Meanwhile, I will contact my superiors to get their approval. If they say no, then nothing more will be done about Brother Kristos, and we have merely spent a pleasant evening together. But I do not think they will say no; I think they will sanction this initiative. But only if you agree to do it, Arnold."

"I'll let you know," Oberfest says.

On his drive back to D.C., he stops at an all-night service station to gas up, use the toilet, and make a phone call.

"You're a fucking genius," he tells John Tollinger.

The young winter has been cold, and already two snow-storms have buried the District of Columbia, halting traffic in the capital and giving unexpected holidays to government workers.

Snow has drifted on the grounds of the tobacco barn in Virginia, but Brother Kristos has hired plows to keep his parking area cleared; there is no fall-off in attendance at his Saturday-night services. Congregants arrive bundled in fur coats and down parkas, but Brother Kristos, wearing his old burlap robe, seems impervious to the cold. In the back room, the iron stove glows red.

The preacher makes his entrance and, as usual, stands in silence a few moments. He gazes at the audience, sweeping them slowly with that incendiary stare they have come to expect. Then, without preamble, he begins:

"We are all born on Monday and die on Friday. Life lasts no longer than a single twinkle of a star. This is as it should be, for who would wish to live forever, enduring all the broken promises of endless existence.

"Brothers and sisters, reflect on the transience of your days. You are blessed with the gift of life and soon enough it shall be taken from you. I plead with you to use your brief hours wisely. To waste them is an offense to the Holy Giver."

Brother Kristos then expounds on this theme, and though he never ceases to remind his listeners of their eventual dissolution, his message stresses the need for joy and committed passion.

"Create!" he cries out to them. "Make your final days— for all days are final—a glory that brings you felicity and is pleasing to God. Do not crab your life, make it small, mean, and sour. Expand your life with love, laughter, and pleasure. Give love to your family, laughter to your children, pleasure to your friends. We are all butterflies and last just as long. I entreat you to fly, to soar, make your short stay on this earth a time for bliss and merriment."

His sermon is well received, for he tells them there is no pleasure they might seek that would offend the Almighty, provided no one is injured thereby in body or spirit. He sends them out into the cold warmed by his words.

When they are all gone, Brother Kristos sits with Pearl and Agnes in the back room, eating jalapeño peppers, raw onions, filets of herring pickled in wine sauce, and passing around a bottle of vodka.

"How did you come up with that spiel tonight?" Pearl asks. "I never heard that one before."

Kristos doesn't answer, but remains hunched over the table, gripping the herring in his fingers as he gnaws. Mustache and beard drip with juices; the stained floor becomes littered with the skins of onions and stems of peppers.

"I thought it was a real downer," Agnes says. "All that stuff about dying—who wants to hear that?"

"You think you're not going to die?" the preacher demands, not looking up from his food. "You are and I am and so is everyone else. We are all the walking dead."

"I just don't want to think about it, Jake," she says.

Then he looks up at her, his strong teeth crunching into an onion. "You don't want to think about anything," he says, "except stuffing your mouth and your pussy. You two sluts haven't got a brain between you. Did either of you ever wonder why there is something? Why not nothing? There is the earth, sun, moon, planets, stars, the far reaches of the universe. Why should these things exist? I don't mean why should there not be a cold and lifeless void, but why should there even be a void? Why not total nothingness, with no form, no measure? Have either of you peabrains ever wondered that?"

"I don't know what the hell you're talking about," Pearl says. "And Christ, you're in a grumpy mood tonight. Have some more vodka."

He drinks directly from the bottle, head thrown back, throat working.

"Hey, Jake, take it easy," Agnes says. "Don't pass out yet."

He throws the empty bottle into a corner. The hound raises his head in alarm, then relaxes and dozes again.

"Get me another jug," Brother Kristos commands. "That herring made me thirsty."

Pearl brings a fresh bottle from the cupboard. She uncaps it, leans over the table to place it before the preacher.

He shoves his hand roughly into the neckline of her robe, fondles her small breast.

"Nice titty," he says. "Sweet titty."

"That's more like it," Agnes says approvingly. "Just cut the shit about dying and why isn't there nothing." She stands, hikes up the skirt of her robe, pulls down her wrinkled cotton panties. "There," she says. "Isn't that something?"

They gulp more vodka. Coal is added to the stove. The air becomes sulfurous and stifling. They tear away their robes. The table is swept clear of food and tin plates. The whitish dog slinks away to a corner.

Brother Kristos pushes Pearl facedown on the kitchen table. He grabs a copy of *Brother Kristos' Prayers for All Occasions* from a stack on the floor. He opens the book on her bare rump. Agnes, giggling, crouches between his legs.

"It is written!" the preacher shouts, wetting his finger in Pearl's vulva to turn the pages of his breviary. "Know the truth, and the truth shall set ye free. Whosoever believeth in me shall never die. I bring everlasting life. Blessed are they who hear the word of Brother Kristos and keep it. Believe in me and all things are possible. Come unto me, all ye that labor and are heavy-laden, and I will give ye rest. I shall die for your sins. Trust in me for the salvation of your soul. Brother Kristos creates something out of nothing. Faith is the answer, brothers and sisters. Faith banishes sin, and no one needs redemption in a sinless world. The arms of Brother Kristos embrace ye all, and he shall make scarlet sins as white as snow. For the peace of Brother Kristos passeth all understanding."

He howls on and on, spitting out his litany, slapping the fleshy pulpit with his book of prayers, the two women yelping with laughter. Until all three tumble onto the fouled floor, inflamed with lust. The pallid hound raises his head again and watches with hooded eyes.

=8=

Former Vice President Samuel Trent's privately commissioned polls show that he is making encouraging progress in his nascent campaign activities. More and more Americans are becoming aware of the wedding of politics and religion in the White House. And apparently just as many are concerned about what Trent calls the "pernicious influence" of Brother Kristos on administration policy. The man who was once dubbed the Rajah of Rant by a political columnist is now earning a reputation of "talking sense."

On January 17 Samuel Trent and his staff are in Manhattan, where he is scheduled to be the featured speaker at a convention of television network executives at the New York Hilton. Trent and his entourage arrive at the Sixth Avenue entrance to the hotel a little before noon.

As he exits from his limousine, a bearded youth steps out from the small crowd of onlookers, points a stubby revolver at the former Vice President, and pulls the trigger rapidly several times. The first shot shatters the Cadillac's windshield, the second tears the chauffeur's left earlobe, and after that there is merely a series of clicks as the handgun, a Saturday-night special, repeatedly misfires.

The would-be assassin is later identified as Simon Czreck, a member of an obscure religious cult that believes in total sexual abstinence and the Second Coming of Christ. "God told me to do it!" Czreck screams as he is overpowered by Trent's aides.

Fortunately for Trent, there are two reporters and a

press photographer on hand to record the attempted assassination. The photograph subsequently published in newspapers and magazines shows Trent standing erect and apparently unafraid during the assault. As one of the reporters later wrote, "If courage is grace under pressure, then Samuel Trent is the bravest man I've ever seen."

By the time he appears on the dais to deliver his speech, news of the attack has spread through the convention. Trent's first words (supplied by his speech writer), "As I was about to say before I was so rudely interrupted . . . ," bring down the house, and the audience rises to give him a prolonged ovation.

"No one has more respect for established religion than I do," Trent declares, coming down hard on the word *established*. "I was born an Episcopalian, have lived all my life an Episcopalian, and have every intention of dying an Episcopalian—but not today!"

(Laughter and applause.)

"Religious leaders of all denominations have contributed greatly to the growth and well-being of our country. But it must be said that occasionally, in rare instances, our spiritual leaders have sought to play a role in the temporal affairs of our government. It is a role for which they are not qualified by education, training, or experience.

"Now we are faced with a situation at the top levels of our government that I do not exaggerate in calling a crisis. The executive branch has become hostage to the insatiable ambitions of a strange clergyman who apparently is not a member of any established religion. He professes to have the powers of a faith healer, clairvoyant, and seer."

Trent then makes it clear that political leaders are and should be free to seek spiritual counsel from whomever they choose. But, he adds firmly, that advice cannot be allowed to intrude on the affairs of state or unduly influence national policy.

"Render unto Caesar the things which are Caesar's," he thunders, "and unto God the things that are God's!"

He then paints a gloomy picture of the future of the country if politics should become a handmaiden of any particular religion, sect, or cult. He predicts a tragic struggle might develop between creeds to gain dominance. "All wars are bad," he says sorrowfully, "but religious wars are the worst."

His concluding remarks, delivered with every evidence of heartfelt sincerity, describe the horrendous effects on American society if the reins of local, state, and national governments are surrendered to political churchmen who care less for the Constitution than for their own dogma.

"Do we want to see Chicago become another Belfast?" he demands. "Or Los Angeles become another Beirut? We can only ensure our continued existence as a peaceable republic if we resolutely banish from the White House, from the Capitol, and from our courts any unwarranted sectarianism. It can only set brother against brother and make a mockery of our democratic traditions.

"All of you here today have the power to affect public opinion. I entreat you as strongly as I can to make your viewers aware of the danger that exists and will continue to grow like a malignant cancer as long as a nonelected religious fanatic is allowed to dictate the laws of our beloved land.

"Thank you."

Trent receives another standing ovation. Later, in private confabs, the television executives discuss the significance of what they have heard. Most agree that Samuel Trent, a man once called the Clown Prince of American Politics, must now be considered a serious candidate in the next presidential election.

On the flight back to Washington aboard a chartered jetliner, Trent and his staff are enormously buoyed by the day's events. The failed assassination and the splendid reception by the TV execs put everyone in a euphoric mood.

That night, at home with his wife, Samuel delivers a detailed account of that momentous and exciting afternoon.

Pacing back and forth before her chair, he gloats on the laudatory publicity that is sure to result.

"I tell you I'm on my way," he exults. "Those party moneybags have got to be impressed. I'm surprised I haven't heard from them already. Nothing can stop me now. I'm sitting on top of the world. Abner Hawkins is finished, and Brother Kristos will be a has-been, soon to become a never-was. I am going to be the next President, and you are going to be First Lady. How does that sound, Matilda?"

"Samuel," she says gently, "sit down for a moment. I have something important to tell you."

=9=

"Good news and bad news," Marvin Lindberg says, uncapping his bottle of seltzer. "I'll give you the good first. I spent the last two days in western Maryland, and I finally found the perfect spot for a burial. It's near an overgrown road on the approaches to Backbone Mountain."

"Much traffic?" John Tollinger asks.

"None at all this time of year. That's really rugged country up there. This particular road might originally have been a logging trail. It's heavily rutted, but it can be navigated. No houses around for miles and miles. You couldn't ask for a more deserted spot."

"You think you could find it at night?"

"Hell yes. It's way off U.S. Highway Fifty, but I drove the route three times, and I could find it with my eyes closed. I can't tell you how wild it is with trees and undergrowth. We'll have to clear a space, but how much room do you need for a grave? Two feet by six feet at the most—right? Less than that if we double him over."

"And you say there's no traffic, no farmhouses, no one to come prowling around?"

"John, if we dig a decent hole and cover the ground with dead branches and bushes, no one's going to find those bones in a thousand years."

Tollinger makes a check mark after an item on the clipboard on his lap. "Sounds good," he says, and takes a sip of his single malt scotch. "Now what's the bad news?"

"On the trip back, my old Buick started to act up. Sounded like the transmission to me. I stopped at a garage, and the guy put in some fluid. He said it would get me home, but a new transmission would be the only permanent cure. I'm not spending another dime on that clunker, so you better not depend on it for transportation. And your Jag'll never hold all of us."

"No problem," Tollinger says. "We'll use Oberfest's car. He's got a big Cadillac."

"Look, John," Lindberg says, "the way you describe this guy, he's a real weak sister. You think we can count on him?"

"Not to worry; I can manage him. He did fine with the Russian, didn't he? Now here's the scenario: as soon as he hears from this Major Marchuk, he'll contact me and I'll contact you. We'll all meet here to get Oberfest wired. Then we'll get to their meeting place early enough to set things up before the Russian arrives. I've rehearsed Michael a dozen times, and if all goes well, we should get a good tape of their conversation, plus the poison—if the major delivers."

"That's a big *if*. We figured we'd scam Brother Kristos the same way, but he weaseled out of it. I hope this Commie isn't as street-smart."

Tollinger stares at him thoughtfully. "Not getting cold feet, are you, Marvin?"

"Who, me? Not a chance. I just don't want to take a fall because we pulled something stupid."

"There's nothing stupid in the plan," John says patiently. "Admittedly, a good deal depends on luck, but so does everything else in this world."

"You can say that again. And the bastard needs killing—no doubt about that. Did you see the revival meeting he emcee'd in the White House? The guy's a loose cannon. Let him run, and he'll be putting atheists in concentration camps."

"I couldn't agree more," Tollinger says warmly. "I saw that spectacle on TV and was shocked that it was coming from the East Room. You know how much I dislike Trent, but I must admit he's making a lot of sense these days. That's another reason I want to terminate Brother Kristos, it'll put the quietus to Trent's presidential ambitions. Now there's irony for you; it's exactly the motive of Major Marchuk of the KGB."

"John, how are you going to explain my presense to Oberfest?"

"I've already told him that you're an electronics technician, and you have to be at the meeting with Marchuk to make certain the equipment is working."

"You think of everything."

On January 19, a little before noon, Oberfest calls John Tollinger at his White House office. Michael's voice sounds shrill.

"It's on," he says. "Tonight at midnight."

"Fine," Tollinger says calmly. "Did he tell you where?"

"Yes, it's going to be at—"

"Not on the phone," Tollinger says hastily. "Be at my house at eight o'clock tonight."

"All right, I'll be there. John, are you sure this is going to work?"

"My house. Tonight. Eight o'clock."

Then Tollinger hangs up and calls Lindberg.

Oberfest arrives first. The man is in a pitiable state, face ashen, hands trembly. Tollinger gets him ensconced in the big armchair in the den and mixes him a double gin martini.

"It's going to be all right, Mike," he says soothingly. "It'll go like silk; you'll see. Did the Russian say whether or not he had the poison?"

"No, he just told me when and where to meet him."

"Good enough. Now just relax and sip your drink. Save your story until the tech gets here, and then we'll plan our tactics."

"I'm hungry," Oberfest says fretfully. "Got anything to eat? No, scratch that; I'm too hyper to eat; I'd probably upchuck."

"You'll be fine," Tollinger comforts him. "I have cold cuts in the fridge, and we'll have a sandwich before we leave."

Lindberg arrives, carrying the transmitter and receiver. John introduces the two men, and then the three conspirators pull their chairs close and lean forward.

"We've met there before," Oberfest tells them. "It's a turnoff on the road to Annapolis. A one-laner, very dark and deserted."

"How long will it take us to get there?" Tollinger asks. "An hour?"

"An hour is plenty, even with traffic."

"We'll give it two hours," John says decisively, "just to make sure. We'll leave here at ten o'clock. Michael, you go first, and we'll follow in my Jag. Marvin, show Mike the equipment."

Lindberg exhibits the small electronic devices. "This is the one you'll be wearing," he tells Oberfest. "It's a microphone-transmitter. All you have to do is switch it on right here. See? It's battery-powered, so leave it off until the guy arrives. Then don't forget to switch it on or we're all dead."

"I won't forget," Michael says, shivering.

"This one is the receiver and cassette recorder. John

and I will handle it. Don't worry; it's our baby. You just remember to switch on your transmitter. When you met the Russian there before, did you sit in his car or yours?"

"Neither. We got out and walked up and down the road."

"Beautiful. Try to do the same thing tonight. It'll improve our reception a hundred percent. Now I figure the best thing is to tape the transmitter to the bottom of your shin. If he pats you down, chances are he won't grope near your ankle. I brought along some wide adhesive tape to attach it to your leg. Any questions?"

"I'm hungry," Oberfest says again with a nervous giggle.

They all move into the kitchen, and Tollinger puts out rye bread, boiled ham, sliced Swiss cheese, mustard, a jar of kosher dills. Michael has two sandwiches and another martini. Lindberg builds one thick sandwich and drinks seltzer. Tollinger has another scotch but doesn't eat anything.

They go over the plan again. Then Oberfest pulls up his right trouser leg, and Marvin tapes the transmitter to his white, hairless skin. They move out onto the patio and test the equipment. Everything works perfectly.

A few minutes after ten, Michael gets into his green Eldorado and pulls away. Lindberg and Tollinger follow closely in the black Jaguar XJ-S coupé.

"I think he'll do okay," John says.

"Let us pray," Marvin says. "He would drive a car like that; it's the color of money."

They're at the turnoff from the Annapolis highway in less than an hour. They see the Cadillac slow and turn; they tailgate down the narrow road.

"Shit," Lindberg says, "it's gravel. If they walk up and down on that, we'll pick up a lot of scrunching."

"No use telling him to walk softly," Tollinger says. "He's spooked enough as it is."

Oberfest pulls onto the verge, switches off his engine and lights. They pull close alongside.

"We're going down the road a way," Lindberg calls. "Out of sight. You stay right here. We'll come back and run a final test."

Tollinger drives another half-mile, around a bend, parks off the road. They lock up and walk back.

It is a cloudless night, a bulbous moon casting a silver sheen on the gravel. A January thaw has arrived; the air is almost balmy. Both men walk with their topcoats unbuttoned.

They come up to the Cadillac and Marvin heads across the field east of the road while John baby-sits Oberfest.

"When your meeting is finished," he tells Michael, "don't wait for us. Head back for my place in Spring Valley. We'll meet you there."

"Jesus, I'm scared," Oberfest says. "What if he discovers I'm wired? He'll kill me."

"He won't kill you," Tollinger says. "You're too valuable to him."

Lindberg comes back grousing. "Nothing there for us," he reports. "All flat land, and that sonofabitch moon is like a floodlight. The Russian would spot us for sure. I'll try the other side."

He heads westward.

"Is the bug comfortable?" Tollinger asks. "It won't make you limp, will it?"

"No, it's okay. Oh God, how did I ever get into this mess."

"You'll be out of it soon with a nice fat tape recording starring Major Marchuk of the Soviet Union."

"I hope so. I haven't been able to get it up for weeks. That Commie bastard is ruining my sex life."

Lindberg returns. "I found something," he says. "It's not the best, but I think it'll do: a shallow ditch, reasonably dry, with a high screen of pussy willows. Oberfest, switch on your microphone, and the two of you start walking on the gravel and talking. I want to check the reception."

He disappears again. Michael bends down to switch on the transmitter, then the two men start walking.

"You still with Trent?" Tollinger asks.

"Oh sure," Oberfest says. "In his D.C. headquarters. You know, John, I'm beginning to think the guy may make it to the Oval Office."

"I don't think so," Tollinger says shortly. "The election is almost two years away. A lot can happen."

Lindberg comes across the road. "Switch off your transmitter," he tells Oberfest. "We don't want to run down the batteries. John, the reception is okay. Less static from the gravel than I figured. How we doing on time?"

Tollinger peers closely at his watch. "About twenty minutes to twelve."

"Then we better get in position. Oberfest, is your bug switched off?"

"It's off."

"Good. Just remember to flip it on again when the guy shows up."

"I'll remember."

"Then let's get this show on the road."

A few minutes after midnight, Tollinger and Lindberg see headlights turn off Highway 301 and come slowly down the graveled road. They scramble into the ditch, prop themselves on the bank, peer cautiously over the edge. They see the approaching car stop; the lights are turned off.

"Do you have your gun?" Tollinger asks.

"Yep."

"We may need it," John says, amazed at how quickly he has adapted to a world of weapons, danger, and potential violence.

They wait anxiously.

"Turn it on, baby," Lindberg mutters. "Come on, turn it on."

Silence.

"Oh Jesus," he says despairingly, "the silly wimp has panicked."

But then they hear a click from the receiver's loudspeaker, a short rush of static, the sound of a car door slammed shut.

"Thank God," Tollinger says softly.

Up on the road, Marchuk climbs heavily from his Lincoln, closes the door, joins Oberfest, who's leaning against the front fender of his Cadillac.

"So," the major says brightly, "here we are again."

"Yeah," Michael says. "Beautiful day today—right?"

"All days are beautiful," the Russian says, "when you can wake up. Shall we take a little walk?"

"Not much of an accent," John whispers to Lindberg. "I wonder where he went to school. Can you turn up the volume just a little?"

Marvin fusses with the receiver. The voices and footfalls on the road become sharper. The tape-cassette reels turn slowly and steadily.

"Tell me," the major says, "have you been thinking about my proposal?"

"*His* proposal," Tollinger says in a low voice. "We suckered him into it."

"Yes, I've been thinking about it," Oberfest says, "but there's something I've got to get straight first."

"And what is that, Arnold?"

"If I do what you suggest, do you promise I'll get my tapes back, Major Marchuk?"

"Major Marchuk?" the Russian booms. "So formal? You may call me Leon if you wish. One of my California girls told me it means 'brave as a lion.' Isn't that nice? But to answer your question, I give you my word of honor as a Soviet officer that I shall return all your tapes as soon as Brother Kristos is eliminated."

"Got him," Tollinger says with quiet satisfaction.

"He just hung himself," Lindberg agrees. "And I take back that 'wimp' crack. So far Oberfest is doing fine."

The two men lean closer to the loudspeaker. They hear the scuff of footsteps on the gravel road, but the voices are still clear.

Marchuk: "Of course I realize that you must trust me, Arnold, but I must also trust you to do this job of work neatly and efficiently."

Oberfest: "Then you got the go-ahead from Moscow?"

"Well, my headquarters are not exactly *in* Moscow, but close enough. Yes, my bosses are quite taken with this initiative, and I have orders to proceed with it as soon as possible."

"What about the poison?"

"I have it with me."

"You must have been very sure of me."

"I know you for an intelligent man. I was certain you would consider the proposal carefully, and then come to a wise and practical decision."

"What's in it?"

"The poison? A little bit of this, a little bit of that. Perhaps some potassium cyanide. Perhaps some pilocarpine hydrochloride. And a few other things. It is a top-secret brew; I am sure you would not be interested in the exact formulation."

"It's colorless?"

"And odorless and tasteless. Less than an ounce will be sufficient."

"How long does it take to work?"

"This particular recipe should produce results within five minutes. Ten at the most."

Then the men on the road are silent.

"Michael is remembering all his lines," Tollinger says. "And his voice is strong. That's a plus."

"What burns my ass," Lindberg says, "is that fucking Red son of a bitch will probably get a promotion out of this."

"Are you sure it will work?" Oberfest asks the Russian.

"Arnold, Arnold," Marchuk says, groaning, "do you doubt a triumph of Soviet science? Here it is. Take it. The little bottle is plastic, but still, treat it gently."

"Five minutes?" Michael says.

"Perhaps ten. It will give you a chance to make your farewell."

"Yes."

"And when may I expect to read of the untimely death of Brother Kristos?"

"I don't know. A couple of weeks. I don't want to seem too eager to see him again. I want to play it cool."

"By all means," the major says, "play it cool—within two weeks."

"And then I get my tapes back?"

"Of course, m'boy," Marchuk says genially. "I gave you my word, did I not? And now I must leave you. I wish you great good luck in your assignment."

"Yeah," Oberfest says. "Thanks."

Conversation ceases. The men in the ditch hear footsteps, the sounds of car doors opening, engines starting up. They see headlights come on. The Lincoln backs onto the shoulder of the road, turns, takes off. Then the Cadillac makes its turn and moves slowly away.

"That's it," Lindberg says, switching off the receiver. "Signed, sealed, and delivered."

"Couldn't ask for anything better," Tollinger says, rising and brushing himself off.

"Now comes the hard part," the ex-FBI man says. "Dealing with Oberfest. He may be a problem."

"Nothing I can't manage," John says. "You wouldn't happen to have a pocketknife, would you?"

"I have a little penknife. Why?"

"I'd like to cut down some of these pussy willows. They're really lovely. Look at the size of those buds! I think I'll take a bunch."

By the time they get back to Spring Valley, the green Eldorado is parked in Tollinger's driveway. Oberfest is standing outside, practically dancing with excitement.

"Did you get it, did you get it?" he demands. "Wasn't I great? I mean, he identified himself and everything—just what we wanted. You got it, didn't you?"

"Come inside," John says. "Let's not talk out here."

He gets them into the den, but he won't answer Michael's questions until he puts the clump of pussy willows into a vase and then serves drinks.

"Mike," he says, "first of all I want to tell you what an excellent job you did. You handled the whole thing perfectly."

"Like a pro," Lindberg adds.

"You have the poison?" Tollinger asks.

"Right here," Oberfest says.

He takes it from his jacket pocket. It is a colorless liquid in a clear plastic vial, closed with a black rubber stopper. He hands it over.

"Get rid of it," he says. "Pour it down the sink or flush it down the toilet. I don't want it around. That stuff scares me."

"I'll take care of it," Tollinger says, slipping the vial into his pocket.

"And what about the tape?" Oberfest says. "You got that, didn't you?"

"Marvin?" John asks.

"Well, we haven't played it back yet," Lindberg says, "but it should be okay. The reception was good, and the reels were turning. I figure we got ourselves a masterpiece."

"Good," Michael says, grinning with delight. "Now if you'll give me the cassette, I'll be on my way. I want to play it at home. Wait'll I tell that Russian bastard what I've got; he'll shit his pants. And listen, I want to thank both of you for helping me out on this. You saved my life, and I mean that. If there's ever anything I can do for you, just let me know."

"Why yes," John Tollinger says with a cold smile, "there is something you can do."

=10=

The January thaw retreats before the advance of a low-pressure front that blankets the entire eastern seaboard. And pushing in behind that pall, weather forecasters warn, is a blast of arctic air moving slowly south from Canada. Variously called the Calgary Clipper and the Siberian Express, this approaching wave is said to pack sub-zero temperatures and sixty-knot winds.

The nation's capital is already shrouded by a thick cloudbank the color of elephant hide. The top of the Washington Monument is hidden by early-morning fog, and gusts of wind snap the flag flying over the White House.

On January 23, John Tollinger calls Jennifer Raye at her office. But her secretary tells him that Jennifer is in Philadelphia with the First Lady and is not expected back until late that afternoon.

"Would you like to leave a message, sir?" she chirps.

"Just tell her John Tollinger called, please. I'll try to reach her later today."

The new Congress is just beginning to get organized, and the office of the Chief of Staff is busy trying to keep up with the membership rolls of congressional committees. No one gets out for lunch, and Tollinger trails Henry

Folsom from meeting to meeting, making notes in his own personal shorthand as decisions are made or, more frequently, postponed.

He tries phoning Jennifer twice more late in the afternoon and early evening, but she still has not returned. He gives up and concentrates on his paperwork, trying to bring order out of the day's confusing events and non-events.

Finally, at ten P.M., he decides he has earned his salary for the day, and tidies his office, putting the most sensitive notes, letters, and memoranda in his safe. Just before he turns off his desk lamp, he calls Jennifer one last time, at her apartment in Georgetown. Unexpectedly, she answers.

"Ellie told me you called," she says, "but I was so beat when we got back that all I wanted to do was kick off my shoes and get to work on a martini."

"Tough day?" he asks.

"Awful. It was cold, wet, and raw in Philly, and our flight was an hour late. And madame was cranky all day because George has the flu but she had to leave him to go open a new soup kitchen in the City of Brotherly Love. How was your day?"

"The usual insanity. I'm still at the office, about to leave. Could I stop by your place for a couple of minutes? I have something for you."

"Oh? Something nice?"

"I think it is."

"Well, I don't want you coming up. This place is a mess. How about parking in front. Give me three beeps on your horn, and I'll come down."

"If that's the way you want it. I should be there in a half-hour or so."

But traffic is murder, and it takes him a little longer than that. When he pulls up outside her town house, Jennifer is waiting in the vestibule, wearing her long raccoon coat. She dashes out, slides into the bucket seat next to him and, surprisingly, kisses his cheek.

"Leave the heater on," she commands. "It's cold." She looks at him critically. "My God, you're thin. All drawn and bony. They must be running you ragged."

"Something like that."

"You sleeping okay?"

"Like a baby."

"I know that gag; you wake up crying every two hours. What did you bring me?"

He reaches behind the seats, lifts up the thick bunch of pussy willows swathed in tissue paper and tied with a blue ribbon. He places the clump of branches on her lap.

"Pussy willows?" She laughs delightedly. "I haven't seen those in years. Where did you buy them?"

"I didn't. I took a drive out in the country a few days ago, spotted them, and cut some down for you. I thought you might like them."

"I *love* them! It was very kind of you to think of me. You know, you can be a sweetheart when you try."

"I guess I didn't try hard enough or often enough."

She doesn't reply, and he turns sideways to get a good look at her. She is as he remembers her: not a beautiful woman perhaps, but with striking features. She is still the only woman in the world with whom he would willingly share his life.

"It's mea culpa time," he says. "But I'll try to make it short and painless. I just wanted you to know that I've come to realize that the blame for our breakup was all mine. You were right; I'm a cold fish. Too set in my ways, too addicted to order, routine, whatever. But I want you to know that in my crabbed way I did love you and still do."

Her eyes glimmer with tears. "Thank you, John," she says huskily. "I know how difficult it is for you to say those things. But the fault wasn't entirely yours. It was a mismatch from the start."

"I suppose," he says. "It's only recently that I've acknowledged that emotion and instinct are far stronger than logic and reason. I always thought the brain should rule the heart, but it brought me a bloodless kind of happiness."

"You can change—if you really want to."

"Can I? Perhaps. But I have a horrible feeling that my poor, desiccated soul will remain as it always has been, without passion."

"You mustn't say that about yourself. It's just not true!"

He smiles sadly. "I know myself better than you know me. Anyway, no matter what happens, I wanted you to know I love you."

She looks at him worriedly. "No matter what happens?" she repeats. "You're not planning to do anything foolish, are you, John?"

"Have you ever known me to do anything foolish?"

"No," she admits, "I never have."

"Except let you get away. If I had been able to loosen up, try to widen my perception of what life is all about, you might have been my salvation. But it's too late for that now. Well, enough of this soul-baring. Thank you for hearing me out."

"I'd like to see you again," she says suddenly. "Could we do that?"

"Of course."

"When?"

"Soon. I'll call you."

"You better, or I'll call you."

She reaches for him, pulls him close, kisses him on the lips. A long kiss. Then she breaks away.

"You always were a great kisser," she says breathlessly. "I've got to go now. You will call? Promise?"

"I promise."

She opens the car door, then pauses. She snaps a bud off a pussy-willow stalk and places it in his palm.

"For you," she says solemnly.

He is left alone, looking down at that single bud in his palm. He touches it with a fingertip. It is soft and warm. He rolls it about a moment, staring at it. Then he opens his window and tosses it away.

=11=

The women arriving at the Mattingly house come scurrying from cabs and limousines, heads ducked against the freezing rain. Only Brother Kristos could bring them out on such a squally day.

Assembled in the preacher's study, the ladies, dressed in black out of respect for a man of God, have the appearance of mourners at a state funeral. As usual, the chamber is overheated, but they still hear the wind's howl and rattle of hail against the windows.

Brother Kristos makes his entrance swiftly from the bedroom. He is clad in a belted robe of silk as white as a winding sheet. He wears no jewelry, not even the golden cross, but carries an ebony crucifix. He sits in the big armchair at the head of the table.

His audience has come to hear him speak of life without sin and pleasure without guilt. He does not disappoint them. "Happiness is contagious," he says, "but misery is a solitary disorder."

He expounds on this theme, telling them it is within their power not only to remake their own existence but also to transfigure the lives of those about them.

"Think of yourselves as evangelists," he urges, "and know that your love of God may transform the world."

He begins to speak of the power of holy love. Suddenly he stops in midsentence. His features freeze, he seems to be staring at a point in space. Fire ignites his eyes, and that blazing glare frightens his audience.

He rises slowly to his feet, still gazing upward, not meeting the glances of his congregants. Then he is standing erect, broad shoulders back, spine stiff. He clutches the ebony cross with such force that his hands tremble. When he begins to speak, his words are so low-pitched that the women must lean forward to hear.

"Who can fully comprehend his own dissolution?" he asks. "Who dares to imagine nothing anymore? In self-protection, the mind slides away from such thoughts. Nothing anymore? Where are we to find the courage to face such a horror? The taste of life, the joys and wonders—all gone. What are we to do? How are we to endure the knowledge of nothing anymore?"

The ladies look at one another, puzzled and made uneasy by the questioning tone of his discourse. He who has always been so certain and assured now sounds confused and wandering.

"On the sunniest of days," he continues, speaking as if to himself, "the shadow is there. It hovers over the cradle and over the bridal bed, over dining table and workbench. It blocks our plans and mocks our dreams. We are all born defeated and take in failure with our first breath. Mortality is the poison that—"

He ends his elegy as abruptly as he began. His gaze slowly lowers, the incandescence fades from his eyes. He seems to recollect where he is and to whom he is speaking. He sits down quietly, puts the crucifix aside and, combing fingers through his beard, takes up his original sermon on the proselytizing power of holy love.

When he has concluded, he retires quickly to the bedroom and closes the door. The women drift away, still disquieted by his strange behavior.

Emily Mattingly knocks timorously on the bedroom door. When there is no reply, she calls, "Brother Kristos, are you all right?"

"Yes," he answers. "Come in."

He is standing alongside the bed, a glass of vodka in his hand.

"Are you all right?" she asks again.

He nods.

"I was worried about you," she says confusedly. "You seemed so . . . so disturbed."

"Did I?" he says with a casual shrug. "Fear not them that kill the body but are not able to kill the soul. Would you like a drink?"

"A small one perhaps."

"Please, help yourself," he says, sitting down heavily on the bed. He waits until she has poured herself a small vodka and added water from the bathroom tap. She seats herself on the bed close to him.

"Sister," he says, "I am going to make an appointment with my attorney to draw up my will. I should have done it before this, but I do not believe it is too late. I don't have a great deal to leave, but I want to make several specific individual bequests. In addition, I wish to make certain that I will be cremated. If it is possible, I would like my ashes scattered over the farmlands of Nebraska. Do you understand that?"

She nods dumbly.

"Good," he says. "I wanted a personal witness to my final wishes in case my will is not completed in time."

"Stop it!" she cries. "You frighten me when you talk like that. You're not going to die."

He smiles, places a hand gently on her breast.

"With faith," he says, "death can be a glory."

It is January 25.

=12=

Persuading Oberfest to join the assassination plot proves to be more arduous than Tollinger anticipated. It takes several days and is made more difficult when Michael starts weeping.

"I'm not a killer," he sobs. "I'm just not *like* that."

"Mike," John says patiently, "I have explained that we are not asking you to kill Brother Kristos. That's my job."

"Then what do you need me for?"

"First of all, we needed you to obtain an effective poison."

"Well, you've got it! Keep the goddamned poison, give me my tape, and let me get out of here."

"It's not that easy," Tollinger says. "If we give you the tape without involving you in the murder, then you have life-and-death power over us. You *must* be a partner. You can understand that, can't you?"

Oberfest takes a gulp of his martini. "I won't say anything," he assures them. "Not a word. As far as I'm concerned, I don't know a thing about any poison or any murder."

Marvin Lindberg shakes his head. "Not good enough," he says. "If push comes to shove, you'll talk to save your ass. I'm not putting you down for that; it would be the natural, human thing to do. We need insurance. If you help us out, then we'll know you'll protect yourself by protecting us. Also, we need your car."

"My car! What the hell for?"

"To transport the preacher to his final resting place. John's car is too small, mine has a bum transmission, and we sure can't use Kristos'. How many silver Scorpios are there in D.C.? It would be remembered by every cop on the road."

Oberfest is silent, nursing his drink.

"Look," Tollinger says, "we've been discussing what *we* get out of it. Now let's talk about the benefits this plan offers *you*. First of all, it gets Major Marchuk off your back. Brother Kristos will be terminated, just as the Russian wants. When that happens, he certainly should return those tapes. And if he breaks his promise, you still have a tape that ties him directly to the actual murder of an American citizen. He'll do anything you demand to get that evidence back."

"I guess," Michael says slowly. "I get the tape after Brother Kristos is eliminated?"

"Absolutely."

Oberfest takes a deep breath. "And all this time," he says sadly, "I thought you guys just wanted to help me out."

"We did want to help you," Tollinger says, "and we *are* helping you. And helping ourselves at the same time. Quid pro quo. That's not so awful, is it?"

"So all I've got to do is supply my car? Nothing else?"

"We'll get to that later," John says. "But you won't have to poison Kristos; I give you my word."

It is then almost two o'clock in the morning. Tollinger has planned it this way, counting on physical weariness to help wear down Oberfest's resistance. And the ploy is working; they can almost see Michael wavering as he considers his options and realizes how tightly he has been snared.

"Just out of curiosity," he asks Tollinger, "why are you doing this? What's your motive in killing Brother Kristos?"

"Let's not get into a heavy discussion of motives. Quite

simply, I'm doing it because I consider the man a threat to constitutional government."

"Uh-huh," Oberfest says. "And the fact that he's banging your ex has nothing to do with it—right?"

"Don't be absurd," Tollinger says. "Kristos is a threat to the country. And he's ruining the political career of Abner Hawkins, an honest, decent man I happen to admire."

"Thank you, professor," Michael says. "Eloquently put." He turns to Marvin Lindberg. "And what's your peeve?"

"It's more than a peeve," Lindberg says angrily. "I think he's a slimy scuzz using the word of God to defraud a lot of innocent, devout people of their hard-earned bucks. If the law can't stop the guy, I sure as hell can."

"Well . . ." Oberfest says, "I guess you both have your reasons, but to tell you the truth, I couldn't care less if the preacher lives or dies. All I'm concerned about is getting the Soviet Union out of my life."

"Then you're in?" Tollinger asks him.

"I don't have much choice, do I?"

"Not much," Lindberg agrees.

During the next four days the conspirators meet every evening in Tollinger's home to refine the plot. As each step of the projected assassination is discussed, honed, and approved, Tollinger puts a neat check mark after the item on his clipboard.

Solving the problem of the cars requires lengthy debate. The plan calls for Lindberg and Oberfest to arrive at Spring Valley before Brother Kristos. But if each man is driving his own car, Tollinger's driveway will look like a parking lot.

"That's unacceptable," he says. "This is a quiet residential neighborhood, and people notice things. They'll see four cars parked outside my house and wonder if I'm having a party. That kind of attention we don't need. I suggest I put my Jag in the garage along with Michael's Cadillac.

But what to do with Marvin's Buick is the puzzle. I think it would be best if Kristos doesn't see any other cars parked outside when he arrives. We don't want to spook the man."

"I could leave my heap at home," Lindberg suggests, "and take a taxi here. Only I don't want a record of the trip on the cabby's sheet."

"I could pick you up," Oberfest offers, "and give you a lift here and then home again when it's all over."

"I don't think so," the ex-FBI man says. "I'd feel naked without wheels. And there's another question that needs answering: after we bury the preacher at Backbone Mountain and return, what are we going to do with his Scorpio? We've got to dump it somewhere."

After an hour of discussion, this is what they finally decide:

Lindberg will drive his Buick to Washington from Alexandria and park in a commercial garage. Oberfest will pick him up there and drive him out to Spring Valley in the Cadillac.

When they return from burying Brother Kristos, Lindberg will drive the Scorpio to a parking lot at one of the airports and leave it there. Oberfest will chauffeur him back to the commercial garage to pick up his Buick.

"Kristos probably won't be reported missing for a day or two," Lindberg says. "Maybe more. If his car is found at an airport, they'll figure he took a flight somewhere. It'll take a week to check passenger lists and interview airport personnel. Every day that passes, the trail will get colder."

"It sounds good," Tollinger admits, "but are you willing to run the danger of being spotted driving Kristos' car?"

"Not much danger. If we stick to our timetable, we should be back early in the morning. Not many people around at that hour. And I'll wear gloves so I don't leave any prints. I think it'll work. There's risk, sure, but there's no possible way of making this thing foolproof."

"All right," Tollinger says, and checks his list. "Now the next item on the agenda is the actual poisoning."

He explains that the preacher likes to drink directly from the bottle. It would be easy to pour the poison into an open bottle from which a few ounces have been removed, but Tollinger fears that a liter of vodka will so dilute the strength of the poison that it might lose its potency.

"I don't know," Oberfest say doubtfully. "According to Marchuk, it's powerful stuff."

"Can't you serve him by the glass?" Lindberg asks.

Tollinger considers a moment. "I think what I'll do is this: I'll bring him his first two or three drinks in full glasses so he mellows out. Then, when the vodka is half gone, I'll add the poison to the bottle and bring it out. I'll laugh and say I'm tired of making all those trips back and forth to the kitchen. He won't get suspicious."

Lindberg nods. "I think it'll fly. What's next on your list?"

They discuss the special equipment they'll need, including two spades, a mattock, a flashlight, a battery-powered lantern, a sleeping bag with side zipper to contain the corpse, and perhaps fifty feet of stout nylon line.

"Let's play this cozy," Lindberg says. "All those things should not—repeat, *not*—be bought at the same store. Each of us should pick up one or two items at different stores."

"Good thinking," Tollinger says. "I'll make out shopping lists for each of us. Now let's talk about what we should wear. From what Marvin says, we're going up into rough country."

By the fourth day, the conspirators have agreed upon a schedule for the murder of Brother Kristos. The final scheme is as follows:

1. Tollinger phones Brother Kristos and invites him out to Spring Valley for drinks and talk. Preferred time: eight

P.M. Tollinger then informs Lindberg and Oberfest what evening the preacher will arrive.

2. Lindberg drives his Buick over from Alexandria and parks in a preselected commercial garage at six P.M.

3. Oberfest picks up Lindberg at the garage and drives him out to Spring Valley. They arrive an hour before the victim: seven P.M.

4. The Cadillac is parked next to Tollinger's Jaguar, and the garage door is lowered.

5. Lindberg and Oberfest go upstairs to the bedroom.

6. Brother Kristos arrives at eight P.M. Tollinger leads him into the den and serves him the first drink of unadulterated vodka.

7. At nine P.M. Tollinger brings his guest the bottle of poisoned vodka.

8. Kristos dies at approximately 9:15 P.M.

9. Tollinger summons Lindberg and Oberfest from upstairs. The keys to the Scorpio are taken from Kristos' pocket, and the body is zipped into the sleeping bag, along with the preacher's hat and coat, and carried through the connecting door into the garage. The bundle is placed on the rear floor of Oberfest's Eldorado. The equipment is loaded into the trunk.

10. Tollinger, Lindberg, and Oberfest depart from Spring Valley no later than ten P.M. with the concealed corpse. They drive northwestward on Highway 270, heading for Frederick, then Hagerstown and Cumberland.

11. They arrive at the burial spot near Backbone Mountain by two A.M.

12. The grave is dug. Brother Kristos is buried. The grave is filled in and concealed with brush.

13. They head back to Washington, arriving no later than seven A.M.

14. The equipment is unloaded from the Cadillac and left in Tollinger's garage. Lindberg leaves, driving Kristos' Scorpio, and Oberfest follows.

15. Tollinger smashes the glass and bottle he and

Brother Kristos handled, and puts the shards outside in the garbage can.

16. Lindberg leaves the Scorpio in an airport parking area, locks the car, and transfers to Oberfest's Cadillac. He is then driven to the commercial garage, where he reclaims his Buick. He and Oberfest return to their homes.

This scenario is completed on the evening of January 29, a Sunday.

"Well, that's it," Tollinger declares. "We can't anticipate everything, but I think this plan is as airtight as we can make it. If we keep our nerve, we should be able to deal with the unexpected."

"All right, all right," Marvin says impatiently. "We've palavered long enough; let's get to it. When are you going to call Kristos?"

"I'll do it right now," Tollinger says.

He looks up the number and phones. It rings five times before the preacher answers.

"Hello?"

"Brother Kristos?"

"I am here."

"This is John Tollinger."

"Yes," Brother Kristos says, "I have been expecting your call."

=13=

On Monday night, the predicted frigid air mass begins moving in from the northwest to cover most of the Atlantic seaboard from New England to northern Florida. It is accompanied by mean winds of twenty to thirty knots, with punishing gusts up to forty-five.

Fortunately, there is little snow, just occasional flurries: hard, crisp flakes that no sooner descend than they are whirled aloft again by the rushing wind. The mercury plummets. In Washington during the day, the temperature is in the single digits. At night, it falls to zero, to ten below.

The freeze continues throughout the week, with no relief predicted until Friday at the earliest. Meanwhile, most people stay indoors. The toll of dead rises as the homeless are picked up from the city streets. One stiff corpse is found wrapped in newspapers near the Jefferson Memorial.

In the nation's capital, many government agencies are closed, or open only during curtailed hours. Both houses of Congress are adjourned.

John Tollinger leaves the West Wing of the White House at 3:30 P.M. on the afternoon of February 2. He plans to get home early, for this Thursday is what the three conspirators call D-day.

Oberfest: "D for death?"

Tollinger: "I prefer D for deliverance."

At home, he heats up a can of mulligatawny and has

that with a bologna on rye. He knows he should be eating more since it'll be his last meal of the day, but the soup and sandwich are all he can manage.

He goes upstairs, takes off his shoes, rolls onto his bed atop the covers. He doesn't expect to sleep, just relax, but he actually dozes for almost an hour. When he awakens at 5:20, he strips down and showers, although he showered that morning.

He dons thermal underwear, heavy whipcord slacks, wool socks, fleece-lined boots, a turtleneck fisherman's sweater. He doesn't believe Brother Kristos will be surprised by his costume; the preacher will probably be dressed just as warmly.

He goes down to the kitchen and places two liters of peppered vodka, a bottle of cognac, and one of Glenfiddich on the countertop. And four ordinary highball glasses. Not his best crystal.

He would like very much to have a drink. Perhaps an extremely dry gin martini. He can almost taste the bite of that, the sharp, astringent flavor, the pungent bouquet. But he does not mix one. It would smack too much of Dutch courage. It would, he decides, be *ethically* wrong.

At 6:30 P.M. he turns on the radio to hear the weather report. He is gratified to learn the snow flurries are tapering off with no appreciable accumulation. All roads and highways are open. But the subfreezing weather continues to grip the eastern seaboard.

Preparations complete, he has nothing to do but wait. And having abjured alcohol to take the edge off his tenseness, he now turns his thoughts resolutely to the act he is about to commit: take a human life. Murder.

He takes the vial of poison from a kitchen drawer, holds it up to the light, cannot resist quoting, "Is this a dagger which I see before me, the handle toward my hand?" Bookish to the last, he ruefully admits, and wonders what man's words he will recite on his deathbed. He cannot decide.

When he considers the enormity of what he is about to do, he curses his lack of fervor, for if ever a moment in his life demands passion, this one does. Yet all he can do is review his motives and conclude that the murder of Brother Kristos is justified. It is, in fact, an elegant solution. But he can feel no more enthusiasm than a mathematician who has solved a knotty problem. Satisfaction, perhaps, but not ecstasy.

He is startled to see that it is several minutes after seven o'clock. When they drew up the schedule for D-day, they allowed what they believed to be more than sufficient travel time. Oberfest and Lindberg were due an hour before Brother Kristos' arrival, but the minutes are vanishing, and there is no sign of them. Perturbed, Tollinger goes to the front window to peer through the gauzy curtain.

By 7:30 his unease and bewilderment have grown to the point where he is beginning to wonder if the entire scheme will have to be scratched. It is 7:38 P.M. when, still staring anxiously out the window, he sees the headlights of Oberfest's green Eldorado turn into his driveway. Tollinger hurries to unlock the connecting door to the garage.

Michael comes rushing in. "He's drunk!" he wails. "Drunk as a skunk!"

"What?" Tollinger cries. Then, foolishly, "Who?"

"Your friend Lindberg, that's who. I finally found him wandering around the garage. The guy's smashed."

Marvin Lindberg swaggers in. "Not smashed," he says with a silly grin. "Just a wee bit boozy-woozy."

John stares at him stonily. "You picked a great time to fall off the wagon."

"Don't rattle my cage," Lindberg says. "I'm mobile, ain't I? One way or another, that scum is going to get popped tonight."

And he pulls a snub-nosed revolver from the pocket of his soiled parka and waves it around.

"Put that thing away," Tollinger says sharply. "We're

going to follow the scenario as planned. Now the two of you get upstairs, and for God's sake, be quiet."

"Yes, boss," Lindberg says, then grabs the bottle of brandy from the countertop. "I think I'll take this beauty along for company."

There is despair in his eyes, rage in the way he blinks continually and shows his teeth. He's on the edge, John decides. Ready to fall.

"Don't drink any more," he commands.

"Why not? You want me to be quiet, don't you? This'll keep me quiet. Maybe if you're lucky I'll pass out."

They climb the stairs, Lindberg cradling the cognac bottle in his arms. Tollinger hurries into the garage, lowers the door, turns on the heat. He comes back into the house and listens a moment. There are no sounds from the bedroom. He holds out his hands. They are not trembling.

Brother Kristos arrives a few minutes after eight. Tollinger, at the window, watches him climb out of the Scorpio. The preacher is wrapped in a greatcoat of black vicuña with a collar of mink. His head is bare.

John opens the door to welcome his guest. He helps Kristos take off his coat. It is surprisingly light.

"Very handsome," he says. "A gift?"

"Yes," the other man says. He is wearing a black silk cossack shirt and trousers tucked into shiny jodhpurs. Around his neck is the golden chain and cross.

"I want to thank you for coming," Tollinger says. "It's so cold I thought you might call and put it off to another time."

Brother Kristos doesn't reply. John leads the way into the den and indicates the big armchair alongside the drum table.

"Make yourself comfortable," he says. "I remembered you like pepper vodka. Will that be all right?"

The preacher nods.

"No ice, no water," John says. "I remember."

He goes into the kitchen, fills a highball glass with

vodka and a small balloon with single malt Scotch for himself. He pours with a steady hand and carries the drinks back to the den.

"Let's drink to a heat wave," he says, raising his glass.

Brother Kristos smiles and takes deep swallows of the pepper vodka.

"Something I must ask you," Tollinger says. "When I phoned to invite you to have a drink, you said you had been expecting my call. Was that an example of your prescience?"

The preacher combs fingers slowly through his beard, staring at his host. "No," he says. "I am not omniscient. It was merely that I hadn't heard from you in some time, but I thought it likely you might wish to meet with me again."

"A very rational explanation. You know, Brother Kristos, you have a reputation as a seer as well as a faith healer. Do all those powers have a rational explanation?"

"I think my powers have been greatly exaggerated. Most people believe because they *must* believe. They cannot endure the emptiness of unbelief."

"But several friends—people whose common sense I trust—have told me you *are* able to do those things. Is there a rational explanation?"

"You are a persistent man, Mr. Tollinger. Yes, there is a rational explanation. Rational to me. I doubt very much if you would consider it logical. My glass is empty."

"Of course!" Tollinger says, springing to his feet. He brings a second vodka from the kitchen. "There is another question I'd like to ask you. It's rather personal, and if you feel I'm prying, simply refuse to answer. I won't be offended."

"What is your question?"

"I have listened to you preach, Brother Kristos, and I presume you are sincere. At the same time, it is generally known in Washington that your private life can hardly be

considered godly. How do you reconcile what you profess
and the way you live?"

Kristos again stares directly at Tollinger. There is no
hostility in his gaze, but it is steady and thoughtful.

"You're referring to my drinking and my love of money
and finery?"

"And your relations with women," John says boldly.
"And please don't give me that mumbo jumbo that we
cannot sin because we are created in God's image. I just
want to know how you can claim to be the brother of Jesus
and live the way you do."

The preacher throws back his head, and his mouth
opens in what Tollinger can only guess is a silent laugh.
But there is no amusement in his voice.

"Mr. Tollinger," Brother Kristos says intently, "it is
possible to negotiate with God. I've done it all my life."

"And you do not fear the final reckoning?"

"I do not fear."

"Your glass is empty again," Tollinger says, as if surprised. "I think I better bring you the bottle. Save myself
all these trips back and forth to the kitchen."

Kristos accepts that. But Tollinger goes first to the
downstairs lavatory, a small room he scorns because Jennifer insisted on calling it the Powder Room.

In this cramped cubicle equipped only with sink and
toilet, he washes his hands thoroughly and dries them on
a stained towel that should have gone to the laundry weeks
ago. Then he stares at himself in the mirror but can see
no change in his appearance.

He goes into the kitchen, unstoppers the vial of poison,
carefully pours it into the half-empty bottle. He restoppers
the vial, returns it to the kitchen drawer. He holds his
thumb over the mouth of the vodka bottle and turns it
briefly upside down to mix the two liquids.

"Here we are!" he says brightly, carrying it back to the
den.

Brother Kristos is standing in front of the bookcase, inspecting the titles. He takes the vodka casually from Tollinger's outstretched hand, but he does not drink.

"You have many fine books," he says.

"Yes," John says with a short laugh, "I'm afraid I'm hopelessly addicted."

Then the preacher raises the bottle to his mouth and swallows deeply. The two men sit down again.

"When I was young," the preacher says, "I read a great deal. But none of the books had the answers I sought."

"Not even the Bible?"

"The Bible does not provide answers. But it asks the right questions. I must confess to you that now when I read the Good Book it is not for the sense; only to hear the poetry."

Kristos takes another swallow of vodka, then lifts the bottle to the light of the lamp and peers at it. "Divine poetry," he says, his voice thickened.

"I know you have published a book of prayers," Tollinger says. "Are you planning to do any more writing?"

There is no answer. Brother Kristos slowly raises his eyes until he locks and holds John's with a stare that gradually grows in intensity.

"The messenger," the preacher says, words slurred, tongue protruding from between his lips.

"What?" Tollinger says. "What are you saying?"

His arm trembling, Brother Kristos brings the bottle to his mouth and gulps greedily. Vodka spills onto his beard, down his shirtfront. He attempts to throw the empty bottle away but it slips from his grasp.

He struggles from the armchair, staggers, stands swaying with feet widespread. Something catches in his throat, his chest pumps. He takes heaving breaths, then rips the gold chain and cross from around his neck and casts them away.

Tollinger rises slowly, staring.

"Whosoever," the preacher suddenly screams, face contorted, "whosoever believeth . . . My God, my God, why hast thou . . ."

His arm flings out. The lamp goes over with a crash. Brother Kristos begins roaring. Not words but animal cries and howls. He rocks back and forth. His fiery eyes start bleeding. The ooze flows down onto cheeks, mustache, beard.

Tollinger, who thought death would be quiet and clean, stumbles back in shocked dismay.

The preacher lurches about the room, grabbing for support to keep himself upright. A chair goes over, a shelf of books comes tumbling down, the table is overturned, the den becomes a shambles.

"Lindberg!" Tollinger yells. "Michael!"

He tries to stay out of the path of Kristos' mad rampage. He is knocked aside as Lindberg comes hurtling into the room, revolver gripped and pointed.

"Die, you fucker!" he shrieks at Brother Kristos, and shoots him twice.

But the man will not die. Tripping, staggering, he lumbers into the living room, heading for the outside door.

"Kill him!" Oberfest sobs. "For Christ's sake, kill him!"

Lindberg fires again, but then Brother Kristos is outside, leaving a bloody trail. They scramble after him, jamming in the doorway. But finally they are through, Lindberg in the forefront.

He empties his revolver at point-blank range, and keeps clicking the trigger again and again. Finally, finally, Brother Kristos is down, sprawled on the frozen ground.

Then they act in ways not panicky but intoxicated with desperation. They grab their victim, haul him back into the house, his heels dragging. They dump him onto the floor, stare down at his bloody eyes, stained shirt, feebly pumping chest.

"Can't he be killed?" Oberfest whines. "Is he going to live forever?"

"We'll follow the plan," Tollinger says dully. "The written plan."

Lindberg whirls on him. "Screw the plan!" he shouts. "There is no plan. The plan doesn't exist."

"What? I don't understand."

"You stupid shit!" Lindberg snarls. "How are we going to bury him? How? The ground is frozen hard. It would take ten sticks of dynamite to blast a grave. You want to drive hundreds of miles to scrape with our silly shovels?"

Tollinger flinches. Not chance or accident. It represents a failure of logical thinking.

"Why do you think I got back on the booze?" Marvin demands. "After all our work, we get snookered by a cold wave. Is that a laugh or is that a laugh?"

"We can still bring it off," John says. "Maybe no one heard the shots. Maybe we can take him out in the country and leave him in that ditch on the Annapolis road."

"Maybe, maybe," Lindberg jeers. "Why don't we zip him up in that orange Day-Glo sleeping bag and throw him onto the White House lawn? There's only one chance—the river."

They put on hats, coats, gloves. They wrestle Brother Kristos through the connecting door into the garage. They jam him onto the floor in the rear of the Cadillac. They open the garage. They move out slowly into the frigid night, sky clear, a zillion stars glistening.

John drives, heading south for Georgetown. Lindberg sits beside him, humming tunelessly and drinking from the bottle of cognac. And in the back, Oberfest cringes blubbering in a corner. We are all clownish bunglers, Tollinger thinks despairingly, and only that crumpled man leaking blood has any dignity.

He goes through Georgetown to the Potomac. There was once a fashionable restaurant on the river. The building, now dark and deserted, has a wooden platform close to the water. There were tables, and young couples sat in the sunshine, drank their kirs and Perrier, and watched the boats move lazily up and down.

They park, haul Brother Kristos from the Eldorado, lug him down to the river. They swing the body twice, then hurl it out. It crashes through the ice. Black water comes gushing up. They see one arm lifted. Almost a wave, almost a farewell. Then the water subsides, the body disappears beneath the ice.

They drive back to Spring Valley.

"Now he's dead," Oberfest says. "Isn't he?"

The other two don't reply.

They turn into Tollinger's street. He leans forward, peers ahead.

"Lights on in my house," he reports in a low voice. "We turned them off."

"Oh-oh," Lindberg says. "Keep driving slowly. Go right on past."

But their headlights pick out a police car ahead, blocking the road.

"Stop and back up," Lindberg commands. "Slowly."

John stops the car, glances into the rearview mirror, sees another police car come out of a side street to obstruct their retreat.

"Someone heard the shots," Tollinger guesses. "The cops must be in the house."

Oberfest begins weeping again. Lindberg finishes the brandy and lets the bottle fall.

"I'm glad we did it," he says. "I'd do it again—wouldn't you?"

John Tollinger doesn't answer. He remembers that earlier in the evening he had wondered what man's words he would utter on his deathbed. Now he knows.

The man: François Rabelais.

The words: "Draw the curtain, the farce is played."

= Epilogue =

In the months after the events recounted here, the following occurred:

The weather having moderated, the Potomac River became free of ice, and the body of Jacob Everard Christiansen, known as Brother Kristos, was washed ashore near Fort McNair. The autopsy revealed bullet wounds and toxic substances in the blood. But the immediate cause of death was given as hypothermia and drowning.

Brought to trial on charges of criminal homicide of the first degree, John Tollinger refused to be represented by legal counsel, pleaded guilty, and is presently awaiting sentencing.

Marvin Lindberg, under indictment on identical charges, was temporarily remanded to a prison hospital for treatment of acute alcoholism.

Michael Oberfest, jailed on the night of the assassination, was not deprived of his leather belt and was found the next morning hanged in his cell.

Two days after the murder of Brother Kristos, Major Leonid Y. Marchuk returned to the Soviet Union. His present whereabouts are unknown.

President Abner Hawkins, dissuaded by his advisers from ordering the White House flag to be flown at half-staff, delivered the eulogy at a small memorial service held in the Roosevelt Room. He is currently attempting to challenge the leadership of his political party by forging a coalition of minority groups, the poor and homeless, and fundamentalist religious organizations. In this endeavor he is being assisted by Lu-Anne Schlossel, who was confirmed as Vice President.

The death of Brother Kristos dealt a heavy blow to the presidential ambitions of Samuel Trent. Nor was his career aided by his divorce from Matilda Trent. However, the former VP has announced his intention of competing with Hawkins in the next election. The former Mrs. Trent is now living in the south of France.

Pearl Gibbs and Agnes Brittlewaite disappeared soon after the murder of Brother Kristos. It has been said that both women are now employed in a bagnio in Tijuana, Mexico, but that report has not been authenticated.

Jennifer Raye, named as executrix of Brother Kristos' estate, sold the tobacco barn and surrounding acreage in Virginia in order to pay estate taxes. The site is currently being developed as a shopping mall. Ms. Raye is working on a book: *The True Story of Brother Kristos.*

Henry Folsom resigned as Chief of Staff following the indictment of his executive assistant for murder. Folsom is now lecturing on political science at Georgetown University.

At her own expense, Emily Mattingly has published a new edition of *Brother Kristos' Prayers for All Occasions.* The book includes a selection of photographs of the preacher. It is said to be selling steadily.

In accordance with Brother Kristos' will, his body was cremated after it was released by the authorities. The ashes were placed in a simple bronze urn. On the night following his cremation, the funeral home was burglarized and the urn stolen. As of this writing, the ashes have not been recovered.

When Brother Kristos' will was filed for probate, it was revealed he had bequeathed his golden chain and cross to John Tollinger.

LAWRENCE SANDERS